ELI,ELY

EZEKIEL TYRUS

hhp
hardheadpress.com

First Edition 2013

Copyright © Ezekiel Tyrus

Library of Congress Catalog Number: 2013943748

Published by
HardHead Communications, Inc
Alexandria, Virginia
www.hardheadpress.com

Editor: Trish Masterson

This is a work of fiction. Though certain products and places mentioned in this novel are real, the people and events are fictional. Any resemblance of characters in this novel to persons living or dead is coincidental. If you think this novel is about you, see: "You're So Vain" by Carly Simon, *No Secrets,* Elektra Records, November 1972.

ISBN 978-0-9860429-0-4

4/25/14
To Zarina,

To James

Thank you for the
support. You are
an inspiration & a
future legend.
Best,
Zeke
Ezekiel

ACKNOWLEDGEMENTS:

A special thanks goes to Michelle Gengnagel, Sean Kelly, and Melinda Bailey. Also to my publisher and editor, Trish Masterson at hardheadpress.com.

Eli, Ely

Sunday 9/7/03

I

The sex this morning was great. Outstanding.

Her back looked amazing: brown, muscular with tattooed flames below her neck and more fire on the small of her back. She was on all fours, with me pulling her hair with one hand and slapping her ass with the other. I felt powerful and large, rocking my body back and forth inside her. I pulled out, peeled off my condom, threw it behind me, and ejaculated on her skin. Jennifer Ely collapsed with her legs slightly apart. There was a towel hanging on the foot of her bed. I reached and grabbed it and proceeded to wipe myself off her body. Then I leaned on top of her and asked if she came. With her eyes closed, she nodded and smiled.

That would be the last agreeable thing my girlfriend would ever say to me.

And even then, she didn't really say anything, did she?

Of course, at the time, there was no way for me to know this.

There above her, I stood on my knees, naked, body sweating and my cock sticky and deflating. "I love her" is what I thought. "I love you, Jennifer" is what I wanted to say. My Jennifer, though she's not mine anymore, is a beautiful woman. A beautiful woman who doesn't know she's beautiful, doesn't think she's beautiful, or doesn't care, I don't know. But she is beautiful and she used to be mine.

Her features are dark, very Mediterranean. Her Poppa was adopted, ergo Ely, a name of which nobody among the family knows the origin. But based on photographs I've seen, he's definitely Italian. Southern Italian. Sicilian. Possibly Greek. The man knew nothing of his birth parents and claimed not to care. Though Jennifer Ely may not sound Italian, she is. Her mother's maiden name is Strazzini.

Ely is a place in Wales. Her dad's adopted family, it's safe to assume, is Welsh. My father is 100 percent Welsh; though born in Florida, his folks were from Pennsylvania. When I legally changed my name, I chose an Italian surname despite the fact I'm not Italian nor do I look Italian. For my first name, I chose Eli, and whenever I meet another Eli, he tells me I don't look like him either. But still, I changed my name years before I met Jennifer Ely, and it was serendipity that the name I chose for myself was my future girlfriend's last name spelled differently.

Through both parents she inherited swarthy skin, sculpted features, penetrating black eyes, and a great, dynamic body that burns fat and muscles up after the slightest exercise. The Elys were college professors at UCLA or USC, I don't remember nor can I tell you what subjects they taught. But they were career academics, and my Jennifer, the twenty-four-year-old grad student with aspirations towards a PhD in philosophy, was headed in the same direction.

The past six weeks my girlfriend had been lying nude by the hot springs found in Yosemite. She looked tanned and sinewy, with muscles gripping her tall, womanly frame. I don't recall her body ever looking better: so firm, so smooth and brown. Her hair, cut short recently, barely came to the bottom of her neck. Wet and messy from the morning sex, it covered much of her face in profile.

I watched the slow, relaxed rate of her breathing and wondered if she had fallen back to sleep. Then I noticed her hands as they slowly crept underneath her pillow.

I was so tired last night that when I crashed over at Jennifer's apartment, that's precisely what I did. I was fighting heavy eyelids and the wounding effects of a bad week on too little sleep. We rented a movie, a two-hour-long English flick called *The Krays*. It was good but not as good as I remembered. The film is based on the true story of the Kray twins, who were notorious gangsters in 1960s London. One twin, Reggie, who was gay, is mentioned in the song "The Last of the Famous International Playboys" by Morrissey.

We snuggled on the couch in front of *The Krays*, but when it was over, it took all my energy to get up and lumber through the halls and into Jennifer's bed. She was wearing a white tank top and panties and I was my usual affectionate hound dog self, holding on, laying my right leg across her hips, right arm draped over her chest, my warm breath damp on her bare skin. She was reading a Greek history book by the light of a lamp she'd had since she was a little girl. The last thing Jennifer said before my eyelids defeated me was "Hey, Eli. Go to sleep, but you better be ready to fuck me good in the morning, boy."

This morning, I'm fairly certain that I did.

II

During brunch, my girlfriend asked me if I had ever had my heart broken.

"Of course. Jana broke my heart. My first serious girlfriend, Tai, she sliced my heart in two."

We were eating at The Squat & Gobble in the Lower Haight. Jennifer was looking down, not really eating her Mexican omelet.

In mock seen-it-all despair, I said, "My heart has scar tissue, baby."

Jennifer smiled.

"And you? Have you ever had your heart broken? Oh, yes, wait, the English guy, right?"

Jennifer nodded her head without looking up.

Since she was only tapping her cold omelet with a fork, I offered to go ahead and eat the damn thing for her.

She nodded. I took her plate and laid it atop my already empty one.

Jennifer was not a storyteller. She remained deep in thought, staring at the now-empty space at her side of the table.

Jennifer, as I partly remember, had a relationship with some English dude she met in San Francisco two years ago. He was here for the summer. They spent every day and every night together. The following winter she visited him at Oxford, where he was a student, and apparently they had mutual friends. The boy came from a moneyed family and was also a major slut, as Jennifer would later find out, shagging as many birds as he possibly could. English dude flunked out of college, went into Daddy's business, told lies, and, to this day, Jennifer suspects he fucked a good friend with whom she's still close.

Mentally, I always visualize him looking like Mick Jagger circa 1965: skinny, petulant, ugly, with dirt-brown hair and pale, pale, spotty skin.

Makes me wonder what Jennifer sees when I mention any of my past relationships, flings, or one-night stands. I am a storyteller, a compulsive one.

During brunch at The Squat & Gobble, Jennifer was quiet and pensive, which wasn't unlike her, but, in retrospect, she did seem more distant than usual. Except for the broken-heart question, she did nothing to engage me. No big deal. We could've had a laid-back, silent brunch the way long-term couples do. However, the atmosphere at our table felt tense and the expression on my baby's face was way too sad for our brunch to be considered laid-back.

4

I began to think out loud.

"You know, Jennifer, I look around at all these hipsters here, heavily tattooed in their thrift-shop clothes, and I'm thinking, 'These are my people.' I don't know what I was thinking this summer, baby. I vow to start spending more time in the Lower Haight. In all the years I've spent in San Francisco, the only times I've hung around this barrio were when I've been sleeping with a chick who lives around here."

Jennifer said nothing.

"Jana lived off Fillmore and I dated another girl who lived just down the street from you on Pierce. In the same apartment building where my new friend Ferdinand lives now. She moved away years ago to Montreal on an Indian reservation to teach. She thought it'd be something worth writing about. She may have been American Indian, too. Had real high cheekbones. Dark skin . . . I guess I do have a type."

I stopped talking. It was obvious Jennifer Ely wasn't having fun hearing me reminisce about women I used to date, women I used to sleep with, who used to live in the same neighborhood as she does now.

Everything was quiet as I finished her omelet.

I asked if she wanted to go for a walk after the bill was paid and she said, "Sure," and gave me a forced, insincere smile.

We walked around Lower Haight, but everything seemed strained. More than once, Jennifer mentioned the Greek she had to study and her room that needed cleaning. I had stuff I needed to do as well. Like clean my room, of which I only have one, considering I live in a residential hotel, a "single-room-only." There was laundry I needed to do and I was also planning to call around and find out if any friends had a black suit I could borrow for my job interview on Tuesday.

5

We both kept talking about going our separate ways, but time was elapsing and we were still by each other's side. My baby kept getting more stoic and withdrawn and my attempts at conversation continued to meander and thud like wounded doves.

When she finally said "I think you should leave now," it came as a relief.

She had been grumpy all day and not good company. Nothing personal. I attributed it to her being a woman. Possibly PMS, time of the month, all that shit. It couldn't be me. Never once did I think it had something to do with me.

We were lying on her bed in our clothes, our shoes off, when she said I should leave. Cheerfully, I got up, put on my shoes, gave her a hug and a simple kiss, and turned around to leave. In the doorway I said, "Thank you so much for Wednesday night. I needed you and you were there for me. Thank you for The Krays last night and thanks for the wonderful sex this morning. And oh, thanks for brunch. I promise I'll treat you next time. Thank you, thank you, and I do love you, baby."

"I love you" wasn't reciprocated, but it wasn't always reciprocated with Jennifer. Her face got even more serious. Something was bothering her. Whatever it was, I figured she'd be fine in a day or two.

Again, I kissed her on the cheek, and walked home.

III

It was late in the afternoon by the time I got to my hotel room in North Beach.

Harvey Wu, my bulldog-like friend (in looks, not temperament), manages The Wash-Out Laundromat & Café and recently told me he owned a solid black sports jacket that I could borrow.

Harvey, a thick, solid Chinese-American fellow, and me are about the same height. He told me the jacket cost four hundred dollars.

I've been a loyal customer of The Wash-Out Laundromat & Café for eight years. Harvey was willing to let me borrow his jacket, but the big guy hadn't even seen his jacket for months. Bulldog Harvey thought he may have let his older brother borrow it, but he wasn't sure. We exchanged numbers and he promised to call me later that night.

When I got back to my hotel room, I called Scott Bonne and asked if he had a solid black tie I could borrow. Scott did. I asked if I could come over later that night to pick it up.

"Absolutely."

Scott lives on Belvedere and Haight. Jennifer lives off Pierce and Haight. Both live in spacious apartments with cool, laid-back roommates. Though our time together, excluding the morning sex, wasn't particularly fun, I decided to call Jennifer and let her know I was going to be in the Haight and see if she'd like to hang out, perhaps finally get a chance to meet Scott.

I called and left a message on her cell phone. "Hey, baby. This is Eli. Hope you're feeling better. Anyway, just calling to let you know I'm going to Scott's pad tonight on Haight and Belvedere. I know you had a shitload of Greek homework, but if you have some spare time, maybe we could meet at Hobson's Choice for a drink and I could finally introduce you to Scott.

Anyway, hope the rest of your day is cool. Call me later. Bye."

And though I knew she already had my number, I left it on her cell phone and even repeated it.

IV

It's Sunday night, and for the walk to Scott's apartment, I decide, for a point of reference, to wear the new sports coat I bought for my now-defunct sales job at Burberry. I was hoping the glen-plaid grey-and-blue sports jacket, though too ugly to wear to work, job interviews, or special occasions, would still be cool and retro to adorn with faded blue jeans and a polo shirt. I've never been one to favor that look myself, but I thought it was a good look for other men. I knew guys in Florida who didn't own a single winter jacket. During the few weeks that actually get chilly, these guys would just put on a sports jacket atop their casual clothes. It looked cool and comfortable on them, why not me?

Walking through Scott's doorway, I said, "So, what do you think?"

"About what?"

"This is the sports jacket I wore to work at Burberry."

He smiles as if looking at a toddler wearing Daddy's clothes and gives me his sympathetic eyes.

"Yeah, that's pretty ugly, Eli. What color pants did you wear?"

"Grey. Red. Almost a burgundy."

"Hm." The same expression remains on Scott's face. "Yeah. That's kind of an ugly look for you, Eli. Sorry. Hey. Are you color-blind? Most guys are a little bit. Well, most straight guys anyway."

I sigh, letting my chin fall to my chest.

"Fuck if I know, Scott. I could be color-blind. Damn. I had no idea this was so ugly. I thought it was retro."

"Now you know it's only outdated."

I make a theatrical woe-is-me sound, only half kidding.

"Old men and panhandlers compliment this jacket whenever I wear it."

We both laugh, but I'm feeling sorry for myself and I'm really telling the truth about the panhandlers and old men. I take the eyesore off my back and throw it on a chair in Scott's bedroom. Scott lifts the jacket by its shoulders like he's lifting a dead rat.

"How much did you pay for this thing?"

"Sixty-five dollars."

Scott laughs.

"Scott, I bought it from an Italian clothing place in North Beach that has been going out of business for six years."

"And the pants?"

"Got them at the Gap for forty dollars."

"Ah, come on, Eli! You know people who work at Burberry spend more than a hundred dollars on a suit. You're not that naïve."

"Maybe I am" is what I want to say. Instead, I give out a thoroughly defeated "I know. I know."

I feel embarrassed. I feel stupid. I feel ugly. How could my night get any worse?

I'd arrived at Scott's at around 9:30. After he breaks the news to me about my ugly clothes and the irrefutable fact that I do indeed have bad taste, he and I chat, nothing serious, but towards the back of my mind, I'm keenly aware that Jennifer hasn't returned my call.

At around eleven, Scott suggests we watch a movie. The man has about a thousand DVDs. We choose *200 Cigarettes*, a movie I haven't seen. Before we sit down to watch, I decide to call Jennifer to see if she's feeling better and to let her know I'm tired and planning to crash over at Scott's. If there's a chance she wants to steal a moment away from Hippocrates, Plato, and the rest of "those ponderous do-nothings," now is too late.

Leaving Scott in his bedroom, I go into the living room to use my cell phone. When Jennifer answers, she sounds tired. I tell her I'm getting ready to watch a movie with Scott and then crashing on his extra futon afterwards.

"Uh, baby, did you get my message from earlier today?"

"Yes, yes, I did, Eli . . . I guess you can say I was, uh, um, avoiding your phone call."

"What?"

She and I have gone through this before.

"Yeah, Eli, I think we need to go on a break."

"What?"

9

"A break. I just need a break."

"Wait. Wait. Are we breaking up?"

"No, no. I care about you too much, Eli. I do. I really do. Just today I wasn't impressed with my behavior at all."

"What are you talking about?"

"I found myself being short and impatient with someone that I love. I didn't like it and wanted to know why I was doing it. I need time to go off and think about it."

My head's screaming "WHAT THE FUCK?" But I just say, "It's called being a human being, baby. Jennifer, you were in a bad mood today. It was no big deal."

Silence.

"Baby, are you saying we're taking a break from our relationship?"

"Yes."

"Like a trial separation?"

"Yeah, I guess."

"Okay, Jennifer. If someone asks me if I've got a girlfriend, am I to say 'No'?"

"Yes, Eli," says Jennifer, "and I've got to be okay with this. You saying you don't have a girlfriend and me saying I haven't got a boyfriend. Look, Eli. I just need to be alone for a little while. One week, that's it."

"Does it have to do with the fact that I'm suddenly an unemployed thirty-two-year-old who can't dress and is afraid of mountains?"

She chuckles but then says nothing for an uncomfortably long time.

I continue, "Hey, baby. If you ever saw me perform or read my fiction, you'd love it. I've got the potential to be a great writer. Really, baby. I mean that. It'll redeem my fuck-ups one day, baby."

Silence.

"You know, it was said about Jack Kerouac by those who knew him, 'Without words or paper, the man was a loser.'"

More silence.

"Seymour Krim said that. Many writers are losers away from their writing."

Is she still there?

"Hey, Jennifer, did you ask me out on Thursday because you wanted to see me or because you felt sorry for me?"

Miss Ely's surprised by my question and reacts with disgust.

"It was to see you, Eli. Absolutely. I can't believe you asked me that."

We both fall silent.

Finally, I say something. "When do you want to talk again? Next Sunday?"

"Yes, yes. You can call me next Sunday if you've got something to say."

What the fuck? Did she just say "if you've got something to say?"

"Hey, Jennifer, that's totally not cool. Not cool at all. Not fair. Think about it."

"Yes, yes. You're right, Eli. I'll call you on Sunday and if you don't hear from me on Sunday, know I just freaked out. If you don't hear from me on Monday, know you'll hear from me on Tuesday because I freaked out on Monday."

"Yeah, yeah," I said, shaking my head. I couldn't comprehend this side of her.

Nobody says anything for the longest time yet, till finally, "Bye, Eli."

"Bye, Jennifer."

Scott stands in the doorframe of the family room. His face is blank, waiting to perceive my emotion, I guess.

"My girlfriend says she needs a break."

His face remains blank but he gives me his sympathetic eyes again.

I place my cell phone on the coffee table, clap my hands together, and on an upward inflection say, "Hey, Scott. Let's watch a movie."

11

I feel nothing. Numb. I sit in a big desk chair while Scott lounges on his bed. His bedroom has a large, flat TV screen. *200 Cigarettes* is about New Year's Eve, 1981 in New York City and it makes me nostalgic for an era in which I barely existed. The music is wonderful, early '80s, late '70s new wave. Ultimately, I just like books and movies about party people from any era.

I remember seeing an independent film called *SLC Punk!* with Jana. We both dug the film and she's originally from Salt Lake City, but I thought it would've worked better as a novel than a movie. Are film and memoir the only media people wish to tell their stories in anymore?

Whenever my attention for the film lags and thoughts of Jennifer Ely threaten to creep into my head, I admire how Scott decorates his room. First you notice the closet, sans door, filled with DVDs, then a 1950s refrigerator in the middle of his room being used as a dresser for his clothes. His walls feature comic book art, some drawn by Scott himself, fascinating nude homoerotic beefcake photographs from the 1880s to the present, and then pictures of various friends, including me with noticeably bloodshot eyes wearing faded blue jeans, a T-shirt, and an old camel-colored V-neck sweater I used to wear. Knowing me, I probably slept in those clothes the night before the picture was taken. I'm laughing in the photo but I'm fairly certain I'm coming off an alcohol or drug binge, as I've got no memory of when or where it was taken, though it was probably five or six years ago based on that damn sweater alone. Still living those years down.

I'm tired, as was Scott by the time the film ended. The living room couch is a futon that turns into a bed. Sleep arrives within seconds, blissfully too fast to brood about any woman whose last name was my first spelled differently.

Monday   9/8/03

I

Around 5:30 a.m., I leave Scott's apartment to find a bus stop. The early-riser tendency is a new habit born from my three weeks at Burberry. I don't see myself abandoning this new habit anytime soon, as I now find mornings the best time to write, exercise, meditate (when I can focus), and get shit done. The later you wake, the less you get done. When you get up early, by midafternoon, you're impressed with how much you've already accomplished.

On the number 7 from the Haight to Market and Montgomery, I try to think about anything other than Jennifer Ely. When you and your ex-girlfriend have the same name, there'll always be something there to remind you, and for a few seconds I sing "There's Always Something There to Remind Me" by Naked Eyes. However, just because a song is old, it doesn't mean it's classic. I get off on Montgomery and cut through the Financial District to Kearny till it leads to Columbus in North Beach. The whole time, I'm laughing, laughing hard, maybe a little forced, but laughing like a schizophrenic with no home, walking quickly through the districts, cackling to myself. At the Sestri Hotel, near the corner of Stockton and Columbus, in room 116, I'm not laughing anymore but I still shake my head in amusement, trying hard to see the humor in my situation and refusing to acknowledge anything else. "This is so funny," I keep saying to myself. "This is so funny."

I live in one of the finest single-room-only residential hotels in the City, which isn't saying much considering most SROs are filthy, dingy rat holes occupied only by recently released ex-cons and prostitutes and alcoholics who've somehow managed to rub enough dimes together to afford a week-long furlough away from the pavement they usually call home. But the Sestri is in North Beach, one of the most interesting neighborhoods in the country. The Indian-American family that owns the place lives at the hotel. That makes the difference. They have a large apartment at the top of the main entrance stairwell, where a Dutch split door leads to their family room. This is where tenants enter and exit the hotel. Mr. Vejapura, the sweet, cherubic patriarch, is the family member I deal with the most. Bald Old Man Vejapura looks like a jolly, brown-skinned Frosty the Snowman. An old man who moved to San Francisco in the 1950s, he seems to genuinely like me.

"I like working people," he always says to me. "We try to prevent the bums and the lowlifes from moving in, but it's hard. We're in the hotel business."

Mr. V. advertises on hostel and traveling-student websites. Many of my neighbors are visiting Europeans and students here for the summer, but others are working-class bachelors like myself, but considerably older, with an even greater capacity for alcohol. There are two public bathrooms on both floors, each with two stalls and two showers. It's embarrassing to admit this, but compared to times in my life when I shared a spacious apartment with friends or even when I had my own one-bedroom, I've never lived in a place with cleaner bathrooms than the Sestri Hotel. There are a couple of Mexican dudes who come in nightly and clean the bathrooms in exchange for a cut in rent. My room is on the corner on the first floor, above a sixty-year-old dive bar called Vieni Vieni. From my window, I've got a view of an alley, the U.S. Bank, and—if I look out the window from an angle—the restaurant Panta Rei. Across the street from the Sestri Hotel is an Italian deli. Below the hotel and next to the dive bar is a Chinese fruit and vegetable stand. I live right where Chinatown and Little Italy meet. The hotel and the area, so rich in atmosphere, feels urban in an exotic way, like being an expatriate in 1920s Paris, or even a Beat writer in San Francisco in the 1950s. When journaling, a habit done nightly, I often feel like I'm in another era: I'm a writer living in various cities, in an old hotel room, writing in a battered diary. There's no computer. My first novel was written on 914 sheets of notebook paper, and then I borrowed a computer, typed it up, and printed out 253 pages. Room 116 is stacked with journals and notebooks of original fiction still written in my chicken-scratch.

With the exception of a small CD player that mostly plays jazz, the setting seems stuck in a much earlier time, and that's how I like it. The wallpaper's got fading stripes like an ice cream parlor from small-town America in the mid-twentieth century. The carpet is charcoal grey and probably never got vacuumed until I began calling room 116 home.

Back in April, I got caught up in the retro thing. This sweet Latina, a mere nineteen and looking for new experiences to eventually fill up her life, was making love to me. To me, "making love" has always meant having sex nice and slowly and sensually and not necessarily actually loving that person. We had already had sex nightly for the last several days, but that afternoon, there she was mounting me, riding my cock, biting her lower lip, top lip curling upwards, eyes closed, hands squeezing my shoulders, her nipples gently rubbing against my chest and a jazz vocal compilation on the CD player.

Sarah Vaughn was belting: so emotional, so real. The curtains were drawn but my window was wide open. We could hear the traffic outside, the alley barflies arguing in Italian, and the Chinese haggling over the price of cabbage. We could smell the garlic roasting at Panta Rei. I told Elena, nearly breathless, that I wanted to remember this moment always, and that in my mind, she and I were lovers of another time. "We were in The Left Bank of Paris, in Greenwich Village of New York, in North Beach of San Francisco!"

Elena was indifferent to jazz and knew nothing of what I spoke about, but she liked what I was saying. With me still inside her, Elena smiled, rocked her body back and forth, up and down, and said, "We're in North Beach, silly."

"Yes," I said, "but I mean we're in North Beach and Paris and New York and this is the 1950s."

She giggled, tongue in my ear, her body consuming me the whole time.

When I came, the second time that day, I thought I was going to pass out. She got up, sweaty and butt naked, and stared at herself in the mirror above my sink.

Elena said, "I know why you like us Latinas. It's because of this," and pointed to her ass, shook it around like a stripper, and smiled seductively, her face the shape of a valentine, dimpled cheeks and full lips.

We went at it again.

We worked together. Elena was, as I learned later, an exceptionally bad decision. She grew to hate me because "He's weird and has major issues with his family and past and shit," and perhaps because I never expressed an interest in a relationship with her from the very, very get-go. Ultimately, Elena saw me as a loser, as many waiters in their thirties are. My friends, while happy for me that I bedded a hot girl, each criticized me for being thirty-one and purposely seducing a nineteen-year-old. "Should've known better," they all said. "Should've known better. This time a year ago, she was in high school, Eli. What were you thinking?"

Don't get me wrong. My life at the Sestri is not all jazz, jizz, writing, and retro ambiance. I wish I could afford more. I miss having a kitchen and wish to move into an apartment as soon as possible, but until then, the Sestri Hotel in North Beach is not a bad place to be. San Francisco is a difficult town to arrive in with no money, and it's even harder to save money once you get here.

I keep my room neat and clean and never leave without making the bed. Nothing is more depressing than walking into a messy room when all you have is a room.

It's around 6:30 a.m. I kick off my shoes and strip down to my boxer briefs and a T-shirt. I peel off my sweaty socks and toss them in my blue laundry bag. I pull some fresh ones from my dresser, put them on, and lie on top of my bed without getting underneath the covers. My lids are getting heavy and my body starts to melt into the elderly twin-sized mattress when I hear the sharp chirp of my cell phone. It takes me a few moments to figure out where I left my cell.

Because it was chilly when I left Scott's this morning, I haven't thrown out my ugly jacket and the phone's in my coat pocket. If you didn't know I had a cell phone in there you would've thought a baby bird had made a nest inside my jacket, and considering how ugly my jacket is, such an event wouldn't seem so unlikely. Quickly, I jump from my bed, grab my jacket from the floor, and find my phone.

So badly I want it to be you-know-who.

It's Harvey. He looks like a bulldog, but on the phone and in person, Harvey sounds like a good-natured little schoolboy: polite, high-pitched, and always laughing, though I don't always know why.

"Good morning, Eli," Harvey says, with a Pillsbury Doughboy giggle. "Did I wake you?"

"Nah. Nah. Been up. Just lying in bed."

"You told me you've been getting up early lately and I've been seeing you at The Wash-Out as early as 7:30, so I thought it'd be okay."

"Harvey, it's fine. What's up?"

17

"Well, I can't find my jacket. The black jacket, the suit jacket I told you about. I don't know what happened to it." More chuckles.

"That's okay. It was a back-up plan, Harvey."

"Yes, well. I'm mad."

I laugh a little. Harvey announcing he's angry reminds me of the cartoon character Droopy Dog.

"Why are you angry, Harvey?"

"Because it was a four-hundred-dollar jacket and I don't know where it is. I let my brother borrow it. He may have let a friend borrow it. I haven't seen it or worn it in a year. Goddamn."

"It's cool, dude. Thanks for looking. Where are you right now? At The Wash-Out?"

"I'm driving right now. Be at The Wash-Out in a minute."

"Okay. I've got to drop off some shirts to be washed and pressed. See you later, dude."

"Sorry I couldn't help."

"Don't be. It's cool. See you in a little bit."

"Bye."

"Bye."

Harvey drives a new BMW and owns a motorcycle. He's a co-owner of The Wash-Out Laundromat and owns a house in the Sunset. He's thirty-five and was born and raised in San Francisco. I've known him for eight years and have never once seen him in a bad mood. Occasionally I've picked up a lonely vibe from Harvey, but who doesn't get lonely sometimes? He's one of my favorite people in San Francisco and I see him almost daily. I appreciate his phone call and know he did in fact look for his jacket and would've let me borrow it if he had it. I know that about Harvey.

"That cheers me up," I think to myself. "But wait a minute! I've been laughing it up all morning, and since I've been home, I've been relaxing as if getting ready to go back to sleep or meditate. Why do I need to be cheered up?" I shake my head fast as if that would prevent me from thinking. I get up, take off my clothes, slip my bare feet into rubber shower slippers and wrap a towel around my waist and another over my shoulders.

I shower down the hall. As usual, it's clean and I have the place to myself. Ten, maybe fifteen minutes of hot water. I lather and scrub and genuinely feel better when the shower's over. I get back to my room and lie down with my towels wrapped around me. My skin feels soft and warm and clean. For a few moments I was happy because the shower was the only thing I focused on while I was inside the water.

But now I think about Jennifer's skin: olive, silky, and dark brown from the sun. How it feels lying on top of her. How it feels to enter her from behind or lie down while she lies on top of me, her tits against my chest. When I sit up on the side of her bed after sex and she drapes her arms around my shoulders, her hands feeling my pecs, sitting behind me, wrapping her legs around my hips, the hot wetness of her pussy warming my tailbone, and she lays her naked chest along my spine and rests her head against the back of my neck . . . and *fuck!* Here I am with a thick, raging hard-on.

Instead of jerking off, I review the previous week.

"This isn't funny," I say to myself.

Depression starts, erection ends.

And then I cry big dumb disappointed tears.

II

Around June, I was waiting tables at California Pizza Kitchen on Geary. I had been working there on and off for years. I was over thirty and waiting tables at a CPK and not proud of it. Being a career

19

waiter at a five-star restaurant is fine—wonderful, even. But waiting tables in your thirties at a CPK is not fun. Even if you get a kick out of waiting tables, as I did, you simply feel like a failure as your co-workers keep getting younger and younger, always at the dawn of their twenties. Customers kept telling me I was too good and too professional to be at CPK, and they were right.

With sixteen years of experience waiting tables, I somehow managed never to acquire fine dining experience. I spent too many months dropping off resumes and pressing for interviews, only to be told I needed fine dining experience. When I'd ask how a person gets experience if nobody's willing to hire him due to his lack thereof, I was told by the managers at several big-name restaurants that the economy wasn't good enough to take a chance on somebody with no experience. But that disappointment didn't last too long.

One day, midsummer, a regular customer who always requested my section encouraged me to apply for a job where he was the manager. The man's name was Cecil, and to a lesser server, he'd be a nightmare. A pretentious, rat-faced, effeminate bully, he was a perpetually hurried and demanding customer. He always came to CPK and insisted to be sat at booth 45—how he knew the number is beyond me. If it wasn't available, he'd pout for a few seconds, then take a second- or third-favorite table, but always of his choosing.

Cecil would never let the host choose a table for him. Cecil's friend Rikki, a fat, pale woman, nicer, but just as hurried, was always with him, always a few minutes late. Inevitably, Cecil would order for both before Rikki got there. "Two bowls of Bolognese penne, add sun-dried tomatoes to one. Add bacon, sun-dried tomatoes, and mushrooms to the other, two orders of iced tea, lots of ice, and keep the tea coming. Oh, and lots of bread and butter. *We're starving!*"

He wouldn't snap his fingers but you almost expected it. Other servers hated Cecil on sight. It wasn't that I particularly cared for the guy, but most homosexuals are good tippers and he was no exception.

A demanding customer, even an asshole, can be forgiven if he tips well. Besides, I had been waiting tables for so long that nothing fazed me anymore. Customers' unpleasantness is not something to take personally, and they are only going to be in my section fifteen to twenty minutes. If somebody is way over-the-top rude, I call attention to it. I'm an intense guy with a muscular build. If I focus my energy on you, you can feel it. If you snapped your fingers or banged your hand against the table or tried to call me and get my attention while I was with another table, I'd tell you pointedly but discreetly that you were being inappropriate and to knock it off. Usually, the customer will stop, maybe even give me a bigger tip than expected. Cecil was pushy and demanding but nothing I couldn't handle.

It isn't saying much, but I was the best server there. When you're lucky enough to get a server like me, you remember it. A fast, dynamic charmer with an exceptional memory and a quick smile, I saw to it that all my customers had a great time and, most importantly, dropped some quality cash. People who came into my section alone, armed with a book, looking forward to a leisurely consumed small salad and perhaps a glass of wine, would instead end up getting an appetizer, a large salad, a pizza, three glasses of our costliest white, a dessert, and a double espresso. My checks were always the highest and I made the most money. My co-workers hated me.

One day, a few minutes before Rikki arrived and seconds after I repeated his order back to him, I could see the wheels spinning in Cecil's head when he looked at me. "Hey, you might be good at this." He pulled his wallet from his jacket pocket, opened it up, and took out a business card: Cecil Duckworth, General Manager. Burberry Fashion.

"Burberry?"

"Oh, yes," he said solemnly, like he was talking about God to a child. "That's Burberry, Eli. We're hiring a new sales associate." He whispered as Rikki was sitting down, "You'll make money. Lots. And I do mean lots. Most associates average over a thousand a week."

I must've made a face, jaw dropping, bug-eyed or something, because he chuckled lightly and said, "Take the card and think about it."

I did and it was all I could think about. I told my managers about it and they seemed impressed but also quiet, apprehensive. The managers didn't want to see their top server go, but they knew I felt stymied and even a little embarrassed about being employed at CPK. My co-workers were excited for me, but most were just delighted to hear I might be leaving soon.

Straight up, I told Cecil I knew nothing about fashion. Cecil said it wouldn't matter because Burberry would eventually supply me with suits to wear. His biggest concern was whether I could handle the lifestyle change. I mostly worked nights or midafternoon shifts and never woke up before 10:30 a.m. I only need four to six hours of sleep. I could adjust myself to wake at any time. I told him in two subsequent interviews that I wanted the challenge of a new job with a new career and also that it was time for me to reinvent myself. And what better way to reinvent than with a new wardrobe?

After my first interview, I sent a thank you card. One and a half weeks later, I did another interview. To both, I wore a pair of cream-colored painter's pants with faded burgundy wingtips, a button-down shirt, and a dark blue tie with red polka dots. The tie was borrowed from the assistant manager at CPK, an old friend, Boston Jerry, referred to as such because his name was Jerry and he did in fact come from the city where people mysteriously drop their R's. This outfit, including Boston Jerry's tie, was the closest thing I had to formalwear.

Mr. C. Duckworth could never claim I misled him into believing I was a fashion plate. He and his assistant, a lovely former 1970s model and airline stewardess named Whitney, did an extensive background check and called everyone on my list of ten references. Of course, I simply wrote down the names and numbers of my closest friends.

Twice a day, I prayed to God to obtain the Burberry sales job. There was a promise that if I got this job, I'd donate twenty dollars a week to a non-denominational church. I meditated and created affirmations: "God, please, may I obtain the Burberry job, dress better, earn a minimum of a thousand dollars a week, and enrich my local non-denominational church." A mouthful, I admit. And strange, too, considering that I've never once been to a non-denominational church since living in California and couldn't even tell you where one was located.

My girlfriend, Jennifer, would ask, "Are you sure you really want this job?"

"Oh, yes!" Then I'd go on to explain to her that I had been poor my entire adult life and I wanted, needed, a nice job, so I could have lots and lots of money to buy nice things for myself and for her. There was a sleeveless silk black dress in the display window that would look "so hot on you, baby."

She caught my enthusiasm.

Jennifer didn't pray and, like many a college intellectual, was skeptical about God. But she loved me and Jennifer wanted me to have the job if it'd make me happy.

We began dating at the end of May, shortly after my one-man show in April. Throughout June, we were inseparable because we knew she was going to be away mid-July and August at Yosemite, where she was working as a forest ranger. By her first week in Yosemite, she was telling me that she loved me via cell phone and I was telling her the same. We spoke on the phone almost nightly and she'd come and spend various weekends making love to me, when making love actually meant "making love."

After my one-man show (just me on stage telling stories), I began to rewrite a novel I'd been working on in some capacity for six years, maybe even longer. A manuscript completed in 2000 got the attention of an established New York literary agent with a Park Avenue address. The manuscript was never sold. However, I got some quality constructive criticism. I was "an extraordinarily talented writer" who'd written an "un-publishable book."

I vowed after my April show to rewrite my un-publishable novel by the end of the year. It's not going to happen. Only now am I coming to terms with the fact that in my personal life, I can't multitask worth shit. Within a week of receiving Cecil Duckworth's business card, it was apparent to me that I could only concentrate on two topics: Jennifer Ely and Burberry Fashions.

"Jennifer Ely loves me. I love her. Almost nightly, we talk on our cell phones for hours. When she comes over, we fuck so intensely, so passionately. Our conversations are deep. She loves my stories. I love her stories. We're so much alike. I can't wait till she's back and living here full-time. We've been discussing moving in together someday," I told my friends. We were consumed with each other like cannibals and it was only the second time in my life where I told a girlfriend I loved her and genuinely meant it.

I'm not the type of guy who falls in love with falling in love, though I probably seem like I would be. No, I loved Jennifer Ely and believed she loved me. I used to say to her, "I want to earn your love, keep your love."

I hated, hated, **hated**, and still hate, being poor. I've been poor my entire adult life and have yet to get used to it. People have alternately complimented and attacked the strength of my personality. All say I ought to be in sales; even those who obviously don't like me say I'm a natural-born salesman.

Shortly after I got fired from United Airlines, Jana Carver looked at me uncomprehendingly and said, "You should live better than you do."

She was right. I can still hear her voice. Disappointed.

For years, I was only interested in making enough money to live hard. Never once did I do anything practical with money earned. Bought lots of paperbacks, CDs, and thrift-shop clothes. Everything else was spent carousing and indulging. But then I started to get older and discovered that my peers had more things than I did. Not just material things, but real things like pride, accomplishments, security, stable relationships, and happiness. They held themselves a little higher, stood a little straighter and in better clothes. My peers, the ones who worked hard, saved their money and had the means to travel, simply lived better than I did. The same people whom I loathed several years before because they were boring yuppies I now openly envied and somehow felt were better than me. I wanted a moneyed job. I gave up on getting a five-star restaurant gig and decided I was tired of year-in, year-out refilling iced teas for a living.

When Cecil Duckworth called me on my cell phone and told me the job was mine if I still wanted it, I accepted, got off the phone, and screamed at the top of my lungs. I was standing in Union Square on a sunny day. Immediately, I called Jennifer's cell. She was still at her Yosemite summer job. My Jennifer shouted over the phone, "I love you. Oh, I love you. I'm so happy. I'm so happy for you. Oh, God, I can't believe you ever doubted yourself."

"I can't believe you ever doubted yourself" would ring in my ears for the rest of the day.

She knew how badly I wanted the job, how I campaigned for this job, and she was there as I often stated the job was going to pull me out of poverty and make me rich. Jennifer wanted it for me. Though the silky, sleeveless black dress did sound appealing, my girlfriend wasn't a Burberry girl. Jennifer Ely was a thrift-shop bohemian like me. Of course, for me, thrift shops have always been more of a necessity than anything else. That aside, Jennifer wanted me to be happy. I recall her saying more than once, in a voice sadder and more doubtful than I'd like, "I hope all your dreams come true, Eli. I really do. I hope all your dreams come true."

25

Her job at Yosemite was coming to an end in less than a month. We spoke with excitement about how great the rest of the year was going to be. She was going back to school to finish her master's degree. I was going to be making shitloads of money and vastly improving our wardrobes. We both said "I love you" multiple times and talked about how cool our holiday season together was going to be. I had to get to CPK to work a lunch shift and to put in my two weeks' notice. We kissed our phones and said good-bye. My phone was shut off during work.

After work, I turned my cell phone back on and discovered I had one message. It was Jennifer. "Hey, Eli, I'm just calling back to say that I love you. I love you so much, Eli. And that I'm proud of you and that I believe in you and that I know all your dreams are going to come true. (*Without a trace of sadness. Exuberant.*) I do, Eli. I'm grateful you're in my life and I'm in yours. I'm starting to gush. (*Laughs.*) Bye, Eli."

III

My days off at Burberry were Sunday and Wednesday. My hours were 9:30 a.m. to 6:30 p.m. The first two weeks at the job, there was nothing but praise. "A natural-born salesman, indeed." Nobody, Cecil said, could believe I had "no sales experience." No retail experience either (except for a brief foray managing a porn shop at 6th and Folsom, but I never mentioned that to Cecil). I couldn't fold clothes or wrap packages but was assured that those things would all come in time. I believed them and was promised that after a month I'd receive, free of charge, my very own Burberry suit to wear to work as well as my very own Burberry business cards. My fellow salespeople, all women, looked like trophy wives of various ages and ethnicities.

The ladies could be friendly and interesting conversationalists when it was slow, but when the store was busy, these same women were aggressive and competitive. I liked that about them. Cecil offered no training period. "You have to hit the ground running and either make quota or not."

I made quota. As a matter of fact, in the second week I outsold a certain employee who had been working there for over a year. She was thirty, beautiful, sweet, and a good saleswoman, just not as particularly aggressive as the others. I hit the ground running. I was giving it all that I had, and I was looking forward to growing and learning and thought for sure that someday I was going to be the top seller in the Burberry family and people would ask me or, more importantly, pay me to teach them the top secrets of the trade.

I was going to save my money, retire at forty, and write novels in a cottage by the sea. There was no wife or children in this vision, but I saw a hip live-in girlfriend who bore a striking resemblance to my Jennifer. More elegant, a little older, sexier, and poised, she was reading a large book while wearing black panties, a white tank top, and fluffy white socks.

Then the third week happened.

On September 4, 2003, Thursday morning, I was called into Cecil's office.

If Cecil Duckworth were a character in a movie, James Woods would be an ideal choice. Like the great character actor, Cecil has the same ugly, pockmarked face, the same dark eyes and total indifference to whether anyone actually likes him or not. Rare for an actor, even more so for a man who works in retail. Of course, this being high-end retail, perhaps the clientele expects a flamboyant asshole to be managing it.

James Woods, an extraordinary actor, has seldom played likable characters, and he certainly wouldn't be changing that pattern with his portrayal of Duckworth. The actor has played a cruel homosexual before, a real-life psycho in the film *The Onion Field*. To play Cecil Duckworth, he could play the same character—fatter, less psychotic and dangerous—and then swish it up, way up, and surely, the underrated James Woods would turn in yet another stellar performance.

After two weeks of solid praise, the man waited until I was seated in his office, then pulled out an aluminum baseball bat and proceeded to slam it into my stomach, then again, then again and again and again. Metaphorically speaking.

CECIL: Eli, we've done you an incredible disservice by hiring you. That is, an incredible disservice has been done unto you.

ELI: (*Did I just hear him correctly?*) Excuse me?

CECIL: Look, Eli. You're a salesman, definitely a salesman. Nobody would ever argue that. You need to be working in sales, *not* at California Pizza Kitchen. However, you don't know a thing about clothes.

ELI: Well, I never claimed to know a thing about clothes.

CECIL: Yes, but you said you had an interest in fashion. If you had an interest in fashion, you'd have developed a style by age thirty-two.

ELI: (*What is he saying?*)

CECIL: Nobody would look at the way you are dressed (*he pointed with his open hand at me like a sideways karate chop*) and confuse you with somebody who knows clothes, or somebody who even knows how to dress. Or, hell, somebody who even has a sense of style. That suit is hideous. The pants are too long, (*rolling his eyes*) the paisley tie and the old man's jacket . . .

ELI: (*A long silence.*) (*I don't wear the paisley tie every day. I look down to see if I am wearing it. I am.*) I didn't know my suit was so ugly.

CECIL: (*Obviously anticipating that I'd say that.*) But it *is* ugly, and that's the problem. You didn't know it was ugly. You are the odd man out around here. Don't you feel it?

ELI: (*I didn't feel like a misfit, believe it or not, until this asshole made me feel like one.*) (*More silence.*)

CECIL: I mean, it'd be like me on a football field. There are things I can do, like running, but I don't know a damn thing about sports.

ELI: (*The fucker is patronizing me, talking down to me like I'm stupid.*)

CECIL: I'm just being brutally honest. You are a salesman. One of the best I've ever seen. You could sell the Brooklyn Bridge, Florida swampland. You should be selling cars, really. But not clothes! Even if you learn the designers' names, the newest tricks, the newest trends, it'd be a waste of time because you have no natural affinity for it. "Affinity" means—

ELI: I know what affinity means, Duckworth. (*In my mind I tell him to go fuck himself.*)

CECIL: I'm just being brutally honest. You don't know how to dress, have no sense of style—

ELI: Are you telling me it'd behoove me to find another job?

CECIL: (*Nodding head emphatically.*) Oh, yeah, you should look for a new job immediately.

I did not make a sale the rest of the day. My hideous suit felt unbearably heavy. The next day, Cecil's day off, I sold $4,000 worth of clothes and merchandise at ten percent commission. Saturday, Cecil was back and I couldn't make a sale to save my life. Cecil, my albatross, had ruined my game. Sunday was my day off. There wasn't a chance in hell I was going to show up to work on Monday.

That black Wednesday when Duckworth swung a bat into my stomach, after work, I tossed the ugly suit onto the hotel floor, showered, threw on my casual clothes, and went for a walk along Washington Square Park to brood, mumble to myself, talk to God, and brood some more. It was sunset and the air was cool. I sat on a bench with my back towards Stockton Street, looking towards the park and Columbus Avenue.

There were various homeless men sleeping under a tree by the Benjamin Franklin statue. There was a smattering of dogs and their owners running around playing. I wasn't sad enough to cry nor angry enough to rage. I just sat down, tired and defeated.

My cell phone rang. It was Jennifer, my Jennifer. She sounded happy. It was her first week back at school and she was pleased. She'd had a good day. "How was your day, Eli?"

I told her everything Cecil Duckworth had said, verbatim. I didn't repeat it angrily, with passion or self-pity. I simply told her as if reporting the news.

"Oh, wow," Jennifer said, stunned and quiet. "I'm really sorry to hear that, *baby*."

I called her "baby" but she usually just called me Eli. There was no other time in our relationship when she had called me "baby." An old girlfriend, a real kind beauty named Leah, used to call me "babycakes." It made me cringe. Another girlfriend, a wild, blonde bisexual named Kathryn Johnson, used to introduce me as her "babe." That was cool. Christine K., an intense lover with a genius IQ, used to call me her "cutie-pie" or "sweetheart." It embarrassed me. Rainey, a god-awful actress I dated with large tits and nothing close to a genius IQ, used to rub the side of my face gently when I was inside her and call me "dear." That was nice, actually. Maybe more intimate than I wanted, but nice. Sexy. Jana, the aforementioned Jana—sexual, funny, party girl—used to call me up at 2 a.m. and say "Tell me a story," but she never called me "sweetie," "honey," or "baby" either. Just now, Jennifer called me "baby." I couldn't believe my ears. Gently, she said it again.

"Baby, how are you doing?"

"Well, I'm disappointed, but you know, it happened. It happened."

"Yeah." A long silence. "But I know you really put out for this job. You were really excited. You worked hard for it. Didn't you say you were making quota?"

"I was."

"Well, shit, Eli. This guy's a first-class asshole. What a fucking dick!"

"Yeah." Sadly, "Yeah."

She began to pep talk me. "Eli, you're an artist, totally an artist, and let's face it, all artists have a tough time holding down jobs. You told me you wanted to sell out, make a lot of money, and then go back into writing. You said that. Those were your words. Fuck that! You're better than that! Be an artist now! Be a writer now! I'm glad your Burberry gig is over."

I said nothing.

"Eli, what are you doing tonight?"

"I don't know. Nothing planned. Did you want to go out tonight or something?"

"Yeah, if you want to. I mean, that's why I called in the first place."

IV

Jennifer and I had seen each other earlier that week. Late Monday night, September 1, Jennifer returned from her summer job at

Yosemite. I arrived at her apartment around 9:30 or so. She lived in a large apartment with four bedrooms, two baths. A new roommate had moved in while Jennifer was in the mountains. I got to meet him before Jennifer. A cheerful guy from upstate New York excited to be on the West Coast for the first time, he was twenty-something and had a teaching job at a local private school. He loved "Frisco" and felt people were friendlier out here than on the East Coast, but the huge homeless population of San Francisco and the aggressive panhandling appalled him.

"It definitely affects our quality of life around here," I told him. "But it's funny, dude. When I moved to San Francisco from Tampa back in '94, if you criticized the homeless for being the indignant assholes that they are, people would get upset, extremely upset. Today, everybody fucking hates the homeless."

"I didn't say I hated the homeless, it's just that—"

"No, dude, maybe you don't hate them now, but you will hate them soon enough."

After that, he really didn't say much. We just sat around watching T.V. Jennifer's other two roommates, people I had met before, Ursula and Alby, had just returned the day before from Burning Man. Both were buzzing and jazzed about the entire experience. The new roommate, very preppy, very East Coast, knew nothing about the art festival that is Burning Man. Ursula and Alby, particularly Ursula, made the mistake of talking to me as though I had never heard of Burning Man. I may be the only person in my social circle who has never been to Burning Man. I've been to umpteen Burning Man parties throughout the City, all wild, all sexual, all druggy, and all supposedly artistic. An old roommate from Theater Bazooka, a fun Scottish dude named MacDougal, is a ranger and organizer at Burning Man.

I personally knew dozens of Burning Man people and almost felt like I'd been there through them. One guy, an artist and performer named Phil Bedlam, a major player at Burning Man, used to be a close, close pal before we went our separate ways. We had to. "He was a drunk. I was a methamphetamine addict. Self-destructive friends don't let self-destructive friends hang out with self-destructive friends." The three roommates each looked perplexed after that last statement. My experience with the Burning Man crowd is that I'm not the Burning Man type.

Ursula argued with me that "there is no Burning Man type!"

"It's all about the artists!" she said.

"But there is a type, girl. And I can't even stand the sight of dirt under my nails. Unless there's a pool or beach nearby, I refuse to go outside. Can you imagine me muddy, dusty, or dirty? It's the same reason I've only been to a handful of concerts in my life. I don't always dig crowds. I love art and artists, but I don't feel a need to go to Burning Man to prove I am an artist. There's nothing wrong with Burning Man and I know people who go there every year, they get laid, they expand their minds, and they love it. It just isn't my thing."

Ursula waved me off and said, "You just don't get it," and went outside to smoke. Alby got up and did the same.

I turned to the new roommate and said, "Ursula's too sanctimonious for me. Do you know what I mean?"

He shook his head.

"Look, if I were to piss in an empty beer bottle and leave it outside, and if the sun set, reflecting great light through my piss and the beer bottle, Ursula would say that it was beautiful, that it was spiritual. When in reality, it's nothing but piss in a beer bottle and the sun reflecting light through it. Also, on the Burning Man thing, my drugs of choice were always speed, coke, alcohol, and rage. Burning Man is kind of a shrooms, marijuana, and free love type of thing. Not my cup of tea, dude."

I felt it was an adequate definition of sanctimonious, even if he didn't. I said nothing else. He finally got up and left the room without saying anything. Jennifer told me that Ursula had a shrine in her room consisting of several candles and a large headshot of herself. Supposedly, she'd chant to the photograph of herself several times a day. Ursula said it was a Buddhist thing, but I don't think so. Neither does Jennifer.

Ursula was definitely hot, a total Southern California body with a Northern California brain, a sexy twenty-seven-year-old with a great natural look. Ursula wore sandy blonde hair parted down the middle. Her body was tanned and toned, and it bounced around in skimpy short shorts and loose tank tops, sans bra. Everything from her was "spiritual this" and "spiritual that." Jennifer liked her and so did I. Everybody, including women, will tolerate absurdity if done by exceptionally beautiful people.

I sat in front of the TV and reminisced about the days when I went to every art opening in the City. Eventually, I was banned from most art galleries because I'd go and eat all the free cheese, hit on the women, get drunk on the free red wine, and flash my penis at everybody. Back in those days, when I was drunk, I did have an exhibitionism problem.

By the time Jennifer made it home, I was already lying in bed. She was tired. She had taken a train into San Francisco and taxied to her apartment in the Haight, lugging nearly two months' worth of luggage. She wasn't talkative and we didn't snuggle. I thought she'd be pleased and pleasantly surprised to come home and find me in her bed. She was too tired.

"Yeah. It's rather anticlimactic, me coming home and you greeting me like this, or maybe it's me greeting you like this that's anticlimactic. It does seem anticlimactic, doesn't it?" she said.

"Nah, it's no biggie, baby. Let's just go to sleep."

I left in the morning before she woke up. It's normal for a couple to be tense and awkward around each other if they haven't seen each other in a little while. Isn't it? On the L train to Market Street, I thought about Jennifer's new roommate and realized he probably

34

thought I was a jerk. I made a mental note to be exceptionally friendly and polite the next time we met.

V

During the first weeks at my new job, new career, I knew Jennifer needed to be 100 percent present at her school. Graduate students are supposed to receive a tremendous workload, and I was prepared to be the trusting, totally supportive boyfriend and give her the personal space she needed. I left her place Tuesday morning with a post-it note on her mirror telling her to call me if she wanted to hang out this weekend. "Perhaps rent a movie?"

I figured she'd call me around Thursday or Friday to plan something for Saturday night. I didn't expect her to want to see me so soon and on a school night. We agreed to meet in Union Square. I told her it'd be easy to spot me: I'd be the bald guy dressed badly.

For a built, tattooed guy with a shaved head, I guess I do dress rather nondescriptly. To meet my girlfriend in Union Square, I was wearing faded, baggy blue jeans, faded Burgundy wingtips, a black belt, and a pink golf shirt with short sleeves. Yes, a pink golf shirt. My girlfriend was dressed cool—hip, even—in a long denim skirt, white leather sneakers, and a striped 1970s-style sweater. She greeted me in the center of the Square with a sympathetic smile. She gave me a long, tight embrace. It was exactly what I needed. Jennifer told me that I dressed fine. The shirt wasn't a shirt she'd wear, but it looked "well, uh, fine on you, Eli."

We walked holding hands, my head down. So profoundly I felt like a dumb-fuck.

"Do I really dress badly?"

"You don't dress bad, Eli. It's just . . ."

Then Jennifer offered to buy me a late-night dinner. We ate at the

35

CPK I had just quit three weeks earlier. I genuinely missed the food and perhaps psychologically felt a need to slip back into my former comfort zone. It was around closing time, the place was nearly empty, and most of my former co-workers were not there. Those who were present were too busy closing up and doing side-work, and they were too busy to say hi and meet my girlfriend. They seemed to think it funny that I had a girlfriend with the same name. Of course, they'd theorize I was only with her for her name, and that I only fell in love with her so I could openly say "I love Eli" without people thinking I was only talking about myself. But then again, considering I was the Ty Cobb of CPK and nobody liked me anyway, why the fuck was I there? Fuck them.

Our waiter was Danny Ryan, 6'3", darkly handsome Danny Ryan, with his thick, spiky, jet-black hair. Danny was a great co-worker with a good sense of humor. Intelligent, laid-back—you never heard anybody say an ill word about Danny Ryan. If he did cause any hostility or resentment in another person, it'd be because of the fact that this Danny happened to be an extraordinarily good-looking young man. Actually, he was classically handsome like a movie star in the league of Cary Grant or George Clooney, but with a faux-hawk. Danny worked three dinner shifts a week, but he also worked full-time for an independent music label that produced albums for most of the Bay Area punk and alternative rock bands that had yet to be signed to a major label, if they ever would be.

I liked Danny. He and I got along well. He knew better than to take me too seriously. He was cool, but ultimately, I was jealous of him, and it is not hard to see why. Danny and Jennifer stared at one another. Simultaneously, they pointed and asked, "Where do I know you from?" They laughed. Jennifer figured it out first.

"Did you go to UCLA?"

"Yes. Yes, I did."

"That's it, then! So did I!"

"Small world." Then Danny looked at me and laughed. "Hey, this must be the Miss Ely that Eli kept talking about." Miss Ely and I smiled. It had been a little while since anyone had made fun of our names. Danny took our orders: sausage and pepper penne Bolognese for me, oriental salad for her. We both ordered water and asked for bread and butter. Later in the meal, Jennifer ordered a beer, Sierra Nevada Pale Ale.

We talked about Burberry, and Jennifer said it was for the best that my time there didn't work out. She was proud of me, she said. It was better for her not to have a boyfriend who was a Burberry guy. Jennifer mentioned to me that Ursula and Alby hooked up over the summer and went from being roommates to lovers. I didn't care. Jennifer wasn't surprised but seemed a little jealous that she wasn't the center of attention anymore. Jennifer once called Alby the older brother she never had and then mentioned that he was still younger than I was. She said that numerous girls, including some of Jennifer's best friends, had expressed an interest in Alby, but it took a real fun hottie like Ursula to catch him.

"What do girls see in Alby?" I asked genuinely.

My girlfriend looked at me like I had asked a stupid question.

"Because Alby is tall, dark, and handsome, Eli! Goddamn!"

"Oh." Fuck me. What the hell? To me, Alby was bland, average-looking, and boring. What the fuck do I know? Was my Jennifer growing out of her "bad boy" phase? For most women my age, that phase is a distant memory, and the sight of me at my regular hangout, The Wash-Out Laundromat & Café, seems only to put more worry lines on their faces.

Jennifer's girlfriends were intellectual academics like her, or they were embryonic yuppies, white-collar professionals right out of college. Every girlfriend I've had since I was twenty-two has said I was an intellectual inside a bad boy's body. Kathryn Johnson said that she dated many guys who weren't sensitive but tried to act like they were. She said I acted like I was an insensitive macho jerk, but truth be told, I was terribly sensitive. Couldn't I be both? Regardless of my interior, these women were convinced I was a "bad boy." Many girls go through the bad boy phase, but most grow out of it.

I asked what she thought of her new roommate.

"Oh, he's awesome. He's smart. He's already got his master's. It's in languages!" Then, for the next several minutes, she did nothing but list the guy's virtues.

I asked if she found him attractive. That's what I meant to say, but it came out as "Do you want to fuck him?"

Jennifer cocked her head with a slightly offended, slightly flattered expression. "Okay, jealous boyfriend, why do you ask?"

I shrugged my shoulders.

"No, Eli, no," she said and made a disgusted face. "No, Eli. I can't imagine getting naked with that guy. Yuck. I like him but not like that."

We were both quiet for a few moments. Then Jennifer spoke again about the as-of-yet-unnamed roommate. I couldn't remember his name, and Jennifer never referred to him by his name, but this guy, whoever the fuck he was, had told my girlfriend that he had found a certain reggae club he liked in the Lower Haight. I'm sure the dude was talking about Nikki's or Café International. Anyway, Jennifer told him that'd be a good place to take her beau, Eli, and that's when the new roommate mentioned that he had met me. Jennifer then said, "Uh oh. He wasn't offensive, was he? Because he can be offensive sometimes." This was what my girlfriend thought of me?

"Did you really say that? Oh my God, Jennifer. Did you really say that? Were you serious?"

"Well, I was half-serious."

"Why?"

"Well, because . . . well, anyway. He said you didn't offend him but it wasn't like you and him were going to be best friends or anything." Then Jennifer smiled like I was going to be pleased to hear that information.

"He said that?"

"Yes." Jennifer seemed to think it was all a very positive thing.

"What the fuck does that mean, 'He and I aren't going to be best friends or anything'?"

"Uh, what it means is that you did not offend him and that he's a totally mellow guy who doesn't say negative shit about people even if he doesn't like them."

"What are you smiling for, Jennifer? Are you laughing at me?"

"Oh, c'mon, Eli . . ."

Silence, though my expression must've been shouting.

"Oh, c'mon, Eli. Don't act like you don't know you offend people."

"Well, maybe I don't want to offend people anymore, Jennifer."

"Then stop doing it."

Silence.

"You can't, can you? Why? Because it's you, that's why."

More silence, a pained expression undoubtedly on my face, Jennifer reached out and touched my arm. "I do love you, Eli." Her eyes looked sincere. Sad. Sympathetic. "I love you, Eli."

"I love you, too." Privately, I recalled the time I complained to my Jennifer that all my CPK co-workers thought I was an asshole. I didn't like being considered an asshole, didn't think I was an asshole, and wished people would stop calling me such. "But you are an asshole" is what Jennifer said to me. "You are, you are." She was being serious. "It's part of the reason I like you, the fact that you're kind of an asshole."

Another time, at Hoover Junior High School, I came home crying because everybody, including the teachers, especially the teachers, was telling me I was obnoxious. And then my Mom looked at me and said, "That's because you are obnoxious."

We passed on dessert. She paid for dinner and I tipped Danny generously.

"Nice to meet you, Jennifer Ely. Again."

"Yes." She laughed, thoroughly charmed. "Likewise."

I didn't have to ask if she wanted to fuck Danny Ryan. I already knew the answer.

We went for a walk, holding hands and talking sweetly, acting like a couple. We went to Post Street. I wanted to look at the display window at Kayo Books, which is a used bookstore and a gallery of vintage book cover art with old paperbacks hanging like paintings. We had gone there on our second date. The display that night was fun. Vintage sleaze books with illustrated pin-ups and horny men. We considered going to Café Royale for a Hoegaarden, but I mentioned how early I had to get up in the morning and Jennifer, on second thought, had to get up fairly early as well. We walked past a spacious, well-lit art gallery and pledged to come back and take a look inside sometime when the gallery was open. Looking in the window, we saw statues of flabby, pot-bellied, bald, middle-aged men.

I said, "I hope I never look like that."

Jennifer said, "Oh, you're totally going to look like that when you get older. Totally."

There's a story about the Krays not portrayed in any movie about them. Once, when a life-long friend and fellow gangster good-naturedly pointed out that the Krays were putting on weight, the twins whipped out their knives and the fellow baddie ended up going to the hospital to get over a hundred stitches fitted across his face. Some may say their reaction was extreme, but it makes perfect sense to me. Luckily for the poor bastard, the Krays weren't losing their hair; otherwise they would've plucked out his eyeballs, too.

We went back to my hotel room.

When we first hooked up back in May, I told her I wanted to move out of the Sestri, but Jennifer said, "Don't. I like it here. It has character, like you. Makes a person feel all bohemian and urban, like you."

She's not the reason I've stayed, but it pleased me that she wasn't ashamed to come over. She spent the night that night and it was lovely. The CD player played a down-tempo, ultra-chilled acid jazz CD. I lit some scented candles that smelled faintly like cinnamon. We had sweet, affectionate sex on my bed by an open window allowing a cool San Francisco breeze to pass through. She fell asleep with her mouth drooling on my skin, pussy against my hip, thigh across my pelvis, arm across my chest, breasts pressed against my ribs, and the cold San Francisco wind cooling our sweating torsos.

I always thought our bodies were something to be proud of, to be envied, but my Jennifer told me she didn't even notice my chest the first few times we had sex. It wasn't until one day when I was changing clothes in her bedroom that she noticed me shirtless and thought "Wow. Nice."

That's the story she told me and I guess I'm flattered, but how does a woman sleep with a man and not notice his chest?

I woke up an hour or so earlier than Jennifer. It was Friday morning. With me trying to do isometrics on the floor and my girlfriend surfing delta waves in bed, I decided to call CPK to see if I could get my old job back. It was 8:30 a.m. Harley, the general manager, was on the phone.

"Oh, hi, Eli. What's up?"

I told him what had happened at the Burberry gig. Harley laughed, stating what a cocksucker Cecil Duckworth was. "What a bad manager. He could teach you. Or he could give you constructive criticism and see if you pull through. Everybody hires somebody they're not sure is going to work out, but they give them longer than three weeks before telling them to go look for another job. What an asshole manager. Hey, isn't he the one who approached you anyway? Fuck, what a douchebag!"

Funny, Harley tended to refrain from that language when I worked there. He never thought much of Duckworth and it was nice to hear him beating the guy who beat me, but when he was done, Harley laughed way too hard at my situation.

"Yes, yes. You're absolutely right. The guy's a prick. Can I have my old job back, Harley?"

"Well, you must remember, the summer's over and we're not as busy anymore." It sounded like he was already anticipating my question. "We've hired a few new servers and hosts to replace all the people who went back to school this fall. Also, let's be frank, is it worth the complaints I keep getting about you, Eli? Boston Jerry calls you the Ty Cobb of CPK and he *likes* you. Can you imagine what people who dislike you are saying?"

Then Harley laughed his ass off.

I like Harley, but fuck me, man. That hurt. Of course, I didn't say that. I just met Harley's laugh, chuckle for chuckle.

"So many people hated working with you, Eli," Harley added. "You are a great server but you used to drive your co-workers insane."

Laugh. Laugh. Laugh. Laugh. I continued to feign laughter. What else was I going to do?

"Look, Harley. I'm in a jam. When your new boss tells you on your third week to go look for another job, I don't know where you can go from there."

"Okay, Eli. Give me some time. Call me back on, let's say, Tuesday. I'll think about it. Weigh the pros and cons and give you a definite answer on that day."

"Thanks, Harley."

"Take care, Eli," Harley said, with finality I didn't appreciate. For a moment, I tried to recall if anybody had ever said "take care" and not immediately disappeared from my life afterwards. No. Never. A pause followed by "take care" equates to "have a nice life" as far as ultimate final good-byes go. I got off the phone knowing I was never going to work at CPK again. A hole had been weathered right through that safety net. It no longer existed for me. Even if I was invited back, it would be too embarrassing, and if Harley told me I was too much of a shit to work with, my heart, soul, and ego would not be able to handle the rejection.

Intuitively, I knew Harley would say no. Who could blame him? If I were in his position, I'd probably reject me, too.

My baby woke up shortly after the phone call. I kissed her cheek and got under the covers to grab some first-of-the-morning snuggle. I thanked her for the night before. I needed her then, and I told her so. She was "beyond good company," I said. "Thank you, thank you, so much, baby. Thank you. I love you." She reciprocated the affection but said nothing. She wasn't grouchy or mean but she wasn't talkative either. Jennifer moved slowly in the morning. More than once, she expressed delight that I was "such a morning person." She said I was the first morning person she'd ever known. "Every morning you wake up all smiles, full of energy, exercising, laughing at the radio. It's really quite amazing. Beautiful, really."

Though she didn't say it that morning, she did say it often, and her comments were generally the first thing I thought about when I woke up. Jennifer never knew the speed junkie, the brawling drunk, the unpredictable party boy, the nocturnal bouncer, or the depressed Oblomov who spent entire weekends in the prime of his Florida college years stuck in bed, too depressed to move, wishing his bones would break. Now I was a grinning, energetic morning person.

After snuggling with my Jennifer, I got up to put on my suit. There was no way I could afford not to finish out my last week at Burberry. Unfortunately, I had no other suit to my name. No safety net was yet secured. As badly as I wanted to, I could not tell Cecil Duckworth to go fuck himself.

"If I had modeled my suit before you went to sleep, you might have had nightmares."

A little giggle from my girl. "I haven't eaten yet."

"Good point." I put on the eyesore and Jennifer looked at me sadly.

"It's not that it is a bad suit, Eli. It just isn't a good suit, or not necessarily a very good suit, a little out of style. The shoulders are too big, too broad. And not really a good color for you, for anybody, really. But don't worry about it. You still look good."

My legs felt weak. I softly landed on my knees and let my face fall onto my bed. Jennifer touched my shoulders. I got up and looked at myself in the mirror. It had been a long, long time since I had felt this stupid.

"You look great, Eli. Really. That guy is an asshole. Fuck him. You don't need him. He doesn't know what the fuck he's talking about. You look great."

I knew I didn't look great and that people had been laughing behind my back for the past three weeks. I didn't believe her. Cecil was definitely a dick but he knew what he was talking about, and I looked a long way from great. She was being a good, dutiful girlfriend, and thank God for that.

"Eli. I do love you," she said. I turned to look at her. Her head sank deeper into the pillow and she spoke almost as though she was talking to herself. "I do love you, Eli."

That empowered me. I believed her. Jennifer Ely loved me. I took in several deep breaths, got up from the floor, washed my hands, and brushed my teeth for the second or third time that morning. I kissed my girlfriend. "I love you, too."

She sleeps naked, and I considered taking off my eyesore and spending the day in bed for some Eli,Ely, but I knew I couldn't do that. I left for work. Jennifer rested a little longer. No classes till noon. We made tentative plans for Saturday night.

Come Saturday, I knew it was going to be my last day at Burberry. After work, I went to a Chinese diner on Kearney to eat an evening breakfast of three eggs over easy, bacon, tomato slices, and wheat toast. It was a $2.99 craving. My cell phone rang. It was Jennifer.

"What are you doing right now, Eli?"

I told her.

"How weird. Well, don't make any other plans because tonight you're all mine!"

"Music to my ears, baby. Thanks."

I went home, showered, changed into casual clothes, and then took the 45 to Market Street. There I caught the 6 Muni to my girlfriend's neighborhood and found her waiting on the corner of Pierce and Haight. When I saw her, after we hugged, the first thing I did was call attention to my clothes. A bright-red teamster jacket I got at Clothes-Per-Pound in the Mission, a blue V-neck sweater I got thrifting somewhere, a white T-shirt, a black belt, baggy carpenter jeans, and my ever-present faded burgundy wingtips.

"Now who says I can't dress? These are cool, aren't they?"

"Yeah, yeah, they look fine. Hey, you're not going to get all self-conscious on me now about how you're dressed and everything, are you?"

"Of course. Who wouldn't be? Can you blame me?"

We rented *The Krays*, a movie I had seen over ten years ago at some art house theater. We snuggled, and, much to her displeasure, I fell asleep far too early. Come Sunday, after morning sex, brunch, asking if I've ever had my heart broken, and spending the afternoon acting as though I were cramping her style, my Jennifer told me she needed a break, a week-long hiatus from our relationship.

Now I want to cry again.

VI

I'm dropping off some shirts at The Wash-Out, chatting with Harvey, who offers me a too-thick-for-San Francisco black winter jacket somebody left to be dry cleaned a year ago and never picked up.

"No thanks, Harvey."

Afterwards, I walk to the Salvation Army on South Van Ness to buy a suit jacket. It's a beautiful sunny day. There's a reasonably attractive jacket in good condition, but I can't tell if it's black or blue. I ask around. Most others can't tell either. Some say it's black, most say it's blue. Others can't speak English and have no idea what I'm asking them. Finally, I decide it's a black jacket with blue threading, a steal for six dollars.

Then I walk to the Ross store on the other end of Van Ness. There I buy a pair of black dress slacks, too baggy, but perfect for twenty-six bucks. Though it can be fun to rummage at thrift and discount stores, it sucks when that's your only option. Afterwards, I have lunch at Little Saigon on Polk Street, neck-deep in the Tenderloin. This place is one of San Francisco's best-kept secrets. You can get tasty French-Vietnamese sandwiches for two or three bucks.

After I eat one sandwich with a Thai tea, I order another to go. I walk to Union Square to browse at Borders. All writers, the professionals and the wannabes, are passionate bookstore browsers. After Borders, I go to B. Dalton's at the Embarcadero, then to City Lights in North Beach, then Columbus Used Books on Broadway. The smell of the BBQ pork and pâté sandwich has been with me all day.

I walk back to the Sestri, drop off my new clothes, take my sandwich, and go back outside. I buy some iced tea at Coit Liquors and walk to a bench in Washington Square Park; the sandwich is still good after all these hours. The sun's setting, the dogs are playing, the

North Beach locals are socializing, and the homeless are drinking, minding their own business, occasionally waving at me. I don't know why. Just being friendly, I guess.

After my park-side dinner, I walk to Barnes & Noble on Bay Street to hang around till closing. After 11 p.m., as I'm walking back to the Sestri, I walk by a muttering wino. As he stumbles past me, I see he's wearing the hideous sports jacket I bought for my Burberry gig. Earlier today, it was ceremoniously thrown into the alley dumpster from my second-story window.

It looks good on him.

Tuesday   9/9/03

I

The tie. The tie, the very item I went to Scott's for in the first place, has been left behind. Like a moron, I forgot and left the tie at Scott's. Around 9:30 a.m., I give Scott a call, knowing full well I'll be waking his ass up.

"Hello?"

"Hi, Scott. Did I wake you?"

"No, been up for a few. Was lying in bed. Needed to get up anyway. What's up?"

"Did I leave my tie behind? I mean, *your* tie behind?

"I don't know. Let me go see." He leaves the phone momentarily and comes back laughing. "Yeah, you did. It was on the coffee table when you were on the phone with Miss Ely. When is your interview?"

"At eleven."

"Well, I'd say come over but I've gotta run to work in . . . Shit! Only an hour! I've gotta go now."

"Nah, it's cool. Don't worry about it. I've got a suit. I'll just wear another tie."

"Okay, Eli. Sorry about it but I've got to go."

"Alright, later."

I have no black tie. No big deal. I do have the new-to-me black jacket (with blue threading) and new black slacks. I have a golden-yellow tie with sliced lemon wedges printed on it. The tie and my shoes are the only items I own that get compliments from young people and individuals who do not live on the streets. Certainly, the lemon tie will go well with the black suit.

II

During my three weeks at Burberry, I befriended the security guards: two undercover security guards who wore traditional black three-button suits. It was comical and I'd joke about it, but truth be told, it annoyed me, because the security guys, Gary and Boone, were young, tall, and handsome. Gary, 6'4", square-jawed, expressionless, with his flattop hairstyle and quiet nature, looked like he should be walking alongside JFK's convertible in Dallas, 1963; and Boone, over six feet and dark, had every bit of race, creed, and color inside his genes, resembling a young, buff, clean-cut Keanu Reeves. Customers, mostly women, would look at Gary and Boone and assume the youthful beauties were sales associates. They'd look at me with my shaved head, broken nose, thick body, and suit and have me pegged as "a bad undercover cop." More than one person actually said that. And despite this, I still had no idea how ugly my clothes were or that I was a misfit, the odd man out.

The boys, both in their early twenties, worked for a security and loss prevention company called The Berserkers. It was started by a small band of nightclub bouncers who decided to form an agency to supply bouncers on demand (B.O.D.s). They'd provide bouncers to dive bars and roadhouses, as well as VIP, high-end nightclubs that catered to the rich and beautiful.

The Berserkers, already a success, dominating the Northern California club scene, decided to branch out and provide daytime security. First, they put uniformed guards in banks, gated communities, and whatnot. Eventually, they got some of their more handsome VIP bouncers who already wore nice suits and got them to wake up earlier and stand inside stores like Gucci, Armani, Burberry, and the like. Their job was to be an intimidating presence and a deterrent to shoplifters.

If someone had the earmarks of a potential thief, the Loss Prevention Specialist was to pay special attention. If he witnessed an individual steal something, he was to alert the retail manager, who would decide to confront and/or prosecute. There were numerous security companies in Northern California. Somehow, The Berserkers had the best contracts with the best high-end retailers.

Boone and Gary had a supervisor named Augustus "Gus" Martinez. Gus would come in periodically to check on "the boys" and to schmooze with Cecil. Part of Gus' duties included making rounds in the Union Square shopping district and seeing that all positions were going smoothly. In each place, he'd check on "his boys" and chat with the managers. Boone and Gary told me several times they could get me work, but I wasn't interested. Nothing Gus could pay me would compare to the Burberry cash I was soon going to be earning.

Boone was on a break when I told him about my meeting with Cecil. Boone gave me a head-to-toe glance-over and said, "It's pretty ugly, dude. We thought you were being ironic."

I must've made a sad face, because immediately he began to backpedal.

"Not ugly, necessarily, but just, kind of like, old man. Or old gent."

"Whatever. The reason I'm telling you this is I can't work here anymore. If in your third week your new boss tells you it would behoove you to find another job, where else do you have to go? And I can't get my old restaurant gig back."

Boone got excited. "You want to be a Berserker?"

"Yeah."

"It'd be a major pay cut."

"I know."

"Cool."

We exchanged cell phone numbers. He called Gus and told him about Cecil's dick move. When Gus called me towards the end of my shift, he sounded both surprised and sympathetic. He recalled meeting me and asked me to come and meet him for a formal job interview at Café Venue on Market Street.

"You know the place, Eli?"

I did.

"Tuesday at eleven is okay with you?"

"Sure."

"Be there with a black suit, okay? Can you get a suit like that?"

"Absolutely."

I was a brain applying for a no-brain job. It was already mine, as far as I was concerned.

III

Without a doubt, the worst part of living in San Francisco is dealing with the aggressive panhandlers. Were the bums of the Great Depression as aggressive as these assholes are? And don't tell me it is only because of the bad economy. I've lived in this town for nearly ten years and the vicious, beer-bellied skeletons I see today are the same ones I saw in the late 1990s when the economy was booming. I've seen street people grope women, steal lunch boxes from kids, and intimidate and menace tourists into giving them cash. They'll become indignant and insult people who've done no worse to the beggar than say "No, sorry, not today."

"Slut! Bitch! Cunt! Asshole! Faggot!"

If you go out and ask people whom you don't know for spare change, you've got no right to get angry if they say no. Does the beggar consider how many times a day the average person in San Francisco gets panhandled? No. They don't care. If they don't care about me, why should I care about them?

I've been homeless, in between spots to couch-surf. I've been drunk. I've been fucked up on drugs. I can sympathize with the wasted and downtrodden. But I hate aggressive panhandlers. They're destroying the quality of life in the most expensive cities in America. Once, the United States funded treatment for the mentally ill. When I see those on the street who obviously need serious attention because they're schizoid or bipolar, I feel deep sorrow for them. Again, they're not the individuals I'm talking about and they're not usually the ones asking for a handout. I'm talking about the scumbag I see almost daily on the corner of Stockton and Geary. Many citizens of San Francisco would openly applaud fate if the 30 bus clipped the Stockton and Geary scumbag and dragged him from Union Square to Candlestick Park.

The man is a terror. He's a 6'5" white guy who, like many a street person, looks as though he was once good-looking. He's got a full head of short blonde hair and he tends to be more clean-shaven than the average street beggar. Perhaps he still has a place to crash, shower, and shave. He hasn't been on the streets that long. He's about my age, underweight, with scary, sunken, bloodshot blue eyes. He jerks his arms and body with the unmistakable characteristics of a tweaking speed freak. His teeth are decaying. His size and unpredictable movements frighten people. This tweaker's modus operandi for begging is reprehensible. The tweaker will ask a child, a woman, an old man, a yuppie, anybody if they have spare change. If they say no, the bastard flinches and throws a fake punch quickly, always stopping about a foot away from the person he just panhandled. Women will scream. I've seen yuppies run away. I've seen children cry. Whenever you look around, there's never a cop anywhere.

I've been incarcerated three times, twice for misdemeanor assault (charges dropped) and once for a suicide attempt. Jail sucks. Psych wards are worse. I've never done more than a few days in either place, but, simply stated, I don't want to go back, regardless of how justified the assault would be. Also, why lie? The tweaker's huge and unpredictable. He scares me.

Tuesday morning, walking along Stockton, I come upon the scumbag's corner. I see him walking towards me. "Twitchy," as usual, is licking his lips frantically. His upper body's twitching and his predatory eyes are bugged out, seemingly extended from his face. He's a sick man but he knows what he's doing. A voice in my head tells me I'm ready.

Not even trying to be friendly, he approaches me. "Hey you! Got any spare change?!"

I say, "Fuck off."

I hate him and see no reason to hide it.

He flexes, but mildly so. He doesn't throw a punch within a foot of my face like I've seen him do to women and children and to men who'd never strike back. He makes two fists, flexes his arms, and lifts his elbows towards the sky. The gesture lasts for three seconds. He puts his head down with a scowl and starts to walk away.

"Hey!" I yell. "What the fuck was that?"

Then I impersonate Twitchy, down to his licking lips and flexing elbows.

This proves he knows what he's doing—immediately the scumbag shouts, "Oh, you don't want me to flinch at you! You don't want me to flinch on you!"

Quickly, too damn quickly, Twitchy throws two jabs at me, stopping within inches of my eyes. Of course, I flinch. See white lights, too. But I don't stumble. Nor am I the type to scream or run away. My fists are cocked and ready to fight.

A real badass would beat me up right there. Instead, Twitchy runs away, waving his arms, yelling, calling me a faggot. As he's crossing Geary, I yell "Good luck panhandling!"

"Fuck you!!"

Twitchy, a schoolyard bully existing in the body of a thirty-two-year-old junkie, starts running faster, until he disappears among the weekday crowd on Market Street. Dozens of tourists and yuppies look on. You can hear people murmuring "Where's a cop?"

What sucks is the fact that I knew I'd see this asshole again tomorrow and the day after that, and he's so high on crank that when Twitchy sees me, he'll panhandle me with no recollection that we almost got into a fight the day before. There are no cops. It's tragic, really. If he had pulled out a knife and stabbed me, he probably would've gotten away with it.

In another vain attempt to find a police officer, I turn completely around and spot three men in black suits standing outside the doorway at Gucci. The one in the center is Gus. I don't know the other two. One is black with short dreadlocks. The other is a white, fat, skinhead type, though surely not the racist kind. All three are smiling at me, eyes wide, definitely amused. Gus runs over with the other two a step behind. Gus and I shake hands. He grips my hand hard. As do the others as we're introduced.

"Welcome aboard, Eli." Gus looks at the men standing next to him. "He's going to make a kick-ass Berserker."

"Yeah, fuck the interview," says the skinhead.

"No need as far as I'm concerned," says Dreads, his massive shoulders shaking up and down with laughter. "We saw the whole thing. He started a fight with you but didn't have the balls to finish it."

Gus says, "Yeah. And then the motherfucker starts flipping out and Eli remains stationary with his fists ready to go. It was great. Fucking great."

We're each in our thirties, some later than others, but there we are laughing, throwing high fives at one another like the macho, brawling children that we are.

"So, the interview's over then?" I'm confused.

"Yeah, who needs an interview?" says the skinhead, a black tribal tattoo crawling above the collar of his suit suddenly visible as he shrugs.

". . . Well, you guys still want to get some coffee?"

"Yeah," Gus says. "My treat."

IV

Gus and Dreads joke that the skinhead and I look like brothers. We're both big white guys with shaved heads, but that's about it. He's ugly, the kind of white guy that doesn't tan but gains additional freckles. His fat fists stick out from the sleeves of his suit like pink, freckled sledgehammers. His head's round, and the expression on his face, even when he's laughing, falls into a perplexed scowl. The skinhead manages the Sacramento office. We also share the same blue eyes, sure, and blonde eyebrows, same height, but he had a solid fifty pounds on me. Thirty-five years old, he'd never done anything else but "muscle work."

The black Berserker's huge, having once done some professional wrestling. Fat and muscular, he more resembles the skinhead's sibling based on body type and facial expression alone. Dreads manages the San Jose office. He tells me he just turned forty the day before, "But I don't look it, do I?" "No, no," I say. Hell, he could be ten years older than that, but he doesn't look like a man you'd consider contradicting. If he tells you he doesn't look forty, he doesn't.

Gus Martinez is "half-Mexican/half-Whitever." He tells me he knows "jack shit" about his white side. Up close, sitting across from me, I notice Gus' two prominent facial scars: one vertical slash by his right eye and another horizontal along the bridge of his nose. His body type's tall and thin, but I suspect Gus is built like a welterweight underneath his clothes, and given his antagonistic smile and the intensity of his concentration when he speaks, I can safely assume Gus doesn't get intimidated easily.

V

ELI: Now you know what career bouncers are like.

SCOTT: Gus sounds hot.

ELI: He might be. He's brown and macho like a beaner, but tall and arrogant like a whitey.

SCOTT: Me like, me like. Four alpha males at one table. Swoon.

ELI: They tell me that they're trying to organize the entire industry of bouncers, security professionals, and whatnot.

SCOTT: Security professionals? Career bouncers? Hm. That's interesting.

ELI: Yeah, so even though I've got enough bouncer experience, it was mandatory that I take a Bouncer Aptitude Test.

SCOTT: A what? There's such a thing as a Bouncer Aptitude Test?

ELI: Yeah, something like that. And then I was to take a Security Guard Test to get my guard card.

SCOTT: How funny.

ELI: So they show me the tests at the coffee shop. They're both take-home tests. I ask if people ever fail these tests. They say it happens almost always. I open the Bouncer Aptitude Test, question one asks, "How many days are in ninety days?"

SCOTT: Did question two ask, "There's a bouncer who's 6'2" and weighs 245 pounds. The solid black T-shirt he wears to work needs to be how many sizes too small? A) One size too small. B) Two sizes too small. C) Three sizes too small. D) Four sizes too small." Were there any questions like that?

ELI: No, that wasn't the second question, but then again, I didn't read the whole thing.

SCOTT: Oh.

ELI: I put the B.A.T. down and looked over the Security Guard Test. Question one: "If you happen to witness a disgruntled employee set fire to his cubicle, this employee has committed: A) rape B) vandalism C) arson D) embezzlement."

SCOTT: Was it really called the Bouncer Aptitude Test? The B.A.T.?

ELI: Yeah.

SCOTT: Well, hell. Why does a bouncer need to know how many days are in ninety days?

ELI: Really. Math was never my specialty either, Scott. So anyway, I put both tests down and see that even Dreads and the skinhead are smirking at me. I'm not totally sure, but I thought I heard Dreads mumble something about me having a college degree so the tests would be no problem. It was noisy in the café, but his mumble sounded condescending. Nobody likes a wiseass, especially a big, bad wiseass. I looked at them and asked if they knew what berserk meant. "Of course," the skinhead says. "Violently crazy." The three looked at one another, pleased, like they were going to slap hands. Gus says, "The Vikings, man. The Norsemen that would overkill

57

their enemies." And then I said, "Yes, but from what is the word derived? Do you know?"

SCOTT: Did they?

ELI: God, no. All three looked at me with no expression. Then I looked at these guys with the most serious face. The term "going berserk" does come from the Berserkers, the intense, violently over-the-top warriors of the Norsemen. But the word really means *behe sekr*, which translates to "bear skin." In other words, it was the rough fur coat these sick, overzealous warriors wore. Berserker originally meant "one who wears bear skin."

SCOTT: What did they say after that?

ELI: They're quiet. Then Gus takes both tests and says, "Hey Eli. You had a tough week. Why don't you just sign both tests and we'll go ahead and waive them and you'll get your bouncer and security guard cards in the mail by next week or so."

SCOTT: How'd he know about your bad week? Did you tell them about Jennifer Ely saying she needed a break? (*It's the first time since we began conversing on the phone that Scott mentions my relationship hiatus.*)

ELI: Yes, yes, I did. They were like, "Cunt! What a bitch! Fuck her! You're better off without her." They were really mad. Gus asked if she broke up with me because I lost the lucrative Burberry gig. I said, "Nah. She's just a little self-absorbed." Gus nodded, but he was contemptuous. When I explained the hold situation, the Berserkers simultaneously said, "Tell her to stay on her fucking break! It's over, Eli! Tell her to fuck off. If she had any real love for you, she wouldn't have done this. Fuck her. It's over. Move on."

SCOTT: Those Berserkers are such barbarians. Look, nobody

would mistake me for either a barbarian or a Berserker, but I'm afraid I agree with them. Totally.

ELI: (*Changing the subject.*) Gus told me I'd be watchdogging the Gucci store on Stockton starting Monday. I'll come at 10 a.m. and he'll show me around the place.

SCOTT: Wow.

ELI: Then I shake their hands, thank them, and as I get up to leave, Gus says, "Oh, by the way. Take my business card and go to the Men's Wearhouse across the street from Virgin Records. You know where it is, right?" I'm like, "What's wrong with my suit?" The Berserkers look at each other and smile. (*Scott laughs at me hard.*)

ELI: Gently but emphatically, Gus tells me I'm wearing a navy blue jacket, baggy pants, and a lemon yellow tie. "You need to get fitted for a suit. We have an account with them. It's a business expense. Go there today."

SCOTT: Were you embarrassed?

ELI: I was so fucking embarrassed.

SCOTT: Did you go?

ELI: Yes, and I can say, for the first time in my entire adult life, I wore a suit, a well-fitted, perfectly tailored suit, and not a suit that was assembled from multiple visits to various thrift shops.

SCOTT: How'd you look?

ELI: (*Quietly.*) Great. Fucking great, man. Handsome. It took me by surprise. It was murder to put back on the ugly clothes I had worn into the Men's Warehouse.

SCOTT: Oh, I bet it was.

ELI: But they had to hem the pant legs on the suit and told me to pick it up on Friday. Man, I tell you, Scott. I almost cried when I saw myself in that great black suit, my first suit, and at age thirty-two.

SCOTT: Do you feel like you've missed out?

ELI: Oh, yeah, Scott. I've definitely missed out. I walked home, gave the bulky navy blue jacket to the black street musician on Sutter and Stockton who plays the accordion. Do you know him?

SCOTT: No.

ELI: Anyway, as I was walking back to my hotel, I thought I was going to cry, and I may have even tried to induce crying, but I just kept giggling.

SCOTT: Why?

ELI: Because self-pity is hard to accomplish when you're too busy laughing at yourself.

SCOTT: Yeah. You've got a lot of material to be laughing at yourself about these days.

ELI: Oh, you've noticed, huh?

SCOTT: Yeah.

ELI: Well, listen. I'm walking and reviewing my entire clothing history. When I was in college in fucking Palatka, a scum-hick town in North Florida, there was this bargain-basement art school called Florida School of the Arts. Oh, it sucked. So, for this one show I helped stage manage, I wanted to wear a suit to the show's opening night. At the time, my dad was sending me monthly $300 checks to cover rent and other things. I told my dad about how I needed, wanted, a suit for opening night. At the Salvation Army, they had used suits for twenty-five bucks. "Dad, this month would you please send me an extra twenty-five so I can buy a suit at The Salvation Army?" My God, damn! Did he put up a fuss! "That's a lot of money, boy! Why the hell do you need a suit? Shit. An extra twenty-five dollars! Jesus Christ!" After much pushing and pulling and begging and pleading—it wasn't like I could ask my mother or stepfather—my father finally relented.

SCOTT: Did you get a suit?

ELI: Oh, yeah. It was a fine, funky, blue suede suit. It was too big for me and had bubble gum stains on the sleeves. Wore it once or twice. Lost it. What floors me is that at nineteen or twenty, I was begging for money from my dad to buy Salvation Army suits. How pathetic. It wasn't like I was this spoiled brat demanding a fucking Gucci suit for my eighteenth birthday. To hear my folks back then, I was a spoiled, lazy bitch, and twenty-five dollars was a shitload of money.

SCOTT: What years are we talking about? Less than three hundred dollars in rent, twenty-five-dollar suits. Did you go to college during the Great Depression?

ELI: Yes, as a matter of fact, I did go during the Great Depression. Not the country's, but my own. We're talking '90, '91, '92. It was a two-year school and I went for two and a half. Never enjoyed it once. Hated it.

SCOTT: Hm.

ELI: So listen. The following year, there's a student-faculty Christmas party. Again, I found myself without a suit to wear. The invite did say formal. Rather than go through the same bullshit with my dad—

SCOTT: You could've saved the money.

ELI: (*Acting as though I didn't hear him.*) My next-door neighbor at the apartment complex I lived in was a sweet high school boy named Boo, like Boo Radley from *To Kill a Mockingbird*. Not a nickname. His real name was Boo. Oh, a real sweetheart. Haven't thought about him in years. He was polite, good manners, gracious with his family, just a sweet, good ole Southern boy. About seventeen and about the same size as I was back then—

SCOTT: You stole a suit, didn't you?

ELI: (*Disappointed my friend would assume I stole something.*) No, I borrowed a suit. Just asked if I could borrow a suit and offered to have it dry cleaned, which I did the day after the party. The suit Boo had was green imitation wool with blue checks. The jacket had shoulder pads and stopped at the waist with two buttons in front like a dinner jacket or a tuxedo jacket without tails. I recall thinking it wasn't particularly handsome, but it *was* a suit, so it would do.

SCOTT: Green imitation wool with blue checks?

ELI: Yeah. On the way to the party, I decide to stop at Walmart to buy breath mints. No condoms because I wasn't getting laid in those days either. When I walk into Walmart, standing about five feet from me is a mannequin wearing the exact same suit I was wearing.

Scott laughs hard, too hard. It isn't nice. My friend wasn't born with a silver spoon in his mouth, but I can tell the middle-class, gay Southern California boy has no comparable experiences of bad suits and the necessities of buying them at Walmart and The Salvation Army.

SCOTT: Oh, my God! What did you do?

ELI: I turned around and ran back to my car. To my credit, I did see the humor in it even then. I was laughing the whole time. Oh, that poor hick spent about forty-five dollars on a suit at Walmart, but my pathetic ass was borrowing that suit. What did that say about me? Believe it or not, Scott, I still went to that party. Was there for about fifteen minutes. Everybody else looked so nice and I may have been the only person at that school who didn't drink.

SCOTT: That's right. You didn't drink then, did you?

ELI: Nope, didn't start drinking till I was well into my twenties. Almost like twenty-four. Shit.

SCOTT: Did you just arbitrarily start drinking?

ELI: No, it was a gradual thing, but it soon escalated. I just felt like I missed out. I didn't party in high school. Most of the weekends at that Palatka acting school were spent in bed too depressed to do a thing. Even at New College of California, I didn't party much. You'd think an easy-A liberal arts college that left me with nothing but student loan payments and a useless BA in humanities would at least be a good party school. It wasn't.

Scott is my friend, not my therapist. The phone moment comes when you become aware of the other person's silence and begin to visualize them at their home reading a magazine, looking out the window, looking at TV, doing anything other than paying 100 percent attention to you. We talk a little while longer, and he encourages me to call him any time this week when I feel like I need to talk.

VI

People don't ever think of San Francisco being hot, but this entire summer, San Francisco's been engulfed in a terrible heat wave. Terrible heat wave for San Francisco, that is. Temperatures rose from the 80s to the mid-90s, and I can only recall once or twice in the past eight years when the City was this hot, even after dark. Long ago, I pushed my twin bed against the window. Now I lie there in my underwear on a threadbare bedspread to feel some faint traces of breeze. My head finds the cold spot on the pillow. My hands are behind and underneath, crunching the pillow, propping my head up, allowing me to look out the window. A weeknight in North Beach isn't that busy. Panta Rei is doing business. I can hear the barflies downstairs pissing in the alley. Bob Marley's on the jukebox. "No woman, no cry," huh?

I was never the diehard William Shakespeare fan that many playwrights and actors claim to be. *Hamlet, King Lear, Macbeth,* and *Richard III* are cool because they feature suicide, madness, bastards, and deformity—all subjects close to my heart. But I'm pretty much indifferent to everything else. Lots of college actors will memorize Shakespearean monologues just to impress sensitive girls who put out. It never occurred to me to impress the chicks at my acting school because they were damn ugly and none seemed to like me much anyway.

For reasons still unclear, I was disliked immensely at Florida School of the Arts. Reflecting upon it now, I feel both sadness and humor. "Isn't it funny that I was so hated?" I think to myself as I quietly laugh. I smile and shake my head because I don't understand why my responses to the same things vary. Some days when I think about how much I was hated at Florida School of the Arts, I cry. It seems I recall reading another man's suicide note somewhere that featured the line "The list of my enemies is very flattering to me." His reactions must've been similar to mine.

It's Shakespeare's sonnets that I love. Memorized dozens but never shared them with anybody. Only one is still with me today. It's my favorite, number 27, and one that feels appropriate right now. Sonnet XXVII:

Weary with toil, I haste me to my bed,
The dear repose for limbs with travel tired;
But then begins a journey in my head
To work my mind, when body's work's expired:
For then my thoughts—from far where I abide—
Instead a zealous pilgrimage to thee,
And keep my drooping eyelids open wide,
Looking on darkness which the blind do see:
Save that my soul's imaginary sight
Presents thy shadow to my sightless view,
Which, like a jewel hung in ghastly night,
Makes black night beauteous and her old face new.
Lo! Thus, by day my limbs, by night my mind,
For thee, and for myself, no quiet find.

I don't want to think about Jennifer Ely but I can so clearly see her face.

This break is a positive thing. It is. An opportunity for two people, two extraordinarily intense people, to take a step back, miss each other, and come back with everything renewed: love, passion, sex. No way is this thing over, no way.

The first date: we spent the night together, me with no condoms, her either. There was lots of oral, though. My God, was there ever.

We drank two bottles of red wine during dinner at an Argentinean restaurant in Little Italy. Her enthusiasm for hanging out and drinking at Vieni Vieni surprised me, since I only suggested it in jest. More wine, then vodka cranberries, and a white Russian here and there. She's mostly Italian. Me? Welsh, Irish, German, American Indian, and my grandfather was a blue-eyed black man. Eclectic jukebox: Hawaiian music, jazz standards, punk rock, grunge, reggae, country, hip-hop—we played everything. Our arms were wrapped around each other as we sang along to Louis Prima. Johnny Cash. Bob Marley. Even Chet Baker. I told her she was beautiful. She told me she had forgotten what I looked like.

She had met me weeks earlier at a dark club; both of us had been drinking. Jennifer never expected me to remember her number, much less call. Two phone conversations indicated to her that this "Eli with an 'I'" would be good company, but she had no real clarity as to what I looked like. We agreed to meet on a bench in Washington Square Park. It was the last week in May. The air was cool and the fog was rolling in; from every view in the City, the Wharf and the Golden Gate Bridge were no longer visible. Shyly, awkwardly, we embraced hello, and she gave me a peck on the cheek. She was the dark, intense young woman I remembered. My memory's sharp. So sharp, I've never written her phone number down once.

Definitely, definitely I was attracted to her, and for Jennifer, as she'd tell me later, naked while climbing onto my bed, when she saw me in the park, she immediately thought "Wow. He's hot. I scored!" Nick Drake was playing on my CD player. She had never heard of him. "Love it," she said. "Just love it to pieces. This is great." She was hunched over my body, holding my cock with her one hand, gently cupping my balls with the other. She tells me, "Eli, you don't understand. You and I totally have the same taste in music." Then she opens her mouth, releases her tongue, and slides it down the tip of my sword with heavy saliva. Slowly, her head bobbing, she makes my toes point, my mouth open, and my neck bend backwards, pushing my head deeper into my pillow. Buzzing with lascivious drunkenness, she rotates her body, landing her torso along mine, her thighs lying on my pecs and shoulders. I lift my head up and kiss her pussy and proceed to shake my tongue inside her like a rattle, and she screams with me inside her mouth.

Didn't I just say I didn't want to think about Jennifer Ely?

Fuck. Damn. And me with a hard-on, too.

I don't want to jerk off right now. But I do, till I cum. I clean my stomach off with a towel.

Did the images that invaded William Shakespeare's head resemble anything like the ones that invade mine? If so, I sure wish he had written about them. Incidentally, the sonnets are dedicated to two individuals. Half are to a woman, a dark woman, as she's described, and the rest are to a man in young Shakespeare's life, either a lover or a best friend; who knows?

I get up, flick on the light switch.

Re-reading books is a wonderful thing. It teaches writers how to write. I grab *Young Adam* by Alexander Trocchi, to be read for the fourth or fifth time. With the thin grey book with the grey cover in my hands, I lie back down. And yes, I named myself after him.

I read until the ink turns blurry.

Wednesday   9/10/03

I

10:30 a.m., I'm downstairs at Vieni Vieni, ordering a Miller Genuine Draft and searching for Stan Getz on the jukebox.

Found it. I can listen to an entire Stan Getz album for a dollar and a quarter. If the only Stan Getz you know is "The Girl from Ipanema," then you're missing out. I request "Waltz for Stan" on the jukebox twice. The sax, Stan Getz' horn, dreamy, sad, pacifying; if I were somewhere else at a different time and with the right company, it'd be sexy. Right now, it's emotional, a substitute for crying in public. I love his sax and wish I could play.

Wherever I am, I can still hear it, in my childhood, in my adolescence, in Melbourne Beach, Florida. There were powerful sea breezes ripping through palm trees and power lines in melodious whistles, and surf sliding and rushing like a brushed drum. Inside the aria, I was there, standing on the dunes, age twelve, thirteen, fourteen, fifteen, alone, hands in my pockets, my eyes staring at my shoes, wishing my head could roll off my chest, gales embracing me, drying my tears, filling my head with jazz.

My stepfather was an asshole, a petulant 6'2" man-child who'd slay me with ear-splitting silences. He wouldn't speak to me. Years went by where we shared the same house and he'd only greet me with belligerent silence, eyes vicious and a mouth gripped so tightly you would've thought it was welded shut. At night, I'd resort to the comfort of the shore. Soon, the cadence of Melbourne Beach took over, and I never heard my stepfather's silence again.

Memories of a close-knit family that never existed and a community I hated are thankfully inaudible, drowned out by the music I hear whenever I walk into an empty room. Wherever I am, I can still hear it.

So similar to my memory is the jukebox jazz that I fear if I keep my eyes closed, I'll be able to see only the shoes I wore when I was fifteen and feel the tears I cried back then.

During my early months in San Francisco, I was twenty-four and there was a girlfriend who'd employ the silent treatment whenever she was angry. "Hey, Leah," I'd say. "I don't know what's going on. I don't, but if I hurt you, I'm sorry, but you've got to let me know. Grab me by the collar and scream real loud. If I anger you, jump up and down, cuss, and throw furniture at me. Break a window. Do something! Light my clothes on fire! Do something! Fucking do something! Just, please, help me. Help me. Just don't ignore me. This I can't handle. You have no idea. This I won't deal with. This I can't handle. Seriously, Leah, stop doing this. I'm begging you." The relationship didn't last.

"Shit, shit, fuck!" I think to myself. It's not yet noon and here I am drinking inside a bar listening to sad music and brooding about an unhappy childhood and bad relationships. "This is not good, Eli, not good." Vieni Vieni opens at 7 a.m., and several barflies stumble in shortly thereafter. Each one is thinking about unhappy childhoods and bad relationships, probably. "This is bad, Eli, this is really bad." After hearing "Waltz for Stan" a second time and with a few swallows left of my beer, I get up and leave.

Today, I must do something constructive. I must do something creative. Today, I need to write. Today, I definitely need to write. Today shall be Writer's Wednesday.

II

Chuck Baudelaire Ambitions

by Elijah Trocchi

Dearest Diane,

Bench-pressing five hundred pounds came easily compared to a relationship with you. You plunged guilt like a rectal thermometer so deep I couldn't stand straight or think normally. I resented your suicide attempts and your eating disorders. You looked at me with either a vengeful glare or a cry for help. At least my looks varied.

Fact: Men are at their strongest when they hate something. It's like getting "psyched up" to "max out" at the gym. When a body builder wants to test his strength, let's say, at the bench press, he'll pose in concentration, breathe forcefully, and remember events that'll turn his skin blood red. Actors call it "emotional recall." Swollen veins and sweat everywhere, the body builder will look like he parked his face in a microwave. To push over four hundred pounds, he'll get psyched up on anger and hatred. Sure, some guys get psyched up on trivial shit like the Tampa Bay Buccaneers or the cystic acne growing on their backs, but believe me when I say abusive fathers and schoolyard bullies have given birth to many a body builder.

For me, whenever I wanted to be my strongest, I thought about you.

You had a mouth like a cesspool. "What's all this fucking shit? Fucking shit! Goddamn fucking asshole! Fucking fuck-face asshole!!" Why did you talk that way? Was it because your family was from Long Island? If a blind dentist mistook my right ear for a mouth and proceeded to scrape plaque from inside my ear canal, it still wouldn't be as painful as listening to you. You and your family put me down because I actually came from Florida and had a tendency to wander around Tampa mumbling in strange voices. Sure, maybe you did catch me speaking in "strange voices," but you never heard me cuss.

New Yorkers make more money than Southerners. They buy up Florida land and patronize the natives. Then they travel the rest of the country and say, "Oh, Florida's not the South!" Meanwhile, full-grown dogs the size of footballs roam St. Petersburg freely, licking the dead carcasses of old Yankees who die playing shuffleboard inside God's waiting room. New Yorkers retire with more money than Southerners. They buy up Florida cemetery plots and push out the locals.

You had no appreciation for my subscription to *MuscleMag*. You never complimented my physique or acknowledged the hours I invested in cultivating the perfect tan. You ignored my body's careful enhancement through horse steroids. I put on sixty pounds of pure muscle in six months and you had the audacity to call me a "fanatic"!

"Do I look fat? Am I fat? Do I look fat?" You were thirty pounds underweight! Thirty pounds underweight! Exactly who's being the "fanatic," baby? Said you were not afraid of dying from anorexia nervosa. What, did you think it was cool to live fast, die young, and leave behind a beautiful skeleton?

Remember how freaked out you were when I went to the cemetery looking for pen pals? You had no respect for my hobby of writing letters to dead people. I'd find a name I liked, write them a letter, bury it under their tombstone, and walk around Tampa looking for a response. The first time I was arrested for desecration of a gravesite, you were, to say the least, visibly upset.

You made fun of my hobbies by telling me body builders were fanatics and dead people couldn't read. Sometimes, to spite you, I wrote letters to dead fanatics and hung out with illiterate body builders. Well, lucky for you, I always bit my tongue and chose not to disclose how much I hated the color black. And never told you the abhorrence I felt for the hieroglyphics you'd draw on your cheeks every time we went out dancing. Eyeliner pencils weren't made so sensitive, self-pitying, darkly clad college chicks could draw on their faces. The Gothic scene is pretentious and stupid! The Goths aspire to an unhealthy, pale, sunken-eyed beauty. Did you honestly think vampires would live in The Sunshine State?

Your crowd works towards frailty and fetishized suffering. And as far as your Chuck Baudelaire ambitions are concerned, for redundancy and predictability, no poetry was ever as bad as your "and-then-my-daddy-fucked-me" series.

> metaphysics, varicose veins & pixie dust
> —and then my daddy fucked me.
> streams of fiery light that push me to
> another realm
> —and then my daddy fucked me.
> moonlight, unicorns & gargoyles
> —and then my daddy fucked me!
> by diane, june 1993

When I offered to kill your daddy, grind him up, and drink him inside one of my protein drinks, you didn't appreciate it. When I threw him through a plate-glass window at the T.G.I. Friday's on Fowler Avenue, you told the Tampa police you thought I was a danger to myself and others, and due to my incarceration, I missed the opportunity to compete in the Mr. Sunshine Florida Body Builder competition. Thanks for nothing.

As a kid, I always got terrible cases of athlete's foot. I'd get these open sores in between the little piggy that cried "wee wee wee" all the way home and the little piggy that had none. For hours upon hours, I'd squeeze and stare into the sores. I'd take strings from my socks and tie them around my toes, letting the strings cut into the open sores. I'd twist and pull at the strings. Other times, I'd simply stab a wound with a tack. It was cool, the way the pain would cause my body to vibrate. Typically, a sore resembled a wet sliver, but sometimes it had hard brown crust along the edges. I don't know what became of that old fungus, but it was the most consistent aspect of my childhood. Don't know how this pertains to you, but I just thought I'd mention it. That's all.

Diane, I thought I could lance your pain like a boil. Stab it into a bloody, pussy mess and eventually it would go away. Soon, you'd forget it was even there. Unless, of course, you lance it incorrectly, in which case it forms a dime-shaped patch of hairless skin. Please, please believe me. Diane, I thought that by hating myself I could love you. They said I could either hate myself or I could hate you. I've chosen what seems most productive.

The only time this boy ever yelled at you was during private moments of desperation. Typically, whenever I did raise my voice, it was preceded by "Diane, please!" But you were a walking temper tantrum waiting to exist. You'd roll your eyes and release a deafening rant about every perceived injustice this world has ever slammed into you. Once anything was intercepted by your paranoia, you'd turn into a blind, rabid dog, attacking whatever moved. Your temper would purge itself in any situation at any time. You'd smack my shoulder with your backhand and scream "What's all this fucking shit?"

Sometimes, during private moments, you'd stop mid-rant and ask, "Why am I being so nasty?" You'd fall to your knees, crying, begging me to forgive you; I always did.

I was punished for your bad dreams. Remember that? I'd hear you tell someone on the telephone, "My boyfriend was bad last night but that's okay because I bitched him out this morning." You split my lip and I blamed myself. You hit me outside your favorite Goth club. I saw it coming and did nothing. I let you do it. If I were a man, I would've killed you. If I were on steroids then, who knows what I would've done. You apologized all up and down and around the block. Caressed my face and cried on my shoulder. A week later, you were bragging about it. Your friends threw high fives and thought it was funny.

Why did you only give me affection in public and never at home? When we went out to dance clubs, you'd grab my crotch and nibble on my ear. So jealous that somebody might find me attractive, you had to declare your ownership. Once you wanted to piss in my face, less of an interest in kinky sex and more of a desire to mark your territory. The moment we got home, you'd make me feel guilty for wanting sex. You'd yell and stare at me with narrowed, accusing eyes. I was your father and every teenage boy with a stiff cock who refused the word "no."

We had lots of sex in the beginning, but five months into our relationship, you told me you've never wanted to have sex with anybody but had come to believe you'd lost the right to say no several boyfriends ago. With me, you relearned that you had a right to say no, and you said it in droves. It killed me, the realization that you had sex with me out of duty. That killed me. The guilt and knowledge that I was so stupid— no longer could sex be anything other than rape in our eyes. Past lays and make-out sessions were harshly analyzed. Nobody could've really wanted to fuck me. For the first time, I remembered being sixteen, seventeen, in my mother's Pinto, getting agitated and surly because a date wouldn't touch my dick. Suddenly, I had memories of wrestling past blocking hands in order to cop another feel. Absolutely no way could I be a rapist, but I didn't know for sure.

One day, I was at an ATM in an isolated, residential area. The machine was warm and magnificently built. It had a screen with vibrating lights and graphics like a video game. I pushed my bank card inside the ATM's slit but I couldn't remember my PIN. The machine kept rejecting and spitting my card out. I kept shoving my card back in, harder and harder, until finally the screen read in bright silver letters, "Please, please stop! You're hurting me!" I looked up at the security camera and just hoped to God the ATM would be too traumatized to press charges. The next day, I presented the ATM with flowers and a letter of apology.

I stopped sleeping. I couldn't read the newspaper anymore. Women get raped every day. Remember the fifteen-year-old girl who got raped by a pair of 12th graders at St. Pete High? The judge wanted to give them a lesser charge so as not to ruin their chances for college. Turns out they were on the football team, or the baseball team. The girl was ridiculed at school and the boys got scholarships. I couldn't sleep for days after reading that article. And others, too: throwaway items that report burglaries and muggings first and mention that the victim was raped in the last line. Read stories about frat boys and Army guys. They're all rapists, you know, every last one of them. I thought that if I began sexually assaulting frat boys and Army guys by the dozen, you'd be proud, that you might even find it amusing. Some of them did. When I proposed my idea to you and went on to describe what such an encounter would be like, I didn't hear you laugh once.

The St. Pete boys grabbed the girl as she was leaving school. They dragged her underneath the bleachers and raped her. Other students knew what was going on and just laughed. Would it have been so wrong if I killed those St. Pete boys? Or how about the judge? It would've been a good idea.

If I had ever admitted to having lust in my heart, you would've pulled my heart out and sliced it open for your fucking

77

ELI,ELY

Goth friends. When you once heard me say
that a certain female had a nice body, you
screamed, beat your fists against your face,
and threatened to commit suicide. Only
after I ate wallpaper, pushed an incense
burner into my palm, and crushed my VCR did
you accept my apology.

Can't you see how hard I tried to be your
boyfriend and what impossible standards you
set for me?

The judge said it was unfortunate that
two emotionally unstable people fell in
love. I said, "It's unfortunate that I fell
in love with an unstable woman, but I myself
am not unstable." Some people in the court
laughed, but the judge didn't. He sat there
and looked at me sadly. I don't appreciate
pity so I threatened to push my fist through
his back. The judge didn't think it was
funny, but he didn't get angry. He ordered
absolute silence in the court. He focused
his attention on my face and said nothing.
He looked sad. It reminded me of my father.

Dad was always despondent about
something. He'd tell his drinking buddies
that having a family was depressing. Or
maybe it was having his family that was
depressing. It came as a shock to nobody
when he finally left. I always felt sorry
for my father. The judge looked like an
older version of how I remember my sad dad.
Dad never wore a robe or sat in a chair
so high off the ground, but the judge's
presence sent me thinking about my dad,
wherever he is. When the judge finally spoke
and gave sentencing, I felt nothing.

Because of my body, the psychiatrists fear me. I'm being observed as I write this letter. Four suited MDs watch me from a plexiglass window. My ankles are chained to the legs of a chair that's bolted to the ground. Both my hands will be handcuffed behind my back the moment I finish typing this letter. The table I'm writing on is also bolted to the ground. The typewriter I pound is welded to the table and invisible. Everything is made of cold metal, bizarre as hell. There are guards armed with ugly sticks standing at each side of this table. It's funny. Guards, orderlies, are only hired for their bulk, and I'm bigger than all of them. They're visibly uncomfortable whenever I'm around. It cracks me up senseless.

They can't keep me here forever. I didn't kill anybody. Your daddy recovered. And even if they send me to a regular prison, like Raiford State Prison, which is what they're threatening, I know they still can't keep me there forever. And when I get out, the first thing I'm going to do is legally change my name to Mr. Sunshine Florida Body Builder since I was a shoo-in to win that title anyway. My mom visited me for the first time since my incarceration. She summarized all that's happened since I've been inside. My brother's joined a hippie commune down south. They're called "the Budd-Judds" because they believe in combining the virtues of Buddhism and Judaism to make one perfect religion. They've built a rock garden in Boca Raton.

And to think, I was always considered the weird brother.

My sister has gotten terribly fat and didn't know she was pregnant until the bastard popped out while she was waiting in line at Stacy's Buffet. He was quickly put up for adoption, and Mom's getting married again. She's marrying her AA sponsor, and this time, I think it's going to work.

And you, Diane, finally offed yourself for good this time; according to Mom, you drove from Tampa to Orlando and hanged yourself from a streetlight in the nude; and sometimes, at night, I can see you dangling above International Drive, the traffic backed up for miles, horns honking and O-town's neon lights reflecting off your pale skin. Mom said you had recently checked yourself into a hospital, but somehow they overlooked your anorexia and the scars stitched across your wrists. The hospital said you exhibited no signs of self-abuse, no signs of mental illness, and no signs of health insurance. The hospital let you go and you drove to Orlando. My doctors were furious when they learned everything Ma had told me. They've kept me chained up ever since. I'm sure it's illegal.

I love you and it's been impossible getting over you. I thought I could save you, but now you're dead and a judge and a shitload of doctors are telling me I'm criminally insane.

People have always said I was crazy.

They'd say, "You're crazy!"

But I always thought it was a fun, good-natured type of crazy. Everyone thought I was funny. I'd hang out at department stores and expose my genitals to senior citizens. Or I'd hang my dirty underwear on the neighbor's tree. You know, basic kids' stuff. My Ma tells me I used to pee on the neighbor's car because I liked the sound it made. The old guy would come over and complain and my stepdad would shake his head and say "That boy ain't well."

The same old man with the tree and the piss-stained Buick had another reason to think I was truly mad. In my early teens, I used to eat laxatives, break into the old man's house, and shit in his cat's litter box. Concerned, the old man brought the litter box to a veterinarian and asked, "Is this normal?" Recognizing human excrement immediately, the vet accused him of pooping in his own litter box just to get attention. The doctor said, "Hey, I know being old can be lonely, but Jesus Christ, man, get a dog."

This habit continued for weeks until the old bastard finally caught me in the act. I must admit, it was pretty embarrassing. Stepdad number two talked him out of pressing charges, but from that day forward, every time I walked through my own neighborhood, people would shake their heads, laugh, and say, "That boy ain't well."

I played it off well. Calling myself the most popular boy at school, my reputation was always good for laughs even if I had no friends. It wasn't a charade. I wasn't out to shock anybody or make people uncomfortable. I was essentially being myself, and people thought that was weird. Today, I'm called insane, and it's never funny. I'm not insane and everybody in this world owes me an apology.

"No More I Love You's" by Annie Lennox was sung, recorded, and released to coincide with our break-up. We had tentatively broken up. You stayed at the Temple Terrace apartment off 56th and I moved to a Suitcase City duplex off of Nebraska Avenue. During the spring of '95, a loser couldn't turn on the radio or watch MTV without hearing Annie's song about a dozen times in one day. Why? Because it was meant to be the catalyst for our relationship ending; Annie wanted to let the world know that a chapter in our lives was over. Annie Lennox is like a fairy godmother to us. To think Annie Lennox thought enough of our relationship that she recorded a song about it. It was a desperate time in my life. A time when I was forced to realize I wasn't going to be your boyfriend anymore and there'd be no more I love you's.

And it was this song that was playing over the speakers the day I happened to run into your daddy eating lunch at T.G.I. Friday's. Baby, don't you understand? It was my love for you, Annie Lennox, and that song that caused me to send your father's fat ass flying face-first through a plate-glass window.

My mom told me you were buried down in South Florida, where Jews and New Yorkers buy up land. I'll be out soon, baby. I'm going to break into your daddy's house while he's taking his morning shower. Pounding his facial scars with my fists is going to be hilarious. I'll easily overpower him. He's notoriously paranoid, and I expect your daddy to whip out a pistol from the soap dish or something. This doesn't faze me. I'm quicker and stronger. He'll be beaten severely and left unconscious. I'll plug the drain and leave the water running, letting him drown in his bathtub in a bloodied fetal position like a homemade abortion.

Your mother shall receive a mercy killing, a quick snap of the neck. After a lifetime of no self-esteem and a marriage to a sick man, that woman died a long time ago.

I'll come to your gravesite there,
I'll fold this letter and bury it under your tombstone.
I'll stand and wait.
Your response could come in the form of a bird singing.
Your message received, I'll take several steps backwards
and broad jump headfirst into your tomb-stone,
cracking my skull and letting the blood seep down into your grave.
Then our souls will ascend into Heaven and we'll be back together.

In our early days, we wrote poetry, drank red wine, and danced all night long.

There'll be no eating disorders in Heaven.
No incestuous fathers. No frat boys. No
Army guys. No high-school-aged rapists.
There'll only be angels, God, saints, and
men with bodies like Greek statues. In
Heaven, nobody will point and whisper "co-
dependent." We'll be angels and eternally
in love.
Oh, Diane, we'll finally be happy again.

Love,
Mr. Sunshine Florida Body Builder
Chattahoochee State Mental Hospital
Home for the Criminally Insane
Chattahoochee, Florida

"Come Visit!"

III

Regardless of how many times this intense little fiction has been consumed, it never fails to break my heart, if only because I wrote it and can vividly recall every thought, emotion, and revelation that inspired "Chuck Baudelaire Ambitions."

I wrote the short story six years ago, loosely based on a relationship that ended nearly a decade before. Interestingly enough, the girlfriend's name was Tai, but I felt it too exotic for the white-trash Florida universe in which my stories were going to take place. Tai, my dear Tai, was not from Long Island but rather the American South. Once, believe it or not, my suicidal Gothic girlfriend had been a runner-up for Miss Teen South Carolina. However, in a tale about incest and its long-term ramifications, I didn't want to perpetuate the Southern incest white trash stereotype.

If the woman was an incest survivor *and* a Southern beauty queen, San Francisco sophisticates would've laughed at the story.

Furthermore, on stereotypes, the preconceived notions people have that body builders are stupid, macho, callous bullies are simply, *emphatically*, not true. Not even close. If I were to compile a list of all the subcultures I've nearly entered but never quite fit into, the one group that I'd say was the most sensitive, sad, and empathetic would not be the actors I went to college with nor the poets and spoken-word artists I've been observing in Bay Area coffee shops for almost a decade. No, the most sensitive people I've known in my life have been the professional body builders I knew. Always remember that most body builders start lifting weights to prevent themselves from being bullied and to prevent bullies from picking on individuals who resemble their former selves. You'll find that on the whole, body builders tend to be nicer people than anybody you'll ever meet who describes himself as an "artist."

Every passionate weight lifter I've ever known will bend your ear with tales about the days in his past when he walked in shame with a body that was always too skinny or too fat. Whenever he sees somebody who resembles his former self, more often than not, he'll treat that person with great kindness and support. I've seen body builders do this in a way that'll bring tears to your eyes. That sensitivity noted, what could be more frightening than a painfully sensitive, emotionally and mentally unstable young man with a chip on his shoulder, juiced up on steroids and capable of bench-pressing over five hundred pounds?

What could be a better dichotomous symbol for a writer than a body builder?

Tai came from money, by the way. Her daddy was a rabid wolf in sheep's expandable-waist pants; a sickening, fat demon made wealthy by being the CEO for a world-famous, world-dominating corporation that shall remain nameless. In my mind, I've slowly pushed a rusty knife into his neck about a thousand times. When she was twenty-one, her daughter-fucker father had the audacity to feel her ass and tits right there in front of me. Tai cowered. I said something like "What the fuck are you doing?" and then he and I almost came to blows. Big regret. I should've shut his eyes with my fists.

Tai had resigned herself to his not-uncommon gropes, and her mother acted as if she saw nothing. Tai couldn't recall her earliest sexual memories. It seems she just *knew* one day that she wasn't a virgin anymore and that it had something to do with the CEO's late-night visits to her unicorn-plastered, girly-girl bedroom with the row of beauty pageant trophies.

In high school, a boy she thought was a good friend knocked on her door when no one else was home; thinking it was cool, she let him in. The next day, he bragged to everybody at school, seemingly unaware that rape is not synonymous with sex.

We met at a Tampa punk club in the early '90s. She was a Goth and I was a skinhead bouncer friendly with the SHARPs and the Nazis both. Though ideally I was closer to the former than the latter, each subculture would congregate at the clubs that employed me. Being muscular, blue-eyed, tattooed, and embracing my premature baldness, the skinhead look was a perfect fit. Tai had to work hard to be a Goth, meaning she had the black leather, the black velvet, the black clothes, the jet-black-colored eyes, and the impossibly black, black hair, but, with the exception of the white scar tissue along her wrists, Tai always had dark, swarthy skin unable to obtain the death-pale sheen those melancholy types strive for.

Writing's cheaper than therapy. Taking the emotion wrapped around a relationship that existed in pain, I wanted to create art. Tai didn't kill herself when I knew her, but she may be dead by now. I was a rather unstable fellow, but Tai was worse. In the beginning, our relationship was passionate and sexy, but somewhere in the middle, I came to realize that nobody abuses like the abused.

She really did bitch me out first thing in the morning if I was "bad" in her dreams the night before. She yelled at me daily for the tiniest reasons. She spat at me and did hit me once, splitting my lip, apologizing profusely but then bragging about it to her friends. I never cheated, nor did I ever hit her. Whenever I stood up to Tai, she'd make me feel guilty, reminding me she was the oft-raped former beauty queen and what was she doing with me since she preferred skinny Goth vampire boys over beefy skinhead types? Sometimes, she'd threaten to commit suicide when I'd criticize her or try to lay down certain boundaries. Never once did she ever take responsibility for her actions. I'd wanted to break up for a solid six months before we did but couldn't because of her incredible skills with guilt weaponry.

Writing an autobiographical short story about a skinhead bouncer and a former beauty queen turned Goth would've been contrived in a *Generation X* sort of way. Close as it was to the truth, it still didn't appeal to me. But a tale about an untalented Goth poetess from New York in a relationship with a chemically imbalanced and chemically enhanced white-trash Florida body builder: *that* was gold—an absurdist tragicomedy.

I turned the story in to my creative writing class at New College of California. The class loved it, even though more than a few couldn't tell if they ought to be offended or not. One chick called it "an exercise in misogyny" and another said she'd have been "more sympathetic if he wasn't a body builder."

Though I know nothing about basketball, Wilt Chamberlain is my favorite athlete of all time, and not just because he claimed to have bedded two thousand honeys, but because he was fond of saying "Nobody roots for Goliath."

Nobody roots for Goliath.

No truer statement has ever been made.

My teacher, a well-respected and frequently published female writer whom I shall refrain from name-dropping, loved it, fucking loved it! Said it was one of the funniest and saddest things she had ever read.

I took that story, and eventually others, and toured around tiny theaters and venues throughout the Bay Area. These other stories (monologues, really) were never autobiographical. Though one character I played, "Tweaker Thomas," was based on an actual drug dealer I knew, I'd have him doing things on stage he never did in real life, like writing a letter to all his neighbors to publicly declare war on sleep. Or I performed monologues, like the one where I played a male runway model with a deformed, amphibian-like, ever-wet, never-hard penis who develops an obsession with The Elephant Man's penis. As fucked up as The Elephant Man was, his left arm, left hand, and penis were in perfect functioning order. Regardless of his pain and loneliness, he could always have sex, he could always masturbate. Now imagine being a drop-dead gorgeous male model who can't do either. There's no way to tell whether The Elephant Man died a virgin, but if Merry Ole England was anything like California in the present tense, then I'll bet my last shilling that surely Joseph Merrick, a celebrity freak at the time of his death, could've located a Victorian-era star-fucker or two.

Then there was a character named Tiberius Cobb (i.e., Ti Cobb) who owned a New Age bookstore and was a serial killer who went around killing people everywhere because he believed that they had tried to kill him in a previous lifetime. And still there were others, including more adventures for my potentially dangerous, mentally ill body builder.

By the time I performed as Tweaker Thomas at the 1999 San Francisco Fringe Festival, I was a fairly well-known figure in the local underground performing arts scene. Of course, I was usually performing while dangerously high on speed, and it seemed I never really came down until I went to a New Year's Eve party that year and 100 percent blacked out, missing the great end-of-the-millennium countdown, only regaining consciousness on my feet around dawn, January 1, 2000 walking around a now mostly empty, cluttered warehouse space with no memory of the preceding hours, and deciding to walk home and overdose on sleeping pills.

A California Pizza Kitchen manager called and heard the suicide note I had recorded as the outgoing message on my answering machine. He dialed 911. The police arrived first and decided if they waited for the ambulance, I'd die. They threw me in the back of their squad car after carrying me down three flights of stairs and drove me to the ER. The CPK manager, Rick, now lives and manages a restaurant in Sacramento. The cops who saved my life? I couldn't even describe to you what they looked like, but if it wasn't for their quick decision-making, I'd be dead right now. There were drugs and drug paraphernalia in my room. The cops could've looked around and dismissed me as a drug-addicted loser, but instead they decided that my life was worth saving. You'll never hear me bitch about the San Francisco Police Department. I've got fantasies that someday I'll be hugely successful and will be able to send a million-dollar check to Rick's Sacramento address expressing my gratitude for his call to 911. To those two anonymous cops who saved my life, I don't know who you guys are, but may you each have long and happy lives.

The emergency room was chaos: stomach pump, tubes in my arms, a hose down my throat, gulps of charcoal juice—waking up there became the most frightening hours of my life. Someday I must forgive myself for the fact that this is how the twenty-eight-year-old me spent his New Year's Day. I spent a single night in a mental ward, though they wanted to keep me there for three days. After much persuasion, they agreed to call me a cab. On the evening of the second, a cheerful, middle-aged, squirrelly Middle-Easterner with a thick accent drove his taxi through the City faster than any driver has ever driven through this town, all the while eating a block of white, pungent gourmet cheese as if it were a hamburger. He dropped me off in front of my old building on Greenwich Street and told me that the hospital pays for the cab. He wanted no money from me. Then he said, "Hey, you're a young, handsome man. Life's too hard to not be happy. Do something interesting with your life. You hear me?"

I heard him.

I've only done speed one other time since that terrible New Year's Eve, and even when I did do it, I walked to Becca Depner's apartment off Howard Street in the Mission and asked her to destroy the rest of my stash. I handed her about seventy-five dollars' worth and she flushed it down the toilet. Even that was several years ago. Haven't done drugs in years. No NA or rehab or anything else. Just decided to stop doing it and I did. Though the drug overdose of the very drug dealer who inspired Tweaker Thomas probably helped enforce that decision.

I took some time off from work, and no, they did not fire me, thank God, and as I lay in bed feeling my vigor coming back, I decided to accumulate the monologues and short stories I'd been performing into one tragic novel. What plot could unite my cast of oddities? How about a national suicide note writing contest?

By June of 2000, I was done, and I gave it the title *Pricks of Conscience,* a term stolen from a Fred Nietzsche, the "God is dead" guy. Said Nietzsche:

"Why does our conscience prick us after social gatherings? Because we have treated serious things lightly, because we have treated light things seriously, because in talking of persons, we have not quite spoken justly or have been silent when we should've spoken, because sometimes, we have not jumped up and run away; in short, because we have behaved in a society as if we belonged to it."

Ever read a better-expressed "outsider" statement in your entire life?

By December 2000, I had accumulated a tiny stack of rejection form letters from various publishers and agents.

By January 2001, I had moved to Seattle.

In June of that year, a well-established literary agent with a Park Avenue, New York address and famous clientele actually agreed to represent me. My agent and I have managed to keep in casual contact through emails and the occasional postcards, and despite his requests for more work, I've yet to send him anything. It's not that I'm afraid or lazy. It's that I've yet to finish a single project.

Even when I did my one-man show at Lance LittleJohn's Theater Bazooka, it was nothing but excerpts from *Pricks of Conscience* and one true story that was told in a straightforward, confessional style, inartistic but funny and self-indulgent and totally heartbreaking, like something you'd hear at an AA meeting.

"Chuck Baudelaire Ambitions" represents the one time that I took autobiography and disguised it as fiction. The body builder's emotional and mental instability and his obsession and love and resentment towards his ex-girlfriend were based on my own. Ernest Hemingway wrote, "Write clear and hard about what hurts."

"Chuck Baudelaire Ambitions" was a short story. However, as a novelist, do I have the balls to truly write clear and hard about what hurts? To write a novel that is but a thinly veiled event list from my own life and not necessarily the events when I shone like a bright-eyed movie star on Oscar night or when, by the grace of God, the prettiest girl at the party went home with me? I want to know if I have the strength to write about the times when I've choked, when I've fallen flat on my face and been forced through disappointments in fate and character, to take a long, hard look at myself and decide where to go next. Do I have that type of strength? Do I have the balls to create a character based on myself, the secret self, the genuine self that I strive so hard to prevent my closest friends from seeing?

I doubt it.

V

Lately, my conscience has felt the prickling of an idea. Something funny, something dark, something bizarre, and something that, if done well, would be thought-provoking:

A young man, who happens to be a repressed homosexual, learns that if you crack open another person's skull at a certain angle that person's life comes pouring out like a hologram. The person with the hammer then can sit back and watch like he's watching television. The images are always brief with no narrative, but somehow, through a montage of dreams, memories, and visions, the viewer gets an idea of the dying individual's character and basic life experience.

It seems the young man, a traveling carpenter, once witnessed a pair of construction workers argue. When one smashes the other's forehead with a hammer, the construction worker runs away, horrified by his actions, and kills himself by driving a pair of electric drills into each of his temples simultaneously. The young carpenter walks over to the man whose head has been bashed. There, to his astonishment, he sees a hologram shoot from the dead man's split skull.

The carpenter sees the dead construction worker as a child being beaten by an outlaw biker father. He then sees him as a handsome, sunbaked teenager getting his dick sucked by surfer chicks, and, later, he sees him on a golden motorcycle with bird wings riding down A1A with a butt naked, in-her-prime Farrah Fawcett holding onto his back. Next, he sees the dead construction worker as he saw him that morning, drinking from someone else's thermos. When confronted, he laughs and refuses to apologize. The last sight he sees is a hammer going towards his face.

Enthralled, the young carpenter becomes addicted to other people's experiences. A shy, seemingly asexual man who has never had a relationship of any kind, he finds himself attracted to older straight men. He hammers men with crow's-feet, laugh lines, worry lines, receding hairlines, leathery skin, and deep, reflective eyes that convey experience and life. The carpenter pleasures himself to images of hard-drinking, hard-living middle-aged men, aging rogues, aging bad boys, and bar brawlers: Edgar Allan Poe, Richard Burton, Sir Richard Burton, Oliver Reed, George C. Scott, Lee Marvin, Laurence Tierney, John Cassavetes, Clint Eastwood, Robert Mitchum, Nick Nolte and the like; these are the types of individuals who give the serial-killing carpenter a boner and those his victims remind him of.

For the carpenter, the only intimacy he ever knows comes through smashing the skulls of the men he finds attractive. He stops watching movies and reading books. For him, there's no greater entertainment than watching the innards of another man's brain, each victim his own Great American Novel, each victim his own epic film.

SETTING: A man's brain.

CHARACTERS: Thoughts, pontifications, obsessions, secrets, loves, desires, prejudices, memories, regrets, depressions, fights, arguments, fears, meditations, mantras, lies, truths.

PLOT: The elusive quests of identity, love, self-esteem, life, perspective of experience, self-awareness. Each victim's story starts with "A hole in the center of a man's forehead is dripping blood, brain, thoughts, secrets, tales, memories, escapades . . ." and always ends with "A hammer is coming towards his face." Sometimes these holograms last for hours into the night, and other times they are over within minutes.

The young carpenter grows older. He travels the country as a master carpenter, acquiring one gig after another. Eventually, his age and appearance closer resemble the men he continually kills, the expressive lines on his face less earned but rather absorbed from the men he has been killing.

By now, in his late thirties, the carpenter feels there must be a greater form of intimacy to be achieved with these weathered macho men than cracking their skulls wide open. He wonders if he could achieve a normal, healthy, perhaps even sexual relationship with the self-destructive, volatile, masculine men he finds so desirable. The carpenter enters a Seattle bar in the U District on a night that lives up to Seattle's wet reputation.

There he meets a thirty-two-year-old writer named Audie Lee Thomas. They talk, drink, laugh, and discover they have much in common. They are a pair of twenty-first-century macho men who agree that feminism did nothing for this country but emasculate men and encourage women to be mean and bitter. Together, they openly consider opening up a Pacific Northwest chapter of The He-Man Woman Haters Club. Audie, ever the audacious mouth, says, "If I ever have a boy, I'll teach him that it is okay to hit girls."

"Yeah?" The carpenter is not offended but is definitely taken by surprise. He looks around to see if anyone at the bar is upset, but the jukebox is loud, playing pure grunge, and nobody's paying attention.

"It's interesting. We're taught not to hit girls. Women are now taught to get into a man's face and bitch him out. Put him in his place. When we back off because we don't hit women, the woman thinks she's a tough guy. She thinks we're intimidated. But truthfully, the only reason she's still standing is because she's a woman. Women are mean bitches. Was it Sean Connery who said 'There are worse things than hitting a woman'? Well, he was right."

Both men emphatically state they love fucking women but could easily live their entire lives without one. The carpenter is lying. He's still a virgin, having never been with a man or a woman. Towards last call, Audie slaps the carpenter's back (he has yet to ask for his name) and says, "Hey, dude. You're my type of guy," then invites the carpenter over to his apartment for more beer, some weed, and cocaine, if he can get some on short notice. The carpenter wonders if he'll lose his virginity to the tough-looking writer (Audie did say he was a writer). He is younger than the carpenter usually likes, but he is handsome in a way and has a good body. Thickly built, like a habitual fighter, a natural athlete, Audie's isn't a gym/health club type of body but is brawny with a definite physical presence: confident, aggressive, predatory even.

The carpenter knows he wants Audie. Knows then and there that he wants to try his first and only real relationship with this man. The writer gives the carpenter a bisexual vibe, and he thinks there seems to be more than a good chance he's going to get seduced tonight. When Audie invites the carpenter over, the carpenter bites his tongue to conceal his excitement. He hopes that his previous form of intimacy with men has become a thing of the past.

Walking the desolate, unlit Burke-Gilman trail just outside the University of Washington campus, Audie Lee Thomas sucker-punches the carpenter powerfully on his jaw. On his knees, the carpenter (the only thing he'll be known as in the story) pulls a small hammer from the side pocket of his cargo pants and jumps up quickly. By thirty-eight, the man has had twenty years of experience as a carpenter and serial killer. Even in the black rain, he gets Audie square in the center of his forehead with an automatic, well-aimed swing of his hammer. The would-be writer dies instantly, moments before he even hits the ground.

Out of breath, the carpenter plops down, his ass falling onto the muddy trail. He sighs deeply, disappointed, though grateful the writer wasn't tough enough to break his jaw. Audie's body lies across from the carpenter. Within seconds, his life unfolds inside a hologram in the dark, wet sky.

Audie's parents fuck with the little boy's head, telling the boy he's bad, conceited, vain, and narcissistic, his mother usually calling him such things as she's looking at herself in the mirror. It escalates into his twenties. A pushed Audie Lee fights, physically fights, his stepfather and his brother. He tells his mother he hates her, tells the biological father he barely knows to go fuck himself. The young man hates everything, more hateful and outwardly more dangerous than the serial-killing carpenter ever was. Audie commits acts of arson, of assault and battery. He's a predatory womanizer, even a bit of a misogynist; he's a drunk and a drug addict. He attacks people violently, both verbally and physically. Audie Lee Thomas attempts suicide often and has a drug overdose. He collects tattoos that are strange, random, and incomprehensible even to himself. Convinced he is ugly, he avoids mirrors. There's no clue as to why women find him attractive. Audie fears his estranged family will take credit for his success. Therefore, success has never been a part of Audie's hateful life. A failed actor who never bothered to give Los Angeles a try, he now calls himself a writer, though he's never been published. He travels the country, one restaurant job after another, hating his mom, hating his life, hating his past, present, and future. He once wrote a poem that was no damn good and signed his byline "The Hateful Hater." To be a writer, a better writer, Audie decides to collect experiences and to have as many different kinds of experiences as possible. He changes residences frequently. He gets into fights, goes to jail, parties hard, does a myriad of drugs, gets locked up in psych wards, and fucks with great abandon and promiscuity, none of which makes him happy. His dreams are all glory—no work, no perseverance. Just reward. He sees himself as a famous movie star, a famous personality, a famous writer—a man rich, gorgeous, beloved, powerful, feared. He has violent fantasies, like having killed his family when they were abusing him, beating up people who are famous, and torturing individuals he knows only casually but who have annoyed him in some way. Starting wars, causing riots—these are his greatest desires. Audie decides one day that he craves a new experience that is also a nod towards a final suicide attempt: to kill a man, and to keep killing until the FBI finally catches him. Washington State uses its death penalty sparingly, but Audie Lee Thomas knows his killing spree will end with the end of his own life, figuratively or literally. "Hell," Audie thinks, "maybe sitting in a prison cell on death row without having to work crap jobs and make ends meet, I'll be able to get some writing done, finish a novel. I'll definitely get published as a mass murderer." Audie knows, just knows, that the man he sees walking into the U District bar is a fag. He befriends the man, talks like a woman hater, and invites him to his cottage. "This is the man I'm going to kill," Audie thinks to himself. Walking along the Burke-Gilman Trail—dark, no street lights nearby, rain—Audie decks the carpenter, hitting him harder than he's ever hit anybody before. The carpenter is on the ground but gets back up immediately. "Was he not surprised?" Audie wonders. Audie Lee Thomas never even sees the hammer coming towards his face.

The carpenter sits in the darkness and says to himself, "I kill men for their experience. He was going to kill me for the experience, and then I killed him in self-defense, which, for me, was a new experience." Then the carpenter laughs a little, shaking his head slowly, the way people do when they're laughing at themselves.

In his maladjusted way, he felt that he was helping the men he had been bludgeoning for two decades. These men did not need to die from natural causes, the carpenter concluded. Robust, volatile men in the shadows of their prime who die by violent randomness are somehow solidifying badass legacies. Nephews will grow old telling and retelling tales about their tough uncles who worked with their hands, got into fights, drank hard, partied hard, and then were found with their heads bashed in. The carpenter never molested anyone's body, alive or otherwise. However, he would scrape up their hands, clothing, and faces. He'd kick and bruise their chests, sometimes crack a few ribs. He wanted to make it look like the men died fighting. "A real man right up to the very end" is what the carpenter hoped people would say about his victims.

Audie Lee Thomas' life and personality left the carpenter cold. He was the first guy that the carpenter disliked upon digesting his experiences. With Audie, there was no need to fake the earmarks of a fight. Audie already had them. People who knew Audie would assume he started the confrontation anyway.

The next day at work, the carpenter aims a nail gun at his forehead and pulls the trigger. After a split second of intense pain, he collapses backwards with a nail stuck inside his skull.

A young co-worker, an eighteen-year-old American Indian laborer, cautiously walks over to the dead carpenter. The Indian pulls the hammer from his tool belt. He places his foot on the serial killer's chest and delicately slips the claw end of the hammer underneath the nail's head. He quickly rips the nail from the carpenter. Nothing comes out but thick blood, bits of bone, and brain. The Indian stays and stares for a few moments. Nothing else happens. He leaves to tell others.

The carpenter just lies there. No hologram. No nothing. He has killed men all over the country, but because of his modus operandi and the lifestyles of his victims, the authorities never recognize the deaths as the acts of a serial killer. He's buried as anonymously as he lived. But then again, glory and fame were never what he wanted. *The End.*

Well, it appears I've got an outline. What exactly are Audie's personal thoughts, and why does the carpenter find them so disconcerting? What could a serial killer find inside the head of a loser like Audie that could be so disturbing he'd go kill himself? Could he simply be fed up with serial murder, or was he offended that he was almost the victim of random violence, and that hypocrisy caused him so much shame that the repressed homosexual decided to kill himself? If I write about a repressed homosexual, won't people assume I'm a repressed homosexual? Would I rather have them think Audie was based on me? Fuck no. I'd rather he die than the serial-killing gay carpenter.

It seems like an awful long buildup for a tiny punch line. In truth, I ought to forget that my one-man show was ever performed, and I need to call this little monster "The Experience Junkies," because these are men searching for an experience fix. Yeah, I like that. "The Experience Junkies."

I continue to write, elaborating on my original idea and outline. Writing, writing, and writing, my red pen against the white paper of one notebook and another and another, trying, trying desperately, to create a sensible story out of an idea that isn't conducive to sensible thinking.

Does it have to make sense?

IV

I'm starved. My eyes are red and swollen. My lower back aches. Someday, I'll probably be dependent on chiropractic help. I stand to stretch. Various joints throughout my body crack; my entire body's sore. Apparently, the great (and usually insane) chess champions burn the same amount of calories as professional boxers. If chess is a cardiovascular exercise, then how many calories does a writer burn?

The jazz CD I was listening to had run its course hours ago, and I was too into my writing to play it again or pick another CD. No noise of any kind distracted me. It was fairly early in the day when I began writing, and now it's 11 p.m.

Ernest Hemingway, in *A Movable Feast*, talks about the story writing itself, as opposed to the writer writing the story. When that happens, the indirect control of a story telling itself, it's pure elation, an extraordinary high. Today, not a single phrase poured out of me. Each had to be pinched and pulled into place. Nothing came easily today. Not a damn thing.

I lie down on my bed and close my eyes. Then a thought comes to me and I sit up. I'm not a pack rat, and because I've never been one to spend too much money on clothes, I've never felt any qualms about tossing them once they've worn out their welcome. One morning, several months ago, I took a green vest jacket I wore too often and threw it in the dumpster parked in the alley below my window. The weather was getting warmer, the hottest spring in decades, and I figured that come wintertime, if I wanted another vest jacket, one could be had at the closest thrift shop for a mere five dollars or so. That night, I recognized my green vest on an extraordinarily regular Vieni Vieni regular named Donovan. Oh, Donovan. Poor Donovan.

Everybody has a story. Donovan's is no more sad or pathetic or unusual than anybody else's. I think Donovan's lack of belligerent self-pity (so prevalent in junkies, barflies, and homeless people) ennobles him. He looks like a junkie, but beneath the tarnish, you can spot a sliver of his former handsomeness. Donovan had been a model and an art student. He had even been the protégé of a well-known Bay Area artist. Sharon, the whiskey-spent barmaid, told me that Donovan had once been physically beautiful and that he did have some talent. Alas, somewhere along the way, he discovered heroin. That was over twenty years ago.

Funny, I used to enviously stare at the thick blonde-grey tresses growing atop his skull-like face and ask God why I had no hair but a homeless fifty-two-year-old junkie had plenty. Donovan and I would drink cognac and Coca-Cola and pontificate on art and jazz and literature at a bar that is basically an old Bowery bar that somehow landed in San Francisco. We agreed that the great Joseph Mitchell, a famous writer from *The New Yorker*, would've been well and content to drink at Vieni Vieni. He knew writers and literature high and low. Donovan devoured everything he could find, material be damned. There was nothing I had read, thought about reading, or simply heard of that junkie Donovan hadn't already consumed. Whenever he couldn't find a book discarded, he'd shoplift at Barnes & Noble.

"Only take from the corporate monsters," he'd always say. He'd take another cognac sip and cackle his gummy cackle. Eventually, all junkies lose their teeth, you know.

He kept afloat by doing odd jobs around North Beach and Russian Hill, mostly for former classmates, the very people who could remember his beauty, his potential, and the great master he once studied under. Donovan told me he lived in a tree house in the backyard of a friend. Who knows if that's true, but he was at Vieni Vieni until closing time every night of the week, and each time I saw him, my old green vest jacket hung on his gaunt frame like a life preserver on a scarecrow.

Another hanger-on whom I care about is Window Jesús, a tiny, 5'4" Filipino alcoholic who may be known to every resident in North Beach. Like Norm on *Cheers*, he has his own special barstool that belongs to him and nobody else. It's in the front window underneath the red neon Vieni Vieni sign, looking out onto Stockton. Jesús stares with a half-smile and a drunken glaze in his eyes. He's North

Beach's most reassuring presence. Friendly locals walk by and wave. They love him. Window Jesús nurses a glass of red, a beer, and a whiskey shot, all simultaneously, two or three rounds a day. Other bar denizens buy him round after round and this determines how late he stays. Even I've bought him a round before. He never says thank you, just nods and waves.

Shortly after Jennifer and I hooked up, we walked past Vieni Vieni and there was Jesús sitting in the window. Miss Ely started giggling. "I love that guy! He's there every day!" Then she blew him a kiss and waved flirtatiously, wiggling her fingers. He nodded and waved back, but the expression on his face remained the same.

"Someday. Someday," Jennifer said, "I'm going to make that little guy smile."

"You ought to show him your tits," I said.

She rolled her eyes at me and said, "You're so crude sometimes, Eli."

Window Jesús gets there every morning, slips a twenty into the jukebox, sits on his stool, and usually leaves just before midnight. The man's taste in music includes Shirley Bassey, Dean Martin, Engelbert Humperdinck—schmaltzy, cheesy ballads that make your head spin. Jesús bobs his head and taps along. The man hardly ever says anything. He sits for hours staring out the window, waving at random people, when suddenly, he'll start yammering loudly, laughing, slapping his knees, and, after several minutes, he stops. Nobody pays him any attention. The other barflies don't even turn around to look at him. His nonsensical yammering simply becomes part of the décor of Vieni Vieni.

Jesús has only said three words to me, and it wasn't at the bar. Once, in Union Square, I spotted Jesús shuffling down Stockton. "Hey, Jesús!" I called out. "How are you doing today?" It was a cold, wet January in San Francisco. Jesús wore baggy jeans with the pant legs rolled upwards. He had an old brown windbreaker and a black knit beanie that read "Fitzsimmons Auto Parts." The hat had once belonged to me. I bought it at Clothes-Per-Pound on Valencia in the Mission, and it seems I had misplaced it somewhere the week before. Jesús looked at me and said, "I'm doing okay." Sad and feminine, his voice could've belonged to an old neglected grandmother.

Jesús wasn't homeless but was, according to bartender Sharon, an SSI-collecting Vietnam veteran who had come-and-go privileges at a nearby nursing home in SoMa. Donovan and Jesús: don't know why, but I care about you guys, I really do. My clothes, my bland, unflattering, unprofessional clothes, shall go to characters who'll appreciate them. Five golf shirts, different shades, different patterns. I always thought they looked good on my thick build with tattoos scribbled all over my arms, but now I know better. The orange Old Navy hoodie must be discarded. The clothes get wrapped up in a solid white towel. At Vieni Vieni, with my clothes encircled in the towel and sitting on the bar like a hobo's pouch missing its stick, I'm asking Sharon about Donovan and Jesús.

"Jesús has left for the day, and Donovan just stepped out to Walgreens to buy some aspirin, but he ought to be back soon." Then she says, "Why do you care?" Sharon has bad teeth, a bone-thin face, and colorless, blotchy skin. The woman's a dive-bar career bartender and looks it. Sounds like it, too. "What, you got a message for them or something?"

I lean closer to the bar. "Look, Sharon. Sometimes I'll toss my clothes in the trash and later on in the day I'll come down here and see Donovan or Jesús wearing them." Sharon's body language relaxes. There's certainly no surprise coming from Sharon's face. "I'm not going to stick around, Sharon. I'm going upstairs to sleep, but I'd like to leave this behind for Donovan and Jesús and anyone else. Just offer it to Donovan in a subtle way that won't embarrass him. Okay?"

Sharon nods. She takes the bundle and puts it behind the bar. The spent woman smiles at me briefly, as if just coming to the realization that I'm not such an asshole after all. I smile back, then leave, running upstairs and feeling lighter, better about myself.

I'm a brooder. Always have been. Losing an entire night's sleep to thought is not uncommon, but after marathon writing and giving away clothes to barflies, my mind is peaceful and clear. Lying down on my flimsy hotel mattress in my socks and underwear with the window open and the San Francisco breeze blowing through, sleep comes easily and happily.

I

ELI: So, Scott. Let me ask you a question again.

SCOTT: Yeah?

ELI: What is your opinion of the whole Eli,Ely situation? I mean, do you think this "hold" thing is a good thing?

SCOTT: Well, it's like, she just got back from Yosemite. Why the fuck does she need to go on a break from her relationship with you when she just got back from Yosemite? And Eli, it does sound like she sort of abandoned you when you need her support right now. You know what I mean? I mean everybody knows how disappointed you were when the Burberry gig fell apart and how that bitch manager, who solicited you in the first place, was really mean to you afterwards. It was totally uncalled-for, totally uncool. I can hear it in your voice, Eli. You're upset. It's not the time to be abandoning you right now.

ELI: Yeah . . . yeah. Yeah. Fuck, you're right. (*A deep sigh.*) I'm going bar-hopping tonight.

SCOTT: (*Silence.*)

ELI,ELY

ELI: Scott, I'm not going to go drinking. I need to get out. Blow off some steam. Need to be around people. Haven't been out all week, and I know that if I drink at all tonight, there's going to be trouble. Reckless binging, fighting, all that shit.

SCOTT: (*Silence.*)

ELI: I'm just going to hang out. Listen to music. Dance, maybe. I'm not going to try to get laid, but I could use some friendly conversation, at least.

SCOTT: Okay, Eli. I'm not your dad. You don't need my approval.

ELI: I know. Want to come with me?

SCOTT: No thanks. Got work tomorrow. Have an appointment with Janice.

ELI: Perverted Janice?

SCOTT: Yeah. Need to go over some illustrations tonight.

ELI: Wow. Perverted Janice is turning into a nice gig, huh?

SCOTT: Yeah.

ELI: (*Silence.*)

SCOTT: (*Silence.*)

SCOTT: Have a good night tonight, Eli. Make a decision about Jennifer Ely.

ELI: Thanks, man. Later, Scott.

SCOTT: Peace out.

* * *

Perverted Janice was a mutual friend who promoted shows at various venues, including Theater Bazooka, which is how she and I know each other. Considering that Janice supplements her income by writing erotica, I doubt that being called "perverted" would deeply offend her. She even has a contract with an S&M publishing house to produce six porn novellas in one year. Short, plump Perverted Janice has a round face framed by a flaming-red bowl cut. She told me she was designing an erotic graphic novel about adults who dress up like sexy, furry animals and stalk each other like prey, always obeying the food chain, in a huge metropolitan city. Not my cup of tea, but I applaud the creativity.

Perverted Janice was a writer, not an artist. She had hired a semi-famous illustrator to draw her characters, but ultimately, she didn't like his stuff. She was bitching about the lost money and the dude's art when I told her about Scott Bonne. I gave her his number and said, "Janice, just tell Scott that Eli referred you. You'll probably like his drawings better. His characters tend to be over-sexualized. All the men are buff with big bulges in their crotches and the women always have tits for days. He did the flyers and posters for my one-man show, 'The Experience Junkies.'"

"Oh, I loved those!"

"Yeah, that's my boy, Scott. Call him."

She called. They hit it off and have been collaborating ever since. One of her erotic graphic novels is now being distributed nationally. She commissions Scott's drawings and pays surprisingly well. Good for them. If only some of my dreams could come true.

Should I call Perverted Janice and get her spin on Miss Ely's "hold"?

No. Truth be told, Perverted Janice and I had little in common. She'd probably tell me to dress like a wolf and go find me a rabbit.

Need to get a woman's perspective though . . . Becca Depner! Time to call her.

BECCA: Eli! Oh, my God, Eli! (*Laughs.*) She's given you no other choice.

ELI: What do you mean, "no other choice"?

BECCA: Look, I don't know this girl. Hell, I was looking forward to meeting another Eli, but that's over and done with. I'm not going to be meeting her now.

ELI: How do you know?

BECCA: Because you've got to break up with her. If you want any self-respect, and if you want her to have respect for you, you've got to break up with her. (*Gently.*) Eli, I know you've had a run of bad luck lately. I'm sorry. It sucks. Like I said, I don't know her, but I know what she's probably trying to do. I've seen both men and women do it.

ELI: Elaborate, please.

BECCA: Sometimes guys who don't have the balls to break up with a girl act mean and short and irritable so the girl will break up with him.

ELI: (*I've done that before, more than once, when I was much younger.*)

BECCA: You've probably done something like that before, Eli.

ELI: I have not! Come on, Becca!

BECCA: Well, maybe *you* haven't (*She doesn't believe me for a second.*), but most people have.

ELI: What's your point?

BECCA: Eli! There's a very good chance that she wants to break up with you but doesn't have the balls, so she kicks you when you're down, makes you appear even more foolish than you already do.

ELI: Thanks, Becca.

BECCA: (*Laughs.*) She's given you no other choice, Eli.

ELI: Have you ever done that? Been real mean to some guy till he broke up with you?

BECCA: Not anymore. When I was mean, the boys became more dependent on me. (*Laughs.*)

ELI: Not all of them, Becca. We've known each other a long time, and I could name a few dudes you got hung up on back in the day.

BECCA: Not *all*, asshole, but most of them did. It must be a momma's complex, I guess.

ELI: Well, maybe after her break, we'll be back together, stronger.

BECCA: It's up to you. But why does she need a "hold" when she just got back from Yosemite? To find out why she was having a bad day last Sunday? Also, it's in the same week as the Burberry guy dissed you. You spent the entire summer harping on about that job. You lost it, and in the same week, your girlfriend, who has been saying "I love you," now decides to go on hold the same week. (*Laughs.*) She's a bitch.

ELI: (*It's painful, but I laugh, too.*) Yeah, Jennifer's pretty much full of shit.

BECCA: She's given you no other choice.

ELI: Shall I call her this week and break up or shall I wait and call her on Sunday? Maybe wait for her to call me.

BECCA: I just wouldn't call her, Eli. Move on, starting now.

ELI: . . . But I love her, Becca. She tells me she loves me.

BECCA: If she loved you (*Very gently.*), she wouldn't go on hold right now. You're in pain. Why was she not able to pick up on it? Is she that self-absorbed?

ELI: (*Silence.*) (*I'm pretty self-absorbed. So is Jennifer.*) *I'm* pretty self-absorbed.

BECCA: (*Laughs.*) Yes, yes, yes you are. Eli, I don't know an artistic individual who isn't, but you're also a totally sensitive person who has a great deal of empathy for others. Maybe you didn't always, but you do now. (*Silence.*) I know you'll make the right decision, Eli.

ELI: I thought I loved her. I mean, I do love her.

BECCA: Oh, Eli. I know you're usually dating somebody. To hear the "Eli-Ely" thing was interesting. What are the odds of a person changing their name and then falling in love with somebody who has the same name? How funny. But everyone used to wonder if you just fell for her because you guys had the same name.

ELI: (*Enough already!*) That's not fair. She loved me, too. She said it all the time.

BECCA: Fine, but she sounds like the kind of self-absorbed girl who'd fall in love with someone whose name is the same as hers. (*Laughs.*) We used to wonder about that.

ELI: Who's we?

BECCA: Me, Buddy (*her boyfriend*), Gladys (*her sister*), Redmond (*her sister's boyfriend*), the Vagina-Calling Girls (*Becca's all-female "boy band"*). Everybody.

ELI: (*Emotionally.*) Jesus fucking Christ, Becca. (*I think about hanging up.*)

BECCA: Eli, I know that isn't the reason you two were together and I know you're not the kind of guy who falls in love with falling in love . . . or maybe you are. But I do know that you've got an addictive personality, and I know you're not doing drugs right now, but you started to feel some intense emotions with this girl and you kind of just went at it full tilt. You know what I mean?

ELI: Whatever.

BECCA: You need to recognize this as a great fling—give it a certain lightheartedness. (*Carefully.*) You do need to lighten up a little bit.

ELI: Why?

BECCA: Because you're too intense. Laugh! Relax! Lighten up!

ELI: (*Silence.*)

BECCA: (*Silence.*)

ELI: Let me ask you a question. Jennifer is only twenty-four, and I'm usually not the kind of guy who gives a fuck about such things, but like, Jennifer volunteered that she had been with no more than thirty guys in her life. Is that a lot for a twenty-four-year-old?

BECCA: Eli, you've probably been with more women.

ELI: Yeah, but I'm thirty-two. Believe me, it doesn't really bother me. As a matter of fact, I used to tease her that she'd been with more people than I had by the time I was twenty-four.

BECCA: How'd she react?

ELI: She'd give me a seriously annoyed look.

BECCA: Girls mature quicker than boys.

ELI: Now you're defending her.

BECCA: No. It's just . . . she went through a phase, that's all. You know what I mean?

111

ELI: Actually, she did once say that she used to be unable to say no. When I asked her about that statement, she nodded and said most girls have that problem when they first start dating. She didn't seem real forthcoming on the subject, so I didn't pursue it.

BECCA: (*Sympathetic.*) Yeah. (*Thinking.*) (*Even more sympathetic.*) Yeah. Most girls have gone through that phase.

ELI: So she went through a sad slut phase. Don't any girls ever go through a happy slut phase?

BECCA: Oh, yeah! Most of us have gone through that phase, too! (*Laughs.*)

ELI: How do I know if I don't love her?

BECCA: Your hurt is genuine. It is. But the relationship is probably too young, and you two spent a goodly portion away from one another while she was up in Yosemite.

ELI: We were on the phone nightly. Hey, when did you and your boyfriend Buddy start exchanging "I love you's"?

BECCA: Just under a year.

ELI: Okay. Wow. So, you think there's a chance that she's done this on purpose?

BECCA: Whether she did or not, she's still giving you no other choice. If you stick around, wait for her call, and she says "I miss you, let's stay together," and if that's what you want, then stick around. But she played with your heart. It shows a huge lack of empathy for you, the guy who's supposed to be her boyfriend.

ELI: (*Silence.*)

BECCA: Another thing to consider, Eli, and I'm giving you

confidential girl information.

ELI: Hope they don't kick you out of your gender.

BECCA: They might. They might. When a guy calls a girl he's pursuing and she doesn't call him back for whatever reason, if that guy calls once and leaves a message, or maybe tries one more time, making a total of two messages, but then takes the hint and never calls back, we girls respect that guy. We do. It means he's cool. He has a life. He's smart. He's savvy. If by chance we run into him somewhere months or even years later, it really isn't that bad. We remember that he's actually pretty cool, and for a moment, we wonder if we should've given him more of a chance. This is as opposed to the guy who calls eight, nine, ten, fifteen times before he gets the hint. With him it's all fear and loathing, baby. He's a loser. He's got no life. He isn't smart or savvy, and if we happen to run into him, we pray like hell he doesn't see us, and we even consider making a mad dash out the emergency exit. Jennifer's not returning your phone calls. Know what I mean? Be the cool guy who can take the hint. And make sure that when she runs into you a year from now, she has nothing but respect for you and wonders if she should've given you more of a chance.

ELI: Okay, Becca. Thanks for the tough love. Bye.

BECCA: Any time, Sick Guy Eli.

Time to get a heterosexual man's angle.

"Fuck her! Fuck her! Fuck her!"

Lance LittleJohn has never been one to hold anything back.

"I can't believe she did that to you. What does she need to go on a break for? Right after that bitch at Burberry dicked you over. You know he wanted to fuck you! You're not that naïve. Come on, Sick Guy!"

"But I love her, Lance."

"No you don't. Maybe you think you do. I don't know. Maybe you do, but she doesn't love you, man. She wouldn't have done that if she did. She doesn't respect you either."

"Yeah?"

"Dude! Are you kidding? It's like the men who beat their wives. The woman keeps putting up with it, and the guy doesn't respect her because she keeps coming back for more. She's avoided your phone calls in the past. She doesn't care about your feelings, dude. Evidently, she doesn't think there's a chance she'll lose you. Tell her it's over. There're so many women out there. Fuck her."

Silence.

"It's like, uh, have you ever met Dave Tribune's sister?"

"No, she good-looking?"

"She's pretty, actually." Lance says it in a way that means she's surprisingly attractive, because Dave Tribune isn't. Women love Dave because he's creative and funny but not conventionally handsome in any way (keep in mind: I typically look like a guy who just got denied parole).

"Anyway, dude, it's like, Dave's sister was in this long relationship with some guy and they'd been together for three years. She's about thirty and says, 'What now? Are we going to get married? Move in together? What?' Guy says, 'I don't know if I'm ready yet.' They agree to go on a break so Dickhead can decide if he wants marriage, cohabitation, or whatever. They go a month not seeing each other or talking on the phone. Afterwards, they meet at a coffee shop, and she says, 'So?' He says, 'I still don't know the answer yet.' She says, 'Yeah, you do. Stay on your damn break,' and then she leaves and it's over. I saw her at Dave and Abby's wedding last year right after she broke up with the dude."

"Oh, yeah. That's the wedding I wasn't invited to. I thought Tribune and I were friends."

"You guys are. He likes you. He just remembers you at Becca's

Christmas party and all those old Popcorn Theater parties. And the Fringe Festival parties and the Bazooka parties." He laughs. "And at my thirtieth birthday bash where you showed your penis to my ex-girlfriend's mother." Lance laughs hard.

"I'm glad somebody remembers my presence at those parties."

"We all do but you, dude." He continues to laugh at me. "But what I'm trying to say is I saw Dave's sister at his wedding and we got to talking and she still loved this guy. It was so painfully obvious. They had been together for years. Her heart was broken but she knew that any time somebody wants to put the relationship "on hold," it's bullshit. They don't want to be with you anymore. They don't. They want to break up with you but can't. Or they want to date someone else from somewhere who's been giving them the eye and see how that works out. He wasn't being fair to her, and though she loved him, she had to be fair to herself. She spent the entire wedding in tears, and the reception, too. Everybody's date had to periodically go over there and comfort her."

"Wow, Lance, did you tell me that story to let me know Dave's sister was available?"

"No! Goddamn!" Lance has a low tolerance for frustration.

Laughing, I say, "I got the point, Lance. Relax."

"So what are you going to do about the Ely chick, Eli?"

"Both you and Becca said the same thing. Basically, she's put me in a difficult position where I can either stand up for myself, be a man, and break up with her, or go back to her after our break and walk on eggshells. Or I could speak to her after this week is over and I could listen to Jennifer when she says she wants us to stay apart longer and I could say, 'Okay, I don't care. It's for the best.' Sad smile. Sad smile. Hold back the tears. Hold back the tears.

. . . You know, Lance, the hold was only for a week."

"Fuck that. You need to be the one to break up with her. 'Let's put our relationship on hold' is bullshit, and can you honestly act like something doesn't bother you when it obviously does? You can't.

It's not in your nature. You wear your heart on your sleeve, always. You always give up what you're thinking, which can be pretty damn scary sometimes."

"Talk about the pot calling the kettle black."

"I know that's an old expression, Eli, but it sounds so racist nowadays, doesn't it?"

". . . Lance, what about you and your women these days?"

"I'm on a fuckathon, dude! A fuckathon."

"Are you with that same woman? That tall girl?" Lance is around 6'6" and his most recent flame is about three inches shorter than him.

"Her name is Angelique, Eli. Learn her fucking name! And yes. We've got an understanding. She's okay with me sleeping with other chicks, and she's into girls, too. So it is all cool—no guys though. We're not into that."

"Does your girlfriend ever talk about me?"

"Only when she's orgasming, Eli."

Lance gives me the greatest belly laugh I've had in weeks.

It's common knowledge that his girlfriend hates me. I once wrote a short story, purely fiction, about having sex with a 6'3" debutante named Ariel Hollingsworth, who, shortly after we have sex, goes to the Philippines and gets a skeletal transplant so she can be a petite 5'2", and then we have sex again, and I graphically describe both experiences while simultaneously decrying the now widespread practice of big-boned American women going to poor, developing Asian countries to buy the skeletons of the impoverished petite women living there, leaving them behind in fleshy blobs inside red wagons and wheelbarrows. I wasn't putting down tall women, nor saying that women needed ideally to be one size or the other. I was making a commentary on vanity and Americans exploiting third-world countries for their culture and natural resources. For the explicit descriptions of having sex with the same woman with two different bodies, I simply mined my own experiences making love to women of various shapes and sizes. After I wrote the short story, which I found very thought-provoking, I suggested Lance adapt it for the stage at Theater Bazooka and cast his girlfriend as "The Big Ariel Hollingsworth" and put out an audition for "her tiny doppelganger." Evidently, the woman read my short story, heard my casting suggestion, and found the entire concept offensive and decided I was equally offensive and, from that moment forward, announced that she didn't like me and wanted nothing to do with me.

I recover myself, laughing the whole time, remembering why his girlfriend hated me, and let out a big sigh. ". . . God, I've got some serious thinking to do."

"I don't know if you got anything to think about. She's made the choice for you, dude."

"I've got to come up with my own answers, Lance."

"Alright. Well, I got to go anyway, but I will leave you with this. Were you ever a The The fan? You know, Matt Johnson? You know, the band The The?"

"Yeah! Loved them. Saw them open for Depeche Mode in Tampa fucking years ago."

"Yeah? Cool. They have an old song called 'August and September.' It's almost like spoken word."

"Love that song! Off the *Mind Bomb* album."

"Great. There's a lyric in that song that goes,"—singing—"'Was our love too strong to die, or were we just too weak to kill it?'"

I sing along, only louder and less on-key. "'Was our love too strong to diiiiiie, or were we just too weak to kill it?'" I have a notoriously bad singing voice.

Then Lance says, "Yeah. People who elect to put their relationships on hold, no matter if it is a week or a month, they're too weak to kill it."

Fuck, he's right. There's a long silence.

"Well, Eli, I got to go."

"Okay, Lance. Thanks, dude."

I turn the radio on. Today is all-request Thursday. I call Live 105's request hotline and I'm surprised how quickly the actual DJ answers my phone call, voice impressive and impossibly clear.

"Hello there! What song do you want to hear today?"

"'August and September' by The The."

"'August and September' by The The!" the DJ shouts, seemingly delighted with my request. "Great! Great song! What's your name, buddy?"

"Eli."

"Eli, Eli! Let me ask you a question." With insincere sincerity, he says, "Is this song dedicated to somebody special?"

Only then does it occur to me that I'm on the air. *Do not say Jennifer Eli! Do not say Jennifer Eli!*

"Uh, um. No. Um, I-I-I just need to hear these lyrics right now. That's all."

With mock sympathy, he says, "Okay. Ah, poor little guy. Take care, little fella."

I hang up the phone. Fucking asshole. I turn up the radio and hear the tail end of my last statement: ". . . That's all." Then the DJ apes the sad nasal sound of my voice, and I laugh until I remember it's me he's making fun of, me on the number one radio station in San Francisco. After the DJ laughs, he goes back to his professional broadcaster's voice and announces, "The The, 1989, 'August and September.' And you listen to those lyrics now, Eli!"

I had taken a shower in between phone calls and was draped in a towel during my entire conversation with Lance. Now, with the curtains drawn, I lie naked in my bed, embarrassed, thinking, "Was our love too strong to die, or were we just too weak to kill it?"

II

Lance LittleJohn's right. A hold is worse than a break-up. To say to your boyfriend or girlfriend "I need to put this relationship on hold for *x* amount of time" actually belittles the other person because you are assuming this person will be there when you're ready to be partnered again. It's disrespectful. It's saying "I've got a life but you don't."

It's different when a person says "Hey, honey, I'm going out with my friends tonight." Or she could've said "I'm going to be so busy with school this week that I won't have much time to talk or anything. Let's plan on doing something next weekend." Fuck, she could've said "Let's call the whole thing off! Let's not see each other anymore!" It wouldn't have made me happier, necessarily, but it would somehow be more acceptable, definitely more respectful. The "hold" thing just makes me feel like a great big loser with nary a backbone in sight.

Jennifer's not a conniving coward who asked for the "hold" to hurt me so I'd break up with her. Becca's wrong, but Jennifer is self-absorbed to a fault, and that's saying something, coming from me. However, I challenge you to find an artist, particularly a writer, who isn't self-absorbed. All artists, even actors, spend most of their lives living inside their heads. A certain level of introspection and self-awareness is healthy, just as a total absence of emotion isn't healthy. It's when your egotism destroys your empathy that it becomes a bad thing.

A former classmate from Jennifer Ely's childhood became a national figure for a very brief time. However, she was a national figure in a way that nobody would want to be. She was "MISSING" and she was an attractive congressional intern for a famous and popular California congressman. The two were having an affair. The girl's family files a report, she's declared "MISSING," and when there's considerable evidence that the married congressman was one of the last people to see her alive and that, according to the young woman's

119

confidants, she was fucking the fifty-something career politician, the authorities naturally want to speak to the man. The congressman backs out, refusing to cooperate with the police, the media lands and sets up camp, and the oft-elected pussy-hound never admits to the affair, claiming not to remember when he last saw the young woman. Tragically, the intern's body is found. Though her assailant has yet to be caught, it's been speculated that she's the victim of a D.C. area serial killer who observed her comings and goings and ambushed her during an early morning jog, a ritual that everybody, including her neighbors, knew she performed every day. She was raped and beaten to death.

While nobody thinks the congressman killed anybody, most of America is offended by the lack of public sympathy or concern for the young woman and her family. He refuses to be interviewed by the police, and when he later agrees to a public interview, conveniently sitting next to his frumpy middle-aged wife, the seasoned politician and former lawyer speaks in bogus legalese and evasive double-talk, and American citizens are disgusted by the sweating congressman, whose only concerns are for his own bullshit. He becomes irritable and defensive when the interviewer quotes the D.C. police, who suggest that had the baby-kisser been more forthcoming about the dead girl's last days, they probably could've found her body much sooner.

The next election year, this politician, a popular incumbent who had held onto his congressional seat for almost two decades, lost to a political novice in a landslide.

My Jennifer knew this young woman. She told me they had grown up together and had known each other since elementary school. Sadly, my Jennifer seemed indifferent to her death, even dishing that when they were in high school, the girl dated a married twenty-eight-year-old cop. Though it was never reported in the news, Jennifer insisted that her classmate bragged about it often. It upset me that my girlfriend simply didn't care. She didn't show even a flicker of emotion for this poor girl. Obviously, they were never friends, and people say the opposite of love is not hate but rather indifference. That's probably true. Jennifer participated in track and the debate team. The doomed young woman participated in track, volleyball, cheerleading, drama, the debate team and the student council. Jennifer shrugged her off as "a total overachiever, a stereotypical preppy popular girl, a total bore." When I commented that what had happened to her was so sad, Jennifer Ely gave another shrug. Then, to my surprise, my girlfriend defended the congressman. "I don't know why everyone got on that guy's case. It's not like he did anything."

"Nobody thinks he killed her. He just should've fessed up from the start. 'Yes, we were having an affair. Her friends are right. We had dinner, she spent the night, and she left my penthouse around 5 a.m.' People felt he wasn't as forthcoming or as sympathetic as he should've been. At no point did he ever publicly show concern for the missing girl or her family."

Again, Jennifer Ely just shrugged and made an irritated face as if to say "Who gives a fuck?"

A woman in the prime of her youth is raped and killed. The crime done to her had nothing to do with her habit of sleeping with older married men in positions of authority. Maybe Ely did resent the girl's overachiever attitude, so prevalent in certain high school cliques, that this Eli hated too, but how could she not be moved by her tragedy, especially considering they were on the same track team? Besides, Jennifer, what happened to your old classmate could've happened to anybody. "Cut her some slack, for fuck's sake."

Maybe it was Jennifer's empathy-free lifestyle that gave her the ability to be so candid about avoiding my phone calls. If she had had more compassion for me, she would've lied, said something like "Oh, I had to wash my hair" or "I fell asleep" or "I was really, really busy." But no, three distinct and hurtful times in our relationship, Jennifer nonchalantly announced, "I was avoiding your phone calls."

It wasn't like I'd ask her if she was running away from my rings, Jennifer would just volunteer it each time. Thanks, Jennifer. Whoever said "Honesty is the best policy" never had a relationship in his life.

III

I remember the first time. The first time she avoided my phone call, that is.

We met at a party at Club Base on Bay Street. The party was called "Rumors" for reasons lost on me. Perhaps it was to imply an underground scene that only an invited, select few would know about. How they got my email, I don't know—at a party, probably—but it seems I was on the mailing list; it was always on the third Friday of every month. After ignoring the email for years (about six), I decided to at least check out one party before I finally clicked "UNSUBSCRIBE."

That Friday, the third Friday of May in the year 2003, I headed over after work at California Pizza Kitchen, clad in bright-blue overalls, wearing grease-filmed black work shoes, a white T-shirt, and a knit cap. (Is it because I'm allegedly a terrible dresser that I now feel it necessary to always detail how I was dressed at any given moment?) I jogged down to the club on Bay Street that I've walked past a million times, across from Safeway, Blockbuster, 24 Hour Fitness, Walgreens, diagonal from Barnes & Noble, upstairs from a less-than-mediocre Japanese restaurant called Bob's Sushi and a twenty-four-hour porn shop. Obviously, I knew the club well, but I had never been inside. There are very few bars or clubs here in the City I can say that about.

"Rumors" was a stupid, cheesy name for a monthly party, which is probably why I had never had the desire to go before. As I was walking up the stairs, shortly after paying ten dollars to get in (so much for being cordially invited to a private party), I immediately thought "This music sucks!" That goddamn relentless drum and bass that's nothing but repetition: no vocals, no melodies, and no clue that at any moment, the song is going to end. I hate it

There were three rooms; one was a lounge and the other two were dance floors. The lounge had a glassy, well-stocked bar. Everything but the counter and the cushions on the stools was made of glass. The television screens flickered in various shades of blue. Comfortable, brand-new plush chairs and couches were all over the lounge, filled with people drinking and leaning on one another in random stages of wallow. I think it's sweet. It seems many people hate public displays of affection; they enforce laws, get angry, and yell fucked-up, never-funny things like "Hey, get a hotel room." But I adore people being affectionate in public. Always have.

There are limits, don't get me wrong. People shouldn't be fucking on the bus, and I don't want to pick up the paper and read about a frisky young couple getting their jollies from mutual oral sex within shouting distance of a public playground. Of course, if it is late at night, dark, and nobody else is supposed to be there, then that's fine. Seeing the young, happy people being affectionate was a turn-on.

Most interestingly, there was a massage table and a massage therapist catering to a line of stiff backs. I recognized the massage therapist as Lance LittleJohn's ex-girlfriend, the girl with whom he first came to San Francisco. He thought he and she were going to be together forever, and they fought all the damn time, always fighting. His friends and I used to laugh about it. Now, what was her name? What was her name? I remember she and Lance used to live together when I first befriended him. She never gave me much attention or seemed to appreciate having me around, but I recall her appearing distracted and almost startled the time I crashed at their pad and awoke shirtless and tried to have a conversation with her in their kitchen, and all she did was stare at my chest the way women accuse us guys of doing, which we do, of course.

I love Lance like a brother but would have no qualms about sleeping with one of his ex-girlfriends. She was my type: dark, exotic, tattooed, muscular, bohemian, and sexual. Lance, God bless him, is a dynamic bragger. I wanted to chat, but there was a line and she was busy.

"Later, Eli, later; maybe her name will come back to you," I thought.

She charged a dollar a minute, with a ten-minute minimum. It felt so good, most people ended up slipping her another ten and getting another massage without getting back in line. She was making bank. Trina, that's it! Trina would hold up a towel so the girls could remove their tops discreetly. However, for every demure young chick, there was another who would come by and couldn't wait to expose her boobies. Twenty-one years old! Bouncy! Firm! Sharp nipples! Oh, my God! Then the exhibitionist would lie down on the massage table, face-first, fully aware of the attention she had just earned.

Watching the masseuse and absorbing the energy of the venue gave me a hard-on.

When I left her area to go back to the bar, I caught Trina looking at me. I hated the sound coming from the first room (drum and bass), and the second room was playing trance, which was also pure crap. The crowd was pretty, the boys and girls both, and didn't appear to dance as much as bounce, over and out, back and forth, from toe to heel. Smoke filtered throughout the space, but this being California, it wasn't from cigarettes but rather a fog machine. The music was not my cup of tea, and the early-twenty-something crowd wasn't doing it for me either. Yes, despite the eager young flasher, the crowd still struck me as being terribly uninteresting.

I had paid ten dollars to get in, and though I knew almost immediately that it wasn't my kind of party, I wanted to get my money's worth. Then, the talent behind the bar pleasantly surprised me by making a quality, kicking double vodka cranberry, all for a reasonable eight dollars.

"Here's twelve dollars. Keep the change." Everybody thinks they know her story when they look at this bartender, a thirty-five-year-old bartender in tight, low-hung jeans and a tank top. Her body was as hard and intensely defined as her face. We picture this: a fun, good-looking young woman takes a bartender job in college, makes too much money, parties too hard; she eventually drops out of school. Then she finds herself in her thirties with no other skills, continuously wrestling a major coke addiction, trying and trying to overcome alcoholism and walking in shame and guilt for the years spent in promiscuity. By the looks of her fatless body, she was probably doing the powder again. She wants to quit her habits but has no other skills, or so she thinks, so it's always back to the environment that got her there in the first place.

She had tattooed stars on her shoulders and somebody's initials under her navel. She was still sexy, but in ten, fifteen years, she was going to look something like Sharon at Vieni Vieni. I already knew her story in all its glory because I once saw her give a speech at an AA meeting back in December. Her name, if memory serves, was Ivy. She nodded with a brief, unopened smile and appreciated my tip, but I saw no recognition in her eyes.

If there was nobody at the party to talk to, I was going to camp out in front of the bar and strike up a conversation with Relapse Ivy, though certainly she was beyond the point where she'd date a customer, even a well-tipping one.

I decided to walk into the trance room because it seemed to be better lit and the music was a little more tolerable. In the hallway, I saw a tall girl in boots, well-fitted jeans—not too tight but not so baggy that you couldn't get a sense of her body underneath—and a man's V-neck T-shirt. Her look was hot, and though ten years ago I'd have written her off as a major dyke, today I've seduced and had flings with women who looked more lesbian than this chick. She was leaning up against a wall in a rare moment when the hallway wasn't

125

crowded. In her right hand was a silver flask, and she was pouring liquid into a half-consumed cocktail she held with her left.

"Hey," I yelled above the music, "what's that? A flask?"

Her eyes were big, a little startled. She nodded.

"What do you have in there?"

"Vodka!" she yelled at me.

A few gulps of my double had already been consumed. It was after midnight when I arrived, and I was in a hurry to get my drunk on.

"Can I have a shot?" I held up my glass. She gave me a shot, the last of her flask. She wore a brooding expression. A preview of what I'd later learn was typical for her.

"Thanks!" I yelled back. She gave me a subtle nod. No smile, no wink. The young woman screwed the lid back on and put her now-empty flask in her back pocket, then walked past me, not seeming interested in further eye contact or conversation.

The music in the trance room was un-danceable, so I just paced in an observing, thoughtful way, not the angry, predatory style in which most pacers pace.

To my great surprise, I felt tremendous sympathy for the twenty-one-year-olds sliding to the crappy music. Evidently, you bounce to drum and bass music and slide to trance. In the early '90s, when the rave scene was in full bloom among my fellow Generation Xers, I was into punk, Goth, and ska. Whenever I partied with my ska friends, all non-racist skinheads, it seemed that every time we got together, we just looked for fights, just as stupid as their racist counterparts. Either way, my scenes were dark, negative, angry, and not especially fun, even if the music was superior.

Is there any era from my past that I'm nostalgic for? No, not really.

In the late '90s I worked as a bouncer/doorman at a retro-lounge, after-hours bar. Most of the clientele, late twenties, early thirties, had been ravers during their high school and college years. All they did was talk about how much fun they had going to raves: ecstasy, shrooms, sex—so much sex—and music, all this at events that lasted six to twelve hours, sometimes for days. These were the happiest ways to waste their youth, and the sentimental value of their rave memories made me jealous.

Nobody on their deathbed wishes they spent more time at the office or getting into fights. They only wish they had more fun. The ravers had better experiences than I did. The rave scene was already coming to an end, so, at age twenty-eight, I wasn't going to run into a rave hoping to recapture some lost youth. I just stood there like the dumb, macho, shithead bouncer that I was and fumed, resenting myself for having never been a raver. "It would've been more fun," I kept thinking. "It would've been more fun."

Then I hit thirty and forgave myself for not being a raver by remembering there were actual reasons why I chose not to go to raves. The music sucked. My friends and I were skinheads, heavily tattooed and muscular. We'd openly taunt the young men we saw who dressed like toddlers in bright, baggy, garish clothes. Women in the prime of their youth looked dopey in baby-doll dresses, sucking Blow Pops, wearing pigtails, and carrying lunch boxes. Remember when it was trendy for chicks to suck on baby pacifiers? Women dressed as children had a disharmonious effect on my hard-on.

To this day, you can keep your goddamn "love drugs" to yourself. Alcohol, coke, speed, and rage were always my drugs of choice, and although I did get laid back then, it didn't happen often enough because I focused on violence. Hemingway stated umpteen times that he liked war because there was always a chance he was going to die. A young man who proclaims that he likes getting into fights does so because he knows there's always a chance that he's going to lose.

I couldn't have been a raver if I wanted to be.

Sadly, these twenty-one-year-olds and various fake ID holders were trying to recreate a rave scene of their own. They were failing miserably. But then again, this is San Francisco: in 2003, neo-hippies still arrive in Haight-Ashbury in dreadlocks, filthy clothes, and dirty feet and wonder what happened to the Summer of Love. At least I had the opportunity to be a real raver. What have they got?

Fully consumed, my tongue licking the hot, fruity taste off my teeth, I knew I was entitled to another double vodka cranberry and to see if I could get more attention from Relapse Ivy.

Her lips still didn't separate when she smiled, ergo she was probably painfully self-conscious of some less-than-perfect teeth, but I dug the way her rapidly aging face wrinkled around her eyes, cheeks, and mouth. It was lived-in and sexy, which is how I'd like my face to be described someday. Sure, she was going to be a nightmare in a relatively short amount of time, it was obvious, but right now, right then would've been the right time to fuck her. Use a condom. Really. Whether they be seasoned bartenders or debutants, always use a condom.

Ivy smiled deeper and more broadly than she had smiled before. Her eyes were actually a lovely shade of dark, dark green. This time there was a smidgen of recognition, but whether it was from an AA meeting or the generous tip from fifteen, twenty minutes earlier, I couldn't tell you. Quickly, another double, another twelve bucks, she grabbed the cash, smiled again, and, from behind the bar, Ivy brought out his and hers whiskey shots. She winked, handed me a shot glass, and we clicked rims in a toast and both swallowed our shots in a flick of our wrists.

Burning, hot, refreshing, I've never met a whiskey shot I didn't like.

To me, Ivy was the lover who'd call me "honey" in a raspy voice while she tenderly rubbed her fingers along my spine as I remained inside her. A man knew, just knew, that Ivy gave stupendous love and would be open to doing just about anything. Women like Ivy always made great storytellers. And they always made great stories. Ivy winked again at me after the whiskey shot and even did a small, bouncy dance around the bar, poking fun at the youngsters, before taking more drink orders. "She digs me," I thought.

That night, was I going to hit on Relapse Ivy the AA girl, or Trina, Lance LittleJohn's ex? I didn't know. Both may have been wondering what an old fart like me was doing there. They were old farts, too. And the coolest people there. Could I sleep with both? How could I work out that deal? To the trance room to come up with a plan.

Weeks later, Jennifer would tell me that when I stopped walking and looked right where she was sitting, her immediate thought was "Okay. This is going to be fun."

"Hey, where's your flask, girl?"

"I put it in my purse. It's in coat-check."

"A silver flask is what every girl in the big city needs."

"I don't want to pay those damn prices and nobody at any of these bars knows how to make a halfway decent drink." My cocktails were fine, better than fine. By SF standards, the prices were reasonable. But I kept my mouth shut. Perhaps sensing this, Jennifer said, "Alright. I admit it. I'm cheap."

Our shoulders were rubbing together. When she spoke to me, Jennifer's lips were close enough to my ears that she could've kissed them. I love it when my ears are nibbled. I always do the same to girls. As she spoke to me, that side of my face and neck felt tingly and sensitive.

She was at this lame party to see a roommate spin and said it was "interesting" being there. By saying it was "interesting," she meant she liked neither her roommate's music nor the faux rave scene. Surely, Jennifer's other two roommates were there: the sexy, sanctimonious Ursula and the blank, bland Robert. But I didn't meet either of them that night.

"So, what's your DJ roommate like?" Was he her boyfriend?

"We're housemates, really. We don't get along. He's kind of stuck-up. He's a fanatical neat freak and I'm a slob. But sometimes you've got to support your housemates. You just got to."

"Well, so far, what I know about you is that you're cheap and sloppy."

Jennifer smiled and looked downward, a tad embarrassed. "Yes— yes," she said, putting her hand on my knee, our thighs rubbing against each other's. "I'm also very smart and very kind."

"Cool. Cool. Kindness is definitely an underrated virtue." Her hand remained on my knee for much of the night. In time, I'd learn she was extraordinarily smart, but I don't recall her being especially kind. Not cruel either, but not especially kind. However, I never saw her being terribly sloppy or cheap. Supposedly, people are never how they say they are.

The conversation is not something I can totally recall, nor is it something I necessarily want to. We talked about parties in general. To my warm surprise, though I played it mellow and cool, Jennifer mentioned she had been to a sex party before, down in L.A., even.

"Why did you go to something like that?"

"Well, I had a friend named Danielle who went to sex parties regularly. This is when I was down at UCLA. She told me and my roommates and we were like, 'Hey, we want to go.'"

"Was your friend good-looking?"

"Oh, my God! She was so pretty!"

"What did you do there?"

"Nothing, really."

That probably wasn't true.

"All that I did was watch people. Did some coke, and there was this couple that tried to feel me up, but I couldn't really get into it. It's funny. At one point, I see Danielle buck naked on a bed with some dude eating her out and two girls sucking her nipples, and she looks up at me and says, 'Hey, Ely! Are you having a good time?'" She laughed. "Have you ever been to a sex party?"

"Oh, yeah." Smartly, I chose not to elaborate. Even when an attractive girl is talking to you about sex, it is still best to remain laid-back and cool. Don't appear hornier than you already are. Don't get aggressive. Besides, she said something that caught my ears even more so than her gang-bang Danielle story.

"Did I hear you correctly? Your friend said 'Hey, Ely'?"

"Yeah, my name is Jennifer Ely. My friends sometimes call me Ely."

"My first name is Eli. Eli Trocchi."

"Wow."

We both laughed and discussed the spellings and ethnic origins, but it wasn't until a future conversation that I'd tell her about my name change. Don't let someone think you're too eccentric too soon. I can be a bit overwhelming at first. Miss Ely told me she was a philosophy major, pursuing a PhD, even. Currently, she was in grad school at State. At the time, I was thirty-one, she twenty-four. Her birthday, November 2, mine, August 2.

"Interestingly enough," I said, "my publishing company is named after a philosopher."

"Yeah? Which one?"

"It's called Kicking Zeno Publishing. We may call it Crying Zeno Publishing or maybe even Zeno's Broken Toe Publishing." Later, I'd change the name to Brooding Drunk Publishing, but the business never came to fruition.

After our third or fourth date, I spent the night at Jennifer's. It was late morning, and we had both showered and wrapped ourselves in towels. I was sitting in a big lounge chair in her room and she was on my lap. There she listened as I described what my publishing business was going to be like. Jennifer's arms were draped on my shoulders, her towel had fallen to her waist, her skin was soft and clean, and her breasts sat firmly in the air, beautiful and distracting. Earlier that morning she'd said to me, "You make me happy. I wish there was something I could do to make you as happy as I feel right now." But now, she said, "I hope all your dreams come true, Eli. I

131

really do." She looked sad and lowered her eyes. To me that meant ". . . but I doubt they will."

"Zeno's Broken Toe Publishing?" Jennifer seemed taken aback, surprised.

"Yeah, because Zeno broke his toe at age ninety and promptly killed himself."

"I've heard that story before. Nobody knows if it's true."

"I know. Who cares? It's a great story. Hey, did you know Zeno is the first person on record to criticize slavery?"

"Yeah, but it was because he was a Stoic. He was the original do-it-yourselfer, Eli. It wasn't slavery he hated, it was laziness. He felt everybody should build their own homes, not get slaves to do it for them. He wasn't what you'd call a true anti-slavery abolitionist type. Zeno also had a thing about being controlled or dominated by one's emotions, henceforth, Stoicism."

"'Henceforth,' a very good name for a do-it-yourself publisher."

"Yes. I vote for Crying Zeno Press." Jennifer smiled at me, impressed.

I then said, "I think the first person of any merit to criticize slavery for any moral reason was the Roman playwright Seneca."

"Interesting. The Romans weren't known for their morality. You sure?"

"Pretty sure." Now I suddenly wasn't. She was smart, a drinker, and sexual? Wow. "What philosophers are you into?"

"Wittgenstein."

"Yeah? Have you ever read *Wittgenstein's Mistress?*"

"No. What's that?"

"It's an experimental novel written by David Markson about a crazy woman who thinks she's the last person on earth. The novel is stream-of-consciousness with the protagonist speaking in beautiful but odd non sequiturs. It's an amazing book."

"Oh, my God! That's so funny. If you know anything about Wittgenstein's philosophy, that's hilarious." She laughed hard, laughing at an inside joke between her and Wittgenstein and David Markson that was totally lost on me, and I was the one who had read the damn book.

We were in various phases of affection when I found Jennifer on my lap, my bulbous erection along my upper thigh underneath her butt cheeks. One arm was wrapped around my shoulders, the other leading her hand as she felt my chest. My right hand was massaging the small of her back while my left rested on her thighs. Jennifer was deeply enjoying herself, making a profoundly pleasured face, even biting her lower lip.

The party had good atmosphere, I'll give it that. Everybody seemed to be hooking up with somebody the moment I walked into Club Base.

At last call, Jennifer got up from my swollen prick to get a Rolling Rock. I asked if she'd get me another double and handed her a ten. She didn't offer to buy mine, but then again, she was a poor college student.

She returned and sat right back on my hard-on and gave me my cocktail with two dollars change. It can safely be assumed she gave Relapse Ivy no tip. Shit, maybe she was cheap.

We made out between sips. I asked for her number and told her not to write it down because my memory was sharp. Though she looked skeptical, Jennifer whispered her number to me. We parted at around two in the morning. She had to hang with her roommates and I was aware that my ever-increasing inebriation was not going to enable me to be the lover I wanted to be that night.

We hugged and kissed good-bye, a damn good kiss with both of us pausing to look at one another. Before kissing, I apologized for my enormous boner, saying it was always embarrassing me at times like this. Jennifer, hardly offended, pressed her pelvis to my body tightly and held on. Her breasts felt firm against my chest. As I'd learn later, she was 5'8" barefoot, and with her boots on, her height was identical to mine. I did not say good-bye to either Ivy or Trina, but I saw both behind the bar, hugging and kissing, mouths open, tongues visible, hands all over each other's asses. (Was it Trina's mom who saw my penis at Lance's thirtieth birthday party?)

My level of drunkenness was getting deeper and deeper. Three doubles and a whiskey shot, an extra shot counting Jennifer's flask. That's eight shots, two for free. I had met a smart, sexy thing whose last name was my first, got the chick's number, and even got to make out with her. I'd call that a night to remember.

That is, if it ended up being a night I could remember. Hadn't I also had a beer or two at work? Bleary-eyed, bleary-eyed, stumble, stumble; last thing I remembered was wobbling back towards the Sestri Hotel and chanting Jennifer Ely's phone number to myself. Two, maybe three days later, an afternoon, I called a happy, pleasantly surprised Jennifer Ely, who never expected to hear from me again. We joked, flirted, talked about everything, but still kept the conversation light. When I asked her for a date, she told me she most definitely wanted to but was going out of town, down to L.A. to visit friends ("Slutty Danielle"?) for one week, and then she was going to start a job at Yosemite (as a forest ranger!) in the middle of July, "So if we were to start something like a summer fling, there'd scarcely be enough time for one."

Yes, she actually said that.

"Okay, Jennifer, good point. But let's play it by ear. You go have a wonderful time down in L.A. When you get back, call me. We'll hang out."

She may have told me the exact date when she was to return from L.A., but I didn't memorize it. A week later, I called her cell phone, leaving a message inquiring when she'd get back so we could plan a dinner date. "I was thinking the Argentinean restaurant Il Pollalo in

North Beach across from Rosa Pistola's. Anyway, give me a call."

A few days went by and I left another message. Now, while I do remember leaving the message, what I don't remember is that I evidently left a somewhat testy message in which I said, "This is it. If you don't call me back, I won't ever call you again."

I said that? Shit, I don't remember.

She called back, leaving a message stating "Hi . . . Uh, I'm not in the habit of talking on my cell phone when I'm on vacation. Sorry about not returning your call. Uh, yes, I still want to go out when I get back to San Francisco tomorrow. I'll call you then . . . Uh, that is, if you still want to go out with me. Yes, well, uh, um. Bye."

"Cool," I thought when I heard the message, as I pushed nine—save—on my cell phone. "But the tone? Why so cautious? Was it something I said?" Only a few weeks ago she told me the second message I ever left for her was an ultimatum. Interesting. I don't remember leaving such a message, but I don't doubt it, either. I drink. With my cell phone on my hip like a gunslinger, I'm prone to drunk-dialing. Yeah, I'm sure I said that.

Our first date was only bettered by our second, then our third. By mid-July, Ely was going to be in Yosemite, and we felt we had limited time to get to know one another, so we chose to fill every spare moment with each other's presence. I planned my schedule around Jennifer Ely and California Pizza Kitchen, and that's pretty much it. We spoke about each other to our friends, acquaintances who really got a kick out of the whole Eli,Ely thing. Methinks it was Danny Ryan himself who first said "I can picture ole Eli fucking his new girlfriend and he says, 'Oh, Eli, Eli,' and she's like, 'Wow, that's different. I've never had anybody say my last name during sex before,' and he says, 'Hey, I'm not talking to you.'"

According to Jennifer, her pals would joke, "Can you imagine our Jennifer mounting her new guy and she's going 'Oh, Ely, Ely!' And he says, 'I love it when a chick screams my name during sex!' And she says, 'Shut up! I'm not talking to you!'"

The fact that we had the same self-absorbed reputation among the people who knew us was something else we had in common, but, for the record, we never said our own names during sex. Well, at least I know I never did.

About a week and a half into our "thing," not yet ready to call it a "relationship," Miss Ely and I had another sojourn at Kayo Books. There, I bought a wonderful expat bohemian novel from the late '50s entitled *Easy Living* by Maitland Zane, a man who never published another novel but ended up a reporter for The San Francisco Chronicle. I've contacted the author, now old and retired and taking up space in Northern California, and told him about my desire to reprint his one and only novel, written over forty-five years ago. He was pleased to have a fan, but even he voiced skepticism, seemingly aware I'm more of a dreamer, less of a doer, and that by the time his young admirer would have the cash and the know-how to publish and promote his long-forgotten novel, he'd most likely be dead. Sorry my shit's not together, Maitland Zane. On the phone, Mr. Zane told me ruefully that he always felt his book should've gotten more attention than it did. The reviews were kind, but nobody bought it. Dismissed, probably as a Kerouac clone, the only good thing that came from it, he said, was that he got a job as a journalist for the San Francisco Chronicle.

My Jennifer bought a pink hardcover book from the 1940s on female etiquette. She knew the book was going to be a wonderful conversation piece on a coffee table someday and that its content would be fodder for future conversations and discussions on feminism.

After Kayo Books, I took her to a store on Larkin Street called The Place for Periodicals. It was a vintage magazine shop that bought and sold old magazines, everything from ancient *New Yorkers* to explicit pornography from the 1940s. Though you could get near-pristine issues of *LIFE* and *Esquire* from forty-five years ago, most of the clientele was there for pornography. Gay, straight, kinky, fetish, bizarre shit—new spreads in last month's *Barely Legal* and vintage copies of *Stag* circa 1958, or even *STURDY BOY*, September 1977, one of Scott's favorite old gay rags. The clientele was made up of men, gross, pasty, older men, who collected porn. Though I've usually gone to The Place for Periodicals to specifically buy long-defunct literary magazines like *The Dial* or *Merlin*, I must also admit that I've gone there to purchase jerk-off material from the early 1980s. There's something about the coked-up, glassy-eyed, heavily tanned, big-haired porn stars that just turns me on so much. Do they somehow remind me of the unattainable adult women who first elicited sexual feelings within me when I was a kid? I've known about The Place for Periodicals for nearly ten years, and in that time, I'm only aware of two occasions when a woman has been inside, and each time she was with me: once with my then-girlfriend, Jana Carver, in the summer of '99, and again in '03, with Jennifer Ely. Each time I thought it funny to neglect informing my girlfriends exactly what environment they were walking into. Jana, to her credit, found it all amusing. She noticed immediately that she had arrived in a room of poorly aging testosterone adding to its filth stash. Jana bravely left my side to look at some hardcore Japanese porn: multiple tiny penises and a lone, beautiful, delicate woman seemingly battered into sex and wrapped in bandages. Jana, half-Japanese herself, just looked at it for a few uncomprehending seconds, put the porn back, and then came and embraced me as if to let any perverts know with whom she had arrived. After that, Jana went to gaze at some gay mustached body builder porn from what had to be the late '70s, judging by the waves of feathered hair parted down the middle. She ended up innocently leafing through some elderly back issues of *Rolling Stone*. Jana kept returning, never leaving my side for too long, always giggling softly at the lonely Joes staring at her. Looking nervous, embarrassed, worried, and excited, Jana would put her hands around my waist and bury her laughing face in my chest. My eyes were chiefly focused on her. I did browse old *New Yorkers* and a *Hustler* circa 1982, but when Jana came back a fourth time, still laughing but shaking her head slowly, I knew it was time to go before one of these loners with boners found the nerve to actually speak to my pretty, petite girlfriend, and believe me, those guys were staring at her hard and trying even harder to act like they weren't.

Hand in hand, we were leaving, but then she stopped me and grabbed a glossy photograph of prisoner porn. If memory serves, whether I want it to or not, it featured three impossibly buff, heavily tattooed prisoners or body builders made to look like convicts, committing acts of sodomy and oral sex. One man was going down on another man's cock from outside his jail cell, while the smoker was getting buggered by his cellmate. Jana laughed out loud, smiling. "Check this out, Eli." She was digging it. Jana, not unlike many women, dug gay porn.

When I pointed at the gay porn star's bodies and said, "That's about as big as I'd like to get," meaning their builds, not their dicks, though that, too, would be a blessing, my Jana shook her head and said, "No, Eli. You're as big as I'd ever want you to be." Then she kissed me as we walked out the door.

When Jana said "as big as I'd ever want you to be," I didn't know if she was referring to my muscles or my penis, but either way, it felt like a major compliment.

The moment Jennifer and I walked in, Miss Ely made a beeline to a small shelf on the ground that held back issues of *Ms. Magazine*. Jennifer was on her knees looking at the magazines excitedly when she looked around, probably to find me, and discovered a room of men—middle-aged, nasty, porn-loving, cry-themselves-to-sleep, pathetic men—staring at her, my Jennifer, my dark, beautiful, athletically built Jennifer on her knees perusing feminist literature.

She rose immediately, walked to me, and hooked two fingers through a belt loop on the side of my jeans. The expression on her face was painful. She wanted to vacate immediately.

Once we were outside, Jennifer yelled, "Oh, my God! Oh, my fucking God! Why didn't you tell me this place was like that?! I thought it'd be cool, like some unique sort of thrift-shop-slash-magazine-stand hybrid, but that was nasty! Fucking nasty!"

I played dumb. "What're you talking about, baby?"

"Didn't you see? I was the only girl in there! I was like, 'Cool, a place to buy old magazines,' but it was almost all porn with nasty, gross-looking old farts staring at me! Nasty! If you knew what it was like, why didn't you tell me?"

"You know I wouldn't let anyone bother you."

"That's not the point. You should've told me."

"I thought I did, and it isn't always like that. I've seen girls in there before."

Then I shrugged like it was no big deal. Jennifer shuddered as if a chill was going up and down her spine.

We ate at a Thai food dive on O'Farrell and Larkin, where we both ordered chicken Pad Thai and Thai iced teas. Everything tasted great. After an early supper—it was just getting dark as we left the Tenderloin—Jennifer's mood was lifting higher and higher as I kept making her laugh, telling her funny stories. We held hands. We were enjoying each other's company, each saying how good the other looked. Intense, angry, disgusted, yelling Jennifer turns me on. So does sweet, affectionate, laughing Jennifer. That day, I had both.

We were looking forward to a good sex-filled evening, but instead, I spent the rest of the night holding onto Miss Ely's toilet, sometimes getting up to puke reddish bile and occasionally to sit on the porcelain to release mud water. Our plans of incredible lovemaking were ruined by a serious bout of food poisoning that only affected me. Was this karma punishing me for not telling my girlfriend, or rather, not warning her, about The Place for Periodicals?

Jennifer did try to nurse me at the start of my illness, but she soon gave up and went to sleep. I awoke in the morning, cleaned the toilet seat—thankfully, there was no mess on the floor—and took a shower. She was still asleep when I left that morning. I've had food poisoning before, but never food poisoning that passed through my system so quickly, nor have I ever had a bout of food poisoning severe enough to make me stop eating meat. Though my stomach was sore like I'd been sucker-punched a few times, I wasn't particularly weak the next day. In truth, it was a busy, productive, financially rewarding lunch shift at CPK, and afterwards, I even enjoyed a complimentary chicken sandwich and pea soup. I always ask the Mexican dudes in the kitchen to make my crew meal extra spicy, and that day was no exception.

However, I anticipated that my phone call to Jennifer that afternoon was going to be tense, and it was, that it was. Her voice on the phone was tired, unhappy, and familiar. It was the voice of every woman who has ever said "I don't think we should see each other anymore."

"What? Why?"

"Because I don't know. I'm leaving soon and last night felt really weird."

"I was sick! I was sick, baby. Hey, didn't you notice?"

"I know, Eli. It's just . . . I don't know."

"Baby, don't you want to see me again?"

"Yes, I do. I do. It's just that I want this thing to be right." A thing? We have a *thing?*

"Hey, baby. Tonight is an art opening at a wine bar off Market Street in Hayes Valley. It's right by Zuni Café. Remember I showed you the flyer the other day?"

"Yeah, I do."

"The artist has taken photographs of all the great jazz artists—Bix, Chet, Sarah, Billie, Miles—and drawn paintings from them. Besides, it's a wine bar. We'll drink wine, eat cheese, groove to music. Do you like art openings, Jennifer?"

"I've never been to one."

"No way! Really? Get out of here! I love them. I used to go to art openings weekly. Love art. Hell, I love jazz, wine, and cheese. Also, I need to see you tonight because I bought you something." That wasn't yet true, but I went with it. "So I need to see you tonight."

"Okay," she said, relenting. "I want to see you, too. I'm just concerned because we spend every moment together."

"Hey, I know. I know. Let's just go out tonight. Tonight's Thursday. On Friday, Saturday, and Sunday, let's part company. You go out with your friends, I'll work and chill with mine. Or better yet, after work, I'll write something. Do something creative. Okay, Ely?"

Laughing, she agreed. "Okay, Eli."

We planned to meet on the corner of Van Ness and Market by the Muni station in front of the Bank of America. After leaving my apartment, I went and did the thing I claimed I had already done. At the tiny flower shop on Columbus that's been there forever, I picked out four large flowers; don't ask me what kind, but they weren't roses. That much I do know. Two flowers were orange, one was red, and one was yellow. They were pretty, and though I wasn't technically in the doghouse, the night before (due to the vomit and the black ass-water), I had been disappointing company. Not to mention bringing my Jennifer to The Place for Periodicals and letting old perverts gawk at her. But she still didn't know I did it on purpose.

There I was waiting for Jennifer Ely, and again I decided to focus on how I was attired. I wore faded burgundy wingtips, faded blue jeans, a nearly threadbare thermal shirt, and a long-sleeved khaki button-down shirt unbuttoned halfway down and tucked-out, with the sleeves rolled up to my elbows exposing the thermal shirt and, hopefully, my build.

Then I saw her. Tall, uncharacteristically wearing high heels, but not too high, and wearing a black velvet top that accentuated her breasts. Was she a large C or a small D? I wondered if the shoes and top belonged to Ursula. Characteristically, she wore slightly faded blue jeans and a serious expression made more intense by her dark hair, which was pulled backwards. Jennifer has a beautiful smile but doesn't smile often. Nor does she smile when she sees the person on the street she's supposed to be meeting. Anyone else would. Even two heterosexual males would if they were to meet somewhere. But my Jennifer doesn't. The philosophy major's always deep in thought. No smiles when she saw me. Was it the way I was dressed? Maybe she still felt tense because of the night before.

From behind my back, before she had a chance to hug me (and she was going to hug me, wasn't she?), I pulled out the flowers I had picked out myself. Her eyes lit up. She seemed startled, like she had to take a step back and catch her breath. Then my Jennifer took the flowers from me and inhaled deeply and smiled a giddy, girly, entirely-not-Jennifer-Ely type of smile.

"Nobody has ever bought me flowers before. Ever."

"Really?"

She kissed me hard on the lips, pulled me to her, embraced me even harder, and held on for several seconds. "Thank you so much, Eli. Thank you." She gushed. She actually gushed.

My Jennifer held my hand and put her head on my shoulder as we walked across Van Ness.

"Flowers are cool. I think the only other time somebody bought me flowers was when my Dad did for my college graduation."

"Really?"

She nodded her head with a sad smile.

I couldn't believe it. How could a twenty-four-year-old woman who's had previous boyfriends, one of whom was a moneyed limey, and "no more than 30 lovers" never, ever have received flowers before? I think that's appalling. Either she only dated thoughtless, inconsiderate douchebags or she just seemed like the kind of girl who wouldn't appreciate flowers.

We found the wine bar off the alley past The Zuni Café. The paintings were cool. Perhaps they'd be better appreciated if they were original renderings, not painted-up interpretations of another artist's vision. We dug the art, silver and black oil paintings, but neither of us could love it for the obvious aforementioned reason. The handsome, goateed, thirty-something bartender was the artist and the proprietor of the wine bar/art gallery, and he told us that he owned a black-and-white photo collection of a well-known photographer and simply made paintings from that guy's pictures. "Interesting," we said. We complimented his art, his obvious love for jazz, and his wine bar. It was dark, with brick walls and candles everywhere, and people with money dressed like bohemians sitting around sipping wine and admiring art. *The Best of John Coltrane* emanated from the speakers.

Jennifer and I each ordered a glass of Chilean Cabernet and I tipped the bartender a five. He snatched it quickly and said "Thanks." We sat down on a loveseat beneath a painting of Jelly Roll Morton. We put our glasses on a small, circular table in front of us. We leaned against one another just like we had on the first night we met, hands on thighs, talking affectionately, sometimes kissing. Her skin felt smooth against my lips; her neck smelled clean, like fresh soap and water. We admired the art from where we were sitting and I said the names of each artist represented, Bessie Smith, Sarah Vaughn, Ella Fitzgerald, Chet Baker, Charlie Parker, Miles Davis, et cetera, and to my twenty-four-year-old girlfriend's credit, she knew and recognized the same ones I did.

We mostly sat, conversed about music, and watched people as the place started to get crowded. Though we were sitting underneath a robust painting, we felt people were looking at us as often as Jelly Roll Morton. A young blonde woman, probably the bartender's girlfriend, came by and dropped off a food menu. It was a list of plates of expensive cheeses. What a wonderful opportunity to discover that a love of fine cheeses was something else Eli and Ely had in common. We ordered a mix plate. Jennifer then told me she wanted to go outside and smoke.

"Okay, babe," I said.

She smiled and gave me a long kiss. When my girl stood and walked outside, sure enough, I watched the guys and the girls alike scope her out. While there's much sexual ambiguity in San Francisco, I recognized the majority of the women as straight chicks admiring another's look, another's style. The men, both gay and straight—in San Francisco there's always a mixed crowd—were doing the same. She's a striking woman, Jennifer Ely. While she smoked outside, I looked out the window and watched as two hipster dudes approached her, probably flirting, making small talk. I was jealous, yes, but I knew she was going home with me that night.

Shortly after she came back inside, Jennifer winked at me with a seductive half-smile and pointed towards the restroom, past the bar. When she came back from the ladies' room, a man and a woman sitting at a small table in the hallway called out to her. She stopped. She didn't seem to know them. The Coltrane jazz was too loud and I couldn't hear what they were saying and it was too dark to read their lips, but my Jennifer was smiling, nodding her head. She came back in high spirits.

"Hey, I made some friends."

"Yeah?"

"The people over there were asking me where I got my top." I looked over at the couple she had been talking to and they looked at me blankly. No smiles, no venom, just blankness. "And then some hipsters outside were talking to me about wine when one asked, 'Are you with that big bald guy?'"

Jennifer impersonated the hipster's deep voice and laughed, kissing me on the cheek.

"You know, Jennifer, today when I bought your flowers, Inez, the old florist who works there, said, 'Hey, is this for that pretty brunette I've been seeing you walking around with lately?'"

Jennifer beamed, lowered her head, and leaned her entire body into mine.

The cheese plate arrived, pungent and tasty, with an additional plate of tiny slices of bread. Jennifer got up and quickly returned with a bottle of Chilean Cabernet.

After the Coltrane CD was spent, the next CD was Tom Waits' *Blue Valentine* album, the one and only Tom Waits CD I've ever owned. Jennifer knew nothing about Tom Waits but was enthralled as I sang "A Christmas Card from a Hooker in Minneapolis" in pitch-perfect Tom Waits, and by the time I sang the odd and beautiful "Kentucky Avenue," a loving valentine from a prankster boy to his wheelchair-bound girlfriend, the bottle was empty and the two of us were a pair of laughing drunks.

I paid our bill and we went out stumbling into the night, up to Market Street, heading towards The Castro, down an alley by the bookstore that only sells travel books. Across the street there's a tiny, well-recommended sushi bar called, called . . . fuck if I can remember at this point. We ducked inside, ordered multiple rolls of spicy mango salmon, two miso soups, and a round of Kirin beer. We ate loudly, laughed loudly, and waved at other customers loudly. None waved back. Jennifer was all smiles and I continued to mimic Tom Waits' gravelly voice as I ordered another roll of sushi.

I got up and left a few twenties under my beer bottle, and due to the lights and too much alcohol, I told Jennifer I had to go outside to consume some fresh air. Jennifer stayed behind to finish her sushi, just a few bites. I sat on the curb by the bookstore and let my head fall into my hands. As Jennifer told me later, the second I left, the sushi bar became noticeably quieter. In a sense, she could tell people were glad my obnoxious ass was gone. For a moment, Jennifer felt embarrassed and self-conscious, but then she saw her flowers lying on the counter. It made her smile, and then she got up, grabbed her bouquet, and stood a little taller, proud of how well our date was going. She found me outside and called my name, and I got up in an instant, as only drunks can do. We embraced, kissed, and proceeded to walk to her apartment in Lower Haight, tightly holding hands, leaning our shoulders into one another.

That night she mounted me, riding my cock, holding onto my shoulders, occasionally screaming, her body vibrating each time she did. When she was through, Jennifer got off, peeled the condom from my dick, and pleasured me until I came. Then Jennifer got up and went to the kitchen naked, not the least bit concerned if her roommates saw her or not, and came back with a tall glass of water, the greatest hangover prevention there ever was. After we each drank half, the glass was placed on her hardwood floor, and Jennifer laid her naked body on top of mine.

The next morning, she woke before I did. The multi-colored flowers sat pretty in a white vase on her dresser, appearing as though professionally arranged and not gripped for several drunken hours the night before. Jennifer was up, cleaning her room barefoot, wearing cutoff denim shorts and a white T-shirt, sans bra, her hair still wet from a morning shower. I got up quietly and put on my clothes. We smiled. I thanked her for the night before. She just kept smiling, with no trace of the seriousness her face is so notorious for. We hugged for a long time and said nothing.

IV

I want to say that I did nothing that weekend but slave at California Pizza Kitchen to make up for the two-hundred-plus dollars spent on our date and to ponder my ever-increasing deep feelings for my Jennifer, but that'd be a lie. I did spend hours at CPK taking orders and refilling iced teas. And Jennifer's skin, her smile, her feet, her tits pressed against my chest, and her voice did enter my mind and devour headspace. But my behavior later that weekend was an earmark of my reputation as an opportunistic, pussy-hound drunk.

I tell myself that it's no big deal because we had yet to use such terms as boyfriend and girlfriend. But I never did and never will tell my Jennifer exactly what happened that weekend. I only remember it in snapshots anyway. When I review the event right now, it strikes me as being nobody's fault, really. I'm only a man, a man totally unprepared for a young woman, a pale, bottled redhead, with a body happily existing between chubby and voluptuous, sitting in my section with another young woman whom I already knew. There's no way I could've anticipated that this woman would come into my section, look at me with eyelids at half-mast, and say "I need some dick tonight." She said that. She actually said that.

Incidentally, the girl I knew was the terribly overweight roommate of Elena, the nineteen-year-old Latina I had so recently bedded. While it is hard to turn down sex when it's being offered, it is even harder to turn down when it's being offered twice. I got drunk after work and met the girls at Diva's, a transvestite Tenderloin bar around the corner from what used to be The Polk Gulch, now Lush Lounge. It was their idea, not mine, but I didn't care because it had good music, high energy, and a well-stocked bar, and I was there to meet the only ladies in the joint. I received blowjobs from both girls in the bathroom, one after the other, and made out with the redhead on the dance floor, her tits soft and plentiful in my hands. But me being me, I got us kicked out of the bar when the flashlight-slinging manager caught the bottled redhead giving me another blowjob while waiting in line for the restroom again. We were so horny that we simply couldn't wait. Outside the bar, I asked her if she wanted to go back to my hotel room. She said "Fuck you" and that she was embarrassed, and "Fuck you" again as she hailed a cab. Stepping inside and flipping me the bird, she said "Fuck you, Eli." That's the short version.

When you have so many tales to live down, you often get tired of telling them, ergo my debauchery-filled summary. The chunkiest girl, who happened to be a co-worker of the bottled redhead, told Elena all that had transpired, who then reported it back to the CPK newswire. They all laughed at me and said "What about your new girlfriend, Miss Ely?" to which I just put my middle finger to my lips and said "Shhhh."

Still, they laughed, laughed hysterically.

I worked the Monday lunch shift, always a lucrative afternoon, until about five. Shortly after getting back to my hotel room and taking a shower, I left a cheerful, beaming message on Jennifer's voicemail. We had agreed that come Monday we were going to talk and possibly see each other.

If I did anything interesting the rest of the night, I don't recall, but when several hours had gone by, I became a little concerned about Jennifer's welfare, as well as my own. Was there any possible way she could've known about me being inside the mouths of various women inside a tranny bar that weekend? (And they were definitely women, too. I did check.) I was fairly certain that there was no way that Jennifer could've known about it. Still, why hadn't she returned my call? Like me, she only had a cell phone. Around 10:30 p.m., I left another message: positive, fun, clearly spelling out my phone number before I said good-bye. Unwarranted confidence told me that something was up, because no way would Jennifer Ely ignore my phone calls like that.

Hoping to appear laid-back and calm, I left another message on Tuesday afternoon, saying, "Hope you had a good time last night. I went out with friends (*not true*) but I'm free tonight. It's around two o'clock. Call me. 415-xxx-xxxx."

11:30 p.m., Tuesday, bleary-eyed drunk and upset that Jennifer had yet to return my call, I was drinking at The Beauty Bar in the Mission. Less than a year before, when I lived at Theater Bazooka, I used to seduce women from this bar and fuck them on center stage of the empty theater with the stage lights, pink and blue, shining above us.

"I like Jennifer Ely and so terribly want to see her again," I thought to myself, my head heavy, hands trembling, ordering a Harvey Wallbanger from a lithe barmaid wearing a baby tee trying to conceal her surprise at my order. She came back with a shockingly stiff Harvey, sweet and burning. Nobody drinks Harveys anymore, but I ordered another, then another, despite the fact that I was already drunk before my first one. Nobody spoke to me, which was fine, because at that level of inebriation, I lacked the ability to say anything nice to anybody.

The music was loud. The Psychedelic Furs. Eighties night at The Beauty Bar, was it? Eighties music in a bar made to look like a 1950s hair salon. "Love My Way." I remembered that song. 1982. My girlfriend would've been a baby when this song came out. Fuck, she wasn't my girlfriend. She wasn't then and wasn't last weekend or the night before. She was not going to call. That was my karma for being a slut with the bold, curvaceous party girls. I was hurt, but I had brought this on myself. Too drunk to fight, too drunk to fuck, too drunk to speak, too drunk to lift my head off my chest, my drinking hours had been spent, and there was no protest when the bartender, a dark-haired boy-man (what happened to the chick?), told me I'd been cut off and that my last Harvey was on the house. He wasn't being tough, just firm, but I hoped he didn't think he intimidated me. Laboriously, I pushed myself away from the bar and off the stool, and for a moment I thought I was going to fall backwards.

There was once a local San Francisco comic called Doug the Alcoholic, used to drunkenly slur the question "Have you ever fallen *up* the stairs?" Barreling through the bar was like falling up the stairs, and knocking people over in my inebriated darkness made me grateful for the thickness of my body. In the smoky entrance, where the bar's doorman and various Tuesday night heel-kickers were sucking down their cigarettes, somebody called out my name and told me to have a good night. I weaved in the doorway like a zombie, my head too low and comfortable to look up and see who said it, though it was probably the doorman, an old friendly acquaintance of mine who wears a black handlebar mustache and vintage suits and plays the guitar in a local band. Somebody pushed me away from the entrance.

Head still facing downward, I felt mild surprise each time the tops of my shoes came into view, like "Wow, am I still walking? Am I still standing? Am I still on my feet?" I wobbled around the corner down 19th Street, past the Baobab, the Senegalese bar and grill where tall, impossibly dark black people spoke French and called out my name while bouncy salsa music boomed from their tiny dance floor. My arms and head wouldn't allow me to acknowledge who called out my name, but the folks who worked there remembered me from when I lived next door, before I moved up a social class by checking into a residential hotel. Theater Bazooka and Art Gallery! I wished I still lived there, if only so I could crash right then. The lights were off and the front door was locked. Damn, damn, damn. My money was running out and I was too poor to hail a cab and too drunk to walk back to North Beach. Lance LittleJohn lived on Capp and 19th and he's a good, generous friend and he'd let me crash on his couch unannounced.

I remember banging on an apartment door yelling "Lance LittleJohn! Lance LittleJohn! Let me in! Let me in! Where's Doug the Alcoholic? Where's Doug the Alcoholic?" (despite the fact that I knew Doug had fallen off the wagon years ago and binged himself into oblivion). "Lance LittleJohn! Lance LittleJohn! Let me in! Doug the Alcoholic, where the hell are you?"

Doug once said, "If you've ever gotten sunburned on the inside of your mouth, chances are very good you're an alcoholic." How about waking up facedown with a mouthful of carpet? Wednesday, late morning, I woke from the kind of brutal sleep that hurts the moment you open your eyes. There was a thousand-pound weight lying across my head and I knew I wouldn't be able to lift my body off the floor without great, strenuous effort. I was fully dressed, still wearing my faded burgundy wingtips as a matter of fact. I forced myself up and "Oh, dear God, Oh dear God, Oh, dear God" I could barely stand I was so dizzy. Taking several seconds to get settled, I stood still and felt the additional pain that greeted me as my body ached inside my clothes.

Down the hallway and into the bathroom, I stared at myself in the mirror, noticing the worry lines stacked on my forehead and the bloodshot blue eyes that lay halfway sunken inside the fleshy, dark half-moons underneath them, and I thought about my grandfather, whom I used to call Papa, and I remembered Papa's eyes.

I'm sitting next to Papa on the couch watching John Wayne kill Indians in black and white. Papa's chain-smoking, tipping his cigarettes into his favorite ashtray, the tall wicker one shaped like a martini glass. The other ashtrays in the house read "GET WELL." Jimmy Carter's president and an ashtray is still a fine "get well" gift. My feet don't touch the floor I'm so small, and I'm bouncing in my seat because I'm so hyper. When John Wayne's manifest destiny begins to lose me, I stare at Papa. Watching him smoke, inhaling then exhaling, fascinates me to no end. His thick glasses remind me of the magnifying glass my brother and I use to burn fire ants. Studying the star-like wrinkles along his neck, I picture straps of soft brown leather stretched and pressed frantically with a Phillips-head screwdriver, leaving behind a million tiny impressions. "Tank top" and "V-neck T-shirt" are foreign words to me. My brother and I always refer to such garments as "Papa shirts." He's wearing a V-neck special right now, snow-white against his leather skin, ankle-high white socks, checked Bermuda shorts, and black canvas slip-on shoes. The TV room is sealed from the rest of the house because it's the only room that's air-conditioned. The TV is loud and smoke is rising to the ceiling and I think Papa is so powerful that he can create clouds indoors. Excited, I ask Papa every last question that enters my head. "Why did that man shoot that other man? Did you eat lots of navy beans in the Navy? How come you've got no hair on your head? How many times have you had your nose broken? How many tattoos do you have?"

Each time, gravelly-voiced Papa would answer, "Yep. I reckon so."

Whenever I have a hangover, I think about my grandfather, can literally feel his presence.

At thirteen, I overheard my Papa talking to my Uncle Jimmy, and somewhere along the line he said, "Every drink I've ever had, every woman I've ever chased, every fight I've ever fought, every sleepless night and every painful morning, appears on this face of mine."

Papa and Jimmy were smoking cigarettes under the carport during a late-night hailstorm on Christmas Eve with pebble-sized hail beating the aluminum like a dozen machine guns off in the distance, possibly reminding Papa of World War II, possibly reminding Jimmy of Vietnam. The former bar fighter had been standing next to my uncle, but after a moment or two, Papa turned to face his adult son.

"Be careful how you live your life, Jimmy, because your face ain't looking too good."

Few people have ever said that the men in my family age particularly well. They go bald sooner than most men, and their eyes, regardless of the pleasure or sleep received the night before, always retain a tired sadness. As a child, I admired my Papa's face and the faces of my uncles. So rich were they in battered character that I always hoped I'd have a face like theirs of my own someday. It just never occurred to me that I'd have to earn it.

Papa was a drunk, a notorious brawling drunk, who somewhere in his fifth decade decided he was never going to drink again. Just like that. No AA or rehab or anything else. Though his binges were gone by the time I was old enough to darken my mother's towels, I was made aware of his lost days and nights through devastatingly quiet, subtle comments from the adults whose childhoods had been savagely marked by behaviors my Papa couldn't possibly remember. Even without those statements, his character and the life he lived were clearly visible on every line in that old man's face. Adults should never forget exactly how much information they themselves were able to perceive when they were just kids.

Papa's been gone the entirety of my adult years, but his presence, his spirit, has made itself known to me whenever my body's been drunk, near-dead, and as connected to the ground as a tree is to soil. It's always been my Papa's voice that tells me to get up.

In the bathroom, taking an enormously long piss, I felt my head draining of fluid. "Oh, my God," I thought to myself. "Oh, my God!" My stomach and my eyes were *angry* and trying to force themselves out of my body. The telephone rang just as the toilet flushed. I walked out quickly so as not to see my grandfather's face in the mirror. The phone was in the hallway, a perfect place to lean my head.

"Hello?"

"Hi, this is Henry. Are you the guy?"

"Huh? What? Who? Who is this?"

"I'm Henry. I live in the apartment you crashed at last night."

"I thought Lance LittleJohn lived here."

"He used to. He doesn't anymore. He and Angelique moved to a place on 24th and Mission."

"Oh, shit." I laughed a little. "I'm sorry."

"No, no. No problem."

"What happened?"

"You were banging on the door around midnight, screaming 'What happened to Doug the Alcoholic?' I look through the eyehole and see this big bald guy banging on the door and I'm like, 'Shit, should I call the police?' But then you started yelling Lance LittleJohn's name so I knew you knew somebody here. Hey, how do you know Fivepockets?"

"What the fuck is Fivepockets? A pool hall or something?"

"Fivepockets is a dude."

"I don't know anybody named Fivepockets."

"Well, he knows you. He's a short Haitian dude who grew up with Lance in Miami. He's an artist. He paints."

"Oh, yeah. Uh, I think I do know him. How do you know Lance?"

"An old college friend. We went to University of Miami together."

"Oh, (*bullshitting*) yes, Henry! I think I have heard Lance mention you before."

"Oh, I'm sure. I just moved here like a month and a half ago. Man, lots of Florida people in San Francisco. Aren't you from Tampa?"

"Yeah, something like that. So, what happened last night?"

"Little Robbie looks in the peephole and says, 'Oh, that's Eli. It's Tweaker Thomas! Let him in!'"

"Tweaker Thomas? Tweaker Thomas is a character I used to play. Back in the days when Lance and I first met and were both members of The Old Popcorn Theater group, I used to perform monologues in venues throughout the city as this insane, manic speed-freak dude. I guess more than a few people didn't know if it was real or not."

"Yeah, I've been hearing about that character and you for years, man. Lance says he even met the guy that character's based on."

"Yeah. That fucker's dead now from an overdose."

"Wow. Little Robbie even remembers seeing Doug the Alcoholic perform."

"Oh, yeah. Ole Doug could've been another Rodney Dangerfield, but he's probably dead now, too."

"All junkies and drunks end up dead eventually."

"As do all good men and women."

"Yeah."

"Hey, Henry, I'm terribly sorry about last night."

"No, don't be. It was no big deal. It was actually pretty damn entertaining. I opened the door and you pushed past me and jumped onto the floor like a belly flop into a swimming pool. Within a few seconds you were snoring. We decided to just leave you there. I went to bed but Little Robbie stayed up to work on a painting. Around two thirty, I'm woken up by the loudest screams I've ever heard in my life. Little Robbie and I come running out of our rooms. Summer Austin and Sherri Bolan had come home from drinking, and when they turn on the lights, they see you on the floor like you're dead, and they both scream in unison. You slept through the whole damn thing." He laughs hard for a few solid seconds. "When they stopped yelling, they could hear you snoring and see your stomach move. Then they're like, 'Why the fuck is Sick Guy Eli Jokey sleeping on our floor?' And we're like, 'He was drunk and needed a place to crash. Leave him alone.'"

"Yeah, those girls hate me."

"No, they don't. They like you."

"Nah, they hate me."

"No, no. So they think you're a little weird, even by their standards, but they think you're a great writer. That's what everybody says about you, actually."

"Thanks, Henry." Then why was I not published? Somehow, even a compliment can make a painful morning worse. "Are the girls here right now? I need to apologize for scaring them."

"No, they're gone. You know those party girls. Drink till two, in bed by four, at work by nine."

"Yeah, yeah, they're tough. Hey, Henry, thanks for everything. I'm going home now. I feel like shit. I look forward to meeting you on better terms."

"Sure thing, Eli. By the way, there's a beer in the fridge if you want one."

"Thanks, Henry."

I'm not a beer-breakfast-equals-hangover-cure type of boozer. I prefer heavy, spicy food. For years, a regular hangover cure for me was a stroll into Chinatown to a place on Jackson called Sam Lok, where I'd order garlic broccoli for a mere five dollars. It was a large bowl of steamed broccoli marinated in garlic sauce. The potent smell would clear my sinuses and make my eyes water. I'd eat the entire batch, even lapping up the sauce with a spoon. Unfortunately, I didn't crash close enough to justify a stroll into Chinatown.

Ignoring Henry's beer, I walked to a tiny sandwich shop on 19th and Mission. It was a place I used to frequent when I lived at Bazooka. It was owned and run by an ever-cheerful Chinese family. It was a place for good, strong coffee and decent, very cheap sandwiches. Actually, their egg sandwiches were better than decent and a perfect steal for a buck fifty. The Chinese lady behind the counter said, "Oh, long time, no see. How are you?"

"I'm sad."

Then she laughed, hand covering her little mouth.

"You eat sandwiches and then you be happy."

I started laughing too and ordered three egg sandwiches with lettuce, tomatoes, onion, hot peppers, Tabasco, and no mayo. I reached into their cooler and grabbed two cans of Pepsi. She was still chuckling when she handed me a plate of sandwiches. The bill still came out to under six bucks. I ate all three sandwiches and drank both cans. Even took a third Pepsi for the road. I paid my bill and walked back to North Beach. I could feel my strength returning and the hangover disappear.

The Chinese lady was right. The sandwiches did make me happier, but my cell phone's silence and my lack of voicemail told me that Jennifer lied when she said she was going to call on Monday, and she was obviously too preoccupied to return my calls. She didn't care. It was over.

I took a shower when I got back to the Sestri, then an afternoon nap. At around 4:30 p.m. or so, my cell phone's chirp woke me from a soft sleep. Caller ID displayed Jennifer's number. Surprisingly, I was reluctant to answer her call.

"Hello?"

"Hello, Eli. It's me, Jennifer."

"I know."

"Will you meet me at Vesuvio's right now?"

I didn't want to, but it seemed urgent.

"Yeah, uh, um, Jennifer, I don't want to meet you at Vesuvio's."

"I don't care where we meet just as long as it is a place where I can get a drink."

"Let's meet at Café Greco then."

"Where's that?"

"It's on Columbus and across from Calzone's. I can get some coffee, and I know they've got beer and wine there."

"Okay, fine."

"I'll meet you there in like fifteen, twenty minutes. I just woke up from a nap. Okay?"

"Okay."

I was displeased with myself because I still wanted to see Jennifer even though she returned my call a day and a half later and assumed I'd be able to stop what I was doing and meet her somewhere. That was when I decided I was not going to be nice.

It was raining heavily when I left my hotel. Outside Café Greco, Jennifer stood underneath the awning looking somber, watching the diagonal sheets of water hit the pavement. I didn't smile when I walked up to her, no embrace, no kiss. She looked at me, startled.

"Let's go inside."

Inside there was a small line at the counter. I turned to Jennifer: "Hey, I'll have a large hot chocolate. You get that and I'll go get a seat for us."

I didn't stick around to notice the expression on her face after I gave her my order, but I knew what I was doing. I walked to a tiny table near a window looking out onto Columbus Avenue and sat down.

She came back to the table with my hot cocoa and a glass of red wine.

"Thanks, Jennifer. Now what's up?"

"Well, I feel like I owe you an explanation."

"For what?"

She cringed, recognizing my feeble attempt at playing dumb. "For not calling you back on Monday."

I shrugged as though it didn't bother me.

"I guess you can say that I was avoiding your phone calls."

She was avoiding my phone calls.

"Why?"

"Because I was scared of getting into a relationship."

"With me?"

"With anybody. You see, my plan was to not call you back and then go to Yosemite without saying good-bye because it'd be too painful. After the summer job was over, I was going to look you up and see if you wanted to start back up where we left off."

Wow. Was she for real? "Did it ever occur to you, Jennifer, that I might have been seeing somebody else by the time you came back, or that perhaps I just wouldn't be interested in seeing you again?"

"That was a risk I was willing to take."

"Then why are you here now?"

"Because I wanted to see you." Jennifer looked like she was about to cry.

My intuition told me maybe someone else had been occupying her time while she was avoiding my calls. "What did you do this weekend, Jennifer?"

"I did nothing. Hung out with friends Saturday. Read a little bit. Did nothing, really."

"Did you think about me this weekend?"

Emphatically, she said, "You were all that I thought about, Eli."

I couldn't believe it. "Really?"

"Yes." Oh, my God. She was going to cry! She obviously regretted not calling me back, and there I was being a cold hard-ass.

I put my hand on her shoulder and whispered, "Baby, it's okay. It's not my intention to hurt you or make you cry. You're all that I thought about this weekend, too."

I was no longer angry. Jennifer avoided my phone calls that first time because she was falling too deeply for me and feared getting emotionally involved with somebody right before her summer job in the mountains.

We finished our drinks and ran in the pouring rain to my hotel room, where my CD player played yet another jazz compilation, and we had sex for two, maybe three hours. In each other's arms, we decided we were boyfriend and girlfriend and that we'd keep in contact through cell phones and letters and the occasional weekend furloughs to San Francisco and a weekend, hopefully my birthday, when I'd come up to Yosemite.

I told Jennifer about my binge at The Beauty Bar the night before and how I had crashed on the floor at the apartment of an old friend only to find out the old friend didn't live there anymore. She laughed, calling me "out of control." Afterwards, Jennifer asked me what I did over the weekend.

"Just worked, baby, and thought about you."

V

My most recent (and probably oddest) tattoo was acquired in mid-August at Tattoo City in North Beach, and I got it for nothing, like forty, fifty dollars. To anyone else, especially the non-tattooed, the symbol would seem random and done without much forethought. However, the theory or philosophy behind the tattoo is one that turns me on, something that motivates me. After consuming several essays by Colin Wilson one morning, I learned that during the Korean War, US military intelligence was bothered by the lack of POW escape attempts. What they soon discovered was that the enemy was taking the POWs and putting them under heavy surveillance. Then they'd pluck out the most assertive, most aggressive, most cunning prisoners and put them under extreme guard. The rest they'd periodically check up on, because without a natural-born leader or instigator to inspire them to escape, these fuckers wouldn't even try. It was always one out of twenty people, or 5 percent. I also learned that if you drop a bunch of rats in a large box with no food or water, 5 percent always kill and cannibalize the rest. It's called the Dominant Five Percent Theory. Dr. Abraham Maslow was also a proponent of this theory. But it doesn't only pertain to badass solders and killer rats. What it means is that there are those individuals with a certain attitude and intellectual proclivity that alienates them from their society and times, but these people, in exceptional cases, become the motivating force for change. Typically, these individuals are highly aggressive, and often they end up occupying important social positions: politicians, entertainers, writers, thinkers, etc. Colin Wilson terms these individuals, the Dominant Five Percenters, "outsiders."

Now, on my forearm is the tattoo, a solid black "5%." To me, it's the ultimate "outsider" symbol.

Bandage and cocoa butter still on my arm, I called Jennifer, still up in Yosemite, to tell her about my newly acquired tattoo and the meaning behind it, hoping that it could be something to impress my philosophical girlfriend, something we could wax poetic about. Boy, was I wrong.

Cheerfully, Jennifer says, "Interesting, but I'd much rather talk about your opinion of *The Giving Tree*."

"*The Giving Tree*?" She wanted to talk to me about *The Giving Tree*? What the fuck? Then I remembered the conversation. On Friday, August 1, a day before my thirty-second birthday, Jennifer and I were in her rented Dodge Neon, driving from San Francisco to Yosemite. Jennifer, to her credit, brought along a *Best of Johnny Cash* CD, and when we got to "A Boy Named Sue," Jennifer was shocked when I mentioned to her that the song had originally been a poem by Shel Silverstein.

"Shel Silverstein?"

"Yeah, baby. You know, *The Giving Tree* guy?"

"I know who he is, Eli. I just didn't know he wrote that song. Wow."

She smiled at me, and that is where I should've just left it, with my girlfriend smiling at me, but instead of stopping when I was ahead, I began to express my pointedly negative opinion of Shel Silverstein's most famous work.

"You know, it's funny, but I always hated *The Giving Tree*. It's a sick story, really, about a sick, co-dependent relationship. It's actually harmful to kids."

Jennifer said nothing then, but now, on the telephone, suddenly Jennifer wanted to discuss *The Giving Tree*.

"Eli, the other day, I was talking to some of the women who work out here in Yosemite and mentioned that you hated *The Giving Tree*. Then one of them said, 'What kind of person could hate a sweet book like that? Adolf Hitler?'"

161

"What did you say?"

"I said nothing, but I think"—cautiously—"they're right. I mean, who in their right mind has a problem with *The Giving Tree*? It's a beautiful story about love, about unconditional love. I mean, here's the story: There's this boy who loves a big, beautiful tree, and the tree loves the boy. Making the boy happy makes the tree happy. When the boy gets older and needs money, she gives him her apples to sell. When he asks for a house,"—talking to me like I'm a child at bedtime—"she offers her branches for lumber. Soon he's older and sad. She encourages him to cut her down to a stump and to build a boat from her trunk. He sails off and the tree stump is sad and lonely. He comes back years later, an old man needing a quiet place to sit and rest. She offers her stump, he sits down, and the tree's happy."

Did Jennifer Ely think by telling me the story in a sweet, maternal voice, I'd suddenly fall in love with *The* goddamn fucking *Giving Tree*? I was quiet on my end of the phone for a long time.

"How can you have a problem with that story? It's not like you're some big environmentalist who has issues with the willful destruction of a tree or something." Then she laughed.

I didn't believe it. We were going to discuss *The* goddamn fucking *Giving Tree*.

"I know the story and you're right, I'm not particularly moved by the willful destruction of a tree. I heard the story as a wee youngster and didn't like it, nor did I understand it the way I loved and understood *Chicken Little*. One of my childhood memories is watching Leo Buscaglia give a lecture on PBS. This would be the late '70s, early '80s. Do you know Leo Buscaglia?"

"No."

"It's okay, he's dead now, but he was a self-help guru whose big message was love. He wrote books with titles like *Living, Loving, Learning* and *Loving Each Other* and *The Fall of Freddie the Leaf*, which was a children's book about grieving. My parents were big fans of his."

"Oh, *your* parents."

There was a long pause. Was she using my shitty relationship with my family against me?

"Yes, Jennifer. They were big fans. When I worked at a bookstore for a little while in the late '80s, his books still sold very well. My point is that during the lecture, Leo Buscaglia brought up *The Giving Tree* and openly hated it. Said it was a terrible little story. I realized he was right. One hundred percent. What he said is that there comes a time in every relationship where you've got to say 'Back off, jerk!'"

"That's bullshit, Eli! If you love somebody through and through, unconditionally, then you'll give that person anything to make that person happy. Do you not understand love?"

"Regardless, unconditional love or not, you've got to tell somebody where to go to get their shit together, and you're not solely responsible for their happiness."

"That's not what the story is about. It's about friendship, devotion, loyalty. It's about sharing, giving, and *unconditional love*! Why can't you see that?"

"No, it's about co-dependent love, and for the sake of the child's growth and the tree's self-respect, the tree needs to say 'No!' Like when the kid needed a boat, the tree should've said 'Go out and earn a boat,' or better yet, 'Go and get a job on a boat.' Then the kid could've gotten a job on a pirate ship. Ah, now that would've been a cool story."

"Oh, my God!" Condescendingly, she said, "You just don't get it, do you, Eli? You're supposed to be this deep, sensitive artist-slash-writer, and yet you fail to recognize that this book's about the unconditional love God gives us or the unconditional love we get from nature or the unconditional love a mother is *supposed* to give to her children."

Again, Jennifer Ely was bringing up my family. On our first date, I told her I didn't get along with any of them. Was she trying to provoke a vicious response from me?

"Okay, Jennifer." Acidly, I say, "God doesn't just give and give unconditionally. If I ask God for a twelve-inch dick, he doesn't automatically grant it to me. Right now, as we speak, there are millions of theater majors praying to God to someday be rich and famous actors, and most of them will never even work as professional actors. Think of everyone who prays to win the lottery but doesn't. I can pray to God to someday be a well-publicized, best-selling author, but that's not going to happen without lots of hard work. I believe in God, which is something I thought you lacked, but my God doesn't act like the goddamn fucking Giving Tree. And let's talk about Mother Nature's unconditional love. Flood, earthquake, volcano, drought, famine. And moms don't just keep giving unconditionally, nor should they have to."

"Goddamn, Eli! People need love and need to love others, and when you love someone, you make sacrifices for them! It's just a story about love for kids!"

"Yes, and I think teaching this story to kids is a harmful thing."

"What do you care? You don't want kids. You've only said so about a million times."

"Yes, I've made the decision not to have kids, but so what? That doesn't mean I don't care how kids are raised. I hate those stingy yuppies who bitch about paying taxes for schools because they don't have kids. Kids are our future, and we childless people have got to live with them. Those little bastards better learn how to converse, how to compromise, how to coexist. You don't have kids. Would it be correct to assume you don't care about kids and what they learn in school?"

"I care about kids but I haven't yet made the decision not to have them. But Eli, you're still missing the point. The tree was only happy when she was giving something of herself. It's through giving that we receive. We can only be truly happy when we give of ourselves to others expecting nothing in return. When we let go of our *egos*, stop wanting to be admired, and think only of other's needs, we attract true love back to us in return. The boy loved the tree, and that was all the tree needed to be happy."

"That's bullshit and you know it. You can give and give and give but you must eventually stop giving if you're not getting anything back in return. The boy gave the tree jack shit. You are never told how the boy felt or where he goes or what exactly he does on these excursions without the tree. He was just a nasty little taker and user who took and took and took. It's just like Leo Buscaglia said."

"That guy was for stupid people!"

What was she saying? That I was stupid? That my parents were stupid? Many things they are, but stupid is not one of them. I took a deep breath.

"Jennifer, Leo Buscaglia was a college professor with a PhD. Your parents probably knew him. They most certainly knew of him. I saw him on PBS, not Jerry Springer. Okay?"

The argument continued. The same points were reiterated, repeated, and shouted. Hours flew by until the arm that held my cell phone ached and my voice became hoarse. We each felt strongly and confidently in our points of view, and neither was willing to concede to the other. Despite being a notoriously opinionated guy, I don't enjoy arguing, and it's not important to me to make people agree with what I'm saying. It was a certain grade school teacher who said to me, "You're not a follower but you're not a leader either." Come along with me or don't, it makes no difference to me. When I state an opinion, it's just an opinion. I'm not out to win a debate. I would've been willing to agree to disagree early on, but Jennifer's patronizing tone seemed to egg me on further.

Sadly, that was the night that I learned Jennifer was my mother: the kind of woman who loved to argue, but only if she was winning, and if you disagreed with her, she'd try to make you feel stupid. But unfortunately for her, I came of age with a woman meaner and more conniving at using the very tactics she was applying. Jennifer Ely didn't stand a chance. My mom would've destroyed her.

Finally: "Jennifer, why the fuck are you doing this? You know what my opinion is. It's not going to change."

She gave an exasperated yell and took a long pause, started to say something, but then stopped. Said nothing at all.

"Why did you do this, Jennifer? Why did you start an argument with me?"

"Because I wanted you to say 'You're right, Jennifer. It's a wonderful story.'"

"But it's after midnight. I hate *The Giving Tree*. I also walked out of *Pulp Fiction*. Are you going to stick up for Quentin Tarantino, too? People are entitled to differences of opinion, even boyfriends and girlfriends."

"I know, I know, just don't lecture me, Eli."

There was nothing else to talk about. We said goodnight with nary an "I love you."

I briefly considered staying up later and writing a short story about the boy from *The Giving Tree,* portraying him as a career criminal who does serious prison time for fraud and piracy, but I was too tired to write it and thought it wasn't such a good idea anyway.

I called every evening and left a message for the next three nights. She never called back. I knew she was avoiding my calls.

When I called Becca for her take on the argument, she said, "I always thought the moral of the story was 'Don't be like the tree,' like the tree was a doormat or something like that. 'Don't be a doormat like the tree,' right? That's what I thought it was about."

"Great. Then I'm right: it's a bogus, harmful, bullshit story about co-dependent love."

"Well, yeah, but so are most love songs. I don't hate the story for it. I thought it was all supposed to be a lesson of some sort."

"Hm."

"Eli, did you really get '5%' tattooed on your arm? That's weird."

I asked Scott.

"I really don't remember *The Giving Tree,* not at all. But it all sounds pretty dumb—the story as well as the argument. You know, whenever somebody starts an argument, it's really about something else . . . So, '5%,' huh? Tattooed to your arm? This I got to see."

I asked Lance LittleJohn.

"Ah, fuck, man. When I first heard that story as a kid, I didn't have an opinion one way or the other, but as an adult, I fucking love it."

"Really?"

"Yeah, Eli. You know why?"

"No, why?"

"Think about it! It's a kinky S&M love story. The boy is a sadist to the tree's masochist. Talk about an odd fetish. The boy falls in love with a tree and the tree loves him back. The boy carves his name into the tree and the tree loves him for it. The boy takes, degrades, and humiliates the tree, and the tree loves it! Taking her trunk and turning it into a boat is like fucking the tree! If you notice, when the boy comes back an old man and the tree offers her stump, the man sits on the stump, a fucking sadist to the end! As a matter of fact, an illustrator ought to redo the book and draw leather whips and chains hanging from the tree like ivy and a black leather vest wrapped around its trunk."

"A pair of black leather boots for the boy with a matching mask. *The Bondage Tree.*"

"Exactly, Eli! Now you get it. It's a kinky S&M story disguised as a story for kids. I fucking love it! The tree-slash-slave is always at the sadistic boy's command. How about *The Giving-It-A-Whipping Tree*?"

Lance proceeded to laugh maniacally.

"Um, uh, yeah, thanks Lance. I got to go."

"Hey, hold up. Did you really get '5%' tattooed to your arm? Haven't you ever heard of The Five-Percent Nation of Islam?"

"No. Who are they?"

On the phone four nights later, Jennifer was soft-spoken and sweet. She said she wanted to call me back when she was ready. Every "I love you" that came from me in that conversation was echoed by her. We didn't bring up *The Giving Tree* ever again.

My girlfriend and I planned to spend the first weekend in August, which fell on my thirty-second birthday, in Yosemite, taking in the great outdoors, breathing the fresh mountain air, and making love underneath the starry, starry night . . . Sadly, seeing the mountains up close scared me shitless. I had to hang my head below the dashboard while Jennifer drove. As a teenager, I'd gone to the mountains of North Carolina, and even camped out. The mountains then did not send me into a heart-accelerating panic the way Yosemite's eyesores did. I'm not afraid to stand on rooftops or fly, but something about those peaks frightened me, as if the mountains were going to suddenly avalanche.

Camping was never an interest of mine. My biological father—the belligerent, un-peaceful hippie I barely knew—loved to camp and forced me to go with him on the rare occasions he took a passing interest in me. Once I was old enough to refuse, I never went camping again.

I knew Jennifer was into camping, the mountains, rock-climbing, hiking, and the great outdoors. Not to say I feigned an interest in those passions, but I did appear more game and excited about those activities than I actually was.

"I haven't been camping since I was fourteen," I told Jennifer, "and would love to go see Yosemite someday. I've never been there."

Jennifer was excited, and the idea of snuggling with her in a sleeping bag in the cold mountain air was appealing. Perhaps my past was lying to me and I secretly loved camping and the great outdoors, if only because I had the right person around to show me how to appreciate the things I was so indifferent to before.

As a park ranger, I assumed her living quarters were going to be in some handsome, rugged ski lodge, like something from a vintage *Playboy* magazine. Instead, they were damp, nasty wooden boxes on stilts with double cots and a hot plate and something resembling a large utility sink. No kitchen. And everybody used public park restrooms and showers. Bazooka was better than this, if only because it was surrounded by art, theater, and creativity and stood inside the heart of a hip neighborhood in a big city.

"I can't sleep here," I told Jennifer.

"Shit," I remember thinking. "Army barracks have got to be better than this dump." Then I walked with trembling baby steps back to the car, not looking anywhere but down. We drove and drove. She pointed at mountains, saying, "I thought we could climb one of those tomorrow," to which I'd mumble from underneath the dashboard, "No way."

She came upon a secluded area in the woods to set up camp, but I was too terrified to leave the car. Due to the absence of city lights, the night sky was darker than anything I was used to, and the mountains' jagged silhouettes taunted me.

Aghast and dumbfounded to learn I wasn't going to leave the Neon to help her set up the tent, Jennifer struggled with a ground that proved too damp, dropped the project in frustration, and ran back to the car. She sat in the driver's side, slammed the door, and proceeded to cry. "You're afraid of mountains, Eli? How's that fucking possible?"

A fear of mountains is related to a fear of heights. When did I develop alpinephobia? Growing up in the flatlands of Florida? Dealing with my father's bullshit in Highlands, North Carolina?

I apologized. "Honestly," I said. "Who knew I'd react like this?"

We talked and held hands.

"I love you, Jennifer."

"I love you, too, Eli."

"And I want you to be in my life."

"And I want to be in your life, Eli, and I want you to be a part of everything in mine."

"I'm really sorry, Jennifer."

Silence.

We fell asleep in forlorn solitude, knowing intuitively that part of our relationship had been irreparably damaged. We slept fully clothed on the Dodge Neon's front seat. When we woke, our backs, our necks and our spirits were in pain, but we made no references to it.

That next day was Saturday and my thirty-second birthday. We drove to a natural hot spring somewhere in the town of Mammoth. The hot spring was on a flat field off a dirt road with the mountains too far from me to cause any real trauma. Nude, I looked city-boy pale, with too much dry skin around my heels and yellowed foot fungus underneath my toenails. My usually well-shaven chest was peppered with quarter-inch prickles. Naked, Jennifer looked tanned and fit with a perfectly muscled hourglass figure. It was my first natural hot spring. The water was murky and warm, and it was like wading in a heated swamp. Altogether, it was neither an unpleasant nor a particularly pleasant experience. Believe me, a Jacuzzi in a lush hotel would've been more appreciated, or even a hot shower at the Sestri.

Earlier in the day, we had stopped at a Mobil station and bought food and drink for a picnic. We had chips and salsa, beer, fruit, and baked tofu. We ate our food on a white bed sheet Jennifer had brought. I bought a package of condoms, and after we ate lunch, I mentioned to her that the night before was only the third time we've spent the night together and not had sex. (The first time was our first date and the second was the time I got food poisoning.) She smiled. Then I smiled, gently pushing her body downward on her back, throwing the remaining food packages aside, and wrapping the white sheet around our naked bodies. Jennifer beamed, her smile large and open, her eyes euphoric, as I pushed myself inside her deeper and deeper. Occasionally, a breeze would enter our cocoon and inflate the sheet around us like a wind tunnel.

We came simultaneously while she held onto my lower back, taking in short, choppy breaths and shaking all over. I released everything and felt my hips and spine twitch and vibrate as I remained inside her. When the aftershocks finally ceased, I rolled off Jennifer's body and peeled the soiled latex off my cock. I tossed it up in the air and heard the unmistakable plop as it landed in the water. Lying next to my nature-loving girlfriend, I hoped to God she didn't hear me pollute the natural hot spring. If she did, she didn't mention it. Instead, we just remained there, saying nothing, feeling the sun embracing our bodies. When we regained ourselves, I asked Jennifer if we could go back to San Francisco that day.

In a voice loving and defeated, Jennifer said "Of course, Eli."

As we drove back, I admitted that I knew I wasn't an outdoorsy person but had no idea that I was actually mountain-phobic. "Someday," I told her, "I'll come out here with you. I know you love the great outdoors and that you love rock-climbing and shit. Give me time, baby. Baby steps, baby. We'll be together for a long time. I took you to your first art opening, though that was hardly a typical art opening. I turned you on to two of my favorite novels of all time." Earlier in the summer, I had sent her copies of *The Sacrilege of Alan Kent* by Erskine Caldwell and *The Razor's Edge* by Somerset Maugham. She liked the former, loved the latter.

"Jennifer, you'll be able to turn me on to the mountains someday, baby. I know it. Someday we'll camp out here together. I just need to work myself up to it."

Jennifer patted my leg as she drove and said "Don't worry about it, Eli. It's okay."

Two weeks later, she started an argument with me about *The Giving Tree,* an argument most likely designed to show how differently we think about things, how much we don't have in common.

VI

To say my girlfriend lacked empathy is not entirely true, considering she seemed to genuinely feel sorry for the people who worked with me at California Pizza Kitchen. Whenever I told my tales about work, the same tales that'd force me to howl and bring laughter pains to my friends and the few friendly co-workers I had, Jennifer would scowl and say something sarcastic like "Oh, you must be a pleasure to work with."

I'd say, "What do you mean?"

My girlfriend would remind me that one of the first things I ever said to her was "Nobody at my work likes me."

It wasn't that *nobody* liked me, but the half who didn't like me tended to be a vocal minority who hated me with a passion. Others, like Danny, Boston Scott, and Harley, liked me, thought I was funny, attended my one-man show and applauded, and chiefly felt entertained by the animated animosity I inspired in others.

"It's the comedy of discomfort," Jennifer would say time and time again. "You get off on the discomfort of others."

A young female server, heavyset, new to CPK, new to the restaurant industry, saw me show up to work in short sleeves. She saw my tattoos and went "Wow! You've got lots of tattoos there! Wow!"

I said, "Thanks for noticing."

Admiring my tattoos, she said, "Is that the only place you've got them? On your arms?"

In utter seriousness, I said, "I've got candy stripes tattooed on my penis."

Her eyes and mouth wide open, she said, "Really?"

"No, but it tastes like a peppermint stick." Then I winked at her, puckered up my lips, and made a loud kissy-kiss sound before walking away. Sexual Harassment Complaint Number One.

Another complaint, though not sexual, is about an intense Eli-hater who may very well have hated me more than anyone else has hated me my entire life.

Jasper Needham was the worst career waiter I've ever known. The man despised me with such a burning passion that he requested to never work the same shifts I did. He wasn't alone in this request, just the most outspoken. His animosity towards me was not bothersome at all. In fact, I rather dug it. Not seeing his ugly, saggy-skinned iguana face during my workdays was something to appreciate. Nobody at work really liked Jasper Needham, and they respected him even less. He was every waiter's nightmare, a living warning of who he might become if he makes the wrong decisions in life. A walking, talking, bitter portrait of Dorian Gray refilling iced teas and coffees and taking orders, hoping for something better than 10 percent of the bill. He was in his mid- to late forties but looked ten, fifteen years older. Jasper's formerly skinny, angular body was hunched over with a small hump on his upper back a la Montgomery Burns, and a tiny paunch over his waist. He had a receding hairline he made more prominent by pulling his dishwater-brown hair into a ponytail.

Whenever Needham's name came up around me, usually in reference to the notorious fact that the man abhorred my very existence, I'd always respond, "I don't hate Jasper. I just don't respect the guy. Can you imagine being a career waiter who's no damn good at it?"

Nobody, not even those co-workers who insisted they got along fine with Jasper, ever said "Oh, no! Jasper's a good server." Nobody ever defended him.

Nice guy Danny Ryan pointed out that he was never late, never missed a day of work, and could always be trusted to complete his tasks. "He may be a good employee," I'd agree. "However, that alone doesn't make him a good waiter."

Jasper Needham had worked at CPK for eighteen years, and yet, he still sucked. He couldn't handle more than two, possibly three small tables at a time, always with his face in a small notebook, writing everything down, something Danny and I never had to do. Despite having three tiny tables, the man still got flustered way too easily, and seeing his frightened face seemingly seconds away from total meltdown reminded umpteen young servers of where they did not want to be in ten, fifteen years.

"I don't want to end up like Jasper" was a common sentiment expressed around CPK.

One cliché among servers is the waiter who is working until he finds a "real" job. Frequently, he performs this "fake" job during college, making money, having fun, sleeping around, and sleeping past noon, all before settling down and pursuing a real career. A second cliché is the waiter who waits tables as a means to support his creative endeavors, the waiter who's really a writer, an actor, an artist, a musician. After a while, either type can become the third type of waiter: the "career waiter."

Jasper was the second type of career waiter: a writer whose creative endeavors never enabled him to quit his restaurant gig. A temporary way to pay the bills turned into a career by default. Whereas a bartender-poet may enjoy his job and appreciate the attention it gives him, Jasper "the failed writer" was never a particularly good server. It was not something that came to him easily, nor did it give him any pleasure. If he smiled or cracked a joke, he certainly never did it at work. He often said, in a voice rueful and dead, "Time just has a way of getting away from you."

If he had any real talent, he probably would've used that line for a poem.

Within weeks of meeting Jasper, the nicest thing I could say about him was "That man's unpleasant!" I got hired at CPK in November, 1999, shortly after getting fired from United Airlines. That became my hell month, when I lost my girlfriend Jana and came to the miserable, irrefutable conclusion that I was addicted to speed. That New Year's Eve culminated with my self-inflicted overdose on sleeping pills. I survived and missed an entire week of work. When I came back, my foolish act and my wanton after-work habits had been printed in the entire staff's mental newsletter. People saw me as an unstable, drug-addicted freak, and while many co-workers treated me with kid gloves, others rolled their eyes whenever I was around.

I don't know what it was about me that Jasper hated so much. If I asked Needham how his day was going, he'd grunt. If I asked the ever-flustered Jasper if he needed help, he'd get angry and shout "No!" If we had an exceptionally busy shift and the servers made mucho cash, I'd ask Jasper if he'd had a good day, if he'd made good money. Jasper would again yell "No!" and say "Don't talk to me about stuff like that. I don't discuss my tips with anyone."

Of course I disliked Jasper. Who wouldn't? But his body sweated so much self-loathing and his badly aging face appeared so strained and frightened among the energetic twenty-somethings that despite how rude he was to me, I never quit feeling sorry for the guy. Thus, I mostly ignored Jasper, but Jasper didn't always ignore me. He never criticized my work ethic or my skills as a server, knowing he couldn't touch me there, but the man did try to attack my character. When I once got two Asian-American co-workers' names mixed up, Jasper Needham called me racist because I obviously couldn't tell the difference between two Asian guys. I pointed out that whenever I got two white guys' names mixed up, people simply laughed. Nobody called me a racist. I challenged him to explain to me why if I get two Caucasian dudes' names mixed up, it's comedy, but if I confuse two individuals of color, it's racist. Jasper had no reply.

Another time, I was having a conversation with a co-worker and said something like "Me and a friend went to the movies yesterday." Jasper, walking behind me, interjected in a loud, condemning voice, "You've got friends?" Nobody laughed. I turned and Jasper looked at me with a scowl and walked away.

At the start of an evening shift, I was in an exceptionally good mood. I walked past Jasper and cheerfully, politely said "Pardon me," just as I would say to anybody. Jasper reacted irritably, like I had done something to purposely offend the guy. "Pardon me? Pardon me? Why did you say 'Pardon me'?"

Still trying to be civil, I said, "Because I'm polite, Jasper."

To which Jasper yelled in reply, "You're not polite! You're obnoxious!"

That did it. That's when Jasper truly fucked up. Not only did that moment destroy my mood, it killed whatever sympathy I held for that man. I rode his ass that night, loudly criticizing everything he did, and his slow, nervous, incompetent body gave me plenty of material, until finally, in front of our tables and on the dining room floor, he pointed his finger at me and screamed "Get back!"

Everyone in the restaurant, customers and servers, reacted, and for a few seconds, the entire restaurant was silent. When people resumed their meals and conversations, and after Jasper gave me a superior smirk and turned around, I said in a calm voice just loud enough for Needham to hear, "Hey, Jasper, you're too old for this job."

Jasper stopped. His shoulders hunched up to his ears and he turned around to face me, and in a voice choking with emotional sarcasm, he said, "Oh, that was real nice, Eli."

Nice? Was I hearing that right?

"Fuck you, Jasper. You are so fucking lucky that people are nicer to you than you are to them." His face more panicked than usual, Jasper turned away from me, walking quickly into a hallway off-limits to non-employees. I followed, and a female server whose name I don't remember ran and stood in between us, fearing I was going to beat his ass.

It has been said that you should never piss somebody off too much because they'll end up telling you exactly what they think of you. What's worse is that you may piss somebody off so much that they end up telling you exactly what you think of yourself. I wasn't going to fight him, but it took all my strength not to. With our co-worker standing between us and our managers nowhere to be found, I raged at Jasper. If I had called him an asshole, a prick, a dick, or a douchebag, he'd have been oddly satisfied. Instead, I went right underneath his skin and told him what he already knew.

"You suck, Jasper! You suck! You're no good at this job! You're no good at this life! You're a fucking loser, Jasper! You're one of life's great fucking losers! You're pathetic! You're fucking pathetic! My average Tuesday is better than your entire life, Jasper! You're a career waiter who's no damn good at it! Pathetic! If God gave you cancer he'd be doing you a favor! That's how fucking pathetic your life is! Again, Jasper, fuck you!" Then I stopped and eyeballed Jasper hard, ready to swing at him if he uttered one more hostile thing. He just looked at me blankly, or as blankly as is possible for a turkey-necked prune-face.

The girl pleaded with me to leave Jasper alone, saying "He'll get you fired!"

I muttered "pathetic" one more time and walked away.

The shift was almost over and we departed not even looking at one another. It was late December, 2000. I was about two weeks away from my move to Seattle and a job waiting tables at a California Pizza Kitchen in Bellevue, Washington. Because I felt I needed a good reference to obtain the job transfer, I exercised my barely used self-control and didn't give Jasper the beating he so richly deserved.

The man surprised me the next day by apologizing. He openly acknowledged that he had been mean to me all year. During our last remaining shifts together, Jasper Needham was polite and cheerful around me. On my last day, we even shook hands like we should've done on the first. Though he did apologize, Jasper never offered an explanation for his attitude towards me. I didn't ask. I didn't care. Yes, I appreciated his apology, but I had already written him off. Remember, the opposite of love is indifference, not hatred. Jasper earned my indifference.

About a year later, I was living in Seattle. I had said "Fuck you" to Bellevue and gotten a job outside the restaurant industry, promising myself I'd never wait tables again. On one cold, wet, foggy night, I noticed a book on display in a bookstore window with the comical title *Pagan Power!* I chuckled at the book cover, which featured a chubby, earthy, nude woman covered in filth and body paint dancing in a forest. "How funny," I thought. Though the book was making me laugh, that surely wasn't the author's intention. "Who wrote this thing, anyway?"

That's when I saw the byline: "by Jasper Needham." "What the fuck? No way!"

When I first got hired at CPK and mentioned that I was a writer, Harley and Boston Scott told me that Jasper Needham was a writer also. However, as has already been established, Needham's personality wasn't conducive to the type of pleasantries that writers use when they first meet, such as "What kind of stuff do you write?" "Are you published anywhere?" "Who do you like to read?" None of that for Jasper and me, and when I looked at his face, old and wrinkled before his time and lacking the character old, wrinkled faces ought to have, I dismissed him, assuming he was not much of a writer at all.

The bookstore wasn't a Barnes & Noble, nor a Borders, but rather a large, cluttered, dusty used bookstore in the heart of the U District. I ran inside and asked the sullen, grunge-clad young bohemian behind a rotting antique desk if I could look at the Pagan book displayed in the front window. He nodded, barely lifting his head from the thick black hardcover he was absorbing: "Go help yourself."

Holding the thin paperback in my hands, I was startled to see Jasper's ugly mug on the back in what appeared to be a genuine smile. "He's published and I'm not" was the first thing I thought. Unfortunately, that statement became a ringing buzz that never left me the rest of the night. The book wasn't great fiction, thank God, and it wasn't compelling journalism either. Needham, a professed Pagan, interviewed others like him and discussed why they became Pagans, the Pagan lifestyle, and the Pagan philosophy. Then he included pictures of nude Pagans, most of whom were unattractive middle-aged hippies with thick, portly bodies and dirty feet. It surprised me to learn that most Pagans were into open marriages with multiple partners and whatnot, because Needham always struck me as unlovable, incapable of maintaining a relationship with one woman, much less several. Though I stumbled across no essays penned by Jasper Needham, it was apparent through his questions that he was very anti-Christian and critical of America's consumer culture and . . . Oh, who gives a fuck?

I looked at the spine and saw that it was published by a San Francisco-based micro-press. The guy, whose name escapes me, ran a single-man production that published fringe-culture type books, anarchist journals, far-left political rants, and reprints of odd things, like books about carnivals and circus sideshow freaks and profiles of people who purposely collect bad music. Ultimately, it's a blessing that there are publishers like these out there producing obscure work and getting people to read it. Bravo. It just pissed me off that Needham was published and I wasn't. I put the book back in the display window, upside down.

Next door was a bar called The Pearl. Its crowd was young and pretty and bohemian and pretentious in a very entertaining way. I got drunk and came to a big conclusion: I should've decked old scrotum-face Needham when I had the chance. Had I known that I wasn't going to be working for CPK in Washington, I could've beaten his Pagan ass all the way to the Golden Gate Bridge. I stumbled home around 2:30 a.m., called Information, and got Jasper Needham's phone number. I drunk-dialed his landline, and despite the late hour, he didn't sound groggy or sleepy, just concerned and unsure who could be calling him.

"Hello?" I told him it was me, and to my surprise, Jasper said, "Oh, hi Eli. It's nice to hear from you. Sorry I was so mean to you. Sorry for the way I treated you, man. It wasn't cool. Sorry. It does bother me, man. It really does."

That took me by surprise. "Wow," I thought, and then I said absolutely nothing.

"Hey, Eli, did you hear me?"

"Yeah, yeah, uh, um, thank you. I, uh, um, I, uh, got to go now."

"Wait a second. Aren't you in Seattle? What did you call me for?"

"Yeah, uh, um, Jasper, I called you because I saw your book at a bookstore here in Seattle and it got me thinking and drinking and it made me realize that had I known I wasn't going to work at CPK in Bellevue, I would've decked you hard, Jasper. As a matter of fact, at the time, it took all the strength I had not to hit you. You're so fucking lucky that I thought I needed the job reference. If you were a younger man, or even looked your age, I probably would've done it anyway. But before I called tonight, I was regretting not hitting you, but now, I'm glad I didn't hit you." A long, mutually uncomfortable silence passed—long enough for me to hear him hold his breath and then let it go in one long, deep sigh. "Hey, Jasper, I'm drunk. Just forget this phone call, okay? But you are really lucky I didn't beat you up."

When I woke up that morning, the phone was off the hook and it felt like a ten-foot jack-booted thug was repeatedly kicking the side of my head, and I knew that at work that day, my secretary and my assistant manager were going to take it upon themselves to warn the others that today was another one of Eli's hangover days. Seeing the phone receiver lying on its side, I knew I'd never completely remember or know absolutely everything I said to Jasper before eventually passing out, probably still holding the phone in my hand and telling Needham how lucky he was.

By December, 2002, I had been back in San Francisco for about three months, living at Theater Bazooka and Art Gallery and using a twenty-four-hour gym for all my hot water needs. Boston Scott and Harley enthusiastically hired me back at CPK to work the busy Christmas season. On my very first day back, I changed into my uniform inside the tiny locker room seemingly only used by the Mexican kitchen staff. After I was through changing, I went to open the door and it was jammed. Not locked, but jammed. I took a step backwards and threw my shoulders against the door, and *bam*—the door slammed Jasper hard, right in the face. It didn't break his nose, but evidently, it hurt badly, because that Pagan screamed, screamed louder and harder and longer than I've ever heard a man scream in my life.

"Oh, shit. Sorry, Jasper. My bad," I said, and I meant it, too. It was an accident. He continued to scream, eyes brimming with tears. "Jasper, lighten up. I said I was sorry." Needham had been carrying an empty tray when the door smacked him. The still-screaming Jasper lifted the tray above him like he was going to smack it against my head. "Oh, come on, Jasper. What are you going to do? Hit me?" Jasper dropped the tray behind him and ran into the general manager's office. He stayed in there for a solid twenty minutes. The shift started without him. He left and took the rest of the day off. He complained about me, of course, but he agreed, eventually and with much persuasion, that it was most likely an accident. "Yes, Harley. Eli did apologize, but what you've got to understand is . . ." And then Jasper proceeded to discuss our entire relationship, from the surly way he treated me in the beginning to the time I cornered him in the hallway, wishing him cancer, to the moment I drunk-dialed him at two thirty in the morning, saying I regretted not hitting him when I had the chance. After he vented, Jasper requested and got the day off, and after that, he and I never worked another shift together again. Jasper would tell the other servers I was an "evil, manipulative bastard," and even though he originally thought my swinging door was a sick, karmic twist of fate (at least, that's what he told the managers), he'd later tell everyone else I did it on purpose.

Everybody knew and would openly joke about how much we hated each other. Our animosity was entertainment for them. Half the staff thought I did it on purpose, and the rest could tell that, deliberate or not, I was glad it happened. Of course, it was an accident. I couldn't have planned it if I tried, but I was also delighted that Jasper thought it was the vengeful act of an evil, manipulative bastard with a grudge. It tickled me. The man displayed obvious discomfort whenever I was around.

I never shared my Jasper Needham story with Jennifer because I intuitively knew where her sympathies would be. She'd express sadness for the man whose youthful ambitions never got fulfilled and who ended up pushing fifty, looking seventy, and waiting tables poorly at a corporate restaurant. He had finally published a book with a small fringe publishing house, and one night it inspired a drunk, macho, notoriously unstable former co-worker who once wished him cancer to call at two thirty in the morning and tell the man he always regretted not hitting him hard across the face. The poor Pagan had worked at a corporate restaurant for almost two decades and couldn't recall another time when somebody else got hit by a swinging door. Therefore, it was too much of a coincidence that the only time somebody got hit by the door to the changing room was when he got hit by a guy who once told him it took all his strength not to hit him in the first place.

Jasper Needham apologized several times. Verbally, I accepted those apologies, but it appears my subconscious remained vindictive to the core. The entire saga with Jasper Needham cracks me up senseless, but if I had told Jennifer Ely, she would've gotten quiet and sad and would've shaken her head slowly and said absolutely nothing. Ear-splitting silences, I do hate them. So we had the same taste in music, but we rarely saw humor the same way.

Another series of complaints:

Nobody thinks of San Francisco as a place that has closeted queers or repressed homosexuals of any kind. People across the nation just assume that all queers in SF are out and about wearing "I'm a Homosexual" T-shirts and talking in flamboyant, lisping voices. My gay pals have often entertained me with stories of their gay conquests with allegedly straight boys who, after enough shots of scotch/gin/whiskey, literally become "Queen for a Day." While I can condone experiments done by consenting adults, my guess is those heterosexuals are actually repressed homosexuals, bi guys whose repressive shields have been clobbered by the victorious armies of alcohol and sexual ambiguity.

Outspokenly confident bisexual men with wedding rings who've accepted my gracious rejections have told me of their need to cheat, claiming that when they cheat on their wives with women, it's too time-consuming and emotionally risky. But a man is a man is a man. Nod, wink, say hi to the right guy, and you can have a partner for the next fifteen to thirty minutes: no phone calls, no dates, with no bullshit lies to the Mrs., who never knew you were gone in the first place.

As long as you're not a rapist or pedophile, I don't care what you do sexually. Even in conservative Florida, I'd always known homosexuals. Gay kids, deeply closeted at school, would come out inside the community theater where I spent my summers. After high school, I attended a small performing arts college where us straight boys would spot the gay freshman and set our watches to when they'd announce their orientation during the first day of orientation.

I've always dug gay people, and the more candid, the better. I love them flaming and I love them butch. I like lesbians fine, but none have ever entertained me or made me laugh quite the way that most gay men do. Besides, as anyone who has ever waited tables knows, gays tip great, lesbians never do. I wasn't the least bit shocked or offended when I moved to San Francisco, the gay Mecca. So perhaps Miss Ely is right: it was the comedy of discomfort that caused me to start singling out the closeted queers at CPK for my own amusement.

Example one: A young gay man named Jody had recently moved to San Francisco. Jody was slight and prissy, spoke with a girlish voice, and swished through the dining area the way the gayest servers did. When I commented on his gayness, Jody's shoulders shot straight up, and emphatically, he said, "Oh, I'm not gay."

With the glee of a schoolyard bully, I said, "Oh, you're so gay. You're so gay." For days, I said things like "It's okay to be gay. Hell, if we were in prison, it'd be an honor to call you my girlfriend." Soon after meeting Jody, I moved to Seattle for no particular reason other than this drifter needed a change of scenery. When I moved back to

San Francisco and Boston Jerry gave me my old job back, there was Jody, still swishy and girly-voiced, but proudly and openly gay. So proud, in fact, that Jody sported gay rainbow flags tattooed to his now hugely developed biceps. Jody gave me a hug and kissed each of my cheeks, saying, "Thank you. Thank you. Thank you, Eli. The relentless teasing from a straight, macho jerk that obviously liked the company of gay men was enough to catapult me out of the closet. Thanks again, Eli. Thank you." Then he kissed me on both cheeks. As he hugged me, I noticed how his left leg popped up behind him and stayed there in midair.

"Uh, you're welcome, dude. Now, who are you again?"

Example two: There was another young man, a host named Jamie, who was handsome with a thick body and large blue eyes with feminine, curly eyelashes. Jamie was a soft and giddy boy/man who seemed to gravitate towards the most boisterous and obnoxious women who worked at CPK. Every day he'd come and laugh with "the girls" and say little, if anything, to the boys. He insisted he was straight, that he even had a girlfriend back home who was surely going to come by and visit sometime soon. His behavior did not scream closeted homo the way Jody's did, but still I perceived something. If you pointed out a good-looking woman to Jamie, he'd say something mundane like "Yeah, she's pretty." If the girls or the gay guys noticed an attractive man and mentioned it to Jamie, he'd go mute, almost too quiet. The gay dudes thought he was gay but didn't know for sure. The women, some of whom had hung out with him socially, thought he was probably gay but couldn't 100 percent tell, considering he did have a girlfriend and they saw her letters, emails, and photographs.

"Maybe the boy is just confused" was a common sentiment about Jamie. If asked, even by his female friends, if he was bisexual, he'd say as casually as possible, "No. Strictly heterosexual. I love girls."

"Okay," everyone would say.

Everyone that is, except for me. I'd talk to him like he was already out of the closet. "Oh, yeah, it sure feels good to be a gay man in the twenty-first century, doesn't it? Yes, sir. Oh, would you look at the firm buttocks of that dude. M-m-m-m-m, good."

He'd roll his eyes, not look at me, and say nothing. Obviously, I was making him uncomfortable. Obviously, that was my intention.

Shortly after I returned to CPK from Seattle, the newly buff Jody quit to bartend shirtless at a trendy gay nightclub in the Castro. About two months later, Jody surprised everybody by coming into CPK for a beer and some pizza. While there, I said to Jody, "Hey, did you know that while you've been away, Sweet Jamie, the host, finally came out of the closet? Yeah, he's gay. Did you know he was gay?"

Jody laughed and said, "Of course I knew he was gay. We've only had sex three times. About time she came out of the closet."

That's when it was my turn to laugh.

"I was only joking, Jody. I just wanted to find out what went on at that wild club you worked at. Poor Jamie—it looks like you just pushed him out of the closet."

In three seconds flat, Jody's expression flashed from panic to "Eli, you fucking asshole." But even he laughed in the end. Begrudgingly. Reluctantly. Eventually. But he did laugh.

Jamie had the night off, but the gay co-workers who heard about the dialogue between Jody and me loved it and applauded my prank, saying sometimes a young man needed baptism by fire and that Jody's accidental outing of their fellow gay man was hilarious and something they had suspected all along.

While I was away the next day, the gloating queers and even some of the straights told poor Jamie what had happened the night before. According to what I've heard, Jamie, a young man who seemed like the type to never get angry, was livid, almost to the point of tears, saying, "Why the fuck does fucking Eli care about my fucking sexuality? Fuck him! Fuck Eli! Fuck Eli! Fuck, fuck, fuck Eli!"

He called in sick the next several days.

When he came back a week later, he was calm and relaxed and told me and "anyone else who gives a flying fuck" that he was a gay and to "mind your own damn business when it comes to my private life."

To his credit, he didn't complain to management about me, and in time, we did become friends. As a matter of fact, Jamie did attend "The Experience Junkies" at Theater Bazooka and told me he loved it. "Vintage Eli," he called it.

When I left CPK, he was moving in with a man he met at The Castro Theatre. Jamie told everybody, including his family, that he was in love.

Example three: A young man named Loren, short and round with a body like a teddy bear, was a host who had moved to San Francisco to come and study the clarinet and flute. He had talent, from what I hear, and serious aspirations to play for the San Francisco Symphony. Loren was a controlled, non-flamboyant sissy who spoke in a soprano voice like Michael Jackson, and he bragged, actually *bragged*, that he was a virgin in all fields of sexuality. He was asexual, or so he said. His love affairs were strictly in music, or so he said. Loren once had a girlfriend in high school, or so he said. A relationship the female herself initiated, or so he said. While he insisted he wasn't gay, he did concede to not being entirely straight either. The girls loved him like a sister or baby brother. The queers did not care for him and frequently spoke of "her pretentiousness."

One time Loren made the statement "I don't feel people ought to be categorized by whom they sleep with," it was the gay guys who laughed the hardest when I yelled in a thick Southern redneck voice, "Shut up, *fag!*" The other straight guys and the management didn't care as long as he was good at what he was hired to do. I cared and recognized a genuine case of coitophobia when I saw it. Gay sex, straight sex, it didn't matter because it all made Loren so damn uncomfortable. It reached its peak towards the end of my stay at CPK when, during a slow lunch shift, I stood next to Loren at the host stand and talked about the anatomy of every last female that walked by, pointing out her attributes to dear asexual Loren and telling the boy what I wanted to do to them. Finally, Loren said, "Eli, you've got to be a gentleman. Girls don't like you when you act like this."

"What would you know about what girls like? Are you a girl?"

Then, later in the day, I told him I was fairly certain I was going to get the job at Burberry but that if I didn't find out soon, I was going to paint my penis in the famous Burberry plaid and just walk into the store and show it to the managers.

Loren was too gay to be straight, but too humorless to be gay. "Oh, no! Don't do that!" he said. "They won't like that!"

"Oh, yes they will," I said. "My dick is huge."

Near the end of the shift, I again approached the virgin's host stand. He looked wounded, like an exasperated parent. "Hey, Loren, don't you ever just find somebody physically attractive?"

"No, Eli, it's the insides that count. I'm into inner beauty."

"Yeah, well how can you tell if somebody's got beautiful insides just by looking at them? I mean, that guy there, he looks like a young Marlon Brando," I said, pointing to some handsome young man eating by himself. "Don't you find him attractive?"

Loren looked back at the guy and smiled involuntarily, but then he looked at me and said, "It's in the eyes. You can see inner beauty when you look inside someone's eyes."

Playing dumb, I said, "Oh, so you judge a person's inner beauty by the look in their eyes?"

"Exactly."

"Well, that makes perfect sense, because I judge a woman's inner beauty by the size of her tits."

I walked away quietly, smiling to myself, listening as little Loren let out a gasp. Not only did Loren complain to management, he stayed in the GM's office and typed up three letters, one for Harley, one for Boston Jerry, and another for the regional manager. I was suspended for three days and forced to watch a poorly acted, unintentionally hilarious sexual harassment video and fill out a surprisingly large amount of paperwork. Everyone at CPK thought it hilarious that I had a sexual harassment complaint against me from another man. The queers, the women, the straights, the Mexicans in the kitchen— all laughed their asses off. My pals outside of work thought it funny, especially Becca. As a matter of fact, Scott Bonne, who happens to be gay and a 6'4" bear, said, only in half jest, "Hey, Eli, you want me to beat Loren up for you?"

Jennifer did laugh when I told her that a guy had filed a sexual harassment complaint against me, but when I told her the full story she looked at me uncomprehendingly and said how terrible she felt for "that fearful little boy."

"What the fuck, Jennifer? The kid was over eighteen."

A week later, I got hired at Burberry.

VII

Just like I told Scott I would earlier in the day, I go out sober bar-hopping and find myself in the Tenderloin at The Hemlock Tavern, where the heavily tattooed San Francisco hipsters drink, smoke on the designated smoker's porch, watch local bands play, and listen to punk, classic rock, and old country on the jukebox. The club's always dark and crowded, with hipsters that treat those who don't conform to them with utter contempt. In other words, I get better service and friendlier conversation when my tattoos are exposed than when they're not. But I still go to The Hemlock Tavern because I like the music there and it's a fine, well-stocked bar, and on any given night, the clientele there is about as friendly to me as I want them to be.

The jukebox is blasting an album of classic rock covers done by The Ramones. The Ramones singing The Mamas & the Papas, The Ramones singing Creedence Clearwater Revival, etc. I sit alone at the bar wearing blue jeans, my faded burgundy wingtips and a white T-shirt with a striped polo shirt on top that I got thrifting somewhere. My tattoos are exposed, I'm built, my head is shaved, my nose has clearly been broken, and my clothes are preppy. Come on, rockabilly dudes. Come on, hipsters. Come on, punk rockers. Come fuck with me. I double-dog dare you. Of course, nobody does, as I order one cranberry juice after another. Not vodka cranberries, just cranberry juice, two, three, four glasses of cranberry juice at three dollars each. I hadn't been out all week, and like in the beautiful song by The Smiths, I spent all day singing "Take me out tonight, where there's music and there's people and they're young and alive." No friends wanted to go out tonight. Not Lance, not Becca. But when I got turned down by Scott, some bullshit about having to draw, I felt compelled to assure him I was going to go bar-hopping alcohol-free. "A teetotaler's Thursday," I called it. Scott didn't care. He said he wasn't my mother or my pastor and I didn't need to check in with him about my indulgences.

"Fine," I said to Scott, but I told him if I got drunk that night, there'd be trouble. However, I couldn't stay home either. I needed to go out and be among people.

So here I am in The Hemlock, flipping back cranberry juice with a fuck-you expression on my face, sitting in my preppy clothes, listening to The Ramones cover . . . No, that album is over, now it's Social Distortion covering The Rolling Stones. I'm feeling wound-up and antagonistic, wanting to verbally abuse the people drinking around me, wishing the music was a tad lower so they could hear my mutterings and try with everything they've got to eject me out of this place. The Burberry world bounced me on my ass, a swift plaid boot to my stomach and a not-so-gentle push into the street, feeling like a fool. I am a teenage retard dressed formally, or in what he *thinks* is formal, for his first day of school, waiting at a bus stop for a tiny yellow school bus that never arrives.

"I'm the long-suffering, oft-tortured writer! I'm the employment-challenged, money-nothing artist! I'm the tattooed San Francisco performance-artist-slash-storyteller! I'm the hard-drinking, body-abusing macho man, and why, why, among the hipsters, the punk rockers, the San Francisco bohemians, the bar denizens, can I not find a place to belong?"

The urge to fight, the urge to fight, where does it come from?

I used to walk down the sidewalk on rare sunny days in Seattle and see serious-faced bicyclists on serious bikes—ten-speed, twelve-speed, fifteen-speed, twenty-two-speed—and they'd pedal with great agility through traffic, and there I'd be on the sidewalk, yelling, fucking *yelling*, "Hey, you asshole! Quit riding in the street! The streets were made for cars! The streets were made for cars! Ride on the fucking sidewalk!"

I did this to see if any bicyclist would come fight me. The bicyclists expected verbal abuse from drivers and were prepared to flip them the bird and to tell them to fuck off, but seeing a shaved madman screaming at them from the sidewalk telling them to get out of the street was not something they knew how to contend with. Nobody flipped me off, nobody told me to go fuck myself. Instead, they just stared at me, some for a long time, but none got distracted long enough to crash into anything, thank God.

Even without my antagonizing the Hemlock crowd (nobody even knows that I exist), if anybody looks at me, they can tell I don't belong here. I don't belong anywhere. "Hey, I live in a residential hotel! And I've got a literary agent!" Though we've never met and only communicate via email and nothing of mine has yet been published.

With my sixth cranberry juice in a Tom Collins glass sitting on the bar, my head in my hands and my palms rubbing my temples, I think to myself, "I'm angry, so fucking angry!"

People who've gone to the edge of starvation, be it through hunger strikes, being stranded on an island or lost in the Alaskan wilderness, these people who've nearly died and come back tell others that there comes a moment when you no longer feel the starvation, the pain, the hunger; and it's reported that the dying individual feels peace, joy, almost elation. I don't want to find out if this is true, and I'm looking forward to my first meal tomorrow morning. My point is that I've been angry for so long, I almost don't feel anger anymore. It's most definitely not peace, but I'm not white-knuckled and red in the face, either. The muscles in my back, head, neck, arms, and shoulder feel tense, wood-thick, and barely able to move. Is this the weight of the world?

"You're nobody until somebody loves you," Dean Martin sang. Jennifer loved me, and as corny as that sounds, I thought I was somebody because Jennifer loved me. My failure at the Burberry gig has embarrassed me to no end. I managed the porn shop longer than I peddled plaid. You become the environment you surround yourself with. The porn grew to disgust me, as did my life at the time. One day, I just did not show up to work and walked into an AA meeting. Did the AA thing for about two months. Then I had a drink, knowing full well I could control myself, just like I'm doing right now.

Funny, early on I got myself an AA sponsor, a kind, soft-spoken, middle-aged gay male accountant who'd been clean and sober for seven years. Through my constant arguments and random phone calls, the poor old guy took up drinking again. I laugh. Damn, do I laugh, laugh in quiet intensity, like cracking up at a funeral. I still hold my head in my hands, and though my stiff shoulders shake and my ribs ache, my eyes drop tears onto the bar. They're not tears of laughter, but rather genuine tears of remorse. I wipe my tears and down the cranberry juice in a gulp, a three-dollar gulp. I order another, "in a tall pint glass with no ice."

"Six dollars?"

Head back in hands, staring at my tall cranberry juice, I think, "Jennifer, you hurt me. Jennifer, you hurt me bad." Then I think, "Jennifer, you've exasperated an exasperating man." I touch the rim of the glass and tip it over, slowly and methodically, so anybody who happens to witness this act knows it was done on purpose.

I get up, expressionless, and stroll away from the bar as the sticky, sweet juice rolls along the counter, wetting elbows and dissolving the beverage napkins parked underneath beers and cocktails.

There's Danny Ryan. Danny Ryan is standing by the front door drinking Rolling Rock, and there's a girl, a babe, Asian, tall, about 5'9", wearing knee-high black boots, long dark hair pulled back. She's tanned and svelte in a denim skirt and a black T-shirt. She's standing next to Danny, leaning intimately, wanting more. Congratulations, Danny, you handsome fucker.

"Hey, hey Eli!" He slaps my left shoulder, quite expansively for Danny. A little alcohol buzz and the mellow, laid-back, peace-punk pretty boy gets slaphappy and animated. Danny introduces me to Mimi, who only looks at me distractedly as I put out my hand and then quickly drop it. I don't think she means to be rude. The woman just didn't see my hand, that's all.

"How's Burberry going, Eli?"

I shrug.

"How's your girlfriend?"

I shrug.

"Hey, hey," he says to Mimi. "This is the guy who had the one-man show where he stood on stage telling stories. It was cool." She nodded again, obviously wishing I'd leave so she could be alone with Danny. "Eli, I wrote a joke. Want to hear it?"

Danny is smiling like a goof. His girl already starts to laugh. Other hipsters, other punks lean towards us. They seem to know and

193

like Danny, smiling, laughing, wanting Danny to be funny, probably prepared to laugh whether Danny is funny or not. He starts yelling the joke before I even say I don't want to hear it.

"What, what, uh, um, what did the—wait, wait, wait a minute—what do you call people who fuck dead people?" Several people shout "Necrophiliacs!" "Okay, okay, that's it! This is the joke I wrote, listen . . ."

Somebody in the crowd says, "I think he's writing the joke right now as he speaks."

"Isn't he cute?" his arm candy says.

"Telling stories is not your forte," I say to Danny with venom totally unwarranted.

"No, no, wait a minute, wait a minute! It's a good joke, you'll laugh! Listen! Listen! What did the necrophiliac say to the narcoleptic?" Simultaneously, several people join in: "I don't know, what?" "Oh, I'm sorry! I thought you were dead!"

Mimi laughs hysterically, wrapping both arms around Danny; she kisses his right cheek, bites his right ear, and gushes, literally gushes, "You're so cute!"

Everybody laughs but me. I tell Danny, "I saw that coming a mile away."

"Sorry it was not up to your standards, homeboy!" This too makes people laugh. My hands are in my pockets and I'm ready to leave, but Danny interrupts my sulking to say, "Hey, Eli! Did I hear you on Live 105 this morning? It sounded like you, and the guy's name was Eli."

I shake my head. My face feels like there's a scowl on it.

"Well, Eli, are you going to stick around for Angry Jimmy?"

"Who the fuck is 'Angry Jimmy'?"

"No, it's a 'they,' and you'll probably like them! Their front man is originally from Sarasota! They're a punk cover band I'm promoting for Sloppy Lard-Ass Records! All they do are Jimmy Buffet covers as angry punk rock! You've got to see it to believe it!"

Danny Ryan is so fucking cool that I want to kick his ass. Throw an elbow to his face, a sucker punch to his stomach. He works at an independent record label that signs Bay Area bands and he gets to go out to bars and promote them. The boy is adorned with an affectionate babe who wants to absorb every part of him. At no point while I've been standing here has she let go, and while he's been conversing with me, dozens of people have walked by and waved at Danny or given the shoulder opposite Mimi a friendly slap. Even while he's talking, Danny nods his head at various individuals making their rounds. Did I accidentally step into Danny's private party?

I sat at the bar in preppy clothes and cried, ordered cranberry juice after cranberry juice, and even tried to start a fight by purposely spilling my drink along the counter, and not a single fucking person even noticed I was alive. And what was worse was the fact that Jennifer, my Jennifer, wanted to fuck Danny. It was obvious, painfully obvious.

Danny's taller than I am, and I consider a quick uppercut to the square jaw that's smiling in recognition at somebody behind me and above my head. This'll get me ejected from this bar, and it'll quench my desire for violence tonight.

Jeffrey Doyle.

Jeff Doyle was a kid I grew up with in Florida. We had known each other since elementary school, and though we were never close, we were never enemies either. Jeff was tall and skinny and good-looking, and he was one of the few white guys who played on the basketball team. Polite and quiet, the boy was genuinely well liked by the students and teachers alike. As for me in high school? Well, if you've been with me this far, you've already got an idea of what I was like as a teenager.

One day, in the 11th grade, we had a substitute teacher named Mr. Maddox, who was an old, blustery moron with an alcoholic's nose, an alcoholic's breath, and a smoker's cough. He wore a nearsighted old lady's glasses that sat on his face like a pair of candy dishes. Old Man Maddox was prone to yelling, and it gave me great perverse pleasure to rile the poor old bastard up. Each time he substituted, I did something to piss him off, usually by calling him Mr. Mad-Dog, and each time he got angry, he'd take me outside the classroom and say "What's your name?" Each time, I answered truthfully, and whenever the regular teacher returned, I'd be given a series of detentions. But one day, the old senile fucker pulled me outside and said "What's your name?" Without skipping a beat, I looked through those thick glasses and into his useless blue eyes and said "Jeffrey Doyle."

My intention was not to get a good kid into trouble. I figured the dumb-fuck would leave a report stating that Jeffrey Doyle was farting in class, throwing spitballs, and simultaneously making fun of his name and notorious drinking habits by calling him Mr. Mad-Dog. The regular teacher would read his report and say "That doesn't sound like Jeff," and she'd simply not believe Old Man Maddox and disregard the bogus report his drunk ass left behind.

Mr. Maddox looked at me, startled, and after a few seconds, he cackled until snot came out his nose. "Okay, kid," he said, wiping the mucus off his face with his own bare hands. "I'm going back in there to find out your name. I know Jeff Doyle. Jeff Doyle is my stepson, and you, my friend, are no Jeffrey Doyle."

Fuck me. I didn't know Mr. Mad-Dog was Jeff Doyle's stepfather. No wonder that kid was so damn quiet. Suddenly my own stepfather didn't look so bad by comparison.

Old Man Maddox told everybody that I tried to get Jeff in trouble. Pretty girls who thought Jeff was sweet stopped talking to me altogether. Tough black kids who played basketball threatened me. My teachers in other classes all expressed their disappointment in me, more so than usual. The regular teacher made me write Jeff a five-hundred-word letter of apology and read it to him in front of the entire class. Interestingly enough, Jeff never seemed to resent me for what I did and thought the whole episode was funny and often told me so. I'm sure he remembers it to this day.

Hitting Danny Ryan on the jaw would be like snitching on Jeff Doyle for something I actually did, only it'd be worse, even less warranted, and the consequences would be far greater, like jail, a lawsuit, or, the least of the possible consequences, getting jumped by all his punk-rocker buddies. Besides, I like Danny. I'm just jealous of him, that's all. I wish I looked like him, wish I had his music industry job, and wish I had the hot babe trying to possess every molecule of my being. Goddamn, I want to be Danny Ryan. Hell, at this point, I want to be Jeffrey Doyle. Anybody but me.

"Eli, are you going to stick around to see the Jimmy Buffet cover band?"

How could I not be curious?

VIII

Angry Jimmy comes on stage: four beefy, heavily tattooed punk rockers with shaved heads, wearing flip-flops on their bare feet, cutoff denim shorts, and Hawaiian shirts. The front man is sporting a six-inch, black, spiky mohawk and carries a well-salted margarita in his right hand and a microphone in the other.

"One-two-three!" The band starts a fast version of "Come Monday," and the hipster crowd screams along and cheers on the opening line: "Heading out to San Francisco, for the Labor Day weekend show!" To somebody who'd cringe whenever his parents played a Jimmy Buffet album, it's amazing how well his slacker lyrics play as strictly punk rock. "Son of a Son of a Sailor" is such a better song when it's done fast, and so is my all-time favorite Buffet song, "A Pirate Looks at Forty." It's about a sad, drunken drug dealer looking back on his life and wishing he were born in another era. In Buffet's signature faux country, it's not my cup of tea, but force it into choppier waters and it elevates his music and punk rock into something better. It's like Jimmy Buffet's lyrics and punk rock are two separate individuals marrying up into a higher social class. Great lyrics, Jimmy! Great song! Great band!

I'm forgetting my troubles, laughing, singing, and jumping to the music. With the exception of stopping to drink his margarita on stage and dabbing suntan lotion on his face inside a dark club late at night in San Francisco, the front man does nothing to engage the audience, which I thought was exceptionally cool. It was all about the image and the music. The drummer wears a pair of papier-mâché parrots on each of his shoulders that somehow stay put as he keeps the rhythm of the band. I love Angry Jimmy, and I think mellow Jimmy would like them, too.

"One-two-three!" And the band breaks into the more obscure Buffet song "If the Phone Doesn't Ring, That's Me," and it hits me: I remember that I have a girlfriend I'm not supposed to be calling, and that if her phone isn't ringing, that's because of me.

I give Danny a hug, finally shake Mimi's hand, and say good-bye.

I try to put off my tears, my angry, bitter, self-pitying tears, by visualizing my very own cover band called Very White; we'd do nothing but Barry White covers as though The Carpenters were the cover band. We'd wear yellow-blonde wigs, argyle sweaters, penny loafers, and khaki pants, and we'd sing "Can't Get Enough of Your Love" in high falsetto voices. Of course, my chuckles and funny ideas are nowhere to be found when I get back to the Sestri and find myself pounding Jennifer's phone number into my cell phone. It's after 2 a.m. when Jennifer answers, and though she does sound like somebody who has just been pulled from a deep sleep, she doesn't sound angry, just tired.

"Eli, is that you?" She does have caller ID.

"Yes, yes it is."

"I heard you on Live 105 this morning."

"Uh, um, yeah, hey Jennifer, what's your address? I want to mail you something."

"It's 309 Pierce."

"Great, great, great. You see, I'm going to mail you all your stuff back, including all the letters you wrote me over the summer from Yosemite. Jennifer, I don't want to talk to you on Sunday. I don't want to talk to you on Monday or Tuesday or Wednesday. You say you need to go on hold, you need to go on break, well, stay on your damn break. It's over. We're through."

Click. She'd hung up on me, but I had nothing more to say.

I

My letter to Jennifer is sealed in an envelope, as are the letters she had written me over the summer. There's a large envelope with six stamps and my furious handwriting on its cover lying in the center of the floor. Though I haven't dropped it into a mailbox yet, it feels like the point of no return. The phone call the night before left no possibility of its effects being overturned. It's over, and sending her letters back is a gesture that speaks louder than anything I could've screamed over the phone.

I wasn't drunk when I wrote my letter, but I was angry, and who remembers everything they say when they're angry? During her summer as a park ranger, Jennifer enjoyed the camaraderie of her predominantly male co-workers, who, she insisted, knew she had a boyfriend. But one guy, a dickhead whose name might as well be Dick Head as far as I'm concerned, bought her a vibrator. She told me it was a gag gift. I said nothing, expressing neither humor nor displeasure, but surely Jennifer could perceive through my rare quiet that I was leaning closer to the latter. We never discussed it.

In my letter, I wrote, "I hope you and your vibrator enjoyed your week without me." That was one of maybe one or two cheap shots I took in that letter. The fact that she told me about the vibrator was typical of a self-absorbed person's lack of empathy for their partner's feelings. She laughingly told me on the phone about the gag gift she got and must've thought I'd get a kick out of a guy buying my girlfriend a sex toy. I've had open relationships before, and though our relationship wasn't an open one, I was prepared to accept that Jennifer might have slept with one or more of her co-workers. She told me she had not slept with anybody else over the summer, and I believe her, for the most part, but somehow, to me, a guy buying her a vibrator is worse than if she had had sex with him. It's inappropriate and a personal affront to me.

I understand cheaters. We all do—lust, temptations, opportunity, whether it's with a co-worker, a stranger, or an old friend—it makes perfect sense. But a guy deliberately insults another man when he buys that man's girlfriend a dildo. It's supremely uncool and worthy of a beating. She had mentioned this character before. Greg was his name, and he, the staff jester, supposedly had a girlfriend back in his native northern Nevada. He, like Jennifer, was using Yosemite as a memorable summer job while he toiled at the University of Nevada. In the same letter, I wrote that if Greg had lived in San Francisco, I'd have walked to his apartment and "hammered the back of his head till his eyes went blind." Funny, if she and Greg had only fucked, it wouldn't have bothered me that much. Maybe they did and he bought her a vibrator as a parting gift, and she, like an idiot, chose to tell me the detail she thought would bother me the least and chose wrong. I wrote that she hurt me and she bailed on me when she already knew I was having a bad week, and fuck being my girlfriend, she'd proven that she wasn't even a worthy friend. I said I loved her and wanted to wait for her phone call next week but that my pride and self-respect wouldn't let me. Accusing her of liking me too much and then pushing me away, I wrote, "Don't worry. You'll get lucky and find a fellow you like a lot less than me and be able to stay with him for a long, long time."

I brought up *The Giving Tree* debate and chastised her for causing such a dumb argument and called it "the greatest single waste of my time and energy I've experienced all year." "I love and hate you right now." That I wrote more than once. "I didn't need to see you this week, but a phone call would've been nice." "We're through, Miss Ely. This is what you've wanted from the get-go!" "Don't get into a relationship unless you're totally prepared to be in one. I'm such a dumb-fuck." "I thought you loved me. I know I was a disappointment to you because I didn't like the mountains and I didn't like camping, but I never meant to hurt you. I'm embarrassed beyond belief around you, around my friends, around myself, around Old Man Vejapura, my landlord!" "I love you, but you're too selfish, too insensitive, too this, too that, blah, blah, blah, on and on and on, etc., etc. . . . Congrats, you finally sabotaged this relationship!" I signed the letter "My first name, your last."

Never did I write "BITCH CUNT WHORE," but no doubt about it, this letter was meant to sting. In the same package was a Johnny Cash CD she had recently bought me. The radio this morning told me "The Man in Black" was dead. Dead on September 12, 2003. Interesting. He'd been unwell for years. Johnny Cash: talk about a face with character and a life well lived. Was it well lived? Who the fuck knows?

After penning and sealing my vindictive letter last night, I took off my clothes and put on a This Mortal Coil CD and went to bed.

II

Sex is over. Emerson wrote, "You are what you think about all day long." Therefore, I used to joke, "I must be pussy because few other things ever cross my mind." Today, for the first time that I can remember, I don't want to get laid. What's become of me?

Having fucked great quantities of women is nothing to be proud of. Unfortunately, I had to fuck great quantities of women to come to that conclusion.

Shortly after we had sex by the hot spring in Mammoth, Jennifer asked me how many women I had been with. It was obvious when weeks earlier Jennifer had volunteered how many lovers she'd had that the gesture was designed to get me to disclose my numbers. Far from any disclosure, instead I teased Jennifer because I had been with less people by the time I was twenty-four than she had. But now was different. She had asked me point-blank.

When Jana Carver asked me, I told her that I had been with lots of women and that I wished it wasn't so. Jana, wisely, did not push for a definite answer. Jana once told me that on a certain New Year's Eve, she surprised herself by banging two different guys at two different parties, and that neither ever knew about the other. Jana was twenty-one when she told me this, and she was delighted that she could tell me such a thing and I wasn't going to judge her. Hell, I was even happy for her.

Christine K., another young woman with whom I had a brief, tumultuous fling, once while lying in bed asked how many lovers there had been. My silence caused her to turn around and face me. She said if it was more than thirty, it was too much, and if it was thirty, it was still too much. My continued silence caused her to turn away and say "I don't want to know." I was twenty-eight when I dated Jana, and I honestly can't remember if Christine K. came before or afterwards, but the truth is I had been with too many women before they came into my life, and there's been a shitload ever since. If I told Jennifer in a reflective, serious voice, "Oh, I've been with too many women and it is not something I feel good about," she would've said, "Okay. So, how many?"

My past promiscuity leaves a stain on me like sun-damaged skin. Intuitively, like most women, Jennifer could tell that I've been around.

"How many lovers have you been with?"

"About a hundred, baby."

Her mouth dropped and she laughed in nervous disbelief. "A hundred! Oh, my God!" She put her head back and I watched her naked body laugh silently in the sun. So, having an enormous amount of sex is nothing to be proud of. Intellectually, I can say it's nothing to be ashamed of, like declaring bankruptcy, something neither to boast about nor deny. It simply is what it is. Surely there have been more than a hundred, but that felt like a good, conservative estimate. How? How did it happen? How did the numbers increase the way they did?

The first person who said "Variety is the spice of life" was talking about food, not fucking. But I bought into that bullshit and wanted to accumulate numbers and experience women by the dozens. Getting women to fuck me and to tell me they found me attractive (I've always been a chronic compliment-fisher and would make them verbalize it) somehow made me feel important, loved, accepted. Beautiful.

Leonardo DaVinci's last words were "I've wasted my hours."

If he could only peek into my journals, he'd see what a real waste of time looks like. Seriously, you only go through life once, and I've got nothing to show for my life's pursuit of pussy but dissipating memory and pounds and pounds of diaries written in furious chicken-scratch that I myself can barely read.

I'd gladly exchange all the sexcapades collected for a few longer, deeper, better relationships; powerful, special, monogamous affairs that'd encompass years, not months, not weeks, not hours. And there'd be former lovers, now close friends whom I could call, talk to, hang out with socially, who could miss me and want what's best for me. It isn't uncommon for me to see women with whom I had one-nighters years ago walking down the street looking past me like they've never seen me before in their lives, and it hurts but it's something I brought on myself. If I had spent the same energies somewhere else, I could've built a better life, a better person. Then I'd have more to give a woman than my cock and a room at the Sestri Hotel.

Sex is over. I don't want it anymore. I don't need it; it's just another demon, another impulse, a vice to be expelled. I've not discovered religion and I'm not going to saunter into a Sex Addicts Anonymous meeting or a monastery. It's just that I'm aware there's yet another aspect of my life that no longer makes me happy, and I question if it ever really did in the first place.

III

9/12/03

Jana,

The following story is going to sound pathetic. I was living at Theater Bazooka in the Mission. It was around December and the air was cold and wet and I had no heat and no hot water and no employment, but at least I could say I was living in the most expensive city in America rent-free. Trying to catch some sleep on the dirty theater floor, I was fully clothed, sans shoes, lying on a towel, using another two towels bunched up together as a pillow. Thank God, I found a thick, dusty blanket and a radio alarm clock backstage. I plugged the radio into an outlet next to my ridiculous palette on the floor. I was able to pick up a soft jazz easy-listening station, loud and surprisingly clear, the kind where the deep-voiced late-night DJ sounds black, seductive, and stoned. When life has gotten so base, so desperate, and your potential has fallen to a standstill, the simplest pleasures, like listening to music, start to mean so much to you. Just as the sounds were starting to relax me, the song "Missing" by

Everything But The Girl came on. Not the remixed dance version, but the original. I knew the remix version, but the more dramatic, profoundly sad original was new to me.

Jana, there's a good chance you may already know the lyrics, but the story could be lost on you. A woman finds herself going out of her way to walk past a former lover's house. She knows he no longer lives there—as a matter of fact, he's been gone for years—and yet she misses this man so deeply that she's walking down his old street just to capture some of his essence, just to retrieve a bit of his memory. She wonders where he's gone. She wonders if he's dead. She recalls the way he would shout to her from his window. When she leaves, she asks why she continuously tortures herself by coming to his old neighborhood. When she got to the part in the song about walking past his door, but he doesn't live there anymore, I began to feel the tapping of emotion. By the end of the song, when she admits to no more insights or great loves since, I was fucking bawling, bawling hard, echoing inside the theater.

It's inexplicable, Jana, but more often than I care to acknowledge, I wake up with an urge to reconnect with you, knowing full well that's impossible. I look for your face in crowds. Where do you live now? Where do you work? Something tells me you're no longer in San Francisco, but where?

I miss you, baby, and know, please know, that you're never too far away from my thoughts. Somebody else has your old phone number from four years ago. Until very recently, like last night, I had a girlfriend who lived only a block or two away from your old apartment. My best friend, Scott Bonne, whom you never met, lives nearby, as does another guy, a newer friend named Ferdinand—a total oddball you'd love. Whenever I'm in your old barrio, your face, smell, skin, and laugh come back to me vividly, and I think to myself, "Even if my shit was together then, our relationship would've already peaked and ended by now." But I do miss you, baby, more so than anybody else, more than women who said they loved me and those with whom I made long-term plans.

Are you in L.A.? New York? Are you back in Salt Lake City?

We would've run into each other by now if you were still in San Francisco, but then again, who knows? If you moved to the Sunset or the Avenues, I'd never see you. Swear to God, I have not walked past your old apartment in Lower Haight just to stare at your door, but I have walked into certain bars you used to frequent (Martuni's, Lucky 13, NocNoc) just on the random chance that I'd see you there, and I know, just know, that you haven't been inside any of these places in a long, long time. But where are you, baby? Do you ever think about me? Who was I in your life? Remember when I told you that you had a tremendous amount of happy-sad, tumultuous shit to experience at age twenty-one and when I thought of all I took in between twenty-one and twenty-eight, my head spun? Remember when I said that?

Jana, at twenty-eight I thought I was wise beyond my years and I was through with failing. Well, wait until you hear about twenty-eight through thirty-two. We never dated exclusively. Your libido was shockingly aggressive, as aggressive as mine. We weren't swingers, which is a shame because maybe we should've been, but we each had numerous liaisons, and fortunately, our lifestyles permitted such. Your trysts with pretty boys, bartenders, artists, hipsters, didn't bother me. I was working at United Airlines as a reservationist for eight bucks an hour and doing minor drug dealing and major drug taking and sleeping with several women in the reservations department and one aspiring airline stewardess, though they like to be called flight attendants now.

You didn't care.

In November of my twenty-eighth year, I got fired, got plagiarized by a close friend, another friend yelled at me for getting fired, and

I found out you fucked a former boyfriend from Salt Lake City, a boy who came to San Francisco just to find you and bring you back. When I broke up with you, you startled me by crying. You said you were surprised you liked me as much as you did. You knew about the drug overdose/suicide attempt that New Year's Eve. Did you know I also declared bankruptcy in March of 2000? And what were your highlights for that year? Oh, yeah, I finally finished writing a novel I had been working on in some capacity since '97. And I saw you standing outside The Stud about two weeks before I left for Seattle. (You always did love those hardcore gay bars.) You looked great, happy, healthy, and sexy. We spoke pleasantly and briefly hugged, and you gave me a peck on the cheek. A shaggy artist dude named Tyler was hanging around, keeping an eye on us. I knew him vaguely from around the local art gallery parties. You encouraged him to go inside while you and I spoke some more. After we departed, I walked home feeling lightheaded, wishing you and I had something more loving, something more exclusive, something more like a traditional, old-fashioned relationship.

I was extraordinarily lucky to have you when I did. Remember when you used to call me up at three o'clock in the morning after you had been out partying just because you wanted to hear me tell a story?

I lived in San Francisco for six years in an apartment on Greenwich and Taylor in an area some people call Lower North Beach. I shared a large apartment with a Chinese family fairly fresh off the boat. They could barely speak English, and I, of course, never bothered to learn Cantonese. We got along famously. My room had a to-die-for view of the bay, including Alcatraz and the Golden Gate Bridge. I loved it. You loved it, too. Remember? Still, my innate wanderlust got a hold of me, and seeing what a mess I'd made of my life in San Francisco, I decided to move on a whim to Seattle. I was never particularly happy in Rain City, which is okay, considering nobody is particularly happy there. Seattle is the city that created a genre of rock 'n' roll based on depression, and don't think it an accident that many of America's serial killers come from the Pacific Northwest.

However, when I was there, I sent my manuscript to a reputable New York literary agent who agreed to represent me. Certainly, that did much for my heart, soul, and ego, but ultimately, the book has yet to be sold, and it's doubtful it ever will be. While in Depressionland, Washington, I did manage to save some cash, and after spending nearly two years there, I decided it'd be a good idea to see my family in Melbourne Beach, Florida, whom I hadn't seen in eight years, and seriously considered relocating back to my beloved Tampa (still, to this day, my favorite Florida city).

Three weeks with my people, old hatred renewed and new hatred discovered, in addition to Florida's humidity and working-class wages, reminded me why I left in the first place. I bought a cheap flight to L.A. to visit actor friends and see one old high school buddy, who was turning tricks as a "massage therapist" in West Hollywood. If only the girls we grew up with knew the best-looking guy and president of The Thespian Club was now a male whore, they'd hang their heads down and cry.

On the way to L.A., I almost joined the mile-high club shortly after a Las Vegas layover. She was a Cuban-American woman named Anna Montero who was on her way to L.A. to work in porn. Sun-bronzed skin, 36Ds, 5'2", firm and stocky, and no inhibitions whatsoever. Unfortunately, I had no condoms with me, and all we did was make out, though my hands were everywhere underneath her clothes and we landed in the City of Angels with beatific smiles on our faces. I should fly more.

I was in Florida for three weeks. During the second week, my then-girlfriend Cassie came down to visit from Seattle. During week one, I picked up a pair of strippers at a rowdy after-hours bar in

Melbourne, Florida. One was dark, one blonde, one very young, the other a little older than I was. They were both named Vanessa, and they both fucked me and watched and whooped and hollered and encouraged the other to fuck me again. It was in their trailer, no lie, in their trailer, in West Melbourne. Week two, Cassie came down from Seattle. It was romantic and fun. We made love every night that she was there. Week three, walking along the beach, I met a fine young woman, around twenty-four, from Louisiana, in town visiting elderly relatives. We met for a drink that night in a tiny bar right by the ocean, and while there, she told me a shocking story about doing a brief prison sentence because, back when she was a spoiled eighteen-year-old, she drunkenly slammed into a car sitting idle at a red light, killing the driver and injuring the passenger. Of course, that tragedy wasn't enough to keep her away from alcohol, nor did it turn me off completely. There was no sex, but we did go skinny-dipping, and she gave me oral as I lay on the shore, the waters lapping up my legs. She was a lithe blonde with green eyes and wonderful, soft, bell-shaped titties.

The reasons I left Florida had nothing to do with the women there.

Ultimately, I couldn't find a job quick enough in Los Angeles, money was evaporating, and couch-surfing options were disappearing. I called San Francisco and got a hold of Lance LittleJohn, an intense dude whom I knew fairly well but hadn't spoken to since moving to Seattle. There are people in San Francisco who consider him a genius. He is somebody, a person with tremendous charisma and passion and talent who'll create some great art before he dies, and host some great events that'll keep people talking about him for years to come. We first knew each other during our days with The Popcorn Theater, a traveling theater group where several different players brought something original to the audience every month.

Lance was a comedy writer who performed with a comedy sketch team called Belching Underwater. He and Becca Depner were definitely the most interesting and daring members of the troupe.

It's such a pity you never saw me perform.

Through mutual friends, I learned Lance acrimoniously broke up Belching Underwater and shortly thereafter bought a theater and art gallery in the Mission called Theater Bazooka. It was an avant-garde theater, home to San Francisco's underground art scene. It featured bizarre performance art, wacky improvisation nights, spoken word, and new plays. Local comedy troupes and solo performances enjoyed week-long runs at Bazooka before making it to bigger, better, more expensive venues. The lobby was an art gallery for equally unknown artists.

"Perhaps I could crash inside the theater for a few weeks, Lance?"

Lance was startled by my random phone call.

"Well, long time, no see, Eli Tweeki. I'd be open to letting you sleep here for a little while. But first rule, dude: no crank. You can't do fucking speed in my space. If you do bring some in, you're out on the street with the homeless."

"Absolutely not, Lance, haven't done speed in over a year." True, actually.

"Yeah." He sounded skeptical.

"You going to look up You Know Who? You going to hang out with him?" You Know Who was my personal drug dealer, my speed connection.

"He's dead. OD'd less than a year ago."

Also true. I once thought the man was invincible.

"Okay," said Lance with a hint of sympathy. "You can come and stay. When are you coming? Are you still in Seattle?"

"No, I'm in L.A. Need a place to stay by tomorrow."

211

Lance laughed. "Eli, you're too much, dude. I'll see you tomorrow. Try to stay out of trouble. Okay, Eli? Try to stay out of trouble."

With my backpacks and sea bag filled to capacity, I boarded a Greyhound with a one-way ticket back to The City by the Bay. It was in September, 2002. I had never done the West Coast drive before. The view from my window was pleasant, relaxing even. Interestingly enough, I was the only white person on the moderately full bus, and every time somebody walked by, they'd double take, as if thinking, "What's he doing here?"

Lance LittleJohn's rule, emphatically imposed, disclosed to me exactly the reputation I had earned. A bad reputation was nothing new to me. It seems I've earned one in every place I've ever been. But now, I was returning to a place where my negativity had not been forgotten. I could either come back and relive it or come back and live it down. I chose the latter, but old habits are hard to break, and while I did stay away from speed, I indulged in everything else.

Oh, dear Jana, I could write a book about my experiences at Theater Bazooka alone. Of course, shortly after my arrival in San Francisco, my Seattle girlfriend and I broke up, a very mutual thing, and I bedded a few sweet, uninhibited bohemian types inside the darkened theater with nothing but blue stage lights and a cheap radio alarm clock to sustain the mood. I partook of a food fight/ orgy, befriended tough Mexican gang bangers who lived nearby, got drunk often, performed an act at Becca Depner's Bazooka Christmas Special, and met dozens of new and old San Francisco underground artists who either knew me before or knew of me.

By January, I was living in a residential hotel, an SRO above a sixty-year-old dive bar, waiting tables, wrestling demons, and trying to write.

In May, I fell in love with a young woman, smart, tall, intense, and beautiful, named Ely. Yes, Ely. That was her last name. For us, "Eli, Ely" was a euphemism for sex. I thought you'd appreciate that. But Miss Ely and I are over now.

As you can see, Jana, since you've been away from my life, I haven't exactly set the world on fire. I wrote and performed more when I was addicted to speed. Fuck, I even completed a novel in those days. If I was wise beyond my years at twenty-eight, like I thought, then why do I keep fucking up now? Armchair psychologists have suggested Ernest Hemingway killed himself because he couldn't live up to the macho image he created. That's bullshit—it's common knowledge that the man was bipolar. But I'm sure there came a day when Hemingway simply said to himself, "I can't live like this anymore."

Relax, Jana. I'm not going to pull a Hemingway, as it wasn't successful the first time, remember?

I did things with you I never did with anyone else, like call you the next day after our dates when I knew you'd be away from your phone and leave a message saying "Thank you for your company last night."

Once, I left a message saying "Every morning we wake up together, I think there's absolutely nothing I'd change about the night before."

Remember when we first met I compared you to a Modigliani painting? When you later actually saw one, you agreed. Modigliani would've loved you.

Remember the first time we slept together? During sex I asked where you wanted me to cum, and slowly, theatrically, you wrapped your arms around my shoulders and whispered, "You can cum wherever you want."

The next morning, you woke before me. You already had your shirt on and you were pulling up your blue jeans as quietly as possible. It was early in the morning, earlier than we were used to as it was still dark outside. I awoke and watched you for a few silent moments. You were being discreet and quiet, hoping, planning not to wake me. When I called out your name, you turned around, a little startled. "Thanks for last night," I said. "I had a wonderful time." Then I fell back to sleep. The sun was up when I woke a few hours later, and you were back in my bed, nude and asleep, with my arms wrapped around your shoulders. To this day, I wish I knew what made you change your mind.

What made you decide to take off your clothes, the same ones you took pains to put on as silently as possible? What made you decide to get back under the covers and lay your nakedness against mine and pull my arms over your body, wrapping yourself inside me? If I knew what it was, I'd bottle it and make a million dollars.

Remember the night it was raining and you came over to my place on Greenwich? I had recorded a Behind the Music episode about Chrissy Hynde and The Pretenders that was followed by a tiny, intimate concert showcasing the band doing an acoustic set. We were watching the video, enjoying it, snuggling in my twin-size bed, and just like any time we snuggled, we began to disrobe each other. You were soft-skinned and petite, with small tender breasts that responded to every touch, every pull, every nibble, and your face was dimpled, with eyes slightly almond-shaped and a sweet smile that never failed to get me excited. You wore your black hair short, usually with a bandana or scarf, letting your hair fall where it may. We had sweet, affectionate sex. Afterwards, lying in bed, watching the rest of Chrissy Hynde's concert, I said, "I love having sex with you because you spread your legs so wide, totally anticipating, totally accepting me."

Then you said, "There's a lot of you to accept, Eli."

When the video was through, the night was still young, so I suggested we get dressed and find something to do. We were walking down Columbus past Bimbo's when I saw the marquee: "Les Nubians, Tonight in Concert. One Night Only." You had never heard of them, but I had heard their first CD and rather liked it.

"Oh, baby. They're fucking awesome. It's smooth French hip-hop. Amazing. You've heard nothing like it before. Want to check them out?"

You were totally game. We located a scalper who sold us a pair of tickets and we got in just as the Nubians were starting their set. The music was sensual, a slow jam, and the club dark. The crowd bounced and swayed, the people nestling into one another. Marijuana was passed around freely, and the smell encompassed the entire show. I'd periodically look at you and you'd smile at me slowly and broadly like a sunset, as if contemplating something sexual, as if contemplating something romantic. Our bodies were pushed together and we danced, our arms encircled and our heads buzzing. You told me you were "so, so unbelievably happy."

When the concert was over, we walked out into the rain holding hands, both declaring we were going to buy the newest Les Nubians CD whenever we had the petty cash, knowing we wouldn't have the petty cash anytime soon. We went to the Chinese restaurant on the corner of Stockton and Broadway and shared a plate of salt-and-pepper calamari over steamed rice. We drank green tea and Chinese beer. The rain escalated into a storm while we were inside and the power went out. The Chinese servers wordlessly placed candles at the tables and we watched the rain and the traffic from our window. We paid for the meal, putting our last dollars together, and then we ran out laughing, getting drenched in the hard Northern California rain.

Back at Greenwich, we threw off our wet clothes, never turning on the lights. I lit a few candles that I always kept around and you told me to put on some Patsy Cline. I did, and again, for the second time that night, you anticipated and accepted me and told me you were so, so unbelievably happy. We eventually fell asleep, quietly watching the rain and the vibrating lights of the Bay illuminating the cluttered walls of my bedroom.

Jana, that was the most romantic night of my life.

I've searched for you on the Internet, googled this and googled that, but I've never found you. Please don't think I harbor any delusional fantasies that we'll get back together. That doesn't even happen successfully in the movies. As are the rules in life, you only get one chance, one opportunity, and when it's gone, it's gone. There's nothing you can do about it. I don't understand why I so often think about you, but I do. Perhaps I feel we ended too soon, but whose fault was that? I didn't mind you fucking other guys but couldn't handle you fucking your ex-boyfriend.

One of the first girls I ever bedded said to me, "All relationships involve one person who likes the other more than that person likes them," meaning no two people like each other equally. She was probably right. In every relationship I've had, I've remained aware of this dynamic of "Who likes whom the most?" I definitely liked you more (which is not to say you didn't like me, because I know you did). Perhaps I fell in love with you but knew I had to give you much space and wouldn't dare utter those three words, knowing that if I ever did, you would've run home before I finished pronouncing the "you."

Unstable, broke, victimized by my senses, my life when you weren't around was chaotic and frightening. It still is. But when I was with you, I thought it would pass, that my life would improve. Shit, I had nothing then, but I still had more than I do now.

How's your life? Has the twenty-first century been good to you thus far? Are you married? Do you have any kids? Do you ever think about me? If you do, do you smile or do you cringe?

Jana, you never knew how special you were to me, then or now.

Love,

Eli

P.S. Remember when I tried to make E.T. a nickname but it never caught on?

9/12/2003
The Sestri Hotel, rm 116
San Francisco, CA 94133

I crumple Jana's letter and throw it in the wastepaper basket by my bed. Then I put on some clothes, leave my room, walk downstairs, and drop off Jennifer's package in the mailbox that stands outside the entrance of the Sestri.

The relationship's over, and now there's no evidence it ever began.

IV

8/12/03

Eli,

Thank you for sending the most beautiful letter my fingers have ever felt. My eyes are still bright from the grin it left on my face. A hundred and eighty miles is all that prevents me from smothering you with kisses and bouncing on your strong body as it bravely occupies that flimsy North Beach bed. Last night, the moon was at its fullest.

217

As I telephoned you, it hung drunk and distended over the meadow, saddled between two dark trees. The August meteor shower painted an occasional chalk line across the sky. Mars was in close orbit, bright red in the distance. My co-workers and neighbors all went for a walk, with the direct goal of sky admiration. I declined and was content to lie in my bed and converse with you.

The universe of your mind was mine to admire. It has not yet failed to satisfy me. You're so complex and wide—just when I find your latitude appearing to shorten, your longitude grips me and I'm left awestruck and in love with this great space of a man I can't even begin to shy away from.

Can I even inscribe my intentions in a letter? I want to lean backwards now and find your shoulders there to rest upon. I miss you, yes, but mostly I miss learning about you. Sometimes on the phone I pretend I am talking to you for the first time—I analyze your voice like a detective, hoping to find some new evidence of Elijah that I haven't noticed before. Please don't squirm at that thought, it's just a desperate move and thus empty and one-dimensional. Other times I don't even hear your tone, just the words and the effect they have on my person/soul/mind/belly/what have you.

I love your stories, but sometimes I want you most when you're quiet. Being near you makes me want to cry—which is a good thing. All in all, I'm nervous as shit about seeing you again, and that's something special. I thought I knew about men when I met you, thought I knew their small ways and desirable waters. If I ever found a man interesting it was an interest I spotted from the beginning and cultivated selfishly.

Meeting you has changed me. You are the first man who has dared to really understand me. You are the first man who has surprised me. You are the first man I have feared will die and leave no trace of himself across my body, which wants his touch so intuitively.

Sex with you is both intimate and exciting. You can hit all the right spots and still add in a few that I wouldn't have expected. When

218

we're fucking, every touch I give you is 100 percent legitimate. I have never lied, exaggerated, or cooed you into false intimacy. Every orgasm blows my heart right out of my thighs. Just thinking of it makes my writing sloppy and my panties moist. I wish I could take various parts of you around in my pocket, feel you on the bike, the bus, in the grocery store line, gross as it may seem to you—but it's the closest I can get to how badly I need you.

I need you with me, and I will need you until I love you no longer, and even then, my heart will always need your memory.

Congratulations on obtaining your Burberry job, wish I could kiss your balls.

Got to go to bed now; you'll be in my dreams.

Your wet and caring girlfriend,

Jennifer Ely

I read her last letter so many times that I memorized it. When I was a theater major I could memorize an entire play by simply reading it cover to cover several times in a row. Even with this brain, unstable, unbalanced, angry, recovering from years of self-abuse and poor judgment, I'm able to recall this letter in its entirety.

At crowded Washington Square Park in the hot sun, I slouch on a bench, close my eyes, and turn my face towards the sun. There I see the intricately folded yellow notebook paper on which she always wrote her letters. There in red ink, I can see her flourished, surprisingly feminine handwriting.

I put my head down and rest it in my hands.

In time, thankfully, I'll forget the letters she wrote me, but I'll never forget that she wrote me letters. Most men will never in their lives receive the kinds of letters I did over the summer, letters romantic and intense and sexual and passionate, written by a young woman whose varied qualities are exhibited in her writing.

Jennifer, why did you declare you needed a break from me when you did? You must've known I was in a bad place at the time. (Have I ever been in a good place?)

After an hour or so, slouching on a bench and letting my head get sunburned, I walk to a Mexican joint and buy a burrito and a Pepsi and go back to my hotel room. I eat, take a shower, read a little, write in my journal, and somehow, hours after the sun sets, when the air cools, North Beach lights up, and the barflies downstairs can be heard pissing in the alley underneath my window, I fall asleep.

I

Running Into Somebody With Whom You Once Had Sex
by Elijah Trocchi

Her name was Carly and we attended the same
easy-A liberal arts college. She was tall,
toned, heavily tattooed, had large C cups,
and would write the kind of angry, maudlin
prose poems that people deny writing once
they get older. She was only twenty or twenty-
one at the time and definitely carrying the
punk-Goth look on her extraordinary frame.
I was twenty-four and looked the same as
I do now, only leaner, with fewer tattoos
and lines on my bald face. But in those
days, we shared a creative writing class,
and not unlike most artists/writers at that
age, my pieces were dark, dark, dark, as
I'd listen to This Mortal Coil and Dead Can
Dance and The Cure and spend hours writing
about catatonic babies, turning dead people

into fertilizer, redneck insane asylum escapees who burn books, and anything odd, disturbing, and tragic that I could laugh at. Carly loved my stories and frequently told me so.

Shortly after my first San Francisco girlfriend and I broke up, Carly gave me her phone number. When I called her, she proceeded to tell me how horny she was, and needless to say, I offered to pay for the cab she took to my apartment. Carly disrobed in my bedroom on Greenwich looking out into the Bay: the Golden Gate Bridge, Alcatraz, the Wharf, everything. Having her nude in my room was a thing of beauty, and she gave herself to me completely, never putting on another stitch of clothing for the next several hours she was there.

The sex was tremendous and powerful and we did it into the wee hours of the morning. We'd stop periodically to read our dark writings to one another butt naked and drink red wine, and then we'd return back to the sex.

Ah, to be young and sexy and pretentious again.

I would've been open to dating Carly casually and, if things worked out, making her my girlfriend. But the next day at school, she (this tall punk chick with long, jet-black hair, shaved on the sides to expose her tribal tats) was telling everybody I was her boyfriend. Considering I had just gotten out of a relationship with a possessive girlfriend, she ended up scaring me away, and the further declarations of love combined with the "You're my man now" statements would've driven some men to file a restraining order against the young woman.

I took to avoiding her at school. I was polite to her in creative writing class, but the minute class was over I'd run out the door to avoid her. Eventually, Carly got the hint, and she never bothered me again.

Years later, I was thirty-one, just returning to San Francisco after some time spent in Seattle, when I bumped into her on Valencia Street. I was surprised by how happy we were to see each other. She looked great, better than before, and though her hair was grown and cut sensibly short, it still retained a nice, spiky edge; and her body, still tattooed, now contained more womanly curves inside her old blue jeans and cowboy boots and the black T-shirt that expressed an anti-war sentiment. She also wore a great big redneck belt buckle, as was the new style at the time.

She was all smiles, asking about my life and what was I up to, and I told her briefly as I could, the good and the bad. I asked about her life. She had worked as a dancer and a model throughout California, New York, and most of Europe, but she said she was tired of modeling, some of which included bondage pictures and soft-core pornography, because she'd gotten tired of meeting people where the whole time they're looking at her thinking "I've seen you naked before." Then I said, "Well, that's what I'm doing right now, Carly. Thinking 'I've seen you naked before.'"

She laughed, her shoulders in the air shaking, her face rollicking backwards—what a delightful laugh that I didn't remember she had. Did I ever see her laugh before? I don't think so. Then she looked at me, her long hands patting my chest. "Yes, that's because you and I once had sex before. Big difference. And believe me, I'm doing the same exact thing right now." We both laughed, our arms leaning on one another. When we stopped laughing, we found ourselves smiling sad smiles and looking into each other's eyes. If I didn't mention it earlier, she had a great face, like a young Elizabeth Taylor with an eyebrow piercing.

One voice in my head said to me, "Seduce her, you fool! Ask for her phone number and rekindle it with a more mature and stable Carly."

But another voice said, "Let this be it. Leave this here. If you ask her out right now, it'll ruin the moment." Carly, probably thinking the same thing, said in a sweet, almost maternal voice I never once heard in our old creative writing class, "It's really nice seeing you again. Take care." Then she gave me a hug and a kiss on the cheek and turned around and walked to wherever it was she had to go.

II

Regret
By Elijah Trocchi

I was twenty-four and had been living in San Francisco for about a month, and I was already dating a local woman named Meredith, who was tall with blue-grey eyes and high cheekbones and earned good money selling cars at a local Volvo dealership. We were dating very casually. I hadn't even slept with her yet. Though the attraction was definite, there were certain aspects of her personality I didn't like. I was able to justify and overlook her materialism because I believe as long as a person is making the money, they can spend it however they desire. What annoyed me was how patronizing and condescending she could be to me, as if treating me like I was some Florida swamp hick who had never been to a city before.

However, she was fun, nice to look at, and knew lots of interesting people and was planning to introduce me to various sites and scenes throughout the Bay Area. Valentine's Day was coming up, so over a drink one evening, I asked as casually as possible if she'd like to do something "fun and romantic" for the fourteenth of February. She said yes, cheerful and flattered, and then "You better take me someplace nice and you better be grateful, because there are lots of guys who'd like to be with me on

Valentine's Day." Afterwards, she laughed
a self-satisfied laugh that disgusted me.

My first California girl and she was a
conceited bitch.

Come V-day, I stood her up.

After calling a day before to confirm, I
purposely chose not to meet her at the Thai
restaurant we had agreed upon. At around
midnight, I called her, and though she
sounded more concerned than upset, wanting
to know where I was and telling me she did
wait for me at the Thai place, I told her I
was so turned off by her egotistical remark
that I stood her up. She said that she was
only joking, "but whatever, no skin off my
nose. Bye." *Click.*

Later that night, I went to a bar and
bragged to some dudes, all straight and
dateless on Valentine's Day, about what I
did. They thought it was hilarious.

I didn't see her again for about a year.
It was at a nightclub and we said "Hi."
She was very cordial, very pleasant, even
introducing me to her new, hunky boyfriend
and fondly recalling some of the short
stories I used to read to her when we
dated. It seems some people really don't
hold grudges. She certainly did not.

Occasionally over the next several years,
we'd bump into each other at nightclubs
and parties, and she was always smiling,
always cool, usually hanging around the
same hunk (was his name Roger?). Then,
after a time, I came to realize I never saw
her around anymore, but I do seem to recall
overhearing somebody at a party saying that

Meredith and Roger moved down to L.A. I'm sure they're married with kids by now.

Flash forward to me at thirty-two, still in San Francisco, living in my immaculate residential hotel room, room 116, laying my towels along the windowsill to dry and knowing intuitively that my time in the City once again must come to an end. Predictably, I find myself reminiscing about my earliest escapades in San Francisco, when the night I stood Meredith up came back to me and I literally shouted "No!"

Why is it only now that it truly hits me?

That was one of the dumbest and meanest and certainly one of the most vindictive things I've ever done. She was only joking, and I now know from personal experience that true egomaniacs are more rare than people realize, and that 95 percent of the time when people utter such conceited things, it is done out of insecurity, not ego, and often the prettiest girls are more insecure than the rest. In retrospect, though materialistic and trying too hard to be my tour guide for San Francisco, Meredith was far too friendly and forgiving to be an egomaniac. Besides, I was lucky to be dating her. I had only been in California for a month and had met this local, sweet-natured hottie my first night out bar-hopping. While I don't think we had enough in common to have had a serious relationship, I should've gone out with her that night, and not just because I would've gotten laid, but because I would've had a wonderful time.

Do you know what the most painful part is? I'll never be twenty-four again. You have no idea what I'd do to be twenty-four years old, new to San Francisco, and to already have a hot date lined up for Valentine's Day.

Now, at thirty-two, and every year after this year, I know that various recollections will warm my heart on lonely holidays and that because of a mean-spirited decision I made nearly ten years ago I've denied myself what could've been a beautiful memory.

Meredith, wherever you are, I am sorry.

III

Though the confessional, autobiographical fiction comes to me with considerably more ease than the odd, dark, speculative stuff I've been flexing for the past ten years or so, I just get so damn tired of writing while reminiscing and feeling like an asshole. I put the cap back on my red-ink pen and throw it across my room. It clicks as it ricochets from one corner to the next. Then I crumple the two short stories I wrote this morning based on actual events and actual characters from my own life. I toss them in the air and watch as each makes a basket, joining the crumpled letter I had written to Jana the day before.

After this, I lie down in bed and do nothing, nothing at all.

I listen to the radio but hear no good songs. I stare at the ceiling and think, but think no good thoughts.

Then Saturday's over; time to go to sleep now.

Sunday 9/14/03

I

It was one of those mornings when you cradle your skull in your hands and stare at the ceiling thinking about absolutely nothing. My week was over. I was defeated. The noise below my window— traffic, people milling about and speaking Cantonese—faded away into not-unpleasant white noise. *Chirp. Chirp.* My cell phone rang while charging on its tiny black podium. I didn't want to pick it up because that'd mean getting out of bed, but I couldn't ignore it either. Pathetic, I know, but I thought it might be Jennifer. I rolled out of bed and snatched the cell phone.

"Hello?"

"Hey, bud."

Ferdinand Noah! The friend I made during my time at Theater Bazooka.

As a fellow writer, I admired Ferdinand Noah. The man wrote nightly, often insightful, wistful, happy-sad pieces that frequently featured displaced Southerners and people wrestling with the hellfire religious imageries that have been beaten into their skulls from an early age. In another incarnation, Ferdinand Noah told vicious, bitchy, vulgar tales as a drag queen performance artist named Titty Titty Gangbang. Ferdinand, half-Filipino/half-English, was born in Louisiana and moved to Seattle in his teens, where he was ridiculed for his Southern accent, a trait he actively dropped. In truth, his voice, well-modulated and polished, is one of his best features, a gift inherited from his Southern Baptist preacher father. Papa Noah's life would certainly make good reading. A conservative Southern boy joins the service, gets stationed in The Philippines, falls in love with a local bar girl, brings her home, becomes a preacher, and eventually comes to terms with his teenage son's gayness. A divorce and a job offer for his mother, who'd gone to nursing school in America, brings Ferdinand's family to Seattle, where Ferdinand (never Ferd or Ferddie, though he did like being called by his surname or even Titty Titty) attends high school and later the University of Washington as a tech-writing major with a lit minor. From what I can ascertain, his relationship with his family is loving, but strained.

Ferdinand supported himself by occasionally writing textbooks and manuals. He'd get one gig and not work for several weeks, later find another gig, and somehow he was able to support himself this way. He wrote life-inspired fiction nightly, separating experiences to be used for the more serious work of Ferdinand Noah and then mining his wicked antics for his Titty Titty Gangbang persona. Just think about all those pupils and teachers skimming informed but dry textbooks and never knowing about the author's Titty Titty Gangbang character, not to mention the notorious stage shows that featured Titty Titty's filthier-than-fuck monologues that stayed stuck in your head for days.

"Ferdinand Noah!" I was happy to hear from him. He'd just returned from a four-week vacation including travels throughout the Southeast and a writer's conference in New Mexico.

ELI: When did you get back into town?

NOAH: The day before yesterday. Didn't you get the email, my most recent one?

ELI: Goddamn, Noah. I haven't. Haven't gone to the library and checked my email in a long time, been having a rough last couple of weeks.

NOAH: Oh, yeah. (*Laughs.*) I heard you had a rough week.

ELI: Yeah? How'd you hear about that?

NOAH: Scott told me. I ran into him at The Squat & Gobble.

ELI: Well, Noah, did you hear? Johnny Cash died on Friday. He had a worse week than I did.

NOAH: Sorry about Burberry not working out for you, but I had a difficult time picturing you there anyway.

ELI: Really?

NOAH: Oh, yeah. Talk about miscasting. And then your young girlfriend breaks up with you. (*Laughs.*)

ELI: Hey, Titty Titty! Did you call me up simply to recap my week or did you want something? Besides, I broke up with her.

NOAH: I'm sorry, Eli. Sorry. I just called to see if you wanted to check out a flick with me tonight.

ELI: A movie?

NOAH: You want to see *Lost in Translation*? That new Bill Murray flick directed by Sophia Coppola?

ELI: Yeah, I do. Is it playing anywhere?

NOAH: Over at the monstrosity multiplex on 4th in SoMa, where Jillian's is, by the Chronicle Books bookstand, you know, the Metreon?

ELI: Oh, yeah. It's like a fucking mall built around a multiplex. Crazy.

NOAH: What time do you want to see the movie?

ELI: Later is always better with me.

NOAH: Cool. There's a ten o'clock feature we can check out. Let's get there early to drink coffee and catch up with one another. There's much shit to tell you, Eli.

ELI: All right.

NOAH: Is nine too early for you?

ELI: Nah, that's fine.

NOAH: Let's meet at The Chronicle Books bookstand, then?

ELI: Deal. See you then.

NOAH: Bye.

ELI: Bye.

Click.

Click.

II

"Hello?"

"Hello, Eli. This is Harvey from The Wash-Out. Haven't seen you in a few days."

"Yeah, been busy this week. Preoccupied. You know how it goes. What's up? Have I been getting a lot of mail or something?"

"Yeah, Eli, as a matter of fact, that's why I called. This morning after I opened up, these two girls came in. One I recognized as the pretty brunette you dated over the summer, the one with the last name the same as your first name, but spelled differently."

"Jennifer Ely? My Jennifer?" (She's not yours anymore, you fucking moron, Eli!)

"Uh-huh. And then the other girl, a real looker, about twenty-one, she looks at me, smiles, and asks me if I'm a Buddhist. I say 'No' and then she frowns and says 'I am,' and I say, 'Well, I am if it turns you on.'"

"You did not say that, Harvey."

"No," he admits, and chuckles, then very sweetly says, "But that's what I wanted to say."

"How was Jennifer?"

"Um, uh, she looked sad, Eli. She seemed upset. Sad. Almost like she'd been crying."

I cringe. But why was I cringing when my intention was to hurt her?

"What did they want?"

"The girls were dropping off a shoebox for you. Jennifer said she was aware that you got your mail here. She said she wanted to leave this shoebox for you. I said 'Okay.' She thanked me and gave me a sad smile that women do where they almost look like they're going to cry. I guess sometimes men do those kinds of smiles, too, but I don't care when men do it. You know what I mean, they're like anti-smile smiles."

"Yeah," I say quietly. "I know those kinds of smiles. Know them well. They're worse when you know you're the cause of them. Ear-splitting silences and sad smiles, the two things I hate the most . . ."

"What? What did you say? I didn't hear you. I'm calling you from a laundromat."

"Yes, Harvey! I know those smiles that aren't really smiles! Know them well!"

"Oh. And then, right as they were leaving, the real looker, the Buddhist chick, looks at me and tells me," he chuckles, "that I've got a beautiful, gentle nature and lots of love in my heart."

"She got all that from just a glance, huh?"

"'So,' I say, 'can I have your phone number?' And she just smiles and shakes her head. Then she tries to say something in Chinese. I don't know if it was Mandarin or Cantonese, but her pronunciation is so bad I couldn't tell you what she was trying to say. After that, they both left."

"Can't win them all, Harvey."

"Can you get me in contact with her? She's into Asian culture. I *am* Asian culture."

"Her name is Ursula and she's my ex-girlfriend's roommate. Sorry, but no, I won't be able to help you. Now, Harvey, did you look in the shoebox?"

"Oh, yeah. Uh-huh. Because the shoebox doesn't have a lid. It's got two paperbacks and a bunch of letters."

My letters, my letters! Bulldog Harvey regularly saw my shit-stained tighty-whities; should I feel violated if Harvey read my personal letters?

When Harvey called, I was exercising, preparing for my first day watch-dogging Gucci by doing an extra amount of push-ups and isometrics. The Cocteau Twins were playing on the CD player. The room was getting hot and my body felt large. My brain was gloriously free of thought; and for me, an absent mind is generally a happy one.

"Harvey, did you read my letters?"

"Uh-huh. Read them all."

"Shit, Harvey."

"Hey, don't worry about it. They were really good. In all the time I've known you, I've never read any of your writing."

Suddenly angry, I say, "I've invited you to all my shows, Harvey, and you've never showed up to any of them."

"True, true. But the point is, these letters, I really like them. They're good! Very good! Some are sexy and blunt, they say things like 'I masturbated three times today thinking about you,' and others are sweet, like, uh (he's obviously reading), 'When we meet again I will ache and tremble. I think about you daily. Nightly. I don't know what to say and I analyze everything I say and write moments after I've done these things with you. I want you here right now so I can feel your breath against my cheek when you speak to me, when you laugh with me.' Wow. I can certainly see why she fell for you, Shakespeare. That's good stuff. And then," he chuckles, "we've also got the break-up letter."

My break-up letter! I guess since it only takes one day for a letter from San Francisco addressed to San Francisco to reach its destination, my letter could conceivably be written in a vindictive rage on late Thursday night, mailed out Friday morning, and read on a Saturday, after which the letter could be returned on Sunday via Bulldog Harvey through tears and forced smiles and whacky misinterpreted Buddhism. Wow. Tough week.

Still chuckling, Harvey says, "That letter was pretty harsh, Eli. 'I hope you and your vibrator enjoyed your week without me.' But maybe that's what happens when you break a writer's heart."

"Harvey, did you really like the way the letters were written? You know, they're just letters. I didn't really work on them. I just sat down and wrote them from the top of my head. They're just private letters. Or at least, they used to be private."

"Oh, I did like them, Eli. It has given me an idea to discuss with you in person."

"What's up?"

"Well, here's my idea. Lots of guys probably wish they could write good love letters like that to their girlfriends and people they're in other long-distance relationships with, mistresses, et cetera. And you know, today, you can buy term papers online."

"Yeah."

"This is my idea. I've got a friend who builds websites for a living. We could take these letters and others you may want to donate and we could create a website selling your love letters to guys who can't write love letters. I figure we could break it down into categories: missing you, sexual, romantic, casual, sweet, and, hell, we could even include break-up letters. Love-no-more letters." Harvey does his Harvey chuckle, boyish and giddy, for a long, long time. Eventually, I start laughing too.

"Eli, I thought maybe we could take inspiration from Cyrano de Bergerac and call it CyranosJournal.com or something similar. You know that story? The guy with the big nose?"

As I was starting to grasp the idea Harvey was pitching, I found myself quietly moved by the fact that Bulldog Harvey with his fat jowls was obviously a fan of that classic love story. Earlier I stated that Harvey was like a bulldog in looks but not temperament, but now I realize that every last bulldog I've ever known, despite its fearsome appearance, was always sweet, fun to be around, and surprisingly gentle with children and adults alike. Will Rogers is remembered for saying "I never met a man I didn't like." I want to be remembered for saying "I never met a bulldog that didn't make me smile." The name "Bulldog Harvey" fits him perfectly, though I still hesitate to call him that to his face. There was a lengthy silence between the two of us.

"Do you know the play, Eli?"

"Of course I do. Yeah, I love that play, too," I say, sitting up, my eyes surprisingly dry. "It's a good idea, Harvey. Of course, I guess I ought to expect only good ideas from a young man in his thirties who owns a laundromat café and a house in the Sunset and drives a fucking BMW."

"Yeah, I do pretty good, I guess."

"Later this week, I'll mine my journals to see if I've got any other love letters in various categories to give you."

"Really? That'd be great, Eli. Hey, sorry about the break-up, but it will be for the best. Maybe it's a blessing in disguise, a way for you to make a profit, something positive out of a negative. She's young. It's for the best, old-timer."

"Yeah."

Despite Harvey's accolades for my writing, depression threatens me like a terrible stench making my eyes water. Nobody, it seems, took my relationship the least bit seriously.

"You going to come over later to the café?"

"No, Harvey. I've got shit I've got to do today, but I'll be there later this week. Go ahead and keep my letters."

"What about the paperbacks?"

The Sacrilege of Alan Kent by Erskine Caldwell and *The Razor's Edge* by Somerset Maugham—I lent both to Jennifer this summer. That latter book, multi-dog-eared, yellowed, and severely highlighted, was a copy I've had since I was sixteen-years-old. Its value to me is immeasurable. The novel changed my life. Was it for the better? Who the fuck knows? Simply, it's still my all-time favorite novel after *On the Road*.

"I'll be there later today to pick up the paperbacks. Lovers come and go, Harvey, but books are forever."

Harvey says, "That may be true, but I'd gladly burn every book I've ever had to get a single date with that white Buddhist chick." It sounds like the Pillsbury Doughboy is at the end of my phone.

Smiling, I say "Later, Harvey."

"Later, Eli."

I'm smiling the best, most genuine smile I've had in days.

III

Standing on the corner of Broadway and Stockton across from the Chinese restaurant where Jana and I had our romantic late-night dinner years ago, I'm waiting to cross the street, standing in a crowd of low-income Chinese people and shock-faced tourists. San Francisco's heat wave is still going strong. My cell phone rings.

"Hello?"

"Hey!" It's a man's voice and a number I don't recognize.

"Who's this?"

"This is Danny. How are you, man?"

Danny Ryan?

"Fine, dude." Danny's never called me before. "What's up, Danny?" The light is green and the crowd I'm standing with is starting to walk across the street.

"Are you sitting down, Eli?" Danny's voice is serious.

"Excuse me, dude. Are you asking me if I'm sitting down?"

"Yeah, yeah, I've got some weird, kind of bad, kind of sad news for you, I think."

Shit, okay. It seems to me that if somebody asks you to sit down before they lay something heavy on you, you should sit down. Neither of us speaks as I walk up Broadway a few yards towards the tunnel and sit on the curb by a weather-beaten twenty-year-old Mercedes parked with a ticket clipped to one of its wipers. Was Danny going to tell me he had run into Jennifer Ely at The Hemlock last night and they fucked and were going to pursue a relationship together?

"What's up, Danny? What can I do for you?"

"Have you read today's newspaper?"

"The newspaper? You mean the Sunday paper?"

"Yeah."

"No. Why?"

"Current events aren't your thing, huh? You know, there's a war going on."

"Heard something about that. The only reason I look at a newspaper is when I'm job-hunting, and even then I just turn to the classifieds."

"Well, if you only look at the paper when you need a job," he says, laughing, "you must be looking at the newspaper all the time."

"Very witty, Danny. Now, what the fuck can I do for you?" I stretch out my legs in the sun and put my head down. Was Danny a friend or not?

"Well, Eli. I guess I'd rather you hear it from somebody cool than somebody else."

Oh, my *fucking* God! Danny *was* fucking Jennifer and it's in the newspaper.

"You see, it's Jasper Needham . . ."

Lifting my head up, I say, "Jasper Needham?"

"Yeah. Jasper Needham committed suicide Friday." I'm quiet on the phone long enough for Danny to say "Hello? Hello, Eli? Are you still there?"

"Yeah, yeah, wow, that uh, um. Shit, fuck. I don't know. Fuck. I'm at a loss."

"Yeah, yeah, it's rather bizarre. For the first time in his two decades at CPK, he pulled a no-call, no-show for a Thursday day shift. Boston Jerry called Jasper, but his line was disconnected. Then Harley got a letter on Friday morning apologizing for being a no-call, no-show, saying something had come up, and then there was a list of co-workers who could possibly fulfill his shifts that coming week, but the letter did say he wasn't coming back."

"Wow."

"Then, apparently, he had given away his cat to Tiffany, who just moved into a large warehouse space in Oakland. Remember Tiffany, the chubby artist chick?"

You mean the chick that filed a sexual harassment complaint against me, despite the fact I wouldn't fuck her if she were the last set of lips and hips on the face of this Earth? "Vaguely."

"Then, on Friday, Jasper's landlord got a letter from him saying 'By the time you read this letter, I'll be dead,' and it further said something like 'I've gone as far as I'm going to go in life,' and some other shit. Pretty depressing stuff, huh?"

"Yeah." It's at this moment I realize Jasper Needham didn't get especially unpleasant with me until my own suicide attempt became public knowledge.

"You don't seem terribly surprised, Eli."

"That's because I'm not, Danny. Hey, remember how he used to always say 'Time just has a way of slipping away from you'?"

"Yeah, he said that all the damn time. I guess I'm not real surprised either, Eli."

"Are you telling me Needham's suicide made the newspaper?"

As if he himself doesn't believe it, Danny says, "Yeah, Eli, it's the damnedest thing. Friday afternoon, some tourists from somewhere in the middle of the United States at the Golden Gate Bridge with a video camera were filming themselves walking around the orange bridge. Suddenly, this shirtless, malnourished-looking, middle-aged man with long brown hair walks into frame, steps over the walkway, and jumps off the bridge."

"So you mean to tell me these tourists ended up recording Jasper's suicide?"

"Yeah, it appeared on the six o'clock news and everything. Bizarre."

"This is bizarre. And me without a TV."

"Believe it or not, I don't own a TV either. But Jasper's landlord, some of his neighbors, and even Harley called the news and identified the jumper as Jasper Needham. Bizarre, man."

"This is all in the newspaper?"

"Yeah."

"Wow. Well, Jasper Needham, the noted author of *Pagan Power* and career California Pizza Kitchen server, made a bigger splash and got more attention and recognition in death than he ever did in life."

"Yeah." Danny isn't laughing but he's not offended either. "You know, you hear stories about people, high school athletes and shit, and you're like, 'Why did this young person kill themselves? They were so young and good-looking, had friends, had a girlfriend, had this, had that, why did they kill themselves? What a tragedy.' But with Jasper, people are not really surprised; they're just like, 'Yeah, well, um, uh, yeah.' It's weird. It's sad, really. You know what I mean, Eli?"

"Yeah, not a whole lot to envy in Jasper's life. You could say life had beaten a whole lot of ugly into him if only he'd had a life in the first place."

"Oh, he wasn't so bad, Eli. And who knows what he was like when he was a young man. He may have been a lot like you and me. He may have been a lot like us."

Again, a surge of depression causes my eyes to water. "Yeah, you're right."

"He just didn't understand you, was intimidated by you. Or maybe he did understand you. I don't know. Maybe he understood you all too well." A long, uncomfortable pause, and then, "You know, Eli. Another reason I wanted to call you before you heard it from someone else is . . . well, uh, um . . . I didn't know this when I saw you on Thursday, I just found out on Saturday that you lost the job at Burberry, or were pushed out of it by that bogus manager there; but earlier during the week, Harley had mentioned to Boston Jerry and some of the others that you asked for your old job back and Jasper apparently pulled a bitch, a genuine hissy fit. Harley and everyone else began to tease Jasper about it, singing 'Eli's coming, Eli's coming,' you know, that old song from the '70s? 'Three Dog Night'? I'm sure you do. But you see, some people at CPK are saying that Jasper killed himself because he thought you were coming back to work there." Danny lets out a small breath, something similar to a laugh.

I say nothing. I don't even breathe.

"But you know that's not fair to you or to him. Come on, people. You could tell Jasper wasn't happy and hadn't been happy for a really

241

long time. Saying he did this because of you isn't cool. He probably had been planning this for months, or maybe even years."

I remain quiet. I feel sadness and rage, but I'm mostly grateful that Danny is calling me, recognizing the true friend that he is and grateful none of my other friends watch the news or read the newspaper, and wishing, wishing I could take back "If God gave you cancer, Jasper, he'd be doing you a favor. That's how fucking pathetic your life is."

"You still there?"

"Yeah."

"Harley told me yesterday he was still contemplating whether to bring you back, but man, fuck it. I put in my two weeks' notice. Sloppy Lard-Ass Records has offered me a full-time position. No more interning."

"You were only interning? I thought you worked there part-time already."

"No, only interning with a small stipend, but now we're talking about full-time with good weekly pay, a nice starting salary."

"Congrats, dude. Congrats. I know that is what you want, a job in the music industry."

"Yeah, thanks. So, Harley may be hiring at CPK soon, but you don't want to work there. You wanted to get out pretty badly in the first place. I mean, you're a grown man and you can do whatever you want, but shit, we lived in fear of becoming Jasper. Fuck, man. Don't go back to CPK. We're both too good for that place. I'll be twenty-nine this summer. I don't want to do shit like this anymore. The economy's bad but you can find something better."

"Yeah, Danny, I've got a full-time security gig working at Gucci starting tomorrow and possibly some bouncer gigs coming up. That'll keep me afloat."

"Cool. You'll be able to focus on your writing and not an intense bullshit sales job—fuck that."

242

I become too despondent to say anything. He gets quiet, too, but then says, "I know you may be a little down this week, but fuck it, Eli. You got the writing thing going. I met a lot of your friends at your show in April. All cool, all of them cool."

He's right. I do have some cool friends: creative, artistic, theatrical, literary . . . Forgiving.

"Also," Danny says enthusiastically, "you've got a cool girlfriend. She's smart, went to UCLA, good-looking. Has a nice rack." Danny laughs. "To tell you the truth, I got your number from the employee directory. You're not going to change it anytime soon, are you?"

"No."

"Great. Did you have fun at the Angry Jimmy show on Thursday?"

"Yeah, I did, actually."

"Great! My friend Mimi, remember her?"

"Yeah, is she your girlfriend?"

"Well, we're definitely seeing each other. Anyway, she said that she thought you seemed like a cool guy and she doesn't like anybody."

"Really?" I find that hard to believe, as she scarcely acknowledged me.

"Yeah. I thought it'd be cool if me and Mimi and Eli and Ely all hung out sometime."

Then Danny laughs like a dork. And I do, too. Eventually.

I don't have the heart to tell him.

"You know, Eli, Mimi's smart, too. She goes to Berkeley and I think she and Miss Ely would hit it off. We'll check out another show together. A couples thing, a double date. It'll be fun."

He's right. Those two serious-faced babes would probably get along exceptionally well, but with Danny's exuberance on the phone and the obvious knowledge he had of my bad week, how can I tell him that Eli,Ely is no more, no more. I'll tell him later on next week, but right now, I can't.

243

"Yeah, Danny, that'd be so much fun, man. Yeah, fuck yeah. We four need to hang out. I'll mention it to Jennifer tonight when I see her. Cool."

Maybe Danny will get lucky some night and catch Jennifer Ely alone when he's hanging out with Mimi, and perhaps the three of them will take off for a ménage à trois, the bastard. Nah, don't hate Danny because he's beautiful. He's calling you and extending these gestures because he likes you, he can handle you, he thinks you're cool and recognizes you as an artist. Lighten up, Eli, fucking lighten up.

"Ah, it's going to be so awesome, Eli. Don't let that bogus Burberry asshole get you down or any of those weaklings at CPK either. Move on."

"Yeah." I get up. "I got shit to do today but thanks for telling me about Needham."

"Yeah. Rest in peace, Jasper Needham."

"Yeah . . . Later on, Danny."

"See you around, Eli."

I stand on the sidewalk and stretch. I'm wearing khaki shorts, ankle-high socks, tan, ankle-high hiking boots, and an XXL brown polo shirt acquired from some Tenderloin thrift shop. The shirt's too large for me and billowy in the sudden Northern California wind. I can feel a bead of sweat roll down my spine. I put my cell phone in my back pocket. Resisting an urge to get down on my knees and pray, instead, with my head downward, my eyes open and staring at grey concrete, I think to myself, "Hey, Jasper, I hope in death you found whatever eluded you in life. Sorry we never became friends. Sorry about the drunken late-night phone call where I'll never know all the terrible things I said. Sorry for the harsh that's-how-pathetic-your-life-is statement I made in the hallway several years ago. And know, please know, Jasper, that when I hit you with the door it was an accident, a major fucking accident. Don't doubt that every time I go over the bridge I'll think about you. Rest in peace, Jasper, rest in peace."

I lift my head up and walk back to the corner and stand among Cantonese speakers and white people looking for someone who can give them directions in English. I ignore an exasperated middle-aged man with a New York accent who asks me "Where the fuck is Little Italy?"

I simply stand there, saliva from his mouth hitting my cheekbones, eyeballing the tourist as hard as a convict, and think to myself, "There's no Heaven, there's no Hell, and reincarnation is a nice theory but just a theory."

Crossing Broadway, walking on Stockton, approaching Old Chinatown, I say to anybody who cares to listen, "Johnny Cash and Jasper Needham are dead. They say things happen in threes, don't they?"

IV

I'm at the monstrosity, the multiplex on 4th, down the street from where the old Trocadero used to be, where I used to go to Bondage A-Go-Go on Wednesday nights and dance shirtless. In an old journal circa '97, on the first page, is me describing a blowjob I scored.

". . . Last night at Bondage A-Go-Go, outside in the parking lot, some strange Goth girl let me feel her tits and they were big and soft and she bit my ears till they hurt and I feared she drew blood. She kept rubbing herself against my cock and reminding me she had said earlier that she wasn't going to 'suck it or fuck it,' but she did just that, sucking me off twice, as she was a total 'good-natured slut,' as she kept describing herself; and when I asked her how she felt afterwards, as we were walking back into the club from the parking lot, she said she felt 'great,' and we kissed only after we fooled around, a blowjob before the first kiss. She never told me her name, nor did I ask for her phone number."

The heaviness I feel suddenly and mildly inside my ennobled tool is not something I desire at this moment—quite the contrary.

Writer Seymour Krim, during his first suicide attempt, burned some ten years' worth of diaries and journals. "Suicide," I keep telling myself in emotional pep talks, "is never the answer." But it was for Mr. Krim, finally getting it right several years later with no journal or suicide note anywhere to be found. No! Suicide is not the answer, Eli, absolutely not. But would burning your journals make you happy? This type of cleansing ritual may be exactly what I need.

Nah, it'd be futile, considering the leaps and bounds my memory can perform. Besides, burning my journals may even be dangerous. San Francisco has been dry this year. Does it really need another Great Fire?

Maybe I ought to quit keeping a journal altogether. Why should I bother keeping a journal anyway?

Where's Ferdinand?

Hearing people describe the first time they encountered you is an incredible opportunity to learn who you are, or, at the very least, how you appear to others.

Scott Bonne and I met innocently enough. We shook hands when I was a sober twenty-four-year-old on Columbus Avenue in North Beach in front of the Ben & Jerry's. We were introduced by a mutual friend whom neither of us has seen in years, a mutual friend that Scott claims to this day had the biggest and wettest crush on me. Before shaking hands, we were introduced in the basement of City Lights Bookstore on Columbus and Jack Kerouac Way. He was hanging out with Miss So-and-So, who was talking about me and said I could probably be found inside the famous bookstore on any given night. She was right. After introductions, the three of us walked towards Ben & Jerry's when I suddenly remembered my manners and grabbed Scott's arm and apologized for not shaking his hand. Scott would later describe me as "polite, a bit of a bookworm, basically a nice guy but a tad inaccessible," especially to our mutual acquaintance. She was a cutie with a decent body but way immature, twenty-one wishing she were fifteen, tearfully gushing about how much she missed high school. I took her home once after meeting her at The Wash-Out because I desired the experience of picking up a woman from a laundromat. The experience was a positive one: Bulldog Harvey Wu has had a loyal customer ever since, and Scott and I have remained friends for years.

Becca Depner says she first got a load of me at a Popcorn Theater meeting and couldn't tell if I was really tweaking or if I was simply in character. Later, she'd come to realize that like a poorly trained, third-rate method actor, I was doing a bit of both, bouncing off the walls, chewing my face, killing my body, and belting out surreal, violently dark monologues. This period of my life was the pinnacle of my drug absorption phase: the brawls, the night crawls, the withdrawals and shouts and screams so loud, my voice crumbled into a hoarse whisper, my eyes bloodshot and bugged out like the squeezed testicles of a white man. Anger and creativity and menace turned me into a metallic, dry-boned zombie. People who were there say my performances were outstanding. I don't remember a goddamn thing.

When I was a featured performer at The Popcorn Theater in the 1999 San Francisco Fringe Festival, Becca Depner, one of the directors, wrote in my program, "For most people, it'll take meeting Eli three times before you realize he's not totally crazy and means you no harm. For some, it'll take fewer occasions. For others, it'll take considerably more."

I met Ferdinand Noah after Becca Depner's Christmas special "Santa Loves Bad Girls." It was funny and every bit as blue and raunchy as the title would suggest. Becca and her all-female boy-band, Vagina-Calling Girls, sang Christmas songs and appeared in a few sketches. Dave Tribune and The Six Million Dollar Band, which only does covers of TV theme songs, played an entire set. I got up and told a story, a confession, really: painful, inartistic, and funny, and because it really had nothing to do with Christmas, I made the story work for the season by stating that if you owed somebody an apology, then perhaps saying you were sorry was the best thing you could do for them this time of year. Later, when I included this monologue in "The Experience Junkies," I knocked the Christmas façade down and simply told it as a shameful tale to end my show, and it was later considered the best part, better loved and remembered than any of the fictional, surreal, violent, dark monologues that preceded it.

Imagine me alone on a dark stage with a single spotlight.

"My name is Eli Trocchi. Legally, my name is Sir Elijah Trocchi. My birth name is Beau Zack. Shortly after moving to San Francisco from Tampa, I started doing lots of drugs, and a famous drug dealer, the biggest in Northern California, looked at me and said, 'Eli, Eli! You look like an Eli! From now on, your name is Eli!' In time, I was better known in San Francisco as Eli or Sick Guy Eli than I was as Beau Zack. I was also becoming addicted to speed.

"After being up for days, one time I came home to check my messages. I've always been a country music fan, so my outgoing message was me singing to the tune of Kenny Rogers' 'The Gambler,' with me impersonating Kenny badly:

> *You've got to know when to call them*
> *Know when to phone them*
> *Know when to leave a message*

248

Know when to hang up
You've got to leave your message
After the beep
There'll be time enough for leaving a message
When the beeping's done!"

Embarrassed laughter. In the darkness, I can see people shaking their heads. I've got a terrible singing voice and at no point do I smile or play anything for laughs, it's just straightforward, serious storytelling. I proceed to impersonate the young man who actually did leave this exact message on my answering machine so many years ago:

"'Oh, Beau, that was so lame! Ha ha! Wait till everybody at work finds out Beau Zack's a Kenny Rogers fan. What a dork! That's fucking hilarious! Oh, my God, that's all good! Dude, it's Billy! We're going to Lake Tahoe this weekend! Yahoo! Lake Tahoe! Hey, Beau, I'm calling to remind you about our weekend, and we've got to meet at Matt's house in the Sunset at 4 a.m. to pile into his Tahoe to go to Lake Tahoe! I can't wait! Yahoo! I'm so excited! Anyway, see you tomorrow! And hey, Beau, maybe you'll get lucky and we can find a Kenny Rogers cassette to put in the tape deck. Later.'

"Who the fuck was Billy and what the fuck was he talking about? There was nothing about my life that resembled that message. I didn't work with anybody named Billy. I don't know anybody in the Sunset. I've never been to Lake Tahoe. I don't ski. I don't snowboard. Then it hit me. There must be two Beau Zacks in San Francisco, one who works with guys named Billy and Matt and goes to Lake Tahoe, another who listens to country music, is addicted to speed, and is better known by his street name 'Sick Guy Eli.'

"Suddenly, I had an idea for a great movie. There's an average young man named Beau Zack who lives in a major city and enjoys an active social life. As fate would have it, this young man shares the same name as a speed fiend, a major freak and a bona fide sociopath with a twisted sense of humor. Because the sociopath is better known by his street names (Eli, Sick Guy Eli), this other Beau Zack, the bad Beau Zack, if you will, decides to go out and purposely destroy the good Beau Zack's name and reputation.

"This would've been the greatest film Alfred Hitchcock never made. I knew I lacked the self-discipline to write the script and lacked the means to make the film, but I could live the film. I could act it out in real life. I called it 'method screenwriting.'

"I used star 69 to trace and redial the call. Using a thick, nasally Southern California accent, I said, 'Hello, this is Beau Zack. This is Billy's co-worker. Is Billy there? . . . Hi, who are you? . . . His girlfriend? . . . And we met . . . at the Christmas party, right, right. Um, I remember thinking you had really nice tits. Maybe some time when your asshole boyfriend's not around I can come over and show you what a real man is made out of. Yeah, I want you to tell your boyfriend that I never really liked him none. He's a dick. But hey, I'm still going with him and Matt to Tahoe, just tell fucking Billy he's not allowed to touch any of my shit.'

"And that's how it all started. Every time a woman called for Beau Zack, I'd sexually harass her. If a man called, I'd threaten to beat his ass next time I saw him. Each time claiming to be the Beau Zack they were looking for. This happened so frequently that I couldn't tell you how many times I taunted his friends over the telephone.

"The two worst things I did to this guy are as follows:

"First: there came a time in my life when I had to rent *Every Which Way But Loose* and keep it for a month. Bear with me, I was working on some project and there came a reason where I needed to watch *Every Which Way But Loose* every day for thirty days. Just believe me. There was one Beau Zack listed in the phone book. That was me. So, I figured the good Beau Zack must've been one of the B. Zacks who came before me. I went over to my drug dealer's apartment on

Filbert and waited for him to pass out. I then took his telephone and called every last B. Zack until I got an answering machine that went (speaking like a Southern California boy) 'Hey, this is Beau. You know what to do and when to do it. Ciao.' When I heard his voice on his answering machine, I knew he was from Southern California. The fact that I got his voice right without even meeting him made me believe God wanted me to fuck with this poor guy. I memorized the number and the dude's address. I went to the Blockbuster on Bay Street and, deciding it was worth the risk, grabbed *Every Which Way But Loose*, and then I thought it'd be fun to have a redneck movie-watching night, so I also took copies of *Urban Cowboy* and *Smokey and the Bandit*. When I got to the cashier, I said, 'Hi, my name is Beau Zack and I don't have my card with me but I did just recently move and I know my address is in your system. My phone number is --- and my address is ---. Am I in there?'

"Cashier says, 'Ah, sure, Beau. You're in here. Do you have ID with you?'

"'But of course.' I kept all three movies for thirty days and sat at home and laughed, knowing that the other Beau Zack kept getting messages on his machine that said 'Uh, Mr. Zack, your copy of *Smokey and the Bandit* is past due. Would you please return it as soon as possible?'

"The second thing I did probably caused more harm.

"One day, I was lying in bed with Toni Rosas. God bless her, Toni was a wild, hot-blooded, possessive, angry Latina who loved me almost as much as she loved cocaine. She and I had been up for days and had just gotten done having sex. We're lying in bed and the phone rings. I let the answering machine pick it up. First you hear the Kenny Rogers thing, which was on my machine for years, then, in a sexy Marilyn Monroe voice, we hear, 'Happy Birthday to you, happy birthday to you, happy birthday dear Beau, happy birthday to you. I love you, Beau. I miss you. Call me, baby.'

251

"Toni knew my real name because she once had to appear in court with me for something totally unrelated, but while she knew my real name, she did not know when my birthday was. She sat up and said 'Who the fuck was that?'

"I stood up, buck naked. 'Baby, this girl and I used to date a long time ago, way before I met you, and you know how much I like to sweet-talk, so one time I said to her, 'Baby, every time we have sex, it is such a treat, it's like my birthday every day.' After I said that, Toni, every time this chick wanted to see me, or more specifically, wanted to fuck me, she'd sing the happy birthday song. Of course, it ain't my birthday, Toni-baby. And I told her to quit calling me, baby, because you're my girl now, but she doesn't know when to stop. I think she's a little obsessed with me. You know, like a stalker, no matter how often I tell her to stop calling me and leaving messages like that, she just keeps on doing it. Baby-Toni, perhaps you could call her yourself and convince her in your own persuasive way to quit calling me.'

"Toni gets up, equally naked, grabs the phone, dials star 69. 'Hey, bitch! Beau Zack is my man! Do you fucking understand me? Bitch, Beau Zack is my man, don't you be fucking calling him again! He don't fucking like you, so fuck off!' Toni slams the phone, pushes me back into bed, and proceeds to ride me for hours, but after that, I start to feel a little guilty.

"That night I'm at Alabama Tom's house. Alabama Tom was a local redneck drug dealer and musician who came from Mississippi. My girlfriend Toni, Alabama Tom and his girlfriend had left to go out and score. I hadn't slept in days and I was coming down off of speed after drinking and fucking all day. When you're coming down from speed, every heartache, heartbreak, depression, disappointment, betrayal, and defeat you've ever experienced in your life is magnified a thousand fold. Nothing is worse than coming down from speed. Nothing. So there I am, drunk, depressed, alone in a room with a telephone.

"By the time I heard the good Beau Zack's voice on the telephone, I began to sob, 'I'm so sorry, so sorry, so sorry, I'm so sorry, and oh, by the way, happy birthday. But I am so sorry, Beau. You see, I'm you, a really *bad* you, and I am sorry, so sorry.'

"On the other end of the phone, I heard 'Hey, asshole! It's three o'clock in the morning!'

"'Oops, my bad.' I quietly hung up the phone, stumbled all the way home, and slept for days. After that, whenever anybody called for Beau Zack, I'd give the caller Beau Zack's phone number. However, when Kristie Silvers, the president of my graduating class and now the president of the reunion committee, called me to verify I was the same Beau Zack she knew back in Florida, class of '90, I said, 'Oh, yeah, Kristie. You've got the right Beau Zack, but while I can't come to the ten-year reunion in August, I'd like it very much if you could put my name, number, and address in the alumni newsletter so people who want to contact me can. I'm moving later this week, so let me, dear Kristie, give you my new number and address.' And yes, I gave her the good Beau Zack's contact information.

"So, for years this poor guy has had to deal with my old Florida redneck friends calling him up and saying 'Hey, Beau Zack, why did you move to San Francisco for? Are you a faggot or something?' I know this happened because when I went to Florida recently, I ran into old friends who told me they had done just that. Sorry, man. Also, I came to find out that he worked at Virgin Records, because people would call me up wanting me to pick up shifts for them. I'd call back and say, 'Dude, you got fired . . . Yeah, you really should've gone to the meeting on Thursday.'

"For reasons too lengthy to describe here, I legally changed my name to Sir Elijah Beau Trocchi. After appearing in court, I went out that night to celebrate my new legal name, and, on a whim, I decided to give the other Beau Zack a call, figuring my name change would be wonderful news to him and all the other Beau Zacks in this world.

"So there I am on the telephone, high off my ass. 'Hey, Beau Zack, you are so cool! You've got such a wonderful sense of humor. Hey, I'm the guy that has been pranking you all these years! Good news! I've legally changed my name to Sir Elijah Trocchi, so unless you change your name to Sir Elijah Trocchi, I don't think we'll get confused for each other ever again! Hey, can I buy you a drink?'

"On the other end, I hear 'Dude' in pitch-perfect angry Southern Californian. 'I know who you are. You are a fucking freak. Don't ever call me again. Do you fucking understand me?' *Click*.

"It's hard to get happy after that one. Look, Beau Zack, the joke was always on me. While friends were inviting you to weekend trips in Lake Tahoe, I was a tweaker in San Francisco. When women were serenading you over the telephone, I was a tweaker in San Francisco. You will never sit through a job interview and be forced to explain why you legally changed your name from Beau Zack to fucking *Sir Elijah*.

"You know, Beau, my entire life, I've considered myself an experience junkie. Somewhere along the way, I mistook peace and stability for boredom and doggedly pursued experience, any and all kinds of experience, until experience began to pursue me. Now I have more experiences than I wish I had.

"I've been incarcerated several times, including in psych wards. I've got no felonies in my background, but there's been a drug overdose, a bankruptcy, suicide attempts, my nose has been broken several times, and I've destroyed every potential relationship I've ever had. And it is nobody's fault but my own. It was my decision to be this way. I would've been this way whether my family was fucked up or not. It has nothing to do with them or anyone else. However, if given the decision of which Beau Zack to be, you chose the right one, dude. Congratulations, you had the better life, and wherever you are, Mr. Zack, I am sorry.

"And for everyone else, thanks for coming and have a good night."

Nervous laughter, uncomfortable laughter, and disbelieving laughter still *count* as laughter, as far as I'm concerned. Performance art is an excuse for people without anything pleasant to say or do to get up onstage and do weird shit. I suppose I'm more of a storyteller, since I just *talked* about this confession, I didn't act it out, didn't even mime it, just told it as it happened, as truthfully and thoroughly as possible. People said my story was compelling, fascinating, and everyone wanted to know if it was true. It was.

After my monologue toward the end of Becca's Christmas show, Noah, as Titty Titty Gangbang, came onstage and told the story of baby Jesus as only an outrageous, trash-talking, sleazy drag queen slut could, and she genuinely brought the house down. We shook hands after the show.

That's how I thought we'd met. Ferdinand Noah tells it another way:

He went to Bazooka one night to watch Becca rehearse and to discuss what exactly was expected from Titty Titty this particular performance. While he was there, he tells me that I walked into the theater from the lobby, tense and uptight, and grabbed a book from the ground and left, muttering to myself the whole time. Noah was there for two hours and watched me come and go, never once saw me crack a smile. My face appeared alternately (his words) "unfriendly and deeply introspective."

As Noah was leaving, he saw me outside yelling at somebody on my cell phone. Walking with Dave Tribune, Noah asked, "Who is that intense bald guy?" Dave, who knew me from Popcorn Theater and was a member of Becca and Lance's old comedy troupe, said to Ferdinand, "Oh, that's just Eli. Don't worry about him. Just leave him be." Noah assumed I was some theater hanger-on pal of Lance LittleJohn, who does have sycophants, by the way.

When Ferdinand Noah finally saw me perform that first time, he was shocked, having no idea that I was a writer or performer. I never attended any rehearsals and nobody mentioned to him that I was in the show. When my one-man show came around in the spring, he came to every performance. I love Ferdinand for that. How could I not?

I pay for my ticket and I'm standing inside the Chronicle Books bookstand, too small to be called a bookstore. The Bay Area publisher specializes in big, garish, colorful books that profile useless things like retro bedrooms, bad haircuts, Airstream trailers, and general kitsch. Though I must admit, a photo book of outlaw bikers from the 1950s and '60s catches my eye. I'm browsing through it when somebody taps me on the shoulder. I turn around and see Ferdinand, who gives me a big hug and says "Hey, E."

"Hey, Titty Titty!" We go to a bench and sit down. The monstrosity is fairly crowded. "Well, Miss Gangbang, tell me what's up. How was your trip?"

"Events and adventures galore! Got material for Mr. Noah as well as Madame Gangbang." Ferdinand looks good. He got some sun while down south, and like most gender illusionists when not performing, Miss Gangbang stopped shaving and has about two weeks' worth of growth on his face. His hair drapes to his shoulders, jet-black and parted down the middle. His dark, almond-shaped eyes smile often, jovial and well-rested, not the sort of eyes I had been seeing around the city lately.

Noah talks about his beloved New Orleans. He talks about Dorothy Allison. He also talks about couch-surfing at the various apartments of childhood friends, many of whom grew up to be gay just like dear ole Ferdinand Noah. When he mentions one pal who has a one bedroom apartment in the French Quarter for 350 dollars a month, I encourage Noah to move down there.

"No, not interested," he says. "I've made the decision to make San Francisco my home."

"Aren't you tired of the City? God knows I am. How many times were you panhandled today? Or how about on the way over here?" Noah winces and nods his head. "Fuck that. I'm ready to leave."

"Just because of panhandlers?"

"There are other reasons I'd like to leave besides the fucking aggressive panhandlers. You know, Ferdinand, living in San Francisco is like going to a great big luxury apartment a day after a great big party took place, one that'll have people gushing for years, for decades to come. The party was so damn decadent and wild that the apartment is in shambles, and drugs and body fluids are stuck to the carpet and the curtains. You missed the party by one day; however, since you are here now, you must clean the mess and pay for the damages."

Ferdinand laughs. "Seriously, though, Eli, if you left San Francisco, where would you go?"

"I don't know. I don't know, really. I'm thinking a medium-sized city, or even a small town with a thriving arts scene."

"You may want to check out Athens, Georgia."

"Yeah?"

Then Ferdinand goes on to describe how much he dug Athens, where he stopped on his way to Savannah, which he also loved. He also had a blast in Atlanta, and though he considered going to Florida, instead he headed to Austin, Texas, where he momentarily fell in love with and deflowered a young, newly gay theater major who will be coming up to Northern California to visit next spring. My eyes must've glazed over when he began to describe his weekend in Taos, New Mexico, because the shrewd Ferdinand, a natural-born politician, brings the conversation back to me.

"Tell me, Eli. What happened while I was gone?" I stare back at him. Did he already forget our phone conversation from this morning? He chuckles. "Oh, yeah. That douchebag at Burberry, what a douchebag! I've heard about some major douchebags before, but that guy, whoa. He's gay, right? If you ever see him at one of my drag shows, point him out and I'll pour a beer over his head and call him a 'filthy cunt.' You don't want to work for that guy anyway. Fuck him. And then your girlfriend telling you she needs to go on hold during the same week, ouch." Noah slaps his knee and laughs again, but is it with me or at me? I can't tell. Skeptical, Noah looks at me and asks, "Did her doing that really bother you that much?"

"Oh, my God, yes. It has caused me so much pain this week. You have no idea." Even to me, it sounds like a statement made in a none-too-convincing actor's voice. Are my emotions already spent?

"Really? You don't seem so upset. Besides, you strike me as the kind of person who falls in love with falling in love."

He doesn't know me well enough to make such a comment.

"That's not true, Noah. It's not like I say 'I love you' to every chick I bang. Not even close. And it's not even like I've said 'I love you' to every girl who said she loved me."

"Okay, then. Maybe I was wrong, but we had lunch at the Argentinean restaurant back in April, a day after "The Experience Junkies" was over, and you said to me emphatically that you wanted a girlfriend. We ran into each other in June, and you had a girlfriend. Just like that, Eli."

"What's your point?"

"Look, it's sad, definitely sad. She wasn't considering your feelings. She was obviously not ready for a relationship. But she's also very young, Eli. And you're a man of the world. You've done so many things with your life. You've traveled . . ."

"She's well-traveled, spent an entire summer in Europe."

258

"So what, you've been to so many places. You've lived in so many places, done so many things. What I'm saying is that you've done so much with your life. Hell, you've done too much with your life." He smiles, meaning it to be funny, but it stings me. I bite my tongue.

"She's young, Eli. And you are an intense guy. You're a lot for anybody to take, especially a youngster like her." Then Noah does a Titty Titty half-smirk and lowers her eyelids. "Besides, E., you didn't seem to be missing Miss Ely too much when we met in front of the Power Exchange. Remember, Eli? Huh?" In Titty Titty's voice, tobacco- and whiskey-stained and about as pleasantly feminine as an elderly whore collecting SSI, Titty pesters, "Huh, sweetie? Ya remembah da night when we met in front ah Da Powah Exchange? Huh, ya made me such a happy woman, let me tell ya, Elijah."

In mid-July, a day after Jennifer Ely left for Yosemite and two nights before Ferdinand Noah was to fly out to the Southeast, I went out drinking with some co-workers from CPK. It was a sports bar on O'Farrell, well lit with multiple television screens—not my cup of tea, but that's where my co-workers wanted to go. There I saw this attractive dirty blonde in a white sweatshirt, denim short shorts, and black flip-flops. She had blue eyes, a dimpled chin, and nut-brown skin tanned by the sun. Her feet were petite and cute with clean, neat toenails. My co-workers no longer existed to me, and I couldn't even tell you who was there. Focused entirely on the dirty blonde, keeping my eyes soft and concentrated, I introduced myself to her. Seated at a table with four friends, she told me her name was . . . told me her name was . . . her name . . . I simply don't recall. (Yes, I can memorize entire monologues and love letters and journal entries, but this girl's name totally escapes me.) All five were from Iowa, and they were traveling the country selling magazine subscriptions to people on the street. I seem to recall being approached by such eager young salespeople in the various cities I've called home.

The dirty blonde was twenty-one and had a prematurely raspy, throaty voice and a deep, mannish laugh. The doors to the bar were wide open and the air was chilly, causing her nipples to poke from underneath her sweatshirt like a pair of perfect no. 2 pencil erasers. Once, when I made her and her crew laugh, I put my hand on her back and discovered she wore no bra. When I made that discovery, the dirty blonde gave me bedroom eyes, sizing me up. Then she smiled.

Outside after last call, three of her friends, less attractive, more blonde, less tan, opted to go back to their hostel and sleep. The dirty blonde, now standing intimately close so I could smell the alcohol on her breath, was telling me that besides helping her cohorts consume three pitchers of Bud, she had done a tequila shot before I'd gotten there.

"Hm," I remember thinking, "my two beers and a double vodka cranberry are just starting to earn me a quality buzz. The night is still young. Let's do something." I told her that I knew of an after-hours club that closed at 5 a.m. Her eyes expanded and she tugged at my arm.

"I wanna go! I wanna go!" Then she turned around to her remaining friend, a guy who was leaning against the wall of the bar with a tiny smile on his face, and called him over. She introduced us. Don't ask me his name either. The boy/man could've been her brother, but wasn't (I asked). Blue-eyed, head gripped by a dirty-blonde Julius Caesar haircut, muscular, and lean, he was corn-fed-Midwestern-farm-boy handsome. The dirty-blonde female told the dirty-blonde male that I knew a club around here that was open until 5 a.m. She then told me that they had been dying to find some local who'd take them to the clubs and bars that locals go to, not dumb tourists.

"Hey," she said to the guy, "you're going to come with us, aren't you?" She gave him a pleading look. She definitely dug me and wanted to party, but she wanted her friend to tag along to make her feel safer, and who could blame her?

"Absolutely! I want you to come, too. The more the merrier," I said. "And believe you me, you'll hook up tonight, good-looking dude like you, totally. You'll meet some hottie to party with for sure." I usually don't speak so Californian, but I felt compelled to do so. He smiled broadly and looked goofy. His choppers could almost have qualified as buckteeth.

"Absolutely, dude!" I continued to shout. "Then we're off! To the after-hours club!"

What I neglected to tell them was that the club was a sex club, the most notorious in San Francisco, and the clientele there was mostly going to be men, paunchy, colorless men clad in only towels, publicly pulling their pricks for everybody to see.

As we stepped into the cab, she smiled the sweetest smile yet, exposing full lips and perfectly straight white teeth. "Can we go dressed like this?"

"Believe me," I said, "the way you two are *dressed* is not going to be a problem."

I'm feeling tears behind my eyes, somewhere inside my skull. They're not falling out of my face and nobody can see them, but they're there. Self-pity is an ugly thing, and I regret watching myself fall into it. However, to dismiss this as self-pity invalidates my emotions. Disappointment is the word. Self-disappointment is the thing.

Imagine, just imagine, that every time we reminisced about getting joyously fucked up and getting laid, that instead of simply barreling through relived moments made more ecstatic by the verve of rose-colored memory, that first we were forced to recall the immediate day afterwards. Think about the physical pain, the depression, the shame, and the eroding shores of your self-respect—and now tell us your story (laugh, laugh) about the time (funny, funny) you got shit-faced (hilarious) and then bedded a virtual stranger (tell us, tell us) . . .

ELI, ELY

* * *

Miss Gangbang's Lower Haight apartment was on Pierce, just down the street from Jennifer's place. I found myself creeping there past 10:30 a.m., almost eleven, tired, body sore, soul and stomach entirely empty, leaving Noah's place. When we had arrived there that morning, Titty Titty was in full drag costume and character, wearing smeared makeup and a trashed, nearly ripped-to-shreds party dress. *Her* wig had fallen onto the slimy, sticky floor when *he* was fucking and refused to pick it up afterwards, and now *his* matted hair stuck up in several different directions, molded by sweat and God knows what else. The queen threw a comforter, a blanket, and two small throw pillows on the ground. He then grabbed the Iowa boy by his belt buckle and said "Okay, Woody!"

Miss Gangbang had nicknamed the Iowan magazine seller "Woody Boyd" due to his resemblance to Woody Harrelson circa his early sitcom days—that and the enormous ear of corn pressed against his pants, apparent to all the gays, sluts, perverts, and drag queens that congregate at the Power Exchange.

"You're coming with me, Mr. Boyd."

They went into his bedroom, and for a little while I heard Roxy Music, bedsprings, and collective male moaning, and then I heard nothing else and assumed they were sound asleep and not dead. The Iowa woman spread out the comforter, grabbed a pillow, and curled into the fetal position under the blanket. Within minutes, her breathing had slowed, and she emanated a low, continuous growl, snoring like an old man whose sinuses need to be drained. Evidently a sleep farter, at regular intervals, the sound of gravel rolling down a wet dirt road came from inside her body, the very same one I had coveted all night. I pulled the blanket away to look at her.

Alcoholic English actor Richard Harris once said, "I've never gone to bed with an ugly woman, but I've woken up next to a few."

This wasn't the case. She was still good-looking, but she was different now, and not just because of the disgusting noises involuntarily produced by her body. The soles of her feet were muddy-black from her flip-flops. Her body remained tanned and youthfully firm, but her clothes needed to be thrown away. Her once-pristine white sweatshirt was now dingy, acned with stains whose origins I didn't want to think about. The natural rugged beauty wore no makeup, but her dirty blonde hair was now oily and sticking to her face. Worst of all, she stank something fierce, like a sickening conglomeration of sweat, bad feet, old sex, lube, farts, alcohol, bad breath, and tobacco. She smoked outside the sports bar, smoked in the cab, and periodically at the Power Exchange she went outside for a cigarette break. There I'd stand with her to provide company and protection, and she'd complain about how disgusting she thought the Power Exchange was (and it is) and what an asshole I was for taking her there (and I am) and "Hey, did you see that skinny-ass scumbag staring at me and jerking off in the hallway?" (I did). But after she was done venting, the dirty blonde always wanted to go back inside.

Despite her great consumption of tobacco (she destroyed an entire pack before my eyes), her nasty odor didn't bother me until we got to Titty Titty's apartment. My nose, oft-broken and out-of-joint, lacks even a halfway decent sense of smell. If I compliment a woman's perfume, it means she's got too much on. I don't notice smells until they are overpowering for everyone else. She *was* different in a way one couldn't observe through sight or smell. It's not like she was ever a prim, square goody-two-shoes, publicly humiliated and freaked out by a Manson-family-like hippie orgy (how many times have we seen that scenario in dumb Psychedelic movies from the 1960s?). But she was different now.

Minutes into the Power Exchange, the young woman with the nipples noticeable underneath her thick sweatshirt knew exactly what type of "after-hours" club I had tricked her into, and eventually, as I knew she would, the dirty blonde did exactly as the Romans do, but in gaining a new experience, unsought and unwholesome, she lost something, something of herself, the same something of myself I've been losing for years.

Later, I would creep hurriedly, painfully along Haight towards Market Street. Apparently, you can't ever look too despondent or too disheveled to keep aggressive street sleepers from standing in front of your feet and asking you to spare a dollar, never explaining to you why you ought to give *him* a buck and not the next asshole standing five feet away. Each person who asked me for a handout right then was a fucking asshole, and I wanted to beat up every single one of them, and if I kept thinking that, I wouldn't think about me, I wouldn't think about the dirty blonde, I wouldn't think about Jennifer Ely, and I wouldn't think about that previous night.

The cover at the Power Exchange is creative and varied and probably makes sense to somebody. Seventy-five to eighty dollars for single straight men, fifty if he strips buck naked and only wears a towel (skimpy, white, terrycloth, heavily bleached hand towels provided by the PE staff), twenty bucks for straight couples, and I don't know about gay male couples or single gay men, but when you walk in, they do ask you at the front desk if you're going to go to the straight side or the gay. Single women, lesbians, and transvestites always get in for free.

I remember being delighted that the two were amused and entertained by Titty Titty rather than shocked or embarrassed. Perhaps it's what they expected to find in San Francisco. We went in, the four of us acting like a pair of couples on a double date. However, I must admit, Titty Titty, happily bumping into me as we were waiting in line, shocked me by the way he gently took the goofy, handsome young man's hand and took him upstairs to the gay area. The boy went with the drag queen willingly, with a perfectly eager smile on his face, not even saying good-bye to us. The dirty blonde was very surprised, telling me the twenty-one-year-old hayseed had just recently lost his cherry a few weeks earlier when they were traveling through Sacramento.

"He's not gay," she kept telling me. "I know he's not gay." But Ferdinand *does* make an attractive woman, I guess, as long as he's not talking in Miss Gangbang's purposely gross spent-barmaid voice. Perhaps the hayseed was just experimenting, but then again, to go from easy Sacramento chick to San Francisco performance artist drag queen on your second time at bat is pretty fucking extreme.

The blonde had nothing going on with Woody. I asked a second and third time, but she was concerned because of his naiveté and because she was being separated from the one person she knew when she arrived in this new and very strange place. However, to her credit, the dirty blonde didn't judge her young friend, she just shrugged her shoulders and laughed, figuring ole Woody Boyd was simply partaking in the other side of the buffet table for kicks, and why the fuck not? Because we were a couple, a fine-looking one at that, we were not expected to disrobe into the bleached hand towels. At least, that's what they told us, but then again, the guys behind the counter did say "If you'd like to get naked, you certainly can."

Obviously, they were hoping that we would.

It's like falling asleep on your couch half inebriated and dog-tired while watching an old movie on the late, late show and waking up the next day hung over and stiff-necked and sick to your stomach, spending the most peaceful moments in the painful sunshine of the following day trying to piece together the images of the film you watched the night before; this is how I remember the dirty blonde.

She held onto my arm. She held tightly to my hand and encircled my bicep with the other hand, partly due to genuine attraction (she complimented my arms several times that night) and partly for security. We walked like that at ground level and watched guys stare at us (at her, really). The men wearing nothing but bleached hand towels visibly reached underneath their loincloths and pleasured themselves with no shame whatsoever as the dirty blonde and I walked by. I do recall her using the unisex restrooms at the Power Exchange while I waited for her. While there, a tall Asian woman gave me a tight hug and put her tongue in my ear. She'd left by the time the dirty blonde came out. We went downstairs and saw the various public bondage displays, where women's leather corsets squeezed their chunky, pockmarked butts into black, thigh-high leather boots. Skinny men in leather briefs and nipple clamps were being whipped into pink skid marks, and there were various open rooms with couples or a handful of exhibitionist females rubbing each other while about a dozen aesthetically displeasing men stood around rubbing themselves underneath their hand towels.

She stared at everything, saying nothing.

By far the hottest thing there, the blonde was eyeballed by everybody, but nobody groped her, nobody spoke to her as she held onto me tighter and tighter and tighter, and I looked hard at everybody who looked at her. Her comfort level, after a cigarette or two, was high enough that she and I made out in a public room made to look like a medieval king's banquet room, complete with royal decorations on the wall and a large wooden table and a throne. Large and theatrical, it was as if props had been stolen from a road company's production of *Camelot*. After making out for a little while, with her French kissing me nicely, passionately, my hands underneath her sweatshirt feeling her firm, plentiful breasts, a crowd had gathered around us with a few assholes cheering and then she stopped. She pushed my hands from underneath her sweatshirt and told me in an irritated voice that she wanted to leave. As we got up from the throne where she was sitting on my lap, the crowd cleared a path for us. The dirty blonde held onto my hand as tight as ever and proceeded to lift her white sweatshirt with the other hand and suspend it by biting the sweatshirt's bottom end, fully exposing her tits while simultaneously flipping the bird to the crowd, telling the perverts and the voyeurs through clenched teeth to go fuck themselves. When a clique of females, most likely voyeuristic bisexuals, maybe lipstick lesbians, also whistled at her, the dirty blonde told them to fuck off, too, and the girls were just as surprised as I was.

Outside by the emergency exit door, smoking yet another cigarette, she proceeded to bitch me out, but not with a great deal of genuine anger. She never raised her voice, and, knowing that it isn't smart to ever interrupt a woman while she's venting, I kept my mouth shut. When a young, fully clothed, conventionally good-looking frat-boy type came outside and tried to strike up a conversation, we remained scowl-faced and unfriendly.

Still, like I said before, despite my offering to take her to the Pinecrest Diner in the Tenderloin and to send a message for Titty Titty and Woody Boyd to meet us there, the dirty blonde wanted to go back inside. After every cigarette, she always wanted to go back inside.

Inside an area that is supposed to be the designated lobby area, there was a cheap forty-dollar CD player playing Eminem and a pool table where some dyke-looking black women were shooting some stick. There were three soda vending machines and one for junk food. Despite the preponderance of naked people draped in a smidgen of terry cloth, the air conditioner was blowing hard, making the room ice cold. The air was having its usual effect on the dirty blonde's breasts cupped in my warm hands. She was sitting on my lap again in a chair that appeared to be part of a patio set. My arms were inside her shirt, my left hand playing down her front, gently stroking her nipples, and my other arm around her back, massaging the muscles along her spine. She was leaning into me, feeling my pectoral muscles, occasionally letting one of her hands fall comfortably atop the bulge in my pants.

Again, she told me how disgusting the place was and how it sucked and what an asshole I was for taking her there and what could her friend and Titty Titty be doing upstairs in the gay area and why were heterosexual couples restricted from going up there anyway, wasn't that "reverse discrimination"? But she said it all in an amused voice, perhaps a wee bit annoyed rather than genuinely upset. In the same tone, the dirty blonde told me a tale that should've been more shocking than it was.

"One time, I was hitchhiking in Iowa, and this businessman picked me up and—"

"What? You were hitchhiking?"

She nodded. "And this guy, this businessman, too old to be a yuppie, picks me up, and as we're driving, he asks if it'd be okay if he could jerk off in front of me."

"What? You were hitchhiking? When was this?"

"Just about a year ago." Then she laughed, communicating to me that she thought it was pathetic and stupid, not the least bit pleasurable or even traumatic.

"So, did you watch him?"

"Yeah."

"He didn't try to force you to touch him? He didn't try to touch you?"

"No."

I'm pretty sure she wasn't lying. She shrugged, our hands still on each other.

"How old was he?

"Late thirties, early forties," she said. I guess that would be old to her.

"Was he good-looking?"

"He wasn't hideous, but he wasn't cute either."

"Was he big?"

"No." Then she let both hands fall onto my cock. "Not especially big. Not like yours."

Her eyes were becoming soft and sexy again, like when she was laughing at everything I said in the sports bar earlier that night.

"Just promise me you'll never hitchhike again."

She rolled her eyes. Fucking change the subject, Eli! Fucking change the subject!

"I know you've never had sex in a place like this, but have you ever had sex in public before? Ever been an exhibitionist?"

She squeezed my cock with one hand while the other crept up and under my shirt. Her hand stroked each of my pecs, back and forth, over and over again. The dirty blonde proceeded to rub my erect nipples with each of her fingertips. The skin around my entire body tingled and I began to visualize her mounting me right then and there, and if we're to believe in ESP, psychic energy, or even mental magnetism, then in whose head did this image first materialize? I believed I was reading her thoughts, and I knew she wanted to fuck me.

"Well, who hasn't fucked outdoors before? In parks, fields, cars. I've never fucked on the beach before, but then again, I'm from Iowa." Smiling, she said, "I'm in California now, though, so who knows? Maybe if you took me to the beach instead of this dump, we'd be having sex right now." A pure naughty-girl laugh. "I've made out with guys and girls at nightclubs and parties and such but never had sex with anybody in front of others." She smiled broadly, in complete control. "I have been known to flash my tits at people in various places: from moving cars, in nightclubs, in bars, at parties. People seem to like my tits, you think?"

I nod my head slowly.

"I know you've been here before, Eli. The door guy and the bouncers seemed to know you. You knew people waiting in line, one of whom is a drag queen named Titty Titty Gangbang who's probably upstairs molesting my friend right now as we speak." Titty Titty was probably doing a lot more than that. "And you, you get off on fucking girls in public with everybody watching you and your big cock, don't you? You're a pervert and an exhibitionist to boot, aren't you? Aren't you, pervert?"

I couldn't speak, and believe it or not, I felt a little too embarrassed to admit what she said was true, so I didn't even nod. The expression on my face disappeared. My skin froze as my body trembled and my erect cock vibrated. Mentally, physically, she was dominating me, squeezing my organ, squeezing my nipples harder than was comfortable, talking to me in a low, angry voice. "Is this what you do? Find an innocent girl like me and take her here? Is that what you see me as, some innocent girl?"

Bold, confident, adventurous, confrontational, her face was three inches from mine. Her arrogant eyes and mouth challenged me. "Well, do you, Eli? Do you see me as being an innocent?"

Very slowly and without much movement at all, I shook my head. Keeping her hands where they were, she let go of my cock and nipples (thankfully, for I was doing all I could to keep from screaming), and then she narrowed her eyes and searched my face, as if trying to gauge whether she ought to be offended.

"Hey, baby," I said, my tone nervous and low, "your voice is older than you are, you're only twenty-one, but your voice is rich with character. It's raspy, throaty, and sexy as hell, experienced. It conveys so much, so much, baby. Almost more than I can handle. Like I said, your voice is older than you are. And you've earned it. You've earned your voice, baby."

Her face lit up. Enthusiastic, roguish, and horny, she dug what I said and attacked me, tongue down my throat, mouth wide open encompassing mine, lifting my shirt to my neck with her sweatshirt to hers and then pressing her naked chest to mine.

Lovers are indeed teachers. Thank you, Aubrey. Aubrey, dear Aubrey, the tall, svelte strawberry blonde who will always be the first girl I ever bedded in California. Six months into San Francisco, in my old room on Greenwich Street, the very one described in my letter to Jana, I was inside Aubrey, doggy-style, with her demanding, fucking demanding, that I pull her hair but not pull it as I was doing, yanking at her ponytail or lifting her hair to watch her fellate me. "No." She was telling me to lay my hand right at her scalp and then to pull her hair in a fist right at her roots. In between the "Fuck me" and "Fuck me harder," she was telling me to "fucking pull her hair" and then releasing a painfully pleasurable scream, all the while, me inside her, my balls slapping the top of her pussy and me pulling her hair until her face became elongated and she pushed her mouth and jaw forward and wide open like an animal, emanating a deafening, agonizing, ecstatic scream. Aubrey climaxed multiple times, shaking, vibrating, wiggling her ass, eventually pushing herself off me and lying on her stomach, twitching, holding onto the corners of my mattress on the floor (sans box springs) and making a breathy, almost laughing, almost crying noise that turned me on like a long, slow lick along the underside of my erect penis. Peeling off my condom, I flexed and pulled my muscle until I ejaculated along her crack. Is there any woman who doesn't love that move? Then, with my naked hand, I proceeded to spank her, letting my own fluid stick to my palm and to her butt cheeks in one long, filmy string. Again and again I hit her, harder. The whole time, Aubrey was filling my apartment with her enormous sound, and to myself I made the mental note, "Women in

San Francisco are kinky as fuck, and women really love it when you pull their hair."

The dirty blonde was losing herself, with her naked chest pressed against mine, softly moaning, softly screaming, with her tongue in my mouth, the humidity between her legs easily surrounding my pelvis, and me pulling her hair as dear Aubrey taught me, when suddenly, I kid you not, I felt somebody tapping my shoulder as if trying to hammer a nail with the tip of his index finger and yelling above the music and above the sounds of the dirty blonde and me.

"Excuse me. Excuse me. Excuse me!" We stopped immediately. The dirty blonde clung tightly to my chest and looked away, more frightened than embarrassed. The Power Exchange was dark but well lit enough with blue and white lights that I could see the guy who had just interrupted us. He was a taut, tall fucker wearing a large white towel wrapped around his waist. Did he bring it with him? He was ugly, with a peach fuzz covered face and shit-breath that hit my eyes like vinegar when he leaned in to say, "I just wanted you to know that there's a whole row of guys over there sitting across from you two here watching and jerking off. That's all. I just wanted to let you two know." Then his armpit-like face smiled, as if I'd be grateful for what he just did. The dirty blonde pulled her sweatshirt down, covering her breasts. She closed her eyes and put her head on my shoulder farthest away from Armpit-Face. She was definitely embarrassed now and getting upset—talk about a buzz kill.

"Dude!" I yelled. Armpit-Face lost his smile and stood rigid and straight like a marine called to attention. "Get the fuck away from us, you fucking asshole!" The dirty blonde got off me, pulling my hand, telling me she wanted to leave. I stood up and glared at the scared-looking prick, who was probably thinking I was going to hit him. Did he honestly think I'd appreciate what he did to us? The jerk-offs, four or five guys who sat at a respectful distance about eight feet away, started to cover their peckers with their towels and proceeded to bitch: "Oh, come on! Please, don't go!"

She was mad and felt stupid and self-conscious, and the thing that really sucked is that she was about to have sex right there in the Power Exchange lobby, in full view of the whacking audience, until that armpit-face destroyed our mood. I recognize a passive-aggressive move when I see one. Public masturbation and sex is the norm at the Power Exchange. In acting as if he cared about us being watched, he purposely interrupted my getting laid and got to see a partially nude babe up-close. Despite the fearful surprise Armpit-Face displayed after I yelled at him, the fucker knew exactly what he was doing.

I escorted the dirty blonde downstairs to a room I knew, where the entrance would be blocked off and "Nobody would be able to sneak up on us like that again, baby." She held my hand the tightest she'd held it thus far, and said nothing. We went into a room away from the bondage displays and performers. It was dark, midnight blue, and illuminated by several screens playing the same hardcore heterosexual porn featuring a wiry blonde with enormous tits and some buff Ken doll packing a schlong so big you didn't know one like that existed in the color white. The room, probably a wee bit too intimidating for the masturbators, was, thankfully, empty. I clicked the chain at the entrance and went to a bed covered with pleather material. Instinctively, we took off our shirts and laid them on the bed, and she reclined atop both mine and hers with her arms extended out towards me. I lay on her, our naked chests against one another; we were kissing, biting, licking each other's neck and lips, when she asked me, "How did you manage to seduce me in a place like this?"

I got off the bed and stood by the foot of the mattress. My body glowed in the blue lighting, and the humping and screaming sounds from the porn all around us drowned out the catcalls and the cheers from the perverts standing by the entrance to the room craning their necks, trying to get a better look at the dirty blonde and me. I kicked off my shoes and dropped my pants and pulled off my boxer briefs and *boing*! I heard what sounded like women's voices cheering. I am an exhibitionist, albeit a guilty and shameful one, but an exhibitionist nonetheless, and hearing one or two ladies cheer at the sight of me naked and erect turned me on immeasurably. I could feel the dirty blonde's naked humidity from where I stood. When did she kick off her shorts and panties? I looked downward and saw her shorts and flip-flops by my ankles. Wow. She was a no panties, no bra type of girl. Nice.

I picked up a free condom from a large, empty fishbowl by the bed. I ripped open the package and slowly unrolled the condom along my shaft onto the base above my balls. Still, I heard people catcalling, cheering among the screaming and huffing and puffing from the porn screens, the same screens that caused the dirty blonde's body to shine in various ever-moving colors. I climbed on and entered her, hard and powerful, and she told me to slow down and pulled my body against hers.

"I'm doing this because I want to, Eli. Just don't be so hard and don't talk to me dirty. Please, please don't do that. I hate it when guys do that." Then she smiled and closed her eyes, her face serene with rows of lights and shadows and sweat. I remained inside her in short, rhythmic, gentle thrusts. "Eli, if you wanted to fuck me, you did not have to take me here. We could've gone someplace else." She opened her eyes and said, as if removed from the scene, "You jerk off too much, don't you? That's why it takes you so long to cum. That or you take a lot of antidepressants or something . . . That's okay, Eli. You can go all night." Pulling my shoulders into her body, she whispered something about how it felt so good that she had to laugh, and that the laughter was a good thing. Then she shook, alternately laughing and making rhythmic, heavy breathing sounds, when suddenly she grabbed my face with both hands and said, "Look at me when you cum."

My spine began to curve upward, but she held my face with both hands tightly.

"Don't leave me! Don't look away! Don't close your eyes! Let me look at them! Let me see them!" I shot an extraordinarily heavy load inside my condom as my pelvic bones pushed farther between her legs and my back tried to arch, but with her gripping my face, my arms, and my back, I could only flex and shiver. I sighed, a long, hard sigh, and was back on top of her, our sticky, sweating bodies fusing together like amphibians. Still inside, slowly I pulled myself out. She proceeded to laugh softly.

The perverts, the voyeurs, the dick-pullers whooped and hollered; the dirty blonde's face went from pleasured relief to pure disgust. Often, girls here will smile and wave after events like public orgasm, but sadly, not the dirty blonde. I got up, pulled off the soiled latex, and we wiped our sweaty bodies dry with our clothes. We got dressed, she grabbed my hand, and we left, the crowd giving us space and several people telling us it was "the best show of the night," which wasn't saying much. Of course, every time somebody walked up to tell us how enjoyable our "show" was, the dirty blonde gripped my hand tighter and seemed to become more and more withdrawn. She kept her head down as I escorted her to the emergency exit door, and all the while I glared at everybody, hoping to intimidate would-be gropers or anyone who wanted to speak to us. Outside, we said nothing and just stood next to one another closely as she stared ahead, smoking her last cigarette. It was a welcome break from the quiet tension when an exuberant and energetic Titty Titty burst through the doors behind us with the much-shagged Woody, saying, "There you two are. We went downstairs looking for you but heard you two left after putting on quite a performance. Yum. Yum. Well, come on now you naughty little sluts! Time to hail a cab and come back to Momma's house!"

A few days later, I received an email from Ferdinand, already dancing, writing, and partying on Southern soil, congratulating me for scoring with Blondie and thanking me for introducing him to Woody, "the sweet, young, not-so-straight straight boy from Iowa!"

It's hard to defeat your demons when your friends are celebrating theirs.

Once, while reading Nietzsche, I stumbled across the phrase "a swamp-soil of self-contempt."

Ferdinand is laughing quietly, smiling to himself, surely encapsulated in his own flashback, sleazy and uninhibited, reminiscing about banging Woody Boyd and being grateful for the guiltless debauchery he can parlay while existing in drag, costumed into another persona, another gender, another human being. Me, I only shudder, aware of the brackish water that turns to sludge inside me, creating worthless land that even the best developers can't build upon.

Disgust passes through me like swallowed phlegm. Again, for the second time in only minutes with Ferdinand, I bite my tongue and try not to show the honest emotion I'm feeling.

Whereas previously the drag queen remained oblivious to my pain, this time, as my teeth continue to press my tongue, my lips stay shut, and my eyes pierce the floor, I become aware of Ferdinand turning his head towards me and saying "Hey, Eli. What's up?"

I'm still looking at the floor, not saying anything for a few seconds, and then: "Noah, I'm not happy with myself."

"Ah, Eli, why are you beating yourself up? Because you cheated on your girlfriend with that slut you brought to the Power Exchange?"

His last question hurts me.

Quietly, I say, "She wasn't really a slut, Noah."

"She was after you were through with her."

I never look up but can hear Noah laughing above my head. Only a few days ago, I would've glared at him, but playing the intimidating badass role has become so tiresome. Instead, I turn my head to look at Ferdinand, increase my worry lines by raising the front tips of my eyebrows, and say, slowly and deliberately, "You know, Ferdinand, it is a pleasure to know the faggot who is going to single-handedly dispel that whole 'sensitive homosexual male' stereotype."

In utter seriousness, with his index finger raised, Noah shakes his head and states, "Watch the 'faggot' stuff, skinhead. I know some queers in this town don't care, but I do. I don't like it. So don't use that word around me, okay? You just remember that I'm a homosexual from Louisiana who was raised by a military man, so it's going to take a lot more to intimidate me than muscles and a shaved head. And besides,"—suddenly morphing into Titty Titty Gangbang—"on the subject of stereotypes: I hate Judy Garland, I hate Liza Minnelli, and Streisand can go kiss my ass. Hey, Babs, is it America's fault that your mother never told you that you were beautiful? Well, that's because you're not, Big-Nose! You're fucking ugly! And your singing is overrated, too."

My eyes return to the floor, but I'm smiling. Ferdinand Noah is cool, and my favorite people are those who are assertive and opinionated. Bravo for putting Streisand and me back in our places. Ouch.

Ferdinand says, "Oh, come on, Eli, lighten up. You're not all fucked up about the Ely girl, are you? What's really bothering you? Is it losing that job? What is it? It can't be that girl."

He's right.

"Sometimes, Noah, when the weather's nice, especially lately, I'll go to Union Square just to chill. You know, write in my journal, people watch, that sort of thing. So there's this guy, this funny old black guy who works security there. You've seen them. They wear khaki pants and red-and-gold shirts that say 'Union Square' on the back."

"Yeah, I've seen them."

"Anyway, this old black guy who works there is named Gene and he's in his early fifties and he's big and paunchy with salt-and-pepper hair and he's funny as hell, with this old Southern accent from Georgia or something."

"Yeah?"

"Yeah. So he sees me hanging out this summer and sits down next to me and chats awhile. Said he moved to San Francisco back in the '70s because he liked those old *Dirty Harry* movies. I asked him if he came here to become a cop, and he said no, he simply came here to party, and that's exactly what he did. But the reason I bring up Gene is because he said something that got me thinking. He told me he was pursuing some woman just a little bit younger than him who lived in his apartment building. She thought he was cute and funny. Then, one day, before they had really had a chance to date, she said, 'You're a security guard. Don't you want more out of life?' And Gene said, 'Honey, I'm fifty-three years old! If I couldn't get my shit together at thirty, I'm not going to get my shit together now.'"

Ferdinand laughs.

I continue. "It's like this: Bing Crosby was a fucking monster who psychologically and physically abused his sons. Bing Crosby set up trust funds for his four boys to collect when they turned sixty-five, and none of them made it to sixty-five. He had four sons from his first marriage and two killed themselves after years of drug abuse and alcoholism, and dig this, they both did it around Christmas time to say to the world, 'Fuck you, Bing Crosby' and 'Fuck you, "White Christmas."'"

"Wow."

"And another son, Gary Crosby—the one who wrote a Daddy-dearest type book in the 1980s detailing what a sadistic prick his father was—well, this poor, hapless son of a bitch dies of lung cancer in his early sixties, like sixty-one or sixty-two. It happened fairly recently." Ferdinand's face is perplexed, wondering what my point is going to be. "I happened to read an interview with the man as he was dying and he bitched about the fact that he was finally 'getting his shit together.' That's a direct quote. He had quit drinking and quit smoking. He said he had finally gotten over all the burdensome, bullshit baggage that came from being the battered son of Bing Crosby. The guy was getting married, was getting some acting work, had money in the bank, and then was suddenly diagnosed with cancer. But the man actually said in the interview, 'The sad thing is, I was just starting to get my shit together.' It's like I think about Gene's line and think about Gary Crosby's tormented life and death, and then I think about myself and take a hard, hard look at this life. I see nothing in particular, dude. I've done everything in this town *but* get my shit together. Don't think for a minute, Ferdinand, that I'm not aware that I'm a bit of a loser."

That last sentence is more painful to utter out loud in front of a friend than it has been to say to myself every day this past week. Even if somebody pointed their finger at me from across a room and shouted "Loser!" it still wouldn't hurt as much as calling myself one in front of somebody I admire. It does seem that the one thing worse than being called a loser is recognizing a loser every time you fill out a job application, every time you hear your name somewhere, every time you catch a tiny reflection of yourself in a store window, having lost the ability to look in the mirror years before.

"This sucks, Ferdinand, and I can't live like this anymore."

Ferdinand lowers his head and says nothing for a moment.

Then he says, "Eli, you don't know Gene's life is so bad. You say he's funny as hell. Obviously a good storyteller, he came to Cali to party and did. He's holding down a job, not living on the streets, he's making friends, pursuing women. You don't know that his life has been such a disappointment. Who's to judge or define another person's idea of success?"

279

"That's just idealistic hippie bullshit and you know it. I like Gene, but I recognize a loser when I see one. Perhaps his lack of self-pity or delusions is admirable, but he's not where he wanted to be. Gene couldn't get his shit together at thirty; I'm thirty-two and I've never had my shit together, and poor Gary Crosby didn't get his shit together till it was too late."

"It's not hippie bullshit, Eli, and besides, who the fuck feels like they've got their shit together?"

"Stop with the well-meaning arguments, Titty Titty. Yes, I'm the Experience Junkie, experience-rich and everything-else-poor. I know who I am, Ferdinand, and I can't stand it anymore. I am a fucking loser!"

"Look, Eli, you're a writer. You've got potential to be a great writer. Everybody I know says you ought to perform more than you do. You've got an agent. If the manuscript you gave him years ago isn't good enough, fix it and send it back. Or give him a new one, a better one. Sell some short stories. Send them out. Perhaps San Francisco is not for you. Move to a more affordable place. They're not hard to find. Believe me, there are a lot more places in America and abroad more affordable than San Francisco. But sitting here comparing yourself to middle-aged underachievers is not going to help you. Make a decision, plan a goal, not for a week, but for your life, Eli. If you want to stop floundering then stop floundering. Living a life without a plan and going from one impulsive move to another is not going to help you. People generally live the lives that they want, whether they realize it or not. If you don't want to be like those guys, then don't be. You're still young. You've still got your health. Quit beating yourself up, and stop beating up other people, too. If you want to change your life, then change it. It's not that hard. You were able to quit drugs on your own. You know how hard that is for some people. Now, I just got back to town, and you're my buddy, but *fuck*, Eli, I got my own bullshit to take care of. You had enough discipline to write a novel and send it to an agent. You developed a one-man show that you could've toured the country with if you had wanted to. It was awesome. You told me last spring that you wanted a girlfriend, and then you got one. You're not exactly the kind of guy that I feel sorry for. I don't feel like I need to be your therapist. You've got writing for that. I don't want to be your personal motivational coach, because you've got yourself for that. Shit! You're a relatively successful person despite yourself. Why are you so self-destructive?" Whispering as if trying to control an urge to scream, he says, "Now quit dwelling in self-pity and be a man, Eli. Do something with your present situation. Don't talk about it. Do something. If you want to be successful, you can be successful. Now, Eli, I came here tonight to meet you, have some laughs, and see a movie. Now, again, lighten up, Eli, and let's talk about something else. Okay?"

The movie was about to start anyway.

V

Outside the movie theater, Ferdinand Noah and I hug for a long time, and he tells me in a soft voice that I can call anytime and that as far as he knows, I'm already in the infant stages of getting my shit together. Then, in a serious voice but in a tone meant to sound light and casual, Ferdinand asks, "Those days are over, right? I mean, you are not going to do something you cannot walk away from. You're not going to pull a Hemingway or act like one of Bing Crosby's kids at Christmas time?"

I smile at Noah and assure him those days are over. He gives me a playful punch on my right shoulder and says we ought to see each other for coffee later this week. I agree.

We go our separate ways on Market Street.

It'd be nice to suggest that the walk home on a warm, cloudless night in San Francisco is peaceful and serene, but in truth, every ten minutes or so, barely drawn human forms creep from the shadows, interrupting my thoughts to ask for a handout.

Enough already.

You can't judge a book by its cover. This may be true, but you can judge a novel by its first and last pages. Whenever I consider purchasing a particular book, I read the first page and skip to the last. Both must be written well enough to intrigue me and compel me to learn everything that happens in between. This has been my practice for as long as I can remember. It makes me wonder if God judges us by our first and last words.

Every tombstone in the world ought to have everybody's first and last words on it, and then we can decide if they're interesting enough to inspire us to learn about the individuals buried underneath.

According to my mother, my first words were "Look at me, look at me."

Only time will tell what my last words will be.

Magic doesn't impress me, be it the white or the black kind, but magician Aleister Crowley, once considered "the wickedest man in the world," fascinates me to no end, if only because his last words were "Sometimes, I hate myself."

I used to think about that all the time.

"Look at me, look at me."

"Sometimes, I hate myself."

"Look at me, look at me."

"Sometimes, I hate myself."

Minutes away from my hotel room, I stop at a drugstore and buy two spiral notebooks of college-ruled paper, each with five hundred sheets. Then I buy a packet of ball-point red-ink pens, and though I know I have to be up early for my first day at a job I really don't want, I sit cross-legged in the center of my room at the Sestri Hotel with jazz playing on my CD player. There, I write "Look at me, look at me" and "Sometimes, I hate myself" again and again, until finally, I write this book down.

The End.

Registered Trademarks

CPSIA information can be obtained
at www.ICGtesting.com
Printed in the USA
FFOW02n0947161213
2715FF